COLONY

Benjamin Cross has a postgraduate degree in archaeology from the University of Oxford. An experienced field archaeologist, he has worked and travelled widely, exploring the remains of ancient civilisations around the world. A member of the Chartered Institute for Archaeologists, he is now Principal Heritage Consultant with a global planning and environmental consultancy. Cross lives with his family in Carmarthenshire, Wales. He has published short stories and academic papers and has written two novels.

Colony is Cross's first novel.

COLONY

BENJAMIN CROSS

The Book Guild Ltd

First published in Great Britain in 2021 by
The Book Guild Ltd
9 Priory Business Park
Wistow Road, Kibworth
Leicestershire, LE8 0RX
Freephone: 0800 999 2982
www.bookguild.co.uk
Email: info@bookguild.co.uk
Twitter: @bookguild

Typeset in 11pt Minion Pro

Printed and bound by CPI Group (UK) Ltd, Croydon, CR0 4YY

ISBN 978 1913551 360

British Library Cataloguing in Publication Data.
A catalogue record for this book is available from the British Library.

For my family

Hannah, Ethan & Ted

Prologue

WHITE DEATH

6000 BC

The hunter's whalebone skis tore across the drift, carving up the surface and thrusting clouds of snow into his wake. The slipstream lashed his cheeks as he accelerated. His eyes watered. His muscles ached. Beneath the thick fur lining of his jacket he could feel the bite of his talisman, the tips of the three teeth probing at his skin.

He threw a glance behind.

Nothing; it was nowhere to be seen.

Ahead, the slope gouged a narrow aisle through the outcrops of rock before disappearing into the blizzard. The snowfall was thickening around him, the mist closing in fast. Gritting his teeth, he drove his ski poles hard into the snow and propelled himself onwards.

As he sped downslope, the storm fed him glimpses of the world ahead. And there was something there, at the bottom of the slope. Like a dark ribbon draped across his path, it grew wider, darker with every glance…

The hunter's eyes bulged with terror.

It was a gorge, wide and deep, hewn into the valley.

With no time to lose, he swerved away, calling on every last fibre of skill to keep his balance, to weave amongst the scattered outcrops now littering the way ahead…

…his ski ploughed into a talon of rock. There was a crunch

as the shaft split open. His heart sank, his legs buckled and he was slung forward. In the chaos that followed, the momentum toyed with him, twisting his limbs around his torso. As he hit the ground, his ski snapped off at the toe and the jagged splinter sheared into his gut.

He tumbled for what seemed like eternity. Then silence.

He blinked his eyes open. The world was now a brutal haze. Blood dripped from his nose and lips, freezing into trails in the snow. He waited, breathed, slowly unfolded himself. As the delirium subsided, pain flared in his stomach, sent a surge of adrenaline coursing through his veins.

He staggered to his feet. His ribs were fractured and his shoulder dislocated, but he had to keep moving. Instinctively he reached for the shaft of bone sticking spear-like from his gut. Then he thought better. Leaving it to plug the wound, he took off as fast as he could along the side of the gorge.

Up ahead he could make out a towering rockface. A low, narrow tunnel was worn into its base where the line of the gorge passed through. It wasn't much, but it was shelter. As he limped towards it, the world bucked suddenly and he was thrown forward. On reflex, he rolled straight over, straining for breath and clawing the snow from his face. He scanned around, his head darting from side to side with every imagined movement, his eyes wide, frantic. But there was nothing, just a thick curtain of white that suffocated his senses.

He glanced behind, searching out the tunnel. It was only a few strides away, and he prepared to drag himself to his feet—

A guttural hiss broke the silence.

The air froze in his lungs.

It was there. Right in front of him. Its head cocked. Its mouth cracked open. Watching. He had never believed the stories meant to frighten him as a child. But here they were: every tale, every description, every warning that he had ever ignored, staring down at him through the flurry.

Plumes of condensed breath fired from its nostrils as it slunk forward a pace, bobbing its head and shaking the snow from its back. Then it froze, its lips curling, peeling back to reveal the teeth emerging from its bloodshot gums. With its face caught in a snarl, it stretched its neck towards him and bellowed.

The hideous sound seemed to bite into his skull, and the hunter scrabbled to his feet in sheer terror. His hand jumped instinctively to the bag hanging from his belt. He fought with the lashings, desperately wrenching them free, until he could tear the fibre sack loose and hold it before him.

The creature's eyes flashed. It screamed out and lunged at him, sending the bag flying from his grip and skidding across the ice into the mouth of the tunnel. With the creature's frenzied screeching ringing in his ears, the hunter dropped to his knees and scrabbled after it, dragging himself in through the narrow folds of rock.

The cold seeped up into his palms. Then the gut-churning stench of putrefying meat wafted in from behind him. Pain erupted in his ankles and panic took hold. He screamed out, struggling as unseen teeth hacked into his flesh and stripped the strings of muscle from his bones. Clouds of steam billowed up into the night as his blood spilt out in rivers, and the freezing air congealed with the crunching of bone.

As the world began to fade, he reached forward and dug his fingers into the surface of the ancient stone. Then, with all that remained of his strength, he heaved himself on into the dark.

Chapter 1

NAM MYOHO RENGE KYO...

1

Harmsworth Island, Russian Arctic

Present day

Starshyna Alexander Koikov ground the gear-shift lever into neutral and brought the forklift juddering to a halt. It was mid-morning and just below freezing. In the new silence he wasted no time lighting a papirosa and taking a long drag. As the tar-heavy smoke tripped from his nostrils, he traced a finger across his scar. The rest of his jaw was covered in coarse, week-old stubble, but nothing had ever sprouted from the distinctive hook of scar tissue gouged into his cheek, not a single bristle, and now the cold was causing it to ache.

It was two months since his detachment had been posted to the *Albanov* icebreaker. As far as Koikov was concerned, being a member of Department V could be the best job in the world. *Could* be. His squad's last rotation had been to Chechnya, where he had spent three months dispatching prominent Chechen rebels, and almost having his balls blown off by a sniper in the process; the proudest day of his life was when he had been promoted from sergeant to starshyna at the end of that tour. But this new detail, working security on some pampered gas tycoon's boat in the high Arctic, it was a sentence not a sortie. It was dull as shit.

He pushed the collar on his jacket up around his chin and tugged at his knit cap, stretching it down over the tops of his ears. And what about his men? Like him, they were no ordinary soldiers. They had all endured the same selection programme, the brutal interrogation exercises, the endless forced marches and night-time parachute jumps. And they had all seen their share of action since. From long experience Koikov knew that charging men like his with tycoon babysitting was a gamble. Hardened, well-trained and well-disciplined they may have been. But they were also human. Humans got bored. Bored humans got sloppy, elite or not.

He watched as Junior Sergeant Sharova and Private Dolgonosov emerged from behind one of the half dozen barrack blocks dispersed around the incomplete runway at the heart of the old military compound. The only other things still standing were a couple of rusting, partially collapsed hangars, an old crane and the three conjoined concrete bunkers peering up out of the bedrock right in front of him. Trails of steam gushed from the men's shoulders as they rolled another enormous metal drum towards the forklift. Moments later they were joined by Private Yudina, whose bear-like stature made a toy of his rifle as he slung it around onto his back and pitched in.

Koikov had half-hoped that the sub-team's deployment onto the island itself might have boosted their morale a little. At least served as a distraction. But the expressions on the faces of the three men only reconfirmed what he already knew: clearing up a bunch of old petrochem containers in sub-zero temperatures was a million miles short of stimulating.

He restarted the forklift's engine and lowered the carriage so that they could heave the recumbent drum up onto the forks. With the clamp secured over the top of it, he then killed the engine once more and jumped out of the cabin. He slapped a palm against the side of the drum. "How many more are there?"

"Fifty or sixty," Sharova replied. "Plus a bunch of smaller canisters. Mostly full."

"Can we be finished today?"

Before Sharova could respond, Dolgonosov let out a loud, indignant snort and slumped back against the side of the forklift cabin. "What the fuck are we doing here, Starshyna?"

Koikov looked hard into the young man's eyes. He was already a formidable soldier, but he was also as hot-headed and restless as Koikov had been at age twenty-one. Ordinarily he would have stung Dolgonosov for the attitude, but on this occasion he was voicing the question on all of their lips. "We're doing what we've been instructed," Koikov replied. "Any day now and the science club will be all over the place, poking their noses here and their dicks there."

Dolgonosov shrugged. "So what?"

"*So* they're coming to check out the environment. How do you think it'll look if they turn up to find the place already littered with chemical drums?"

"But this is a job for a civilian contractor."

"Look, Dolgonosov, I don't like this any better than you, but Major Rabinovich gets what Major Rabinovich wants. You have an issue with that, feel free to take it up with him. Otherwise, you're next on watch." Koikov pointed to a steep-sided moraine to the north-west of the compound, where Yudina had spent the last two hours scouting for polar bears. "Get up on top of that ridge. You know the drill, half-hour comms."

"And keep your eyes peeled," Yudina added, his deep voice echoing around the compound. "The last thing any of us needs is to be shit out of a bear."

Dolgonosov spat on the floor, careful to direct the globule away from Koikov's boots. "Bear watch," he grumbled, slinging his hazchem gloves at Yudina. Then he shouldered his rifle and stomped off towards the moraine.

Koikov's orders had been to pack the drums into the bunker and detonate them, burying what the official brief had termed *evidence of AEPM 'Anomalous Environmental Policy Mismanagement'*. He shook his head at the conceit. There had been no environmental policy to mismanage, that much was obvious, and the only anomaly was that whoever built the place hadn't fucked the environment up even worse.

It was a shame. For all its remoteness, he couldn't deny that the island was a beautiful place. To the west of the compound was an expanse of icy, rock-strewn tundra, beyond which, if he raised himself up and peered across the bunker's concrete roof, he could make out icebergs, distant islands and the ocean shimmering through fissures in the melting ice floes. To the east, further inland, the relief rose steeply towards the foot of a mountain range, half covered by an immense glacier. He followed the lie of the surrounding peaks as they jostled into the distance. The sight drew a whistle of contentment from him; the wind had blown him a hell of a long way from the grim tower-block estates of suburban Moscow.

He slotted the second of his explosive charges into place and made sure that it was firmly attached. Then he set to work on the wiring. As he began stripping back the plastic coating, something caught his attention. He stopped and listened. There it was again: a distant wailing. He pulled his head up out of the doorway and listened hard.

After a few moments, the noise gave out and he dropped back inside and refocussed on the charge. It was probably just a gull, that or one of the other poor creatures that called the island home—

It started up again, low but definite. The more he listened, the less animal it sounded, until he could no longer ignore it. He strode back out of the bunker and cast an eye towards the lookout post on top of the moraine.

His heart sank. Dolgonosov was nowhere to be seen.

He snatched at his radio. "Dolgonosov? Over."

Silence.

"Private Dolgonosov. Answer me now, over!"

Silence.

"Junior Sergeant Sharova!"

"Starshyna?"

Koikov chased Sharova's voice to the rear of the bunker. "Any word from Dolgonosov?"

Sharova shook his head. "Nothing, Starshyna."

"Me either," Yudina said.

"Either of you hear that noise?"

They looked blank.

"Just now. There was a noise like screaming, from beyond the ridge."

"There's a walrus colony further up the coast," Yudina said.

Without responding, Koikov took off towards the hovercraft and leapt up behind the controls. Sharova and Yudina exchanged a glance. Then they dropped what they were doing and followed on.

"Junior Sergeant, man the gun turret."

"Yes, Starshyna."

Koikov keyed the ignition and within seconds the armoured vehicle was tearing around the moraine and on along the coast. He scanned the horizon. The landscape was as eerily still and calm as ever. There was no movement, nothing to suggest a human presence, until something shifted on the very periphery of his vision. It was faint, barely perceptible through the incessant glare of the midnight sun, but he could make out what appeared to be a thin trail of smoke leaking from behind a rock cluster north of the moraine.

He veered sharply towards it and slammed his foot onto the accelerator. "Hands on!"

A metallic crunch and slide rang out behind him as Sharova readied the mounted gun.

Rounding the side of the rock cluster, Koikov brought the hovercraft to an abrupt halt and cut the engine. He jumped down and shouldered his rifle. Yudina joined him and together they approached the smoke trail.

Koikov's body went numb. "Jesus Christ!"

Obviously a dud, the standard-issue warning flare had not deployed properly. It dribbled out a thin trail of coloured smoke secure within the user's hand. But the hand was no longer attached. It was severed a few inches above the wrist, and two splintered prongs of bone protruded from the pulp. The skin had been flayed from the palm and the ends of the fingers, as if somebody had gone at them with a grater, and the surrounding rocks were streaked with blood, still steaming into the cold.

As the men stared on in disbelief, there was a groan from behind a nearby rock.

Dolgonosov's torso was twisted back against the outcrop. The rest of his arm had been removed at the shoulder and both of his legs had been reduced to shreds of flesh, which trailed like red tentacles from his groin. It was hard to believe that he could still be alive, but as Koikov dropped to his side he could see the young man's chest staggering faintly up and down.

"Dolgonosov... what in God's name?"

Dolgonosov's head turned slowly. His lips and nose were bleeding and his eyes were bulging, grotesque with terror. He looked about ten years old. His mouth quivered as he attempted to force a word out, but all that emerged was a long exhalation that gurgled from the bottom of his throat before his head flopped forward into Koikov's hands.

Instinctively, Koikov made to check his pulse. But before he could, a screech pierced the silence and a shadow dashed between the outcrops on the facing slope.

"Sharova!"

"Yes, Starshyna!" The hovercraft's gun erupted into life and fire raked into the side of the opposing slope, sending clouds of residual ice and rock billowing up into the air. Back on his feet, Koikov trained his rifle in the direction of the barrage, and he and Yudina joined in, unloading magazine after magazine at the shadow as it darted up the incline.

Koikov's heart pounded with adrenaline. Adrenaline, and something else. He could feel his hands shaking as he tried to aim, spraying rounds that he knew would normally have hit their mark, ineffectually across the barren slope.

At last the roar of the mounted machine gun, and the percussive thump and whine of high-calibre rounds on rock, ceased. Koikov looked down; his rifle magazine was empty, had been for some time. But his finger was still cramped back against the trigger, willing it to discharge.

He glanced across at Yudina. The private's rifle was also poised but silent, quivering below his pale cheek.

Slowly, the two men lowered their weapons and watched in silence as the sediment thrown up by the barrage gradually resettled.

"What the hell was that?" Yudina half-whispered, his voice strained with fear.

Koikov said nothing but reached slowly for a papirosa.

Whatever it was, it was nowhere to be seen.

2

Loch Ness, Scottish Highlands

Callum Ross knelt down and selected a pebble from the shore. He looked it over, rubbing away the patina of ground-in silt and smoothing his thumb around the edge. It felt cold and granular. Instinctively he rolled it in his palms, warming it before handing it to Jamie. "That's the sort you want, son."

Jamie took the pebble and gave it his own, much more rigorous, inspection. The little disc of water-worn stone looked suddenly very large as it flipped through the boy's fingers. The day after his mother had been rushed into the maternity unit in Edinburgh, those fingers had barely folded around Callum's thumb. He smiled at the memory. That tiny, insistent grip had changed his life forever.

Callum walked to the water's edge and motioned for Jamie to join him. "You want to try and keep your body low," he said. "Try and throw *across* the water." He looked up to see that Jamie was beside him, knees bent into an exaggerated right angle, swinging his arm wildly back and forth towards the loch.

He was his father's son alright, from his deep-set hazel eyes to his soft jawline and pale skin. His face bore the same intensity that Callum recognised in his own when he was concentrating, and it was already framed by the same mop of dark curls that enveloped his ears and licked at his brow.

"Do you want me to go first?"

Jamie nodded.

With an exaggerated sweep of his arm, Callum snatched up a stone and sent it skipping out across the silt-rich water.

"...nine, ten, eleven, twelve!" they counted together, watching as the stone tripped away, the trail of circular ripples feeding one into the other.

"My turn!" Jamie yelled. His face wrought with focus, he positioned the pebble precisely in his fingers, then crouched down and launched it out into the loch.

It sank without a single jump.

"No matter," Callum said, watching as the disappointment spread across Jamie's face. "You see all these pebbles?" He gestured along the sweeping shoreline. "That's how many goes you've got."

Disappointment morphed into a guarded smile, and Jamie dropped to his knees and gathered up a handful of new skimmers. He seemed to consider the multi-coloured stones carefully before selecting a thin, white one from amongst the greys and pushing it into Callum's hand.

"Quartz," Callum said, holding the pebble up to the light. "Ancient tribes used to make arrowheads out of this stuff, you know?"

Jamie's brow wrinkled. "It's just a stone, Dad."

Callum laughed and closed his fingers around the gift. It was one of the things he loved most about his son. When they were together, he was no longer Doctor Callum Ross, Professor of Archaeology. He was just plain old 'Dad'.

"Are they not scared of Nessie?"

Seated on a pebble-and-jacket throne later that afternoon, Callum followed Jamie's gaze. His eyes were fixed on the water, where a group of young men were busy sculling around on their backs amongst the ranks of wooden piles. Beyond their shoulders, the loch stretched on into the distance like a vast pupil ringed by the iris of the Great Glen.

"I guess not," he answered.

"He's not real, though, anyway, is he?"

There was part of Callum that felt he ought to play it straight, just like his own father back when he and his brother had descended on the loch each year, determined to hunt the beast with nothing but wooden spears and a knackered-up old dingy. *Chances are it's nothing, son. You're dreaming if you think it's a dinosaur. Probably a freak sturgeon...*

"Nessie? Of course he's real," he replied. "How can you not believe in Nessie?"

"But why don't more people see him then?"

"Well, did you ever think that he doesn't want to be seen?"

Jamie slurped up a mouthful of ice-cream. "Suppose," he said. "Do you really think there's a monster?"

"Of course I do." Callum lowered his voice to a whisper, "Between me and you, I think there's more than one."

"More than one Nessie?"

"Well, there'd need to be for them to survive all this time, wouldn't there?"

"Why?"

"Well, because..."

The boy's brow was furrowed. The ice-cream cone hovered just below his chin and a tear of melted raspberry ripple was creeping for his knuckle.

The desire to come clean was there again: *Because there'd need to be a viable breeding population, that's why, son. Daddy Ness would need his and Mummy Ness would need hers and one thing would lead to another...*

"Because he'd be too lonely to live on his own all this time, wouldn't he? He'd need his family with him."

"Why do you not want to live with me and Mum?"

The question struck Callum in the gut.

"Jimmy Bevan says it's weird that you don't live with us," Jamie continued, "and so did Fraser."

"Did they now?"

He nodded. "And Fraser called me a dicknose as well."

Callum offered up the remains of his cone. "I wish I could live with you, Jamie, but you know it's not that simple."

"But why?"

"Well, for a start you and your ma live in Edinburgh, and I live in Aberdeen some of the time and in Norway some of the time and all over the place the rest."

"You could take us with you. I want to see all over the place."

"What about your school and your mother's job?"

"But I want to dig up treasure like you."

"Well, if that's what you really want, then you've plenty of time." Callum felt relieved that the conversation had moved on before he'd let slip the other reason why he no longer lived in Edinburgh: the simple fact that he and Moira would have ended up throttling each other. "It's not all about finding treasure, you know. I spend much more time in the library reading dusty old books."

Jamie looked as unconvinced as ever. But before Callum could say any more, his phone rang and he hurried to answer it.

"Jonas, hi…

"…I'm on Dores Beach with Jamie…

"…you're where?"

He stared along the crowded beachfront. Sure enough, Doctor Jonas Olsen was standing in the garden of the Dores Inn, set just back from the shore. Phone pressed to his ear, he was waving his trademark straw boater methodically from side to side.

3

Callum reached out and shook his colleague's hand. His grip felt weak and he seemed even thinner than usual, but Callum kept his thoughts to himself. "Jonas, to what do we owe the pleasure?"

In his thick Norwegian brogue Jonas replied, "You have told me so much about this monster of yours over the years that I just had to come out and meet him for myself."

"But I thought you were supposed to be in Tromso for the summer?"

"I was supposed to be, yes. But things have changed."

There was something about the word *things* that set the alarm bells ringing faster. It had been twelve years since Callum had first met Jonas Olsen. He had already established himself as a world authority on the archaeology of northern Eurasia and he had been one of the main reasons for Callum joining the department at Aberdeen. The result of over a decade of close collaboration was that he knew Jonas well and he was a specifics man, not a *things* man. He searched the pale blue of his friend's eyes.

"Surely not again?"

Jonas nestled his boater back on top of his thinning grey hair. "Can we talk?"

Having settled Jamie back on the beach, Callum returned to Jonas, who motioned for them to sit at a nearby table. On it already were his favoured white jacket, lichen stains on the elbows where he had been leaning, and two glass tumblers, both containing generous measures of single malt. He slid one across the table to Callum.

"What've they said?"

"They think six months, a year at most."

Callum slumped back in his seat. "Jonas, I don't know what to say."

"You can say whatever you like, my friend, but what you cannot do is feel sorry for me, please." He assumed that same commanding gaze with which he fixed his students year on year. "You know, you should never feel pity for a dying sixty-year-old. He has enjoyed the things that are here to enjoy and now he gets to skip out on the bill. You should envy this man. You should refuse to drink the expensive whiskey he has bought for you and give it back to him on principle." He grinned and held out his glass. Callum clinked it and they downed their measures.

"Is there really nothing they can do? Last time they said it was hopeless and then you came through."

Jonas shook his head. "Three years ago it was a pussycat. This time it is a tiger. And besides, I'm afraid this time it has spread."

"Where?"

He tapped the ends of his fingers against his hairline. "Straight to the old think tank."

His words hung swollen and grotesque before them, as the shock passed from Callum's stomach up into his chest and back again. They sat quietly together, the air cut with the familiar squabbling of gulls and the shrieking of children playing down on the shore.

"Is there anything you need me to do?" Callum said at last. "If there is then just name it, okay, anything at all."

Jonas's features hardened suddenly and his elbows forced a creak from the table-top as he leant forward. "As a matter of fact, there *is* something," he said, "and it is the reason why I am here ruining your holiday like this."

"You're not ruining anything," Callum replied. "I meant what I said. Do you need me to look out for Sarah? She knows, doesn't she?"

"Yes, yes, she knows, and no thank you, she is far too headstrong, I mean stubborn, I mean *independent* an old girl to accept anybody's help."

Callum could feel a tear building in the corner of his eye. He turned his head and saw that Jamie was still sitting quietly down on the beach. Hand outstretched above his eyes, he was scouring the loch for movement.

"You have heard of a place called Franz Josef Land, of course?"

Callum nodded, still watching his son. "Off the north coast of Russia. Why? Are they developing a new treatment there?" No sooner were the words out than he knew they were absurd. There was no *they* in Franz Josef Land, let alone any advanced medical facilities capable of treating metastasised pancreatic cancer. For many years one of his major research foci had been the archaeology of northern Siberia, and he was familiar with the off-shore islands. Those that made up the Franz Josef Land archipelago were remote, uninhabited and glaciated. There was only a smattering of abandoned Cold War outposts, the odd meteorological research station and a handful of ramshackle nineteenth-century explorers' hovels to show that man had ever given the place a second thought.

"No, nothing like that," Jonas chuckled. "This is nothing to do with me knocking on heaven's door. This is much more serious. This is research."

Callum stared at his friend. "A field survey?"

"On Harmsworth Island. It is in the extreme north-east of the archipelago. Nobody even knew that it existed until recently, not even the Russians."

"But it must be at eighty degrees latitude. The whole place must be under ice."

"Eighty-one," Jonas corrected. "But apparently this island has only a single, comparatively small glacier in the centre. The rest is open tundra, which can be surveyed like anywhere else during the summer. At least that is what I am told."

"And you want me to go there instead of you?"

"I have suggested you to the powers that be, yes, and they have said that if I am satisfied you are the most qualified replacement then they are happy for you to climb aboard, pending all the usual checks."

"And who are *they* exactly? I mean, who's proposing to fund all this?"

Jonas threw a glance around the nearby tables. Then in a low voice he said, "One minute I am working on the report for the Malsnes excavation and the next minute head of department Clive Berridge is in my office telling me that he has had a phone call from the Arctic Council and that they have requested me to go to Franz Josef Land and carry out the survey."

"The Arctic Council?"

"It is an inter-governmental department promoting cooperation in the Arctic. All eight of the Arctic nations have signed up."

"I know who they are, Jonas, but what have they got to do with archaeological research?"

"Nothing. At least not directly. But what they *do* have to do with is regulating the impact of the Arctic oil and gas industries."

"They've struck oil then?"

"Close. The G&S Consortium have found gas in the seabed around the island. A substantial volume by all accounts. They will build a large processing plant and other facilities on the island itself, no doubt making a great big mess of the place. Then they will build a huge underwater pipeline to transport the gas to the mainland."

Callum whistled. "Sounds like they're throwing some serious ruble around."

"Like you wouldn't believe! This will be a true sea monster." Jonas cast another glance around, evidently relishing his involvement in something quite so hush-hush. "But also, the company involved is interested to do things properly. They sold Clive a line about wanting to be a responsible twenty-first century corporation, etcetera etcetera, but what it really comes down to is them trying to avoid the condemnation of the international community, though I happen to think that this is inevitable. Anyway, they have commissioned a full environmental impact assessment on the island in accordance with the Russian Federation's energy strategy and the stipulations of the Arctic Council. They want ecologists, marine biologists, geologists, archaeologists, the full works."

"An island-wide environmental survey?"

Jonas nodded as if it wasn't unprecedented.

"And they think there might actually be some archaeology out there?"

"Do you not agree?"

It was not the question. It was Jonas's bluntness that told Callum the man's mind was already set. "Look, I can understand them getting eco-geeks and rock-botherers out there, but the likelihood of there being any ancient sites at that latitude is remote, you know that."

"Prehistoric reindeer antler has already been recovered on at least two of the islands."

"Yes, I heard about that, and I'm not doubting that there were reindeer there for a second."

"Where there are reindeer, there are reindeer hunters."

"Maybe—"

"And just look what Berg's team turned up on Svalbard only last year. There we are thinking that the earliest inhabitants are seventeenth-century whalers, but then they discover one small prehistoric settlement on Nordaustlandet and suddenly the human history of that island is back ten thousand years!" He banged his palm down. "Just like that and we push back the date of man's relationship with the Arctic not by years or centuries but millennia. People were living in these areas. You know it and so do I. So why not Franz Josef Land?"

"Okay, but if we're talking *why nots*, then why not use Russian archaeologists? Why have they asked a Norwegian? More to the point, why are you asking a Scot?"

Jonas's eyes flashed. "Well, this is where it gets interesting. Not only have G&S agreed to the Arctic Council's request for an environmental impact assessment, but they have also agreed that the team will be an international one and not just a bunch of home-grown yes-men. Representatives from all of the Arctic nations will be involved to one extent or another."

Callum sat back. "Sounds like one big political powder keg."

"Welcome to the Arctic," Jonas beamed. "Now, unfortunately time is not on our side. You can appreciate that suitable survey conditions are fleeting at such high latitude, certainly no longer than two months in the year. There is a very narrow window of opportunity for you to get on the ground."

"So when exactly do you need me there?"

"Two days from now."

Callum's heart sank. "Two days? Jonas, I can't. It's the first time this year that I've had any real time to spend with Jamie." Their eyes moved in unison to where the boy had kicked a mass of pebbles into a pile and was now attempting to knock the top one out into the loch with a driftwood golf club.

"He is a gorgeous boy and I am sorry to have to ask this of you," Jonas said, holding Callum's gaze, "but this is the opportunity of a lifetime for you *and* a lifeline for the department. Like you said, the company is throwing some serious ruble around and," he lowered his voice again, "as you know, the department's future is far from certain right now."

"I appreciate that, Jonas. But is there nobody else? What about Professor Cunningham?"

"Duncan Cunningham has never been north of Inverness," Jonas spat. "He has half your field experience and even less knowledge of Russian archaeology. No, you are the only person qualified, the only person that I would trust to take my place. And at best we have only August and September. That's two months for your survey and that is if the conditions hold out, which I think would be unprecedented. Two days from now is—"

"The first of August," Callum said, his voice low with resignation.

"Yes, and they have already been very patient with us, given my personal circumstances. The rest of the team are out there as we speak, but they have agreed to hold the show until your arrival."

Callum released a long, drawn-out sigh. "I don't really have a choice, do I?"

"There is always a choice," Jonas replied, placing a hand on Callum's shoulder. "The hard part is making it the right one."

5

"This is Ptarmigan."

For a few seconds the line was silent. Ptarmigan stared out of his cabin window and waited, watching as another fissure opened up in the remnant pack ice. It was melting fast, and the grinding of the fragments against the hull of the icebreaker produced a deep, constant groan that was as much a sensation as a sound.

"You are all set?"

Ptarmigan's jaw clenched at the sound of the familiar robotic drawl. "I think so."

"You sound uncertain."

He caught sight of himself in the polished steel surrounding the window. He looked uncertain too. He also looked like shit; he always did when he was stressed. His skin was pale and clammy, and a finger of shaving rash glowed on the side of his neck. He rubbed at it. "You sound like a machine."

"The voice distortion is for both of our protection."

"Bullshit! What's protecting me?"

"I am."

Ptarmigan snorted into the receiver. They had spoken only once before, but it had been enough to get the measure of the man who called himself Finback. He was an irritating know-it-all, overly fond of the sound of his own voice. But he was also a visionary. He was like some kind of goddamn activist messiah, at least in the circles Ptarmigan moved in. More importantly, he had proven himself to have the money and the resources to make things happen. The rocket launchers the group had used to blow up the new Barranquitas nuclear power plant on Puerto Rico prior to the installation of the reactor, the motorboats and charges used to board the Japanese whaling ship *Shonan Maru III* and send it to the bottom of the Southern Ocean, the information about Biocorp Research Laboratories personnel in Mexico, all of it, every last scrap, had come from Finback.

"It is okay to be scared."

"Well, I'm not, it's just—"

"It is nerves," came the metered reply. "Remember what you are doing this for."

"I do remember!"

"Those bastards at G&S can pretend to be as green as they like, toeing the environmental line. But you and I know that they are both about as green as an oil slick. Greed is what they are about. Profiteering and looking after themselves. There is no reasoning with these people and there is certainly no regulating them."

"Look, Finback, I know all this. Do you think I would've come this far if I didn't hate the way those corporate cocksuckers are raping this planet? I'm with the programme, okay, I just have an issue with the fact that innocent people are going to get killed on this one."

"The cancer of capitalist ignorance can no longer be restrained by empty words and signatures on bits of paper. If we are to save this planet then blood will need to be spilt, and we must not be afraid to spill it."

"I said there's no need to keep feeding me the party line! I already told you I'm on board, literally. It's the only way to open people's ears, I know that. But then it's still me setting the charges and then sneaking away, so cut me some slack, would you?"

Finback cleared his throat loudly. "Let me make this very simple for you. The race for the Arctic has begun. The Russians, the Norwegians, the Danes, the Canadians, the Americans, all of them, they are all poised and waiting to move in on the North Pole. Before the rest of the world has woken up to what is happening, the place will be covered with wellheads and tankers, and any remaining space will be disfigured with pipelines. A few years later and gone will be the wildlife, and one day, of course, gone will be the ice itself.

"*We* have the chance to try and end the whole ugly little relay. We lose the Arctic and we lose this planet. We save the Arctic and we give the best of humanity time to teach us all how to adapt and survive without the need to extinguish its beauty and exterminate its creatures and lay waste to the whole region. We save the Arctic and your children's children, and mine, the children of anybody who dies on that ship, will have a shot at a future here." He paused. "We must all die someday, somehow. I think that those who die for *this* cause will have died well. B—"

For an instant the line cut out and when it picked back up, Finback's tone had changed. "…if you are no longer interested then say so now. There is still a chance that I can make alternative arrangements."

"Look, for the last time, I'm in, okay?" Ptarmigan snarled. "You're right. It's just nerves, that's all. Just tell me what next."

"You received the plans I sent you?"

Ptarmigan fanned the pages of the book on the desk in front of him. It was called *Ship of Fools* by a woman he had never heard of. "Right here," he said, adding, "Interesting choice."

"You should read it," Finback replied.

Ptarmigan was damned if he would.

Finback: "On the reverse of the back page, top corner, there are two eight-digit codes written in pencil. The first is the GPS coordinate for your explosive drop. You must collect this as soon as you can before the elements do what the elements do best and make it disappear. The second is the GPS coordinate for the rendezvous point. When it is done, make your way there. You may have to wait, but I will have somebody pick you up. An associate. If you really must contact me again, then of course you must only use this handset."

"Is that everything?"

"It only remains for me to wish you good luck, Ptarmigan. Remember, you will be a hero to those who count."

The line went dead.

"Patronising bastard!" Ptarmigan snarled after him. He crammed the wafer-thin handset back into the converted external drive port of his laptop. Now that he knew the secret compartment was there, it seemed to stick out like a sore thumb. But when the on-board security team had carried out their searches, it had been more than effective. They hadn't suspected a thing.

He sat on the edge of his bed, feet planted squarely, hands clenched around his knees, and took a deep, energising breath. His pulse hammered in the side of his neck. His skin crawled.

"Patronising bastard," he repeated, lower this time but still pointed. As he exhaled, he closed his eyes and imagined the negativity leaving him, anger and fear gusting out across his lips like toxic smoke, flowing from his fingertips like poison drawn from a wound. Then he began to chant the Buddhist *daimoku*: "*Nam Myoho Renge Kyo, Nam Myoho Renge Kyo, Nam Myoho Renge Kyo...*"

As the seconds ticked by, his pulse slowed from a hammer to a tap, until he was no longer conscious of it. A deep calm washed over him. His mind focussed. He was no longer a practising Buddhist, but the devotion he had experienced in his youth had left him a valuable legacy. It had taught him the power of the mantra to recharge a man's soul.

25

"*…Nam Myoho Renge Kyo, Nam Myoho Renge Kyo.*"

He reopened his eyes, took his reading glasses and slid them gently onto the bridge of his nose. Then he picked up the book again and thumbed through to page fifty-four. As he parted the leaves, the content raised up off the page towards him. Only it wasn't text. It was the first of twenty-three detailed 3D architect's plans of the *Albanov* icebreaker, superimposed upon the print.

He slid the glasses to the end of his nose and peered over them.

Text.

He reaffirmed them.

Hull of the *Albanov*.

He slid them down again and skipped a few pages.

Text.

He reaffirmed them.

Albanov deckhouse elevation.

Though he had already studied the concealed plans in some detail, he couldn't help but smile. "Finback, you piece of work!"

He refocussed and searched out the ship's engine room. The amount of high explosive he would be planting there, nothing could be left to chance.

6

Murmansk Airport, Northern Russia

The man who greeted Callum in arrivals was short and dark-haired, with the familiar high cheekbones and pale-bronze skin of the indigenous Siberian people. He wore traditional beige trousers and a padded knee-length parka, both made of black-stitched, inverted hide. His nose and cheeks were wind-lashed, and his fur-lined hood was pushed back off his head, leaving a ribbon of paler skin encircling the centre of his face.

He shook Callum's hand. "Hello, Doctor Ross. My name is Lungkaju. How are you, please?"

In truth, Callum felt sick. Just about as sick as he ever had. It was partly the turn of events. The shock of Jonas's relapse. The physical exhaustion of the last two days travelling from Loch Ness to Edinburgh, Edinburgh to Amsterdam, Amsterdam to St Petersburg, Russia, and most recently the twenty-six-hour train journey from St Petersburg to the northern port city of Murmansk. But mostly it was the look on his son's face when he had cut short their holiday together. There had been no screaming and shouting, no tantrum. Just an unbearably silent four-hour car journey back to Edinburgh followed by a look of undisguised betrayal as the boy had slipped away from their perfunctory hug and into his mother's arms.

"It feels like somebody's replaced my brain with a bowling ball," Callum replied at last.

Lungkaju looked blank.

"I'm tired, that's all," he said, failing to conceal a yawn. "Did my equipment arrive?"

"Yes, Doctor Ross, it is already on board. Now come on and I will get you to the outpost so that you can rest."

As they approached the aircraft, Callum realised two things. The first was that it would not be an aeroplane transporting him to the ends of the earth, but what appeared to be a converted military helicopter. It was white with black engines, and a Russian logo was emblazoned on both sides in black and gold.

"We're travelling in that?"

"Yes," Lungkaju replied. "It is a Kamov, a military helicopter adapted to fly important people to the island and also back as quickly as possible. We are expected to land on the *Anna Ioannovna* research vessel in one and a half hours to refuel."

The second thing Callum realised as they approached the Kamov was that he and Lungkaju would not be unaccompanied. Staring at them out of the rear passenger window were two pale eyes amidst a mass of mottled white and grey fur. Below the eyes, a damp nose was squashed up against the window, fogging up the glass with great gusts of breath.

"Do you like dogs, Doctor Ross?"

"I'm okay with dogs," he replied. Not that it was an entirely relevant question. The beast panting away in anticipation as his master went to open the side door was clearly ninety per cent wolf.

"His name is Fenris," Lungkaju said, throwing open the door. "He is very friendly."

The dog immediately bounded onto the tarmac and advanced. Callum had seen large Malamute dogs before, but by any standards Fenris was enormous. His back was easily waist height, and as if to put his stature beyond doubt, he proceeded to plant his forepaws squarely on Callum's shoulders and lick the side of his face.

Callum stumbled backwards with the weight of the animal, and Lungkaju tugged the dog down by his collar and led him back into the cabin. "He likes you," he said, reclosing the door.

Callum wiped the saliva from his cheek. "Thank Christ."

Once both men were seated, Lungkaju wasted no time firing up the Kamov's engines. The roar of the rotor blades was quickly reduced to a background hum within the insulated cabin, and moments later the aircraft rose smoothly up and away from the airport.

Below, Callum could see the landscape thrown into sharp relief. The line of Kola Bay disappeared into the horizon, the fjord gouged deep into the rugged peninsular. Either side, the tundra was uneven, cut by rivers, lakes and gorges, and the thin cover of greenery was strewn with forbidding grey-brown outcrops of serrated rock.

As they accelerated north, the city of Murmansk itself puttered into being and then sprawled along the eastern side of the bay. Its concrete aura barely dwindled before merging into the next great scar. "The naval settlement at Severomorsk," Lungkaju said.

From here the land either side of the estuary shattered. A chaos of islands, rivers and fjords tussled for space, and the waters of the bay teemed with commercial vessels. Then before long the whole fragmented scene thinned away, until only a solitary tanker remained lonely against the vast blue-grey expanse of the Barents Sea.

With the coast behind them, Lungkaju seemed to relax. He shuffled back in his seat and reached inside his coat pocket, withdrawing a small leather flask. He unscrewed the top, took a draught and then offered it up to Callum. "Vodka?"

Callum had worked in Siberia enough times to know that vodka was practically a dietary staple for many indigenous peoples, part and parcel of a different cultural mind-set. But then none of his previous Siberian acquaintances had ever been flying him a thousand miles in a turbo-charged helicopter before. He nodded at the flask. "When you're flying?"

Lungkaju belched out a laugh. "Do not worry, Doctor Ross. I have flown many times. Many, many times. You are in very safe hands."

Not feeling overly reassured, Callum finally accepted the flask and took a gulp. The burn of the neat vodka was as unpleasant as he remembered.

"So how long is it going to take us?" he asked, handing back the flask.

"Four hours," Lungkaju replied. He took another swig. "We will be on the *Albanov* in time for dinner."

Lungkaju was Nganasan, the most northerly of the indigenous Samoyedic clans in Russia. Callum had co-directed an excavation on the banks of Lake Taymyr seven years before, so he already knew a thing or two about the culture. This delighted Lungkaju so much that he awoke a snoring Fenris to tell him the news.

"Doctor Callum Ross has been to Lake Taymyr, Fenris! That is very brilliant because our family are from Lake Taymyr!"

Evidently not sharing his master's excitement, Fenris looked around, nonplussed, before replacing his massive head in-between his paws and falling back to sleep.

They passed the next hour in conversation about Callum's job as an archaeologist, the other specialists already waiting on the *Albanov* and the project ahead of them. Attention then turned to Lungkaju and his involvement. At this he frowned, straining to remember something crucial. At last he exclaimed, "Statistic! I am what you call a *statistic*. The company must give a small number of jobs to Nganasan and our neighbours or they get into trouble with the government. I am useful to them because I can fly and because I speak different languages."

"You seem very well educated," Callum said.

"Because I am lucky," he replied. "And old. Did you know that I am fifty years old?"

Callum had figured late thirties, maybe even younger. But now he knew the truth, a few tell-tale creases did seem to emerge on the pilot's cheek, crumpled as it was by his trademark grin.

Lungkaju set them down on the *Anna Ioannovna* as scheduled. Callum stretched his legs for a couple of minutes, but the icy wind soon drove him back inside the cabin. He waited as Lungkaju directed the fuel crew and Fenris relieved himself furtively against the back of the fuel car.

The vessel was enormous, easily a football pitch in length, with a large bronze-coloured deckhouse and its own helicopter perched alongside the Kamov on the helipad.

"The *Albanov* is bigger," Lungkaju boasted, as he re-entered the cabin and initiated the engines. "Very soon we will be there, Doctor Ross, and you will see. Soon your journey will be over."

Inside his pocket, Callum's fingers closed around the quartz pebble. He watched out of the window as the helicopter accelerated and the endless grey ocean disappeared into the horizon. "I wish I could believe that," he replied.

Chapter 2

ICEBREAKER

1

"Well, if it isn't Indiana McJones!"

Callum did his best to smile as the American man with adolescent sideburns and horn-rimmed spectacles skipped towards him across the dining room. His hair was jet black and he wore a thick, gold chain around his neck.

"Dan Peterson," he said, hand outstretched. "It's good to meet you at last."

"Callum Ross."

"Of course you are. Come on over and let me introduce you to everyone. We've been expecting you." He turned and strutted off back between the tables.

The main dining room on the *Albanov* icebreaker was on the eighth floor of the deckhouse. Panoramic windows were set within the outward-facing walls, overlooking the southern end of the island and taking in the rugged coastline. From the helicopter, the inland tundra had looked as if it had been churned up by a massive plough. Much of it was still covered in snow and it looked as beautiful as it did inhospitable. It also looked a hell of a lot larger than Callum had expected. In the distance, a massive ice-cap squatted over the southern half of the range, the northern half emerging as a tangle of peaks, which stumbled on out of sight.

Lungkaju had set them down on the *Albanov* late afternoon. He'd been right about the size of the vessel. It was enormous, much larger than the *Anna Ioannovna*, easily the largest ship Callum had ever been on. No sooner had they stepped foot on board, than he and his equipment had been subjected to half an hour of stringent security checks. Despite his protests that it was sleep and not food that he really needed, he had then been whisked straight up to the dining room to play meet-and-greet with the rest of the team. He fought and failed to stifle a yawn. Then he forced a smile and followed after Peterson.

The table Peterson made for was one of thirty or forty, all lavishly set. It was surreal. Having spent the afternoon heading ever further from civilisation, dinner in the equivalent of a five-star restaurant was the last thing Callum had expected. The people awaiting him at the table were well dressed, as if attending a conference at a plush hotel rather than embarking on fieldwork within spitting distance of the North Pole.

Peterson gestured Callum towards the remaining laid place at the head of the table. As he manoeuvred himself into the appointed seat, a portly, older-looking man with bushy white hair spoke out in a Russian accent. "It is a beautiful view, is it not, Doctor Ross?"

"It's like something out of Tolkien," Callum replied.

"You are probably wondering why the glacier sits only to the south?"

Callum had not been wondering that at all and the directness of the question took him by surprise. Should he have been wondering that? Was it something the others had all immediately wondered? What he had actually been wondering was how on earth he was going to survey such a vast area in only two months, glacier or not. Out of politeness he replied, "It crossed my mind."

"The answer is simple," the man said, running a hand through his wiry moustache. "There is a high density of tectonic fault lines here, radiating from the Gakkel Ridge."

"Gakkel Ridge?"

"The large oceanic fault line running to the north-west."

"Of course," Callum replied; he had never heard of it before in his life.

"This is why Franz Josef Land is divided up into so many islands," the man continued, "and why there is such a high level of local geothermal activity. It is my belief that the northern end of this island sits on top of a hydrothermal circulating convection cell. There may be fissure swarms in the bedrock allowing the groundwater to penetrate and form vertical convection systems." Looking pleased with himself, he added, "I will be interested to try and verify this."

Before Callum could reply, Peterson said, "That's Doctor Semyonov. Don't worry, none of us understand what the hell he's on about most of the time either. Isn't that right, Nikolai?"

Doctor Semyonov did his best to ignore the remark and returned to prodding a fork disconsolately into his side salad.

"Now," Peterson continued with a flourish, "this here's the beautiful Doctor Ava Lee, our resident—"

"Yeah, okay, take a seat, would you, Dan, we're all quite capable of introducing ourselves." The lady seated to the left of Doctor Semyonov stood up and held out her hand. She looked to be in her forties, with dark eyes, thin lips and short brown hair. "My apologies," she said. "Ava Lee, vertebrate palaeontologist," she shot a glance at Peterson, "and resident Canadian. Nice to meet you."

"And you," Callum replied, noticing that Peterson seemed oddly invigorated by his dress-down. "I read through a couple of your papers on my way to Murmansk. I never thought dinosaurs would have lived at such high latitudes."

She smiled. "Most people don't. It's because it doesn't fit in with our notion of T-rex wandering around humid swamps full of tropical insects and ferns."

"You suggested some of them may have survived the meteor strike as well."

"This is, of course, complete nonsense," Semyonov broke in. "There is not a single secure example of a non-avian dinosaur fossil known from a Tertiary context."

"Well now, that's not exactly true, is it, Nikolai?"

"Oh, boy, you've started something now!" said Peterson with undisguised glee. "Better have yourself a seat, those two'll be at it for hours. Let me introduce you to Doctor Lebedev, ecologist with the Russian Academy."

It was the first time since entering the room that Callum had really noticed the girl seated to the right of Doctor Semyonov. Evidently the youngest member of the group, there was a stillness about her that Callum found immediately calming. Her features were strong, and her eyes were green and searching. She smiled pleasantly and nodded acknowledgement.

"Nice to meet you, Doctor Lebedev," he said.

By the time the meal arrived, Callum's appetite had returned with a vengeance. As they ate, they discussed his journey and then his work as an archaeologist, before he brought the conversation back to the island itself. "So what sort of wildlife can we expect out here?"

"Oh, there's nothing much living way out here, old buddy," Peterson replied, the hint of mischief on his lips. "There's the odd gull, maybe, but otherwise it's a lot of barren rock—"

"Actually, there are over a hundred varieties of native flora alone," Doctor Lebedev corrected him. "I would expect chickweed, buttercup, poppy, one or two saxifrages and many different species of moss."

"What about animals?" Callum asked.

"Mainly birds. There may be as many as forty species, but the rock ptarmigan is the only year-round. Also Arctic fox, possibly Arctic squirrel, and of course polar bear, genetically distinct population."

"Then there's your marine mammals," Peterson added.

"You've got your pinnipeds, so bearded, ringed and harp seals, and your whales, beluga, killer and Greenland right. Then you've got walruses and narwhals."

"I guess they come under your remit then," Callum said, tucking into his dessert.

"Hell no! Those critters are far too big to do anything for me. No, I'm here for this little guy." He sat up and stretched the sides of his T-shirt out to display the monstrous face emblazoned on the front. "This little fella's an arrow worm, a form of microscopic carnivorous plankton."

Callum cast a glance through the window and across the remains of the surrounding pack ice. Glistening and criss-crossed with deep fissures, it besieged the island off into the distance. "And they live at these temperatures?"

"They don't just live here; they thrive. And they're a doozy of a bio-indicator. Arrow worms are healthy, the ecosystem's healthy. Period. Say, you'll have to drop by the lab when I've collected a few samples. It'll be love at first sight, guaranteed."

"Labs are on Deck 3," Doctor Lee said. "I'll show you later if you like. Or if you're beat already then there's a tour after the director's briefing tomorrow. You know about the briefing?"

Callum shook his head.

"Mr Volkov's giving us a briefing first thing tomorrow. Then it's pretty much a full day of safety inductions. You know the score." She paused. "Have you met Mr Volkov yet?"

"Not yet," Callum replied.

"Ha!" said Peterson. "Then you're in for a real treat." Without drawing breath he continued, "Say, when we've finished up here, do you wanna come check out my baby?"

"If it's all the same, I'll come and see the plankton another time."

"Not the arrow worms," Peterson replied with a snort. "This is something much prettier."

2

The elevator stopped on Deck 1 and Callum followed Peterson along the corridor. They stopped at a door next to the main entrance and Peterson tapped a code into the security keypad. The door clicked open and they proceeded through to a narrow staircase leading below the main deck.

"We could've taken the scenic route," Peterson said, his voice echoing in the close confines, "but I figured neither of us was dressed for it."

"So says the Hawaiian surfer," Callum replied, following the flip-flopping of sandals down the stairs.

"Texan, actually. Grew up on Galveston Island on the Gulf Coast. There's plenty of good surfing off Galveston, and diving. It's where I first fell in love with the ocean."

A doorway emerged up ahead. Peterson entered the authorisation code, pushed through it and hit the lights. Holding it open for Callum, he extended his arm out towards the centre of the room in a dramatic gesture. "Et voila!"

The room was extensive and largely empty of furnishings, giving it the appearance of a vast car body repair shop. Around the edges were a few collapsible tables bearing a scattering of mechanical components. More parts were stacked up in boxes in the far corners and against the walls, alongside compressed gas canisters, lengths of corrugated hose and racks of scuba gear.

In the centre of the room stood Peterson's baby.

"Let me introduce you to the *Sea Centaur*," he beamed, adding, "*Sea Centaur*, allow me to introduce Callum 'Indiana' McJones."

It was a marine research submersible, state of the art by the looks of it. Oval in shape, the craft appeared to be about eight metres long from the tip of its nose to the end of its rear-mounted propeller cage. It was perhaps half that across, including the lateral projections, like pectoral fins, on either side. Several panes were set within the vessel's grey upper body, with its surmounting dorsal fin, and the underbelly was lined with pipes and set with numerous hatches. 'SEA CENTAUR' was written in bold letters along either flank, while 'NOAA' was printed in a smaller font towards the tail.

"NOAA's short for the National Oceanic and Atmospheric Administration," Peterson said. "That's who I work for. If it'd been up to me I would've christened this baby *NOAA's ARK*. But I guess I'm just too far ahead of my time." He gave Callum an enthusiastic slap on the back. "So what do you think?"

"I think it looks like a mechanical shark," Callum replied.

Peterson's eyes lit up. "That's exactly what it is! The designers tried to combine the capacity and manoeuvrability of Mir-class and other modern research subs with the aerodynamics of a Seabreacher."

"What's a Seabreacher?"

"A play-thing for the rich and famous. They're quite a recent innovation, personal watercraft that can skim around on the surface like a regular motorboat, submerge a short distance, maybe five or ten feet, and leap out of the water as well. Their body form simulates that of a dolphin or shark."

Callum re-examined what was obviously a very heavy, very

complicated, undoubtedly very expensive contraption. "Are you telling me this thing can leap out of the water?"

"Hell no!" Peterson answered. "Not unless the operator has a hankering for a free lobotomy, which I can tell you he doesn't. But it *is* a good deal faster and more manoeuvrable than most other research subs, and it can operate fine on the surface as well."

He paused to gauge his audience's reaction. "Technologies are advancing rapidly to allow us access to the Arctic safely and affordably. The enhanced speed of this baby means that in ice-locked conditions the host vessel can drop us off at a distance from destination without having to muscle its way through to drop us exactly in position. If the water's a sufficient depth, the *Sea Centaur* can be deployed somewhere more accessible and then travel quickly *underneath* the ice sheets. And if she meets with obstacles or the ice becomes too thick then we can retract the fins and try to circumnavigate whatever's in the way. If it gets too messy or shallow down below then we can even breach the surface, travel across fissures and polynyas if need be. It's like survival here. It's all about versatility."

"What sort of speeds are we talking?"

"Oh, she can shift," Peterson said. "She'll push eighty or ninety knots sweet enough."

Having wheeled over a moveable staircase, he heaved open the access hatch on the roof and allowed Callum a look at the interior.

"It's designed for two, operable by one, but you could fit four, maybe even five people inside of her without much trouble. The instrumentation can be isolated so that nothing gets activated by accident." He hoisted himself up onto the rim, dropped down into the cabin and seated himself in front of the control panel. "Otherwise it's pretty much like driving any other vehicle. Here's your steering, brakes, acceleration, which can be switched to foot-pedal operation." He took Callum through the operating procedures as if he were teaching him to drive the thing. Then he indicated the mass of switches, levers and dials to the right of the steering wheel. "It looks a bit busy on here, but really most of these controls relate to the operation of the mechanical arms. Why don't you hop down front and I'll show you?"

Apprehensive, Callum descended the staircase and walked to the front of the craft. Next thing, there was a loud whirring and various lights flashed as Peterson powered up the sub. The craft rested on its rails, elevated about half a metre off the floor. Her nose sat just above Callum's head. He watched as inlets opened up on either side and two large mechanical arms tipped with tripartite metal pincers inched towards him.

The pincers began to open and clench rhythmically, and Callum took a step backwards, out of range. Peterson's voice boomed out over a PA. "Step back where you were, would you? I wanna show you what this baby can do."

Callum hesitated. The *Sea Centaur* was impressive and everything, but he didn't fancy losing an eye to it. Against his better judgement, he stepped back forward.

"Good man. Now keep perfectly still. I'm gonna do you a favour."

Callum watched as one of the arms extended nearer and nearer to the top of his head, until it was only a fraction above his hairline. At this point the pincer opened with a barely audible squeak and reclosed.

The form of the demonstration suddenly became clear, and Callum braced himself for the inevitable hair-plucking that was to follow. Instead, the other arm now moved forward, arched around the side of his head and came back in to meet with its counterpart. The second pincer clunked open and closed with a pneumatic whistle. It then moved upwards, before the first pincer opened and retracted painlessly. The second lowered down in front of Callum's face.

He examined the prongs. Unable to see anything, he shrugged.

43

"Look closer," erupted from the PA.

Callum looked closer. This time he saw that caught within the pincer was roughly a third of a single grey head hair.

Peterson's laugh filled the room. "Getting old, buddy!"

Callum couldn't help but smile. "Where's the rest of it?"

"The rest of it's your problem," Peterson replied. "I only just met you."

3

"What's the password?"

Silence.

"Come on, the password."

"You don't need the stupid password."

"Of course I need it. How do I know it's you I'm talking to and not a clone?"

"You can see it's me on the webcam."

"Could be a clone."

"It's not a clone, it's me!"

Silence.

"Jamie?"

Jamie made a show of staring past his computer screen, as if reading something on the wall behind. He said nothing. His face was sullen and drawn, and his chin was perched resolutely on top of his knuckles, forcing his lips into a pout. Beyond his hunched shoulders, Callum could make out the little wooden bookcase that stood in the corner of his bedroom; in a rare moment of unity, he and Moira had assembled it together, shortly before the split. The boy's football trophies were lined up across the top, along with a die-cast Lamborghini sports car minus a door, some kind of hideous feng shui bowl thing that his mother had no doubt forced on him, and a mini desk globe that Callum had bought him as a stocking-filler last Christmas. The picture on the high-spec monitor in front of him was so clear that he could read the spines of the comic books crammed into the upper shelves.

"Your mother let you have your Batman comics back then?"

Jamie sighed but made no reply.

"Jamie?"

"Not all of them," he mumbled.

Softer. "Jamie?"

"I said *not all of them.*"

Callum took a deep breath. *Just be patient.* He glanced around the communications centre, a cosy, lounge-like little room, with computer bays and wall-mounted phone terminals divided by felt screens. He turned the volume up on his monitor. It wasn't the first time that he and Jamie had spoken via video link-up. Over the last couple of years it had become a key part of their relationship. Like clockwork, every other Friday at six Callum would connect his webcam and dial through. Jamie would answer pretty much straight away, they would exchange passwords to make sure that neither of them was a clone, and then they would talk for as long as they could. It was no substitute for being together in the flesh. But, as Jamie had once put it, *at least we can pull faces at each other and the other one can see.*

"I'll have a word with her," Callum said. "About your comics."

Jamie dropped his gaze, still determined not to look at the screen, and tapped at his keyboard.

Callum took another deep breath. "Jamie, I'm sorry."

No response.

"I'm sorry that I had to take you home early, I really am. I'm sorry I'm not there with you now." He watched as the boy's gaze moved from the wall briefly and flashed across the screen. "I won't be gone forever, you know. I'll be back before you know it, and then we can go somewhere else, somewhere special, just you and me."

The boy shifted in his little desk chair, and his eyes flickered back towards the screen.

"I love you, Jamie, and I never meant to make you sad. It's just really important that I help Jonas out right now, you know?"

The boy finally looked directly at him. His usually bright hazel eyes were dull with hurt. His brow was crumpled into a frown.

"Can you forgive me?"

"Where are you, Dad?" There was a quiver to the boy's voice that Callum never wanted to hear again.

Out of the corner of his eye, he saw the communications assistant shift uneasily. Of all the new things he had experienced over the last few days, this was the weirdest. It was straight out of Kafka: an armed, po-faced guard *assisting* him with his conversations with his son. Jamie would have loved to hear all about it, to be a part of it, but of course he couldn't.

Callum traced his eye across the man's narrow features. Were it not for his immaculately ironed combat smock, and the pistol holstered at his hip, he would have seemed an unlikely soldier. He was tall and slender, his face was gentle and his eyes gleamed with a rare intelligence. He stood in the corner with his back to the wall. His tattooed knuckles were clamped around the waist-height railing that ran to either side of the main entrance, and his head was tilted inquisitively. On entering, he had helpfully suggested a list of subjects that Callum might not wish to discuss. Unsurprisingly, these comprised anything at all to do with the project, including its location.

"I'm in Russia," Callum answered at last.

"Where's Russia?"

He thought about it. Then, with half an eye on the comms assistant, he said, "Why don't you grab the little globe?"

With a sigh, Jamie edged around on his desk chair, scuffed

across to the bookcase, grabbed the globe and slumped back down in his seat.

"Can you find Scotland?"

"Duh!"

As the comms assistant stretched his legs, coincidentally as far as Callum's computer booth, the boy turned the globe around its axis with a slow, precise twist, scanning across the surface as he went. He stopped and jabbed his finger down somewhere between Aberdeen and Inverness.

"Okay," Callum said, "now keep turning…"

With the little globe placed directly in front of the webcam, Jamie turned it slowly from the top until his finger was hovering somewhere east of St Petersburg.

"…aaaand stop. That's Russia."

Jamie picked the globe back up, held it up to his face and studied it. "It's massive."

"Biggest country in the world."

He plonked the globe back down. "How long for?"

"I'll be back before you start school again in October."

Jamie flopped back in his chair. "October's ages away."

"It'll come around sooner than you think."

"But it's ages and I never see you anyway."

Out of reflex, Callum threw another glance at the comms assistant, but he had retreated back into his corner. "That's not true, Jamie. You're seeing me now, aren't you? Do you know how difficult it was for me to arrange this?"

"Pfff."

"We see each other for real every other weekend, and when we don't see each other we talk like this. You know you can phone me whenever you like—"

"Yeah, but it's not the same. None of it's the same."

"I wish I could change it, son. But it's the best I can do right now."

Jamie went to reply, then closed his mouth, humphed and

stared back down at his keyboard.

Callum sighed. "Come on, what's going to make you feel better? Do you want to shout at me? Do you want to call me names?"

The boy's nose wrinkled and a faint smile flickered on his lips before he stifled it.

"Go on," Callum continued, "free hit. You can call me anything you want and I promise I won't tell your mother."

"What? Anything?"

"Anything at all. You want to call me a great big jerk…" Jamie sniggered, "…that's fine, I deserve it. You want to call me a butt-face…" the snigger turned to laughter, "…go on and call me a butt-face."

Callum glanced over to see the comms assistant looking at him now with undisguised interest; he probably thought that it was all some kind of secret code.

He looked back to see that the grin had disappeared from Jamie's face. His eyes were dull once more.

"Jamie?"

"Got to go."

Callum's heart sank. "What's the matter? Have I said something?"

The boy shook his head. "Mum says it's dinner."

"But we've only just…" Callum stopped himself. *Patience.* "Okay, well, have a nice dinner."

There was a short silence before Jamie said, "Can we talk tomorrow, Dad?"

"You bet," Callum replied, trying to keep his voice steady. "We can talk every night if you like?"

Jamie shrugged. Then he reached a hand out to close the link.

"I love you, Jamie."

The screen went blank.

Callum fell back in his chair and clasped his hands on top of his head. For several minutes he sat quietly, staring at the empty screen and replaying the conversation in his mind. He rolled his eyes. *Have a nice dinner.* Was that really the best he could do?

He watched as the screen went onto automatic standby, then he got to his feet and walked back over to the door. The comms assistant monitored his approach; the intensity of his gaze made Callum feel increasingly self-conscious. Had he said anything wrong? Revealed anything he shouldn't have?

As he pulled the door open, a hand fell on top of his shoulder. He turned around. "Look, I didn't say anything—"

The man gently squeezed his shoulder. "Give to him time," he said, with a warm smile that took Callum completely by surprise. "Just give to him time."

4

"Ladies and gentlemen. Good morning and welcome to Franz Josef Land."

A hush descended as the tall, balding man rose to his feet and cast an imperious glance around the audience. His smile was awkward, incompatible with the focus in his eyes. It caused his brow to furrow and the ends of his neatly trimmed moustache to flare beyond the corners of his lips. His skin was pale and taut, stretched tight across his prominent cheeks, chin and brow ridges, giving his face a skeletal aspect. "I am Mr Volkov, G&S Chief Executive and director of operations here on Harmsworth Island."

Callum was seated towards the middle of the induction group, between Doctors Lee and Lebedev. Doctor Semyonov and Dan Peterson were seated behind, and there were at least twenty or so other specialists and research students packed into the surrounding rows. Around the lavishly decorated, wood-panelled walls stood G&S officials, all wearing similar blue outfits, as well as a rank of soldiers and a handful of Siberian guides.

"For the benefit of our foreign guests," Volkov continued, "I will be giving this talk in English. I presume most of you clever people have a basic grasp. If not then please come to see me afterwards and I will speak properly." He gestured an arm around the room. "This is the *Albanov* outpost. A full tour of the ship is next on the itinerary and later today you must also put up with me telling you all how close to death you are." He perched on the edge of his desk. "For those of you who are unaware, you are now part of the most ambitious infrastructure project ever undertaken. The proposed plant here on Harmsworth will be at the highest latitude of any plant anywhere in the world. The construction energy requirements will be so considerable that power will be supplied, at least initially, by one of a number of pioneering floating nuclear power stations currently under construction.

"Russia, of course, has the largest known natural gas reserves in the world, and we are also already the largest exporter of natural gas. You may be wondering why, then, we are undertaking this project, and the answer is that the geographical pattern of our gas production is set to change dramatically over the next few decades. There will be reduced output from the current primary production sites, for example at Urengoy and Yamburg, and increased exploitation of Arctic resources."

"In other words, they're running out," whispered Peterson.

"Aren't we all," Doctor Lee replied.

Volkov continued, "The gas fields identified in the waters off Franz Josef Land have an enormous projected capacity. The volume of gas that we expect to extract and process will be enough to ensure a continuous, reliable gas supply for northern Russia for many years to come. It will also make a substantial contribution towards our European export commitments."

"Nothing at all to do with making money then," came Peterson's next instalment. This time Doctor Lee said nothing, but turned her head and shot him a warning glance.

Volkov: "Drilling and wellhead installation will get underway within the next few months and are anticipated to be complete by June 2024. This will *hopefully* coincide with the completion of the environmental impact assessment and any other scientific studies, though I appreciate that the timescales involved will rely on the results of your on-going investigations. As a representative of the G&S Corporation, I would like to thank you all for your expert participation. Thank you."

After a few more words of introduction from Volkov, the assembly was invited to reconvene up on the bridge for the start of the guided tour. The bridge itself was a narrow building, the many windows providing a complete arc of vision for the ship's navigators. It was perched on top of the deckhouse, curving slightly across the beam. Behind the bridge, rising up out of sight, stood the main telecommunications mast, with receiver dishes and aerials running up along its length. The centre of the ship's deck was taken up with a series of superstructures, several stories high and forming an extension to the main deckhouse. From their centre rose the wide, rectangular funnel, beyond which the main mast rose to an even greater height, a beacon flashing on its pinnacle and a series of cables trailing from the cross arm. At the very rear of the ship Callum could just make out the raised helipad and the tail of a dormant helicopter.

Callum nudged Doctor Lee, who was standing next to him, and whispered, "Could you imagine trying to reverse park this thing?"

She said nothing. All the colour had drained from her face and her fingers were clamped around the underside of the console.

"Doctor Lee?"

"It's okay," she whispered back, forcing a brief, unconvincing smile. "Not great with heights, that's all."

After touching on the *Albanov*'s research history, Volkov conducted the tour down through the deckhouse, eventually drawing to a stop beside the ground-floor entrance. He rapped the back of his knuckles against one of the doors. "Beyond these doors, you may of course walk the decks and I would invite you to please do so. But all other buildings are restricted. As our guests, we are trusting you to move around unescorted as necessary. *I* am trusting you. Please respect this arrangement and be careful not to enter restricted areas unless you desire an encounter with security forces," he pointed across at the plain, austere frontage of the security headquarters, "which, believe me, you do not."

After lunch the group reconvened in the lecture room. It was roughly the size of one of the University of Aberdeen's smaller auditoria, and Callum guessed there was capacity for around three hundred people at a squeeze. The assembly filed noisily into the first few rows, as Volkov took to the stage and his entourage of officials positioned themselves to either side.

"Thank you for relocating yourselves and your full bellies, ladies and gentlemen, and welcome to our humble lecture room."

He signalled for the lights to be dimmed, and the enormous screen on the wall behind him lit up. "Harmsworth is one of the smaller of the 191 uninhabited islands that make up Franz Josef Land, the world's most remote Arctic archipelago."

He produced a red dot pointer. Then, with a swift about-turn, he aimed the pointer at the image of the Arctic Circle, which flashed up on cue behind him. He circled the little cluster of specks below the 'Barents Sea' label.

"Only two other land masses on earth are as far north as you are now – Canada's Ellesmere Island and Greenland's extreme north." The image flipped to a close-up of those areas, and Volkov indicated each in turn. He then slid the pointer back into his pocket and turned to face his audience once more. "Make no mistake, ladies and gentlemen. This is the edge of the known world. If you believe in Santa Claus, then this is your chance to meet him."

There were a few titters of laughter, notably from Peterson. Then Volkov continued, "When you step outside of these walls, the most important thing to remember is that nature does not want you here. The peoples of northern Siberia call it 'the Land of White Death'. And for good reason. It has survived undiscovered by science for longer than any other landmass on the globe, and it will work hard to defend that isolation. The temperature can reach as low as minus fifty degrees. Last year's average was..."

He looked to Lungkaju, who replied, "Minus fifteen, Mr Volkov."

"Minus fifteen. If you stay here long enough, you *will* get frostbite. If you venture out without the correct clothing and equipment, you *will* get hypothermia and die. If you feel the urge to lick metal, your tongue *will* get stuck, and I and everybody else on board *will* laugh at you."

There was another rumble of laughter. This time the officials joined in as if fondly recalling the times when this had actually happened.

"But it is not all doom and gloom. You lucky people are with us to enjoy the summer, which means that you can expect only minus one or two degrees on most days, perhaps even plus one if you are very lucky. But if you are anticipating any romantic sunsets to photograph and post on Twitter then you can think again. You will experience no such thing. What you *will* experience is the midnight sun. The cold light of day, twenty-four hours a day for the rest of the summer. After this, if any of you are fortunate enough to remain here with us, you will experience polar night conditions, continual darkness and the Arctic winter.

"I'm sold! Where do we sign up?" Peterson called out.

Volkov eyed him cautiously. "If, like Mr Peterson here, none of this is bad enough for you to want to leave us directly, then I must warn you that there is also a killer on the loose. Latest reports indicate that he weighs approximately 1,500 pounds and stands approximately three metres tall. His name is Ulmus. Ulmus Maritimus. But you will know him better as... the polar bear."

A murmur of excitement passed around the audience.

Volkov continued, "This is the largest land carnivore our planet has to offer. He is hungry and he has made his home here. His sense of smell is so well developed that he has already sensed your arrival. Whenever you venture out to look for your rocks or to take your samples, you will be accompanied by an armed patrol. Especially you, Doctor Lebedev," he pinioned her with his gaze, "as you will be seeking him out directly, I presume."

Doctor Lebedev replied to him in Russian and Volkov answered back. The exchange was short, and, though he didn't understand a word, Callum could tell that it was a long way from amicable.

With a snort of irritation, Volkov ended the conversation and brought his attention back to the rest of the group. "One last thing. We have been told to expect unusual solar flare activity over the next few weeks. This is nothing to worry about, but our satellite communication systems may be affected. I am told that any interruption will be infrequent and minimal, but you should be prepared for some short-term disruption to internet and radio communications."

"Will there be any warning?" Callum asked. "Only, I've promised my son—"

"I repeat, Doctor Ross. Any interruption will be infrequent and minimal. There is unfortunately no way to predict if or when this might occur." Volkov checked his watch. "Now, I see that it is almost time for your tour of the island, so I will say nothing further. If you could collect your emergency supplies and reassemble by the helipads at the stern, the guides will be waiting to introduce you to Harmsworth."

"Great," Peterson said, springing to his feet. "Let's get this show on the road!"

"*In the air*," Doctor Lee corrected him.

5

By the time the group had changed into their outdoor gear and reassembled at the stern, the Kamovs were fired up and waiting. Beyond the nose of the nearest aircraft, Callum could see Lungkaju, shades and headset already dwarfing his face, priming the controls. Lambie, another of the indigenous guides, was busy with the controls of the other craft.

Driven by the wind, the group divided itself quickly into two and boarded.

The main cabin had a high ceiling and four rows of detachable seating. Callum followed the first few people on board and sat next to the window on the forward-facing second row. Beside him sat Doctor Lebedev. In front of him, also beside the window, sat Dan Peterson. Callum could hear the other two members of the team, Doctors Lee and Semyonov, already embroiled in a fresh campaign of academic sniping in the rows behind.

With the door secured, the helicopter lurched up off the deck and hummed its way out over the water. Within moments they were approaching Harmsworth's southern shore, and Lungkaju's voice boomed out over the PA: "I will fly around the whole island so that you can see all of him." He then repeated himself in Russian, before banking the helicopter and beginning to pass over the bay. "Valerian Cove," he announced.

Callum watched as the parallel helicopter shadows crossed the expanse of shingle side by side and then manoeuvred into file. Lungkaju in front, they were following the rugged coastline west. Close to shore the ice was fragmented and thin; in places it was absent. Where the surf broke free it clawed against the beach, flecking the light grey pebbles with slush.

"The ice will melt quickly now," Lungkaju said. "In a few weeks it will mostly be gone."

"Death throes of the ice floes," Peterson remarked.

Further westwards the shingle gave way and the relief rose up to form a series of bluffs. Stumps and stacks of exposed rock clustered just off shore, forcing their way up through the residual sheets.

"Harp seal colony," Peterson said, pointing a gloved finger towards the foot of the cliffs.

Callum could see several clots of white fur between the rock pools. The seals' black eyes and huddled pug snouts turned upwards as one to investigate the sound of the helicopter, while several of the more cautious members heaved themselves to the edge of the rocks and slipped away into the safety of the water.

As Callum looked on, Doctor Lebedev leant past him towards the window. In her eagerness to catch a glimpse of the seals, her nose squashed up against the glass and she almost swiped Callum as she brought her hand forward to try and protect her eyes from the sun's glare.

"They look healthy," she said.

"I bet they don't look so healthy once all the building work starts," Peterson replied, with a smirk. He made the sound of a pneumatic drill and held his hands up to grasp the imaginary handles.

Doctor Lebedev turned to Callum and muttered something in Russian. Her face was close enough that he could see the fine grain of her make-up and make out the few pale freckles dotted around her eyes and nose. To his surprise he found that he could also understand her.

"*Mu'dak!*" she had said. *Arsehole!*

For Callum, the days of being able to hold any but the most basic of conversations in Russian were long gone. The years since his last visit had chipped away at his vocabulary until all that remained were the most basic of phrases and a colourful lexicon of curse words, which still came surprisingly naturally.

"*Da, mu'dak,*" he replied. *Yes, arsehole.*

She stared at him, uncertain whether he was just mimicking her. Then her eyes brightened and she laughed.

Callum laughed too.

"*Suka!*" she said, holding his gaze.

"*B'lyad!*" he replied.

"*Khui!*"

"*Piz'da!*"

"What are you guys on about?" Peterson broke in. "What the hell's so funny?"

Callum's eyes searched the vital green of Doctor Lebedev's, just inches away.

She mouthed something that he didn't quite catch, but which he took to mean, *Please don't tell Peterson I just called him an arsehole.*

"Nothing," he replied at last. "Just my shameful Russian."

The Kamov made its way north along the low-lying serrations of the western coast. When Callum returned his attention to the world below, he found that the thin scatter of harp seals had been replaced by a heaving walrus colony. Alarmed by the helicopters' presence, they had churned themselves into a frenzy and were now stampeding out into the water.

"It is not good to scare them like this," Doctor Lebedev said.

Sensing her concern, Lungkaju steered them away.

The relief rose sharply inland, creating a wide coastal plain. Beyond this the island dissolved into a series of rock-strewn valleys stretching on towards the foot of the glacier. As they passed over the centre of the plain, Callum spotted something below. He strained to make it out, but it looked like a cluster of derelict buildings organised around an area of hardstanding.

"Is that an airfield?" he called through to Lungkaju.

"This is an old military base," came the reply over the PA. "The Soviet army built it, but it was never finished."

Callum felt a twinge of disappointment. "Did anybody else think we were the first ones here?"

There were murmurs of general agreement from the rest of the team.

"The government would not tell you about these things," Doctor Lebedev said.

"Did *you* know?" Callum asked.

She shook her head. "I was told nothing either."

As they reached the island's north-western extent, the helicopter banked sharply around a long isthmus jutting out into the sea and ending in an ellipsis of craggy islets.

"Nansen Rocks," came the announcement.

Doctor Lee said something about eroded late cretaceous sediment, while Doctor Semyonov counter-claimed almost reflexively for mid-Jurassic.

From the centre of the northern coastline all the way across to the east, a row of massive cliffs fronted onto the sea.

"This is Svayataya Point," Lungkaju said. "There are many birds here. Very many birds."

The helicopter moved out over the edge of the precipice, descended and flew low along the face of the cliffs. In places they rose to a height of over two hundred metres or more. Time and the elements had gouged fissures into them, and landslides had left great overhangs as well as islands of fallen stone off shore.

Just as Lungkaju had predicted, the face was alive with

nesting birds. Silence descended in the cabin as the helicopters disturbed more and more of the birds from their ledges, and they became so thick in the air that the pilots were forced to swerve out to sea.

"Here's your forty species," Callum said to Doctor Lebedev, somehow recalling their conversation at dinner the night before.

"This is funny," she replied with a knowing smirk, "I count only one."

Past Svayataya Point, as the birds thinned out and the land descended sharply back to sea level, the helicopter continued south along the east coast. Then Lungkaju turned inland once more and made towards the central ridge of high ground. It rose swiftly in vertebral chunks. To the south, the Hjalmar Cap held dominion over the turrets of ancient rock. Up close, the ice revealed its infinite, angular faces, some purest white, others an intense blue. It was a cascade suspended and frozen in time.

To the north, the ice dwindled away to nothing and the base of the ridge was riddled with tunnels.

"In there," said Doctor Semyonov suddenly. "In there you will find the thermal fissures!"

"That's great, Nikolai," Peterson called through to him. "But what do we need hot springs for when there's a sauna on the ship?"

"Because that sauna will not power the Harmsworth facility."

"What the hell are you talking about, *power the facility*?"

"You mean you haven't heard?" said Doctor Lee, sensing blood. "Doctor Semyonov here believes that there's enough thermal energy on this island to provide a fully renewable energy source for the processing plant. He's been pitching it to the powers that be from day one. Only thing is, he's still got to prove it. Oh, and they'll never buy it either."

"Typical western cynicism," Semyonov retorted.

"Typical eastern short-sighted bullshit!"

"Ladies and gentlemen, I will land now," announced

Lungkaju, "and you can walk for a while." He took a furtive swig from his vodka flask, radioed through to Lambie and spoke to him in Nganasan. Soon afterwards, the helicopters set down on Valerian Cove.

"Please be familiar with your survival kits," Lungkaju said. "There is an emergency tent, very strong, a bolt gun for securing him to the bedrock, some flares, a can of bear spray and a survival tin. Hopefully you will not need any of these things, but you should keep your rucksack close whenever you are on the island."

As soon as the side door was thrown open, the wind whipped into the cabin.

"Jesus H Christ!" Peterson said, pulling his hat down around his ears. "I hope you've packed your thermal kilt, McJones."

As the team jumped out, Lungkaju handed each member a thin adjustable strap with a red LED set centrally. "It is an emergency locator," he said. "If you are in trouble, then please press the button and your signal will be picked up on the *Albanov*. Watch for bears and do not wander off the beach."

Callum fastened the locator around his wrist and then began picking his way across the shingle towards the shoreline. The stones crunched underfoot. Splinters of gnarled driftwood were scattered widely. Excreted by the receding floes, cracked by the salt and bleached silver-white by the sun, they were formed into loose piles, like the skeletal remains of long-dead sea creatures.

He reached the water's edge and stopped. *So this is it. The Arctic.*

The *Albanov* was anchored majestically off shore. The surrounding sky was clear and endlessly blue. A number of other islands were visible in faint outline along the horizon. Their features were dulled by the matt sunlight, giving them the appearance of distant icebergs, dark and mysterious, lurking on the edge of existence.

He reached down, selected a pebble and skimmed it along

a fissure in the ice. Below the ripples, the shallows were smooth and crystal clear, and he could make out the edge of a kelp forest, the brown strands bowing with the current. Along the edge, and in between the belts of kelp, the seabed was strewn with multi-coloured rocks, rust reds, greys, blues and blacks, all glowing green with algae.

As the ripples widened, a second stone tripped through them and dropped into the water. He looked around to see Doctor Lebedev standing next to him.

"Your turn," she said, another pebble waiting in the palm of her glove. Her pale cheeks were red with cold, and where the few fine strands of ebony hair had escaped from below her hat, the wind picked them up and whipped them underneath her chin.

He skimmed again, watching as the pebble caromed off a chunk of ice and disappeared without a jump.

"It's the gloves," he said with a grin.

Doctor Lebedev frowned playfully. Her follow-up attempt managed only two small skips.

"You are right, Doctor Ross. It must be the gloves."

"Callum," he replied.

She smiled. "Darya."

"Can I ask you a question?"

"Of course."

"What did you say to Mr Volkov earlier, in the meeting?"

Her eyes narrowed. "I told him that Harmsworth is dangerous enough without a lot of frightened people wandering around carrying guns."

"And what did he say?"

She tutted at him. "Now that is two questions, Callum."

6

Ptarmigan lay stretched out on his bed. Technically it was one o' clock in the morning. But with the goddamn sun up at all hours of the night, it might as well have been one in the afternoon.

The day's induction had left him feeling totally drained. Volkov could've talked forever, and being cooped up in the helicopter with all those corporate cocksuckers was almost unbearable. He took a deep breath.

On top of the chest of drawers beside him was an irritatingly pointless bedside lamp, next to which sat the copy of *Ship of Fools*. He stared along the book's spine. Then he reached out and ran his hand absent-mindedly across the cover.

Since speaking to Finback last, he had studied the plans in such minute detail that they were practically burnt into his visual cortex, complete with annotations. He needed to be prepared for anything. He needed contingency.

The ability to memorise images and text like this was a skill which he had always had. His whole life, people had been crediting him with a photographic memory, but he knew that it wasn't quite that simple. For Ptarmigan, memory was more a matter of discipline and determination. It was the sad fact that these were virtues most people lacked in abundance that made him a goddamn memory magician by comparison.

If there was something to be learnt, say the plans to an icebreaker, then he would read them… and then he would read them again… and then again… and again… tirelessly, as many times as it took to commit them to memory. That was why he had given a seamless rendition of *Hamlet* in the school play, and that was why he now knew the layout of the *Albanov* as if he'd built it himself from scratch.

He yawned and turned over onto his side in preparation for another *night* of broken sleep. Yessir, he had to hand it to himself: sleep-deprived or not, he was all over this project like a rash.

Tomorrow he would pick up the explosive and then… zero hour.

* * *

The red and white pills dropped into Finback's palm. With a deft flick of his thumb he resealed the chrome-plated dispenser and slipped it back into his top drawer. The headaches were the result of a blow to the head that had left him fighting for his life as a young man. They weren't migraines. There were no hallucinations, no sickness or disorientation to accompany the head pain, only intense flashes of blinding agony, as if somebody was slamming an ice pick repeatedly into the front of his skull. They had all the usual triggers, primarily stress and fatigue, and tonight Finback was feeling both.

He tipped the pills back onto his tongue and felt the bitter sting as they began to dissolve.

In front of the flat-screen monitor on the desk before him were three evenly spaced items. On the left was a large hexahedral bottle half-filled with Rodnik Gold, the most delectable and expensive vodka money could buy. Beside this, in the centre of the desk, was the print-out of an email, adorned at the bottom with the official footer of the Russian Government. To the right, resting with ironic delicacy on the polished wooden surface, was a combat knife.

Finback reached out and took hold of the bottle. He unscrewed the top and drank, throwing his head back to force the pills down. It pained him to be so uncouth as to not use one of his crystal tumblers, but the warning twinges were already beginning to pique and every second counted if he was going to avoid an episode of debilitating head pain.

He placed the bottle back down and reached for the email. There was no greeting, no sign-off and no text. There was just a simple table:

	Team I	Team II
2020	3.64	0.32
2021	6.94	0.95
2022	8.59	1.31
2023	4.31	0.16
2024	2.49	0.03
Albanov	-	3.2
Total	25.97	5.97

Finback ran his eye down each column, carefully adding and re-adding the numbers. Then he took a pen from his top pocket, scribbled '20,000,000,000 rubles' beneath the table and slowly underlined it. He did a quick mental calculation. That was nearly three hundred million US dollars, 200 million British pounds; two billion Chinese yuan. He pursed his lips. The figures were not unpleasant reading, but in truth he had hoped for an even larger differential.

He glanced down at his wristwatch just as the platinum minute-hand nudged onto the hour. It was time. He creaked back into his leather armchair, took out his phone and dialled.

"Good evening, gentlemen… Yes, I have seen them. I thought it might be more, but there will, of course, be further reductions as a result… You are happy to continue…? Of course. Everything is in place. Tomorrow he will pick up the explosive… because it needs to seem as real as possible. He is no fool… No, he suspects nothing… Of course. Good evening."

He dropped the handset back into his pocket and slid the document back onto his desk.

His gaze moved to the knife. The handle was made of solid black birch with a gold-plated metal butt, and a gold-plated, S-shaped hand guard. The admittedly brutal-looking six-inch blade was also black, with serrations along the lower part and a narrow clip point. He wrapped his fingers around the handle and gently lifted it off the lacquered surface. After thirty years, it was like a fifth limb; the feel of the weapon – the grip, the weight, the balance, even the difference in temperature between the wood and the steel – was as familiar to him as the sound of his own voice.

He jumped suddenly to his feet, simultaneously tossing the knife a short distance into the air. He caught it with practised ease, spun it across the back of his hand and then flipped it several times on end as he reached out with his other hand and reclaimed the email. With a fluent sweep of the blade, he sliced the paper in two and let the two halves drift back down onto his desk. Then he flipped the knife one last time, caught it by the back of the blade, turned and propelled it into the wall behind him.

The knife slammed into the cork throwing board with a loud thunk that shook the adjacent lamp housing and drew a satisfying rattle from the glass. He walked over and eased the blade free. As he did so, the photograph that had been pinned to the centre came unstuck and spiralled to the floor.

Finback watched its progress as it fluttered downwards and settled onto the carpet.

Staring up at him was Ptarmigan, his dumb, unsuspecting face precisely cloven.

Chapter 3

ICE MUMMY

1

Harmsworth Island, Russian Arctic

Nothing could have prepared Callum for the sense of isolation he felt on Harmsworth. If it hadn't been for the slow, steady trudging of Lungkaju day after day, and occasional distant glimpses of the *Albanov*, he could easily have imagined himself the only man on earth. He struggled to understand it. He was no stranger to remoteness. Bleak Hebridean landscapes had been on his doorstep his entire life, and his job had taken him to the frozen tundras of Scandinavia and mainland Russia many times. But this was different. It was the deep stillness here. The intense quiet. Inland, away from the lapping of the waves and the groaning of the remnant icebergs, there was no movement. No sound. Not even time intruded on the vast, desolate sweeps of tormented rock. *A place for ghosts*, Callum thought. *If ever there was one.*

He checked the mapping on his GPS tablet. After two weeks, he and Lungkaju were still in the south of the island. On paper it had looked so simple. But in practice the terrain was slowing progress to a crawl. Beyond the shingle-strewn beaches, scoured into gentle inclines by the timeless clawing of the surf, the inland valleys were wide, steep and unforgiving. The rock appeared solid, but in reality it comprised overlying crusts of loose, pitted stone, always brittle, often slick with ice or moisture, which shifted unpredictably with the weight of every pace. The successive valleys rose and fell like rippling dunes, from light grey eructations to banks of pewter and charcoal scree. Angular upright and recumbent boulders huddled on the valley sides, barring the way ahead, their faces weathered flat and dimly glowing in the unrelenting radiance of the midnight sun.

It had started as a curiosity. On his first night aboard the *Albanov*, Callum hadn't minded being woken by the laser beam of sunlight that had somehow penetrated a chink in his cabin blind. As the clock turned 01:16, he had thrown the blind up and looked with wonder out across the deck and the ice-flecked ocean beyond, still bathed in the same intense, white light as when his head had first hit the pillow. But after a few days, as the sun persisted, circling and circling the sky overhead without ever setting, the relentless light had become an issue. It was surreal to the point of disorientation. It was constant to the point of distraction. The medics had warned the entire team to expect two things: sunburn and mood swings, and within days they had all been struck down with both.

By the end of the first week, they had also each come face to face with the mist.

"This is very common at this time of year," Lungkaju had said, as it descended rapidly and unexpectedly for the first time. "Do not panic, please, Doctor Ross."

Don't panic, Callum had thought. It was an inconvenience, for sure, but why would he panic over a bit of mist? He had then watched with a mixture of awe and deepening unease as the rocks around him thinned, fractured and finally disappeared behind a suffocating pall of grey. He'd expected tough terrain. But the severity and regularity of the mists on Harmsworth had taken him entirely by surprise. The reduced visibility was one thing, but the freezing *sea smoke*, as Lungkaju called it, was something more, a far cry from the fingers of atmospheric *haar* that rolled in off the North Sea from time to time and hugged the lowland coast of Aberdeenshire.

This mist, the sea smoke, carried a strange scent, a bitterness that clung to his nostrils, stung his eyes and left him with a dry mouth. It didn't hug, drift or drape. It billowed and pulsated. There was nothing picturesque about it. Nothing redeeming. At times the proximity and constant motion of the vapour induced a sense of suffocation, and a queasiness that Callum could only liken to the travel sickness he'd suffered with as a child. At other times sound was amplified and distorted into distant wails and shrieks; the world would come alive with echoes, and dark shadows would flicker in and out of being like spectres in the haze.

"The sea smoke is very thick," Lungkaju had informed him, his knowing grin barely visible through the murk. "Sometimes it will not clear for many hours, sometimes days."

When the sky was clear, the two men walked in single file, pitching snippets of conversation at each other, lost in their respective tasks. Lungkaju kept to the rear, rifle cradled in his arms, scanning for tell-tale bear tracks and scat. Callum recorded the predicted lack of archaeology in his field journal, stopping every so often to take photographs and to try to puzzle out their precise location with the help of his increasingly temperamental GPS tablet. It was tough going, physically and mentally. Only Fenris seemed free to enjoy the island, disappearing for hours at a time, reappearing with gifts of mouth-sized boulder for Lungkaju before vanishing back among the outcrops.

By midday they had picked their way down into a valley. Where the ice had relaxed its grip, moss flourished; it carpeted the valley bottom, toupees of spongy green fibre stitched to the head of every boulder. Tufts of buttercup sprouted in between, as did other red and purple blooms that would have looked more at home in the meadows of the Scottish Lowlands. It was just as Darya had insisted that first evening at dinner. The abundance of life in such an extreme environment was extraordinary. While Callum needed insulated clothing, sun cream and shades, the daintiest of flowers simply shook their heads at him and thrived.

Lungkaju drew to a stop and lowered the rucksack from his shoulders. "Let us eat."

Callum gladly shed his pack and sat down next to him. As he reached for his water bottle he felt his emergency locator slip down his wrist. He shook his head and fumbled through his jacket sleeve to tighten the strap. Only two weeks in, and the island had already taken half a stone from him, not to mention his foot blisters, which had made him a regular in the infirmary.

Lungkaju leant his rifle down and hollered out for Fenris.

"Don't you worry about him getting lost?" Callum asked.

"It is us that I am more worried about," Lungkaju answered, "me and you, not Fenris." He took a swig from his flask. "Do you have any pets, Doctor Ross?"

"Does an ex-wife count?"

Lungkaju laughed. "You were married?"

Callum poured himself some soup. "I was. We were together for ten years."

"And then you did not love her anymore?"

"Oh, I loved her alright. I loved her more than anything. Only thing was, she didn't love me. I mean, she stopped loving me."

"That is very sad."

"My fault," Callum said. "I could see it coming. My career was taking off. I was spending more and more time in the department. Less and less at home. She kept telling me that she was unhappy."

Lungkaju took another swig from his flask and offered it over. "Why did you not listen?"

"I've asked myself the same question a thousand times," Callum answered, accepting the flask. "Just young and foolish, I guess. Didn't know what I had until I didn't have it anymore."

Lungkaju smiled, understanding.

"So, what about you? Are you married?"

"I was," Lungkaju replied. "My wife died giving birth to our daughter."

"I'm sorry."

"We were married for sixteen years."

"Happy years?"

"Happy years."

They ate in silence for a while, Lungkaju picking the raisins from the tattered bits of malt loaf that seemed to be all that he ingested besides vodka.

"My daughter looks like her mother," he said at last.

"My son's got his mother's temper," Callum replied. "Otherwise he's like a little version of me."

Lungkaju stared at him as if trying to imagine such a thing. "What is his name?"

"Jamie. He'll be nine in November."

"My daughter will be fifteen next March."

"You must miss her, working so far away."

Lungkaju nodded. "I miss her very much. But I write her a letter every month. When I first came away I wrote every week, and emailed. But she told me to stop. She said that one week left me nothing to say." He grinned. "She said that I was boring after just one week."

"I don't see Jamie very often," Callum said. "We talk online a lot, using webcams, but he's right, it's not the same. We were on holiday a couple of weeks ago. It was the first time I'd seen him properly for ages and he was so excited. I taught him how to skim stones." He paused. "Then I had to leave him to come here."

"He will forgive you, Doctor Ross. You have a good heart; I can tell because Fenris likes you and he does not like bad people."

"I hope so."

Lungkaju retrieved another slice of malt loaf from his

rucksack. "Now, will you tell me something? What is *to skim stones*?"

There was a sudden scuffling sound beyond where they were sitting and in an instant Lungkaju was on his feet, rifle in hand.

Fenris trotted into the clearing.

"Where have you been?" Lungkaju said, relaxing his grip. "You have worried Doctor Ross."

With a snort, the dog paced over, slumped down between the two of them and commenced chewing. Callum watched as he grasped one end of an off-white stick between his paws and gnawed at the other. With a loud snap, he crunched the tip off his new toy and dropped the broken end to the floor.

Callum's eyes widened at the sight. Handing the flask back to Lungkaju, he got to his knees and leant slowly towards the dog. Fenris stopped his chewing and growled, his top lip quivering back to expose the first warning flashes of tooth.

"He thinks you want his stick," Lungkaju said.

Without moving his gaze, Callum replied, "He's right."

There was a confused silence, before Lungkaju gave Fenris an order in Nganasan. The dog barked in protest. Then he sat back up, dropping the object from his massive jaws with a snort.

No sooner had the object hit the ground, than Callum had reached forward and grabbed it. His heart picked up as he wiped away the film of saliva and turned it again and again in his fingers.

"What is it?" Lungkaju asked. "It is driftwood?"

Callum shook his head. "No, it's bone." He turned it again, exploring the splintered end. Then, slowly, he turned his head to face Lungkaju. "It's *old* bone."

2

The object was no longer than twenty centimetres, half that wide and a couple of centimetres thick. The intact end curled upwards into a lip, while the other end had been snapped off into a point and splintered by the best efforts of Fenris.

Callum ran his fingers over the pattern etched into the face of the shaft. The mesh of intertwining strands had been chiselled with such finesse that even a modern-day sculptor would have struggled to replicate it. The harder he looked, the less he could believe that the item in his hand was ancient, and yet the more certain he became.

As he inspected the bone more closely, he could make out traces of paintwork. The recesses had once been blacked out and the ridges painted gold. There was also a strange brownish hue to the broken end.

Lungkaju was peering intently at the item.

"I don't suppose you've lost this, have you?" Callum asked.

He smiled and shook his head. "I don't know what is this thing."

"Can Fenris take us to where he found it?"

Lungkaju took the item, flipped it over in his palm and nodded affirmatively. "This is archaeology?"

"It just might be."

"What is it?"

"I'm not sure," Callum answered, noticing the traces of resin on the bottom surface. "But it looks like the tip of a ski."

Steam trailing from his back, Fenris bounded in between the fallen pillars of rock. Collapsed with age and moss-encrusted, they littered the valley floor beside a wide stream channel.

"Water flowed here once," Lungkaju said, jogging to keep up.

"Yes, it did, but not for many years by the look of it," Callum replied. "It's what archaeologists call a palaeochannel. An ancient riverbed."

"A *palaeochannel*," Lungkaju repeated. "You speak a strange language, Doctor Ross."

The channel rounded a bend and descended sharply. Callum could see that the rockface revealed up ahead formed a foothill to the Hjalmar Ridge. If it hadn't been for the previous fortnight, he would have found it strange that such a prominent feature could go unnoticed until a person had all but jogged into it. But life on Harmsworth had been nothing if not a steep learning curve. Little was what it seemed in this guarded and demanding place. Like a large optical illusion, the land itself seemed to shift by the second. High became low. Low became high. Far was near, and near could take forever to reach.

At the base of the rockface was a narrow opening, partly obscured by a rock-fall, where the river had long since chiselled its way through. Straight away, Fenris leapt up and over the obstructing boulders and began sliding his way in.

"This is where he found the bone," Lungkaju said. He beckoned the dog back with an ear-piercing whistle. "But I am not sure that it is safe."

Until now, Callum had feared they were on a wild Malamute chase. But the fact that Fenris had led them here made a believer of him fast. There was no way that the object could have survived so well preserved if it had been rolling around in the open for centuries. Protected from the elements, within a tunnel, such preservation was much more likely.

Callum's mind raced in tandem with his heart as they approached the opening. If he could find evidence of human occupation here, it would be one of the archaeological discoveries of the century. Jonas's conviction that ancient people *had* lived at these latitudes would be vindicated. There was even a chance that he could justify himself to Jamie.

The entrance to the tunnel rose to just below waist height. Callum knelt down and peered inside. An icy draught yawned its way between the cheeks of ancient rock, causing him to shiver. "Well, I think we've safely disproved Doctor Semyonov's hot springs," he said, removing his rucksack. "This place feels more like a walk-in freezer." On his hands and knees he started to creep forward. "Make that *crawl*-in."

"Are you sure it is wise to enter this place, Doctor Ross?"

There was consternation in Lungkaju's voice. The grin that Callum had grown accustomed to was nowhere to be seen. In fact, for the first time, Lungkaju looked his age. Fenris shuffled awkwardly from paw to paw beside him, a low, impatient whine escaping his jaws.

Callum himself would normally have been the first to preach caution over curiosity. If it had been one of his students creeping headfirst into an unknown tunnel in the middle of God knows where, he would have given them hell. But the possibility that there was something ground-breaking so close at hand was too much for him. It had that same gravitational effect that had brought him into archaeology in the first place. It was the scent of discovery, the opportunity to see what no other human being had seen for so many years.

"I'll be careful," he said at last, holding Lungkaju's still-cynical gaze. Then he crawled on into the tunnel.

3

The smell was overpowering. It was the fug of wet stone, like a dank medieval cellar. Callum moved forward, his elbows scraping past the naked ribs of rock, the torch beam fluttering ahead like a pale moth.

In the closeness of the confines every sound was amplified, from the faint whistling of his breath to the scraping of his toes on juts of stone. When Lungkaju called to check on him, his words were accelerated by the tunnel's natural rifling until they flew past, deafening and garbled.

Up ahead the torchlight met with something.

Callum stopped. He searched the obstruction out and homed in. Whatever it was, it was sizeable, propped against the right-hand side of the tunnel and spreading out into the centre. It might have been a rock. But something about the shape and the glimmers of colour feeding back to him along the faint beam made him think otherwise.

He edged forward until it was within reach. Then he refocussed the torchlight. There, dimly illuminated, was another piece of bone. Only it was not carved or smoothed off on the surface. Instead it looked brittle, jagged where it had been roughly snapped off. The shaft disappeared into a brownish oval, overhung by shreds of fabric. To the right was another almost identical arrangement of bone, oval and shreds, though in this case the shaft was even more badly splintered.

It took a while for Callum to realise what he was looking at. He recoiled suddenly, knocking the back of his head against the roof of the tunnel. Behind him, Fenris barked and Lungkaju's voice echoed past once more, prompting Callum to reply that he was okay.

The two yellowing lengths of bone were clearly the remains of human femurs, thighbones, a honeycomb of marrow at their centres. Their distal heads had been snapped off, neither fracture appearing fresh. The dark ovals into which they disappeared were stumps of thigh, discs of quadricep and hamstring muscle left in cross-section around the nubs of bone, where both legs had been roughly hewn above the knee.

Callum reached out and prodded at the flesh. It was frozen solid. He moved the torch along what was left of the thighs. The beige trousers were made of animal skin. The fur was on the inside for insulation and the outside had been sown with black thread and treated with oil of some description, presumably for waterproofing. Strands of the material hung over the ends of the severed thighs, frozen to the muscle.

The corpse lay on its front, arms outstretched. Around the torso was a fur parka, similar to Lungkaju's. The hands were frozen into claws, and a large hood concealed the head.

Callum's brain flooded with a thousand questions. Most pressing was the matter of when exactly the person had died. Some Samoyedic peoples had maintained a traditional lifestyle for so long that a person alive at the time of Christ might have appeared identical to one alive today. There was nothing Callum wanted more than to accept that this was one of Lungkaju's earliest ancestors, perfectly preserved in time. But it was not that simple. When it came to human remains, getting the distinction right was crucial. It was the difference between an ancient burial and a modern murder victim, between archaeological excavation and the forensic examination of a crime scene.

He thought on it. The corpse was frozen solid, which might have suggested age. But then in these temperatures most things *were* frozen solid. The bone was an off-yellow colour, a sure sign of age under normal circumstances. But these were not normal circumstances, and whatever mechanism had removed the lower legs in the first place may have had a part to play in any colour change. Even the waterproofing agent from the clothing might have affected the bone composition. Then there was plain old scepticism. Just as he had argued with Jonas, the likelihood of anybody ever living at this latitude in the distant past was as remote as the place itself. But then was it any more likely that a modern Nganasan, Dolgan or Nenet had ended up lost out here, alone and unreported?

Strictly speaking, the process now would be to record the body as it lay, before disturbing it. But on both a professional and personal level, Callum needed to be sure. He moved his hands gently along the sides of the thighs to the base of the jacket. Around the top of the buttocks was strung a thick belt of hide. He followed it, patting his hands around the hips, feeling more like a police officer frisking a crook than a professor of archaeology.

The fingers of his left hand closed around an item dangling from the belt. He shifted his position and, as carefully as possible, peeled back the frozen flap of parka.

In his palm was a leather sheath, no more than ten or eleven centimetres long. Within it sat a knife with a beautifully crafted bone handle. The patterns adorning hilt and handle were similar to those on the ski-tip, though in this instance the paintwork was still pristine. Undoing the toggle clasp, he jiggled the blade upwards just far enough to reveal what it was made of.

He held his breath. If it said '*Clydebridge Steel*' he would have his answer.

It was an unadorned, smoky-blue flint blade that met Callum's gaze. It was as skilfully fashioned as any he had ever excavated before and still as sharp as the day it was knapped.

He let out a massive sigh of relief. In front of him was a genuine ice mummy, the archaeological equivalent of a lottery win. The freezing temperatures had prevented breakdown of the body's soft tissues by fungi and bacteria. Hair, nails and skin survived, as did stomach and bowel contents, clothing and other organic personal effects. In front of him was a near-complete picture of a past life frozen up into a human time capsule.

Other famous examples flashed through his mind: the mummified Inca children discovered from time to time, high up in the Andes of Peru; Oetzi, the Bronze Age man discovered on the Italian/Austrian border in the European Alps; the two ancient Inuit women preserved at Barrow in Alaska; the family of eight discovered in a communal tomb at Qilakitsoq, north-west Greenland. The mummy in front of Callum now was easily as well preserved as any of these other cases that he had read about. Better even. The summer temperature on Harmsworth may have crept above freezing over the last few years, but the tunnel's sheltered interior and the constant sub-zero through-breeze had effectively freeze-dried the body.

A short distance beyond where the mummy lay, something else caught his eye. He resecured the flint blade back within its sheath and then crawled over to inspect.

It appeared to be a fibre sack, open at one end, empty. In front of it were a bird skeleton and a scatter of yellow-white pot shards. He reached out and carefully lifted one from the rock. It was unlike any ceramic he had ever seen before: fine and delicate with a nobbled outer surface. He placed it back down. Whatever these items represented, there was little doubt that both the dead bird and the pottery had originally been within the sack, perhaps forming part of some magical shamanic rite.

After carefully examining a couple more of the shards, his

attention moved back to the mummy. He inspected the frozen flesh of the thighs once again. His heart raced with excitement. Desiccation of the most vulnerable outer soft tissues was virtually nil. Jonas had been right after all. *Where there are reindeer, there are reindeer hunters.*

He brought the dim glow of the torchlight back down over the severed leg bones.

"And reindeer hunter *hunters*," he whispered.

4

At sixty-six years of age Doctor Semyonov was finding Harmsworth a challenge. The helicopter had set him and his guide down on the plateau overlooking the cliffs at Svayataya Point earlier that morning. He had then spent the last couple of hours slipping around on scree, battling his way through marsh and scaling deceptively steep inclines on his way to the Hjalmar Ridge. The whole damn thing had looked a lot simpler from the air.

He sneaked a couple of fingers up below his jaw and checked his pulse. It was rapid, but no more so than he'd expect for a man of his age clambering around in the wild. Truth was, he'd had no option but to keep his angina a secret. There wasn't a chance in hell that he would have qualified for such a remote research posting if he'd declared it. And it was nothing serious. The whole thing had been a massive over-reaction. The occasional and really very mild chest pain was a holiday compared to his wife's nagging about it, her conviction that he was going to drop dead suddenly and leave her a widow. It was all nonsense. He felt perfectly fine. Even so, he dropped his fingers from his neck to his top pocket, where they found the comforting bulge of the small sublingual nitro-glycerine canister, issued to him in case of an acute attack.

Over the last fortnight Semyonov had spent the majority of his time quite happily in his laboratory, determining the index properties of old rock core samples. These had been extracted, somewhat more crudely than he would have liked, by the previous prospection team. In due course he would need them for comparison with the sixty scientific samples he was to take himself over the next two seasons. In the interim, having given the outside temperature time to achieve its yearly maximum, the moment had been ripe for the first of his field observations.

So far that day there had been no great surprises. The whole island appeared to be formed of successive tiers of basalt. Now that the majority of the ice cover had melted – an oddly accelerated process which he had observed with some interest through the safety of his laboratory portholes – Semyonov could confirm that they were Jurassic to Tertiary in age, with a handful of late Triassic strata outcropping in places. Much to his dismay, Doctor Lee's prediction that the majority of the sediments would be late Cretaceous was also confirmed. Still, it had obviously just been a lucky guess on the part of that infuriating know-it-all Canadian bitch.

"This way," he called to the Dolgan security guide following behind. The man's rifle looked comical against his tiny frame, and he was made to seem all the smaller by the size of the doctor's rucksack. Semyonov snorted away the guilt that this inspired. There was too much western-minded liberality displayed towards Dolgans and Nenets and the like these days. He certainly felt no remorse for his opinion that they were still little better than cannibals. They were a pain in the Federation's arse with their determination for unjustifiable equality; though, in fairness, they would always be more tolerable than the blacks.

As the two men approached the base of the ridge, the gradient increased once more and the land bucked itself into a series of steep foothills. Semyonov smiled at the sight of the ice-capped crags towering beyond. Already he could make out the first of the caves, its gaping mouth navigating him across the melt-water marsh. An hour later, he was standing beside it, perspiring heavily and peering into the darkness.

The guide chirruped away, entirely unhelpfully, about the likelihood of bears. But Semyonov ignored him and fumbled open the backpack on his shoulders to retrieve his headlamp. Speleology – *cave exploration*, as it was known to the ignorant – wasn't strictly a part of his assessment scope. But nobody would give a damn after he had proven once and for all that there was a convenient, easily extractable source of geothermal energy on Harmsworth. G&S would save millions, the world would have one less coal-fired plant to fret about and he himself would be wallowing in acclaim.

He handed the protesting Dolgan a second headlamp and led the way.

Semyonov estimated the cave to be thirty metres across by eight or so high in places. It was probably a relict littoral cave, the result of wave action on an ancient shoreline. And it was likely to be extensive. Other examples that he had visited in Norway had reached lengths of over three hundred metres, and they were labyrinthine in their complexity.

As his eyes adjusted, Semyonov could see that roof collapse had left dollops of rock scattered widely. The floor was uneven with rifts, channels, pools and spreads of stone. Moisture dripped from the ceiling and patted off his jacket. The sound was eerie and annoying. But it wasn't half as distracting as the stench. The reek was incomparable.

"What is that?" he asked, his moustache wrinkling in disgust.

"I do not know," came the reply. "It is like the guts of a whale."

Semyonov had never had the misfortune, but he was unsurprised that the Dolgan had, and the description seemed very apt. Another few paces and he felt his foot sink into something soft. He looked down to see the heel of his hiking boot disappearing into a mound of pulp. He bent down to inspect. A second beam of light appeared as the Dolgan knelt beside him.

It was excrement.

"Bear, I presume?"

The Dolgan moved his face revoltingly close. Then he removed his glove and held his hand palm down over the dung. "This was a large carnivore, yes. It was here recently."

"How recent?"

"One hour." The Dolgan rose to his feet. "Doctor Sir, we should leave to be safe."

Doctor Semyonov was tired of the man's whining. But at the same time he was in no hurry to antagonise a bear, genetically distinct or not. Besides, from what he'd seen already there would be no shortage of other carnivore-free caves to explore in this part of the island.

"Fine," he replied. "Let's move on."

As they picked their way back towards the entrance, Doctor Semyonov panned his headlamp across the floor to either side. What he had thought were scatters of stone he now recognised to be more animal droppings. What's more, he could see that practically the entire floor of the cave was caked in them. Some were greying, evidently quite old. Some seemed much more recent. The observation was unimportant. It was nothing really, barely worth the brain activity. But it still made him want to pick up the pace. "I think there may be more than one bear—"

Something bolted suddenly across the entranceway. The two men froze.

"What the hell was that?" Semyonov demanded.

The Dolgan held a finger to his lips and crouched down, motioning for Semyonov to do likewise. He did so, watching as the man aimed his rifle towards the entrance.

They waited.

Nothing.

The Dolgan slowly stood back up. "Wait here, please, Doctor," he whispered.

With not the least intention of moving, Semyonov remained crouched as the Dolgan inched towards the nibbled disc of daylight that formed the cave's entrance. He drew closer and closer, stopping just beyond the mouth. Steam rose from his silhouetted body, spiralling into the cold as he scanned around.

In an instant something launched itself towards him and knocked him out of sight.

Doctor Semyonov jumped to his feet, but he remained silent, rooted to the spot. He listened as a scuffle took place and a shot rang out from the Dolgan's rifle.

Then silence.

What the hell had just happened? Semyonov had no idea. All he knew was that he was suddenly alone. On instinct, he bolted from the illumination of the entranceway and made his way into the shadows. Excrement crunched underfoot as he fled. Not that he was really fleeing, of course. His clamber into hiding was strategic. There was nothing cowardly about it. He just needed time to reassess the situation.

He turned off his headlamp and prayed that the Dolgan was okay. There had been no screams *and* he had fired a shot off, so why wouldn't he be? They knew their business, these Dolgans. Cannibals or not. No doubt he had killed the bear, felled him with a single bullet, and any second now he would return to the cave ready to carry on as if nothing had happened.

Semyonov waited for him. By now the pounding of his heart drowned out the drip-dripping of moisture from above, and it was suddenly accompanied by twinges of discomfort: not quite pain, but almost.

He reached a hand towards his top pocket, his eyes remaining glued to the cave entrance. As he fingered the zip, he felt his own defencelessness more and more keenly. As well as the rifle, the Dolgan had been carrying everything else of any use in that rucksack: the bear spray, the flares, even the damn survival tin.

His thoughts were interrupted by a sudden rustling and then movement at the cave entrance. Semyonov's skin was clammy despite the chill. Discomfort churned in his chest. He held his breath. *Please be the Dolgan, please be the Dolgan, please be the Dolgan...*

It was not the Dolgan.

Callum watched as Lungkaju craned over the mummy's legs. How would he react? He was proud of his Nganasan heritage and as faithful to his traditional customs as Fenris was to him. But he also piloted a helicopter for a gas company. He had a smartphone and, so he assured Callum, Facebook and Twitter accounts. Would he be upset to see one of his ancestors like this? Or was he more likely to want a selfie with the archaeological find of a lifetime so that he could post it online?

"I know this man."

Callum stared at Lungkaju. His face was barely illuminated in the torchlight. "He's carrying a prehistoric flint blade," he said. "If you know him, then you must be a hell of a lot older than fifty."

Without taking his eyes off the mummy, Lungkaju pushed his hood back and reached inside the neck of his parka. He withdrew a stone pendant with the image of a man carved into the front. "It is him," he said in a low voice. "It is Ngana'bta."

"Ngana'bta?"

"It is a sad name. It means *to be forgotten* because he was an orphan. But thousands of years ago he was a great Nganasan hunter."

Callum had a vague memory of being told the story by one of the host families that he and his team had stayed with in the summer chum settlement in Taymyr. But by now it was a distant, vodka-infused memory. "But Ngana'bta is only a myth."

For the first time that Callum could remember, Lungkaju frowned. "The only difference between myth and history, Doctor Ross, is that we *choose* to believe history. My grandfather taught me this and he was a very wise man."

He was right, of course. The fact that a culture's history was spoken rather than written didn't make it any less valid. "I'm sorry," Callum said. "I didn't mean to offend you."

"It is funny," Lungkaju said. "Ngana'bta also did not believe in myth. Would you like to hear?"

"I'd love to."

Lungkaju settled back onto his haunches and drew a deep breath. "He was an orphan. He was taken in by the people of the Taymyr Lake, my ancestors, and brought up as one of them. He was taller than most of the other boys in the village and he was also very smart. He would sit and learn from the shamans whenever he had no chores. He was an expert skier and hunter, and he could shoot his bow and throw his spears while moving at great speed. He could do this even as a child."

As he spoke, Lungkaju kept his body perfectly still and his eyes closed. But the remainder of his face became oddly animated. His eyebrows bobbed up and down, his forehead crumpled as he strained for the right words and his voice turned increasingly sonorous.

"Ngana'bta was given the job of protecting the clan's reindeer from wolves. He did this with great courage by charging the wolves on his skis and killing the slow ones with his spear. His work made him fearless, and he led many hunting parties into the far, far north where most Nganasan were afraid to go. Then, in his twentieth year, the sun disappeared from the sky."

"An eclipse?"

"Yes, but to my ancestors this was a very bad sign, Doctor Ross. The leaders of the Twelve Clans that hunted along the northern sea coast called a council. The earth told them that she was angry and that the greatest hunter-warrior in the land would have to perform for her a sacrifice."

Callum had heard of the twelve clans. They were roughly equivalent to the modern Finno-Ugric peoples of northern Scandinavia and north-western Russia, and the northern Samoyedic peoples living between the Urals and the River Yenisey in north-eastern Russia. He waited as Lungkaju took a swig from his flask.

"To find the champion, each clan called for their best hunter-warriors to take part in a sacred contest. Lots of men, young and old, went along. Those that were chosen faced many very difficult tasks to test their strength and their speed and their skills with weapons. In the end, the last five men were given a final task. They had to hunt and kill three animals: a wolf, an ice tiger and a white bear. The hunters were allowed no help, not from men or dogs. It was very hard. Soon three of them were dead and another was not able to finish the task and went back to his village in shame.

"Now only Ngana'bta was left. He laughed and boasted, 'Not only will I hunt these creatures, but I will hunt and kill them all in one day!' The elders shook their heads and the shamans cursed him. Even the Nganasan, who knew of his skills, still doubted him as he vanished into the snow.

"He had only his skis and his ski-pole spears, but he had spent his life on the trail of wolves and he quickly found this first animal. He chased it from the rest of the pack on his skis and then killed it with his spear. Then he skinned it and went to the land of the ice tiger.

"He knew that ice tigers were smart and that they were afraid of men. He knew that they would never show themselves while they could see him and smell him. So he took off his skis.

He threw the wolf skin over him and howled like a lost wolf. He knew that the wolf and the ice tiger were enemies because they both hunted the reindeer. And soon a very big tiger followed his howls. As the tiger pounced, Ngana'bta threw off the wolf skin and speared the tiger through the heart. Then he skinned him and went north towards the ocean and the great white bear.

"The bear was the hardest animal to hunt of all. He was twice the size of Ngana'bta, with sharp teeth and sharp claws and a very thick skin. The bear and the tiger were enemies, just like the tiger and the wolf, so he put the tiger skin around him and roared like a lost tiger until a very big white bear followed the roars. It had big claws and even bigger teeth, and when it saw the tiger, it roared also and then attacked. But Ngana'bta was on the ice and he had dug a hole in front of him. He had hidden this hole with snow, so when the bear was very close it fell down through the hole into the water.

"When he came up for air, Ngana'bta took off his tiger skin and stabbed his spear into the bear's chest again and again until he was dead. Then he took out his knife and cut off the bear's head. He went to the council, dragging the wolf skin and the tiger skin and the bear's head with him. The elders did not think that he would live, so they were sitting in a circle drinking and laughing together when he returned, and he threw the bear's head into the middle of their circle.

"Those that did not know him were now very scared. They knew now that there was a young Nganasan hunter of great bravery and skill. They were scared because the clans were not always at peace and Ngana'bta would be a very great enemy in war. They honoured him as the youngest-ever champion of the Twelve Clans, and after much talking they decided that he must go north. He must go further north than any man before. He must go to the Land of White Death. There he must hunt the monster called *Tansu Taibaa*. To please the earth, he must kill the creature and bring back one of its teeth.

"Ngana'bta laughed and said, 'I do not believe in Tansu Taibaa. He is a myth. A simple myth for simple men. But I will go to the Land of White Death, and if I am wrong and he lives, then I will cut out his skull and swap it for my sleigh and ride it back to you!'

"The very best carpenters made him a strong wooden sleigh. The Twelve Clans gave him their strongest sleigh dogs. The very best craftsmen made him a pair of whalebone skis and they made him two ski-pole spears from the tusks of a double-tusk narwhal. The shamans made him a very powerful talisman with a carved tooth from the wolf and the ice tiger and the white bear that he had killed and hung it around his neck. Then he said goodbye to his family and to his friends and left for the Land of White Death."

Lungkaju reopened his eyes, reached into his pocket and withdrew his flask once more. He unscrewed the cap and took another draught.

"So what happened to him?" Callum asked.

"Nobody knows this for sure," Lungkaju replied. "Some say that he let the dogs go and threw away the weapons and went to find his real mother. Others have said that he asked a killer whale to carry him across the sea, but that the whale was jealous of such a great hunter and so he still swims around and around with Ngana'bta on his back, pretending not to know the way. I do not believe this one, Doctor Ross." He peered into the torchlight. "But my grandfather, he used to tell me that Ngana'bta did reach the Land of White Death, but that Tansu Taibaa caught him there and ate his flesh." After a few seconds he added, "I believe my grandfather."

With the end of the tale, the cave was plunged into silence. Could it be true? Callum had no idea. There was no reason why Lungkaju would make up such a story and there was no reason to distrust him. All he knew was that, if it was true, and if this turned out to be one of those rarest of instances when history, archaeology and legend held hands, then he was staring at one of the most important scientific discoveries of the century.

"Say I believe the story," he said. "I still have a couple of questions."

Lungkaju met his gaze and waited.

"What makes you so sure that *this* is Ngana'bta?"

Without speaking, Lungkaju leant forward and grasped at the mummy.

Ordinarily Callum would have had a heart attack at the thought of even touching such a find, let alone manhandling it like this. But, not for the first time that afternoon, his curiosity had the better of him.

Carefully, sensing his friend's anxiety, Lungkaju rolled the mummy over onto its back. The face that had been pressed into the stone floor for so many years crept into the torchlight. It bore an expression of pure horror. The skin was pale. The eyes had receded back into the skull, leaving wide-open sockets. The tip of the nose had been creased upwards and to one side, and the lips were bent open in an unnatural grimace, revealing the front teeth.

Callum had excavated many dead bodies over the years. But this was different. This was death in a very loose sense, and it was a fearsome sight. If Lungkaju was at all moved by the spectacle, then he hid it well. As the face had rolled into the light, Callum had half-expected him to drop the mummy in disgust and flee the tunnel. But instead he had kept calm, his own expression unchanged.

Callum's eye was drawn lower, to where the parka fabric appeared to be pierced through. The cavity, slightly smaller than a fist, continued on into the stomach, and around the edges a rust-coloured halo was dyed into the garment.

"It's a stab wound," Callum said. Whoever this was, it looked as if they'd been impaled as well as having their legs hacked off. *But what could've...* His mind moved back to the carved bone object, the possible ski-tip, salvaged from Fenris. The splintered end was similarly discoloured, and the dog must have tugged it free from the mummy's gut.

Lungkaju said nothing but began feeling around the top of the mummy's chest. Callum watched as he undid the drawstrings at the base of the hood, loosened the neckline and reached inside. A second later he withdrew his hand, two strands of a hide thong now trailing from it. Slowly, he unfurled his fingers.

Callum could hardly believe his eyes. In the centre of Lungkaju's palm were three strung canine teeth, ascending in size. The teeth were separated by two silver spacers, and a series of symbols was carved around their roots. Surely it could only be the amulet that he had described just moments earlier; the amulet that the shamans of the twelve clans had made for Ngana'bta before sending him to his death. Single teeth from a wolf, a tiger and a polar bear.

"You had a second question, Doctor Ross?" Lungkaju asked.

Callum's gaze remained glued to the amulet, the shock of this latest revelation still reverberating inside his brain. "Tansu Taibaa," he whispered at last. "What was it?"

At this, Lungkaju shifted uneasily. "I do not know. I thought that it was not real also." He draped the amulet across the mummy's chest. "But I know what it means."

Callum looked up.

"*Tansu Taibaa*," Lungkaju continued. "It is strange. A very strange name. It means *lizard bird*."

Chapter 4

TUSKING

1

The centre of Callum's laboratory on board the *Albanov* was taken up with surfaces and storage units, map tables and field plan digitising palettes. Computer terminals were positioned around the edges. Sinks with attached gas extraction chambers stood at either end and a large, glass-door specimen refrigeration unit hummed away in the far corner.

Having mooched around it as part of the initial tour and returned only once in the fortnight since, this was only the third evening that he had been there. Until yesterday, there had been no reason for him to be there. His field survey had identified precisely nothing of archaeological interest. Not so much as a flint flake. His only regular task had been to keep his field diary updated, which he had done on his laptop from the comfort of his own cabin.

The discovery of the ice mummy had changed everything.

Callum pulled on a pair of latex gloves, took the bone object and placed it on one of the work surfaces. The more he'd looked at it that day, the more confident he'd felt in his original assessment. It *was* the end of a highly ornate, ancient bone ski and it *was* the most probable cause of the mummy's stomach wound.

He reached up, grasped the head of an anglepoise and brought it into position above the artefact. After a great deal of trial and error earlier that day, he'd managed to affix the digital camera to a robotic arm extending from a unit above the workstation. He now returned to the computer, where the shutter image was relaying in real time. Grinning like a child with a new toy, he remotely manoeuvred the arm until the camera was in the perfect position. He then took a number of shots at different resolutions and from different angles; the photographs were automatically uploaded and saved to the computer's hard drive ready to be emailed back to the department.

He'd attempted to contact both Clive and Jonas as soon as he and Lungkaju had returned to the *Albanov*. But Volkov hadn't been kidding about the predicted solar flare activity. It had been playing havoc with the ship's transmitter and all external communications were down. This was disappointing, but no great disaster. Lungkaju had agreed not to mention the find to anyone until official arrangements could be put in place to deal with the logistical, financial and publicity fall-out, and Callum had no problem taking him at his word. In truth he was more concerned about missing his video call with Jamie; the *intermittent and minimal* disruption Volkov had talked about had actually been regular and prolonged, at least over the last couple of days.

As he went to rearrange the ski-tip, there was a sudden crashing noise and the sound of raised voices from Ava Lee's laboratory next door. Callum rushed out into the corridor and knocked on the door. "Ava? Are you okay in there?"

There was no response, so he tried the handle. The door was unlocked, and he went ahead and cracked it open.

Ava was on her knees collecting up a scatter of beige-coloured stones from the floor. A tray teetered back against the side of a storage unit and Dan Peterson was bent over a stool, his face contorted, clutching at his lower back.

Ava looked up suddenly. She blushed. "Doctor Ross."

"I heard shouting," Callum said. "There was no answer when I knocked…"

"Oh, it's all been a bit Chaplin meets the Marx Brothers," she said, fishing the last of the stones out from underneath a cabinet. "I was showing these to Dan when I went and dropped the tray. When I tried to pick them up I knocked into him and he hit his back against the desk there." She attempted a laugh.

"Are you okay, Dan?" Callum asked.

"I'm just fine, thank you," Peterson replied, unable to conceal a wince. "It's like Ava says. It's my own damn fault for being such a doofus."

"You should go to the infirmary and get it checked."

"Oh, hell no, it's just a little knock to the pelvis, that's all. I'm gonna go lie down a while and it'll be fine." Still clutching at his spine he stood up, wished them both a good evening and made his way out.

Callum walked over to Ava and took the tray. "Here, let me help you." He went to place it back down on the nearest countertop only to find that it was already strewn with books and stacks of papers. He scanned around. The whole place was in a state, clutter spread across every surface.

He placed the tray down on top of an open textbook. "Busy evening?"

"Oh, this is nothing," she replied, the redness retreating from her cheeks. "You should see my office back home. I put half a bacon sub down in there once and it was a full week before I found it again."

Callum studied the beige stones scattered across the surface of the tray. They were shark fin-shaped with serrated edges.

"They're teeth," Ava said.

"Dino teeth?"

"You betcha." She moved over to stand beside him and gently lifted one of the larger specimens. "They're from a troodontid, a

103

late cretaceous bipedal species we find quite commonly at high latitudes. It's possible they're all from the same individual."

Carefully, Callum accepted the tooth into his palm. It was about six centimetres long and a plaque of surrounding rock still clung to its surface.

"No, they haven't been properly processed yet," she said, reading his thoughts. "At the moment I'm just collecting a sample of the material I've located eroding from the cliffs at Nansen Rocks. They can be cleaned up after the field season, but for now I just need to be able to prove the scale of the palaeontological resource here."

"Looks like you've hit pay dirt."

"Put it this way. I located all twenty-four of these in a single day, along with a sizeable number of other much larger bones. That's more than some palaeontologists recover in an entire season."

Callum ran a finger along the serrations. "I'm guessing Mr troodontid was a carnivore."

"You'd think so, wouldn't you?" she replied. "He's a therapod for sure, a predator, and the name *Troodon* is even taken from the Greek for *wounding tooth*." She pointed a nail at one of the denticles. "But these prominent serrations are apically oriented, which is unusual in other therapods. They're actually much more similar to those of herbivorous species."

"So he was just a plant-eater with bad teeth?"

"More likely he was an omnivore, ate whatever he could sink those bad teeth into."

"Presumably that's why they survived well here, because they could eat whatever?"

"It's one of the reasons, sure. But not the only one. They were also fast, agile and hugely intelligent. People have themselves convinced that the velociraptor was the most intelligent dinosaur, and they were smart alright, don't get me wrong. But in reality they were also the size of a turkey, and their brainpower was nothing on Troodon's. As far as we know, Troodon had the largest brain relative to body mass of any known dinosaur, and they also had enormous eyes and stereoscopic vision, which would've given them a huge advantage during the polar night. We can tell that they thrived here because they got bigger."

"Their eyes?"

"All of them, the animals themselves. That tooth you're holding now is twice as big as one you'd expect from a southern Troodon."

"Steroids in the water?"

"Even better," she replied. "Rich pickings. Even during the Cretaceous the polar environment would still have been harsh enough to deter most predators, so there would have been plenty of fresh meat for those that could stick out the low temperatures and light, and Troodon was one of them. Evolution took over, and badabing-badabum the Arctic Troodon packed on a few extra pounds of lean, toothy muscle."

Callum went to place the tooth delicately back beside the others, but Ava took his hand and folded his fingers over it. "For your kid," she said, smiling. "I know you've got a lot of making up to do when you get back. Maybe this'll help some."

"Are you sure?"

"It's not like there's a shortage," she beamed. "Just keep it to yourself, yeah? I'm not planning on opening a souvenir store."

Callum slid the fossil into his pocket, where it clinked against the quartz pebble. "He'll be over the moon, Ava. Thank you."

Somewhere in the office one of the internal phones began to ring. Ava searched it out from under a pile of oddments and answered it. She turned back to Callum. "Spread the word, communications are back up and running. For how long, nobody knows."

"Let's hope they stay up a while," Callum said, checking his watch. "I've got a call with Jamie in an hour. Night, Ava." He went to leave.

"I meant to ask you," she called after him. "Did you see Nikolai today?"

"Doctor Semyonov? No, he wasn't at breakfast."

"I missed him at lunch too," Ava said. "Only I took a couple of rock samples for him from Nansen, and he was supposed to pick them up earlier this afternoon."

Callum smiled. "You know what he's like. He's probably stapled his moustache to the desk or something."

"True. But it'd take more than that to keep the obsessive old grouch from breakfast."

She was right. Today was the first day Callum could remember when Semyonov hadn't marched into the dining room at eight sharp, poured himself a coffee and a bowl of cereal, and plonked himself, alone, at the far table overlooking the island. "Have you tried calling him?"

She nodded. "No reply. You're right, though. I don't know why I agreed to help the crazy old bastard in the first place."

"I'll keep an eye out," Callum said.

2

Back in his own laboratory, Callum stowed the ski-tip away in a locked cabinet and powered down his computer. In all the excitement earlier that day, he'd forgotten to quiz Lungkaju about the possible symbolism of the dead bird and pottery. The more he'd thought about it since, the more convinced he'd become that they must have formed part of some shamanic practice. There wasn't much about Nganasan culture that Lungkaju didn't know, so maybe he could shed some light on it.

Having locked up, he left the lab once more and made his way to the deckhouse elevator. Up on Deck 5, he headed past his own cabin and knocked on the door to 502. "Dan?"

A low voice answered, "That you, McJones?"

"Yes, it's me, Callum."

With no attempt whatsoever at a French accent, Peterson called out, "*Entrez!*"

Entering the room, Callum was as struck by the neatness of the place as he had been by the unexpected disarray in Ava Lee's laboratory. It was as if the two of them secretly switched personae in private. There was no clutter, not so much as a misplaced sock, and even the air smelt oddly sterile.

Peterson lay stretched out on top of his bed, his arm draped across his face. The midnight sun streamed in over him through the window.

"I brought you these," Callum said, placing a box of painkillers on the bedside table.

Peterson looked up from underneath his arm and adjusted his horn rims. "That's very good of you."

"No bother," Callum replied. "Archaeology and back pain are bedfellows, so I keep some handy."

"You keep anything stronger handy? Morphine, maybe?"

Callum laughed and made for the door. "I'll leave you to rest."

"McJones? You ever been in love?"

Callum looked back to see Peterson's eyes wide with anticipation. "Yes, I've been in love."

"At first sight?"

"No, it took me a while to realise."

"How long's a while?"

Callum shrugged and perched on the arm of an easy chair facing the bed. "Couple of months, maybe. Something like that."

"Do you think you could be in love with a person after just a couple of weeks?"

Callum laughed. "Is there something you want to tell me, Dan?"

"No not you, you lamebrain!" He lowered his voice to a whisper. "You know. *Ava*."

"Ava Lee?" The team had spent a lot of time together over the last few weeks and Callum had got to know the others well. At least he felt as if he had. And the thought of the no-nonsense Ava Lee and the younger, much more erratic Dan Peterson together was strange to say the least. They seemed so incompatible. Height-wise, age-wise, wise-wise. More like mother and son.

"I saw her once before, at a conference a couple of years back," Peterson said. "Watched her give a paper on some ancient beast or other. Truth is, I didn't give a goddamn what she was talking about, I was too busy looking at her and wondering whether I'd ever see anything so beautiful ever again. Felt like somebody had clocked me upside the head with a nine iron." He sighed. "Then I turn up here and damn me if she isn't the first person I meet, after security, that is."

"Well, does she know how you feel?"

"What, that I'm sweet on her? She ought to." Peterson eased himself up into a sitting position. "You know that was a load of bullshit she sold you just now, right? About dropping things and knocking me into tables and everything."

"It did sound a little far-fetched," Callum replied. "So what's the real story?"

"The real story is she dropped something in that room alright, but it sure as hell wasn't her fossils!" He looked away and lowered his voice once more. "We were... you know... *messing around.*"

It was the first time that Callum had seen the man look genuinely embarrassed. His face was pale, and he looked as if he might just up and flee the room at any moment.

"It all got a bit heated," Peterson continued. "I was hoisting her up and then I felt something crack. Truth is, I dropped her on her ass and upset her tray of whoosits trying to pick her back up. I thought she was plain gonna kill me."

"Did nobody ever tell you love hurts?"

"Yeah, yeah, laugh it up," Peterson sneered. "But seriously, do you think I'm talking crazy? Come on, this is important. I thought it might be... well, I figured it might just be the real thing."

"I'm not the best person to ask about this sort of stuff," Callum replied. "I managed to screw up my own marriage and then I managed to screw up my relationship with my son, the two people I was supposed to love. So my track record's not exactly great."

There was a long silence before Peterson said, "You're a

straight shooter, McJones. I could tell that about you when we first met. Truth is, that's why I'm interested in your opinion. I can be sure it's an honest one, see?"

"Well, if it's my honest opinion you want, Dan, then yes, I think you're talking crazy." He watched as Peterson's smile melted. "But I suppose that can only mean one thing."

"That I'm a lovesick fool?"

Callum cleared his throat and assumed his broadest Scottish accent. "*But t'see her was t'love her, love but her and love forever.* Robbie Burns."

Peterson reached for the painkillers. "Now there's an opinion I can trust."

3

"What's the password?"

"Great white shark! What's yours?"

"Hmm…" Callum scratched his head and pretended not to know.

"Clone!" Jamie shouted.

"Whoa, hang on! I'm an old man, my memory's not as good as yours. What are you? Fifteen? Sixteen?"

Jamie laughed. "I'm eight, Dad!"

"Ah, so you do think it's me?"

"No, I don't! One more go or you're a clone."

"Well, in that case…" Callum drew himself up and did his best Arnold Schwarzenegger impression. "*Hasta la vista, baby!*"

Jamie repeated it as usual, then said, "Okay, it's you."

Callum looked over to see the comms assistant smiling at him, and he smiled back. The man's name was Gavriil, and he had the names of his own two children tattooed on the back of his knuckles in a thick black Cyrillic font: **Антон** and **Наталья**. Anton, aged six, and Natalya, aged twelve. Over the last couple of weeks the two men had got to know each other. No matter how tired or disheartened Callum had been after the day's survey, he had made certain to speak to Jamie every evening before dinner, making him practically part of the furniture in the comms centre. Gavriil spoke only broken English, but the language barrier had barely been an issue, because they both spoke a shared second language: that of the remorseful absentee father. As the days ticked by, Gavriil's interest in offering *assistance* on behalf of the company had quickly transformed into the concern of one struggling father for another.

Gavriil looked around. With no-one else in the room, he nodded at Callum and then stepped outside to allow them their privacy.

"Got something for you."

Jamie's eyes lit up. "What is it?"

Callum held the fossilised tooth up to the webcam. "Dinosaur tooth."

"Whoa! A real one?"

"Sure is. I had to swap him one of mine. Look." He opened his mouth wide and pointed to his wisdom tooth gap.

Jamie laughed. "Is it from a T-Rex?"

"No, it's from a…" he racked his brain, "…a *Troodon*. But they were meaner than any old T-Rex."

"When can I have it?"

"Not long. I'll keep it safe for you until I get back."

"Promise?"

"Promise."

They talked about school for a while – one of Jamie's poems had been put up on the classroom wall, which was great, but Fraser had called him a dicknose again, which was not so great – then Callum leant forward and whispered, "Want to hear a secret?"

Jamie nodded.

"I found something cool."

"What?"

"A mummy."

"What? Like an Egyptian? We did Egyptians last year with Miss Summers."

Callum smiled. "Not quite. This is an *ice* mummy. A frozen man."

"Is he dead?" Jamie asked, his nose wrinkled with curiosity.

"For a long, long time." Callum checked the doorway behind Jamie's shoulder to make sure that Moira wasn't listening in. He could hear her voice clearly inside his head: *Don't you fill his mind full of horrid things before bed, he'll have nightmares and I'll have to pick up the pieces, blah blah blah...* He was nearly nine, for God's sake, and there were worse things than mummies on the news.

"His name was Ngana'bta. You want to hear what happened to him?"

"Unga butter," Jamie said.

"Close enough, son."

After saying goodnight to Jamie, and showing him the dino tooth one last time, Callum made his way over to a phone terminal and rang Jonas. They had spoken a number of times since his arrival on the *Albanov*. But the conversations, though comforting, had always been a disappointment, as there had been nothing at all to report back. This time things were different. Not only did he have something to report, but it was something big, potentially massive.

As the dial tone started up, he couldn't wait to hear the excitement in his friend's voice. For somebody who had dedicated his entire life to archaeology, news of the ice mummy would be like a restorative shot in the arm for Jonas, and just when he needed it most.

He shook his head. A fortnight ago if somebody had told him he'd be enjoying himself like this, there was a good chance he would have punched them in the face. But it was undeniable. He was enjoying himself. In fact, he couldn't remember the last time he'd felt so engaged with his own life. Not only was he on the verge of something massive with the ice mummy, but he was somehow managing to patch up his relationship with Jamie too.

"Hello?"

Callum recognised the voice as that of Sarah Olsen, Jonas's wife. "Sarah? It's Callum. Callum Ross."

"Oh, Callum, hello."

"How are you?"

"I'm…" Her words trailed off and she began to sob.

"Sarah, what is it? Is it Jonas?"

"They… he…"

Callum closed his eyes. Her meaning was loud and clear.

4

Callum drained his glass and poured himself another whiskey. It was nearly one o' clock in the morning. The lounge on Deck 8 of the *Albanov* was empty and silent. The electric shutters were fully lowered, leaving only the light of the muted television set to come between the gloom and complete darkness.

As he tipped another shot across his tongue, the door to the lounge cracked open and Darya poked her head through. She entered and walked over. She appeared to be dressed in full outdoor gear. "I thought I could hear somebody."

"Sorry," he replied, "I was trying to keep it down."

She looked at him puzzled. "Keep what down?"

It was easy to forget that English was not her native tongue. "The noise," he replied, forcing a smile. "I was trying to be quiet."

She sat next to him on the sofa and watched as he poured himself some more whiskey. "Your plan is to get drunk alone in the darkness?"

"So how come you're all dressed up?" he asked, changing the subject.

"I am going over to Harmsworth."

"It's one o' clock in the morning."

"This is not a problem." She raised one of the blinds a

fraction, allowing a band of sunlight to stream into the lounge.

Callum watched the light reflecting off his measure, before swirling it around and downing it. "How could I forget?" She seemed unaffected by the relentless daylight. Where he and the others attempted a regular sleep-wake pattern, as recommended by the on-board medical team, she carried out her research at all hours.

"Besides," she continued, "wildlife does not wear a watch."

Callum made no reply and instead refilled his glass.

"There is something upsetting you," she said, her eyes meeting his. "I can tell this."

"My friend, the man who was supposed to be here instead of me, I just found out that he's gone. Passed away."

The touch of her hand on his told him that, this time, she understood his chosen phrase. "That is very sad, *solnishko*," she said. "He was not in great pain, I hope?"

"No, if there's one good thing it's that there wasn't any pain. From what his wife told me, there was some kind of complication related to the tumour in his brain. He was unconscious in his armchair when she found him. They did what they could for him in hospital, but he never woke up."

"This is very sad," she repeated. "I am sorry that you were given this news."

"So am I."

She squeezed his hand. "I lost a good friend also last year. I did what you do now and drank. Tried to forget. Then I realised that they did not want me to be that way. They would not have liked me that way."

"Yeah, well, trust me," Callum replied, "Jonas would want me to drink this whiskey. Every last drop."

"Even if you are throw it all back up again and waste it?"

The logic was sound and Callum couldn't help laughing. "Jonas would've liked you. I'm sorry you never got to meet."

"Yes, but then I would never have met you," she said.

Their eyes met, but before Callum could reply, she released his hand and stood up. "I know what you need."

"And what's that?"

"You need distraction," she answered. "Go and put on your boots and jacket and meet me on the deck. Ten minutes."

She strode off towards the door.

"But, Darya, I'm drunk," he shouted after her.

"Not for long," she called back.

Emerging from the deckhouse in his outdoor gear, Callum checked his watch. Nearly half past one in the morning. The sun was up – *as ever* – and the sky was clear and blue. Over the last few weeks the ice had largely melted from the bay. Where there had been fissures, there were now vast polynyas, areas of open water with only a few diminutive icebergs lolling on their surfaces. The water itself seemed unnaturally dark, as if its long winter concealment had been enough to shield it from the bleaching effects of the sun.

He stared over at the island. Even though it was no longer new, the sight of the mysterious hunk of twisted rock, with its coves like hatchet gashes and its peaks like worn molars, still sent a shiver down his spine, half-excitement, half-fear. The image of Ngana'bta fleeing from Tansu Taibaa flashed before his eyes. He could think of no more fitting a place for an ancient monster's lair.

Darya was waiting for him. He followed her along the deck, past the row of lifeboats strung along the funnel-house wall and towards the helipads. Then they descended a long staircase onto the lower deck.

The asphalt platform, on which the two helicopters were perched, now formed a canopy overhead. Its considerable girth was supported by a row of thick, white-painted steel girders. Darya strode towards the first of these. A small control panel was mounted centrally at head height. She tugged the lid open to reveal a confusion of switches.

"What are you doing?" Callum whispered.

She said nothing but reached out and tapped the black button in the centre.

"Darya?"

There was a low clunking sound before the stern ramp uncoupled itself and began to lower onto the water's surface like a drawbridge. Callum stared down at the water lapping against the end of the ramp. "If it's all the same, I think I'll stick to the pool."

"Come and help me," she replied, heading for the vehicle bays.

Callum followed her to the end compartment. The tambour door rattled as she slid it up to reveal one of the two Czilim hovercrafts that Mr Volkov had mentioned on the tour. Callum had seen them on more than one occasion over the last couple of weeks, patrolling around the island manned with Spetsnaz.

"You're not serious?"

"No, not that," she replied, with her half-smile half-frown, "that."

He followed the line of her finger to the roof above the hovercraft. There, upside down, hung a wooden canoe. It looked to be at least four metres long, and it was suspended from the ceiling by a system of elastic cables.

Callum turned to her. "Okay, now you really are joking! I haven't been in one of those things since I was a lad."

"Then the distraction begins now."

"But can you even… I mean, do you know how to—"

"Of course. It is not difficult."

"But we're supposed to have a guide with us," he said, casting around for new excuses. "What if we run into a bear?"

"Hah!" She laughed. "Please to trust me. The most dangerous animals on that island will be you and me. And besides," she reached back over her shoulder and patted the top of her rucksack, "I have my bear spray."

5

The sea was like a millpond, calm and still. With a little guidance, Callum soon got into the rhythm of paddling, and with every stroke the island seemed to grow. The canoe was surprisingly nifty, dodging in and out of the remnant ice, skirting around the larger chunks that glistened and rocked like buoys from side to side.

As the exertion burnt away the alcohol from his system, it was replaced by the feeling of intense jet-lag that came with continued exposure to the midnight sun. *Light-lag*, Peterson had called it at dinner one night. *"Anyone else feel like there's a goddamn balloon inside their skull?"*

When they were only a few hundred metres from shore, they turned and began to follow the lie of the east coast northwards. There was no breeze. The current was gentle but insistent, urging them towards the shoreline and forcing them to maintain momentum.

"How deep is the water here?" Callum asked.

"It is shallow," Darya replied. "Perhaps only fifty metres."

When Callum and his brother had paddled across Loch Ness as children, the water had been over four times deeper. Yet it had felt no more than a shallow pool. This was different. Fifty metres or not, it was fifty metres of Arctic Ocean. He focussed on paddling. "Are you going to tell me where we're headed?"

"You'll see."

They continued on in silence, with nothing but the sound of the oars patting into the water to either side.

There was a sudden splash and something broke the surface up ahead. Callum stopped paddling. Scanning around, he thought he could make out a confusion of shadows, mostly dark, some pale, all clustered in the same area. But as the canoe drifted closer, they melted into the depths.

"We have arrived," Darya said.

Callum was about to ask where exactly they had arrived, when a brownish-white spiral, two metres long, pierced the water to his left and scraped across the prow. He dropped his paddle in shock, almost causing the canoe to capsize as instinct drove him up onto his feet. "Did you see that?"

"Sit down!" Darya yelled. "Do you want us to go over? It is a narwhal. They will not harm you."

Callum dropped back onto his seat and watched as the horn re-emerged, joined by another four, five, six. As if choreographed, the creatures dove together and then resurfaced, their horns aloft.

Fear turned quickly to wonder as more and more of the porpoise-like creatures revealed themselves. Each of their horns was a different shade and size, and there must have been twenty or thirty now piercing the air around the canoe.

"They are beautiful, aren't they?" Darya called out.

"They're fantastic," Callum answered. He reached out to stroke one of the passing horns, trilling his fingers across the grooves before it pulled away.

"Some people think that this is where the myth of the unicorn is coming from," Darya said.

"Yes, I've heard this one," he replied. "Norse seafarers would hunt them and sell their horns, then the connection with the sea would become lost over time and inland communities developed the unicorn myth to explain them." He peered over the side and watched the dumpy, mottled-marble shadows gliding beneath them. "It's not surprising," he added. "Most landlubbers would never have seen the ocean in their entire life, let alone a narwhal."

"They are *tusks*, not *horns*," Darya said. "A narwhal's tusk is just an elongated tooth. Sometimes they will even grow two, one from each incisor."

"I've heard something about this too. Lungkaju was telling me an old Nganasan myth, and the hero's ski poles were made from a double-tusk narwhal. I'd imagine they're pretty rare?"

"Extremely rare. I have seen it only once before, and I have studied the narwhal now for many years."

There was a loud slap as one of the creatures, small enough to still be a youngster, smashed its tail down beside Callum and showered him as if on purpose.

"This is a young female," Darya said. "She is very playful. She must like you."

Callum wiped the freezing spray from his face. "No, I have that effect on all the girls. Only, they usually throw the water from a glass."

She laughed. "We are lucky. The narwhal can be shy animal and usually there are not so many together at once. Three different pods are together here to feed. During winter they live out in the deep water a long way from shore. They only move to the shallow water here in summer. These three pods have maybe made the same migration to Harmsworth for many, many years now, and they will stay here until the ice starts to form again." She pointed to a particularly large narwhal, much paler than the others. "This one I call *Grandfather* because I think that he may be the oldest."

Callum watched as the creature turned on its side as it glided past the canoe and examined him with one eye. "How can you tell how old he is?"

"It is simple. They turn paler as they grow older, and you can see his colour is very light. Also I know that he is male because usually the females do not have a tusk. Some of them do, but it is shorter. I have also seen him tusking. Look."

A short distance from the side of the canoe, several of the larger animals had congregated. They were busy grinding their tusks together, high above the water.

"They look as if they're sword-fighting," Callum said.

"This is tusking. The males rub their tusks together like this. Nobody knows why, but it is probably a way to decide who is in charge and attract a mate."

"So they're sizing each other up? My tusk's bigger than yours?"

"Yes, this is what they do. This is how I know that Grandfather is a male, because I see him do this often."

"He must have a complex," Callum said.

After staying with the pods for a while longer, they continued northwards. The current had driven them to within fifty metres or so of the shore, so they moved back out to sea and held their course. Several of the younger narwhals continued to follow alongside them before turning as one and heading back to the safety of their family.

"We can head back also, whenever you like," Darya called to him.

"I'll be okay for a while yet," Callum replied. "I thought you were mad when you suggested this, but I think I'm getting the hang of it."

"You are doing very well, *solnishko*. If you are feeling strong then we can go and see the bird colony at Svayataya?"

"Okay," he replied. "Svayataya it is."

Soon the shoreline began morphing into the northern cliffs. A succession of coves bore their way inland. Seals lolled on the outcrops and the tooth-like headlands were interspersed with pocket beaches and pebble shores, strewn with silver driftwood. Beyond, the Hjalmar Ridge towered over the coast, the ever-present peaks standing guard at the island's heart.

On one of the beaches, something had caught the attention of a couple of dozen gulls. Some of them scuffled over it, while others circled patiently above them on the breeze.

"What do you suppose it is?" Callum asked.

"The birds are little auks," Darya replied. "I am trying to see what they are feeding on."

Callum looked around to see that she was already examining the shore through a pair of expensive-looking lightweight binoculars.

"Anything?"

"At first I thought it was a dead seal," she said.

"That's what I thought."

"But actually," she stared intently into the eye-pieces, "I think it may be a bear."

She handed him the binoculars.

The birds themselves were black on top with white underbellies, and through their strobe of wings he could make out nothing more than the odd flash of yellow-white. When he looked back, there was an ominous expression on Darya's face. Her lips were pursed, almost pouting.

"You want to check it out, don't you?"

She flashed him an embarrassed grin. "It would be very useful for me to take some photographs and a few measurements. I have only seen one of these animals so far this season, and he was far away. It is not very often that I have willing subject."

"Do you mean me or the bear?"

"If you would like not to stop then we can carry on."

He sighed. "Okay, but you owe me."

She leant forward and kissed gently at the side of his mouth. "This is down payment."

6

As they approached the shoreline, the seabed got shallower and shallower until their paddling gave way to punting and the gentle surf finally eased the canoe up onto the beach. The gulls took off and hovered at a respectful height as they arrived at the carcass.

It lay on its side, soggy and bloated. The ribcage had been picked open by the gulls and a horrific smell emanated from the stomach. It was the first time Callum had ever seen a polar bear outside of the zoo. Dead, desiccating, with its tongue lolling out, it was not exactly the way he'd imagined.

"You're not going to touch it, are you?" he asked, trying his best not to gag.

"Unfortunately I must. But it is okay." She slung her rucksack off and delved into it, withdrawing a box of single-use hygiene gloves and a tape measure.

"I love it when a girl comes prepared."

With a roll of her eyes, she pulled on a pair of the gloves and handed another pair to him.

He stared at them and then at her.

"It will be a lot faster if you can help me with some measurements, please." She produced a small Dictaphone and attached it to her lapel. "Then we can get away from this horrible stink as soon as possible."

Her argument was compelling. They set to work taking measurements, Darya dictating a record of them and presumably any other observations. They measured the limbs, head and paws. Darya then forced back the creature's jowl to examine the gums and teeth. As she came to measure across the chest area, she stopped suddenly to inspect a number of holes made by the probing of the gulls' beaks.

"They were making quite a meal of him," Callum said.

"It is *her*," she replied, "and..." she hesitated, digging her fingers into the neatly circular wounds one after another, "...this was not the gulls."

"What was it then?"

She turned and looked at him, her eyes suddenly aflame. "Somebody has shot this animal. She died recently, no more than a few weeks."

"But there's been nobody else on the island. Only us and the security forces."

"Her tissues are swollen," Darya continued, ignoring him. "Whoever shot her must have put her body into the sea afterwards and now it has come back to shore. Look, the fish have nibbled at her tongue." She knelt back down and re-examined the bear's head, pointing to another wound behind its ear. "You see. This is bullet hole too!"

She stomped back to her rucksack, grabbed a digital camera and began to photograph every last inch of the swollen carcass as if it were a homicide victim. "I will show these to Mr Volkov and *make* him find out who is murdering this creature!"

As she strode around the animal, muttering to herself in Russian that even Callum could understand, a tendril crept its way down the shore and out over the surf-line. Before he had time to react, it was followed by another, thicker tendril and then by a dense blanket of grey-white, which poured over the top of the cliffs encircling the beach and tumbled towards them like an avalanche. Within seconds the sudden mist had reduced the daylight to a haze overhead and visibility to no more than a few metres. In her fury, Darya seemed not to notice.

"Oh, great! Come on," Callum ordered her, "we need to leave before we get stranded."

She looked up at last, face shrouded in white. "You are right," she said. "We must be quick, before it goes too far out."

The temperature had dropped and only small pockets of visibility remained. Callum shouldered her rucksack and they raced along the beach to the canoe. Barging the vessel down into the surf, he slung himself back into the front seat and felt a thud as Darya leapt into the back. Then he punted the canoe back out into deeper water and began to paddle.

As he fought against the current, he could feel the mist overtaking them. It was riding the wind out across the water and thickening by the second. "We need to break through it or we'll lose the ship!"

At that moment a mechanical splutter sounded behind him. He turned around to see that Darya had dislodged a wooden cover to reveal a concealed outboard motor. She had thrown the propeller over the back and was now tearing at the pull-cord. A final yank and it roared into life.

"I think that we should not fuck around any longer," she shouted, noticing the look of disbelief on Callum's face.

"Fuck around? You mean we've been paddling all this time for no reason?"

"Not for no reason," she shouted. "You needed a distraction!"

Callum gripped onto the gunwale as the canoe burst forward.

Chapter 5

ZERO HOUR

1

Everything was ready.

The improvised explosives.

The remote detonators.

A route through the engine room.

All of it.

Zero hour was meant to be the following night, but the last half hour had changed everything. Mist had descended around the *Albanov*. In an instant it had turned the entire outside world into one large smoke chamber.

With the help of Finback's intelligence, Ptarmigan's every movement had been meticulously planned. The only element that relied more on luck than judgement was the very first: accessing the observation room. It was from here that security surveillance was maintained for all areas of the ship, making it the necessary first port of call for anybody wishing to sneak around with a pack full of explosives. To access the room, he would have to make his way to the door at the front of the deckhouse and punch in the code. This was an immense gamble in plain view, so the cover of mist was an opportunity not to be wasted.

Ptarmigan had waited patiently over the last few weeks,

maintaining his cover during the day and constructing his devices late into the night. But even now he found himself dogged by the same reservations. Innocent people were going to die as a result of his actions. Whatever the intention, whatever the outcome, *that* was the reality. He was going to deprive parents of children, destroy families. But then, he consoled himself, it was like Finback had said: *Those who die for this cause will have died well.*

Now that the time had finally come, his adrenaline production had gone into overdrive. He turned from the grey swirls churning up against the porthole and seated himself on the rug in the centre of the room. He crossed his legs and placed his hands, sweaty palms upwards, on his knees. He drew a deep breath in through his nose... one... two... three... four... five... and released it through his mouth... one... two... three... four... five...

He repeated the breathing pattern, feeling his heart rate slow.

"*Nam Myoho Renge Kyo, Nam Myoho Renge Kyo, Nam Myoho Renge Kyo...*"

Ten minutes later, Ptarmigan placed his explosives into a small rucksack, left his cabin and took the stairs down to Deck 1. The only person likely to be up at this hour was Doctor Lebedev. He'd never warmed to Lebedev. In fact, she bugged the shit out of him. She was like the energiser bunny for one thing, up at all hours, never seeming to need sleep. In a word: unpredictable. For another, she seemed to spend half her time in a surly silence and the other half flirting with the goddamn archaeologist. But thankfully she was nowhere to be seen.

Outside, the mist enveloped him, suffocating his senses. He had heard the others talking about what a strange sensation it was. But, so far, he had managed to avoid being out in it himself, and the sudden realisation that this really was some heavy-duty vapour stopped him in his tracks. It made the skin on his face feel oily, and the cloying bitterness tickled at the back of his throat making him want to cough.

It's just mist, he told himself, forcing his mind to refocus. He closed his eyes and listened. There was the sound of the wind and the lapping of the ocean at the side of the ship. Somewhere in the distance there was a groan and a faint splash as the top of another iceberg bit the big blue. But nothing else. No conversation. No footsteps. He carried on around the deckhouse, feeling his way along the railing at the side of the walkway until he reached the door to the observation room.

He checked his watch. The last shift would've left on the hour. The standard operating procedure was for the replacement shift to turn up first. But there was complacency amongst the on-board Special Forces contingent, again, just as Finback had predicted.

Over the last few weeks he had observed the replacement shift arrive consistently ten to fifteen minutes after the previous shift had departed. No doubt they'd review a portion of the CCTV footage that they had missed and then consider everything to be rosy. After all, what could possibly go wrong out here? Well, tonight Ptarmigan was going to show them and show them good. That extra hand-job they were giving each other when they should have been on duty was going to cost them their lives.

He punched in the code and entered.

2

"Cut the engine!"

The growling of the outboard gurgled out as Darya released the accelerator and brought the craft to a stop. "What is it?"

"It's no use," Callum replied. "Look."

They had barely left the cove, but already visibility was less than half a metre. Harmsworth was gone. The *Albanov* was gone. The sky itself was gone. It was as if the whole world had shrivelled up and retreated into the canoe. "I say we head back to shore before we lose our bearings completely."

"You want for me to turn around now?"

"If you're sure you know where you're going then carry on," he said, waving his hand through the murk and trying not to sound either sarcastic or on the verge of panic. "Otherwise, yes, I think we should turn around. We haven't gone that far. We can set up a shelter and wait for it to lift."

There was a long silence before the engine roared back to life and the canoe began to turn.

Mist. Distance meant nothing. They could have been two metres or two miles from the shoreline and the world ahead would have been the same unyielding grey swirl.

Callum's eyes were watering. "*The sea smoke will find the*

weak points," Lungkaju had told him. And he was right. It clung to his face like a mask, and he could feel an intense cold around his wrist and neck lines.

After a burst of speed, Darya had cut the engine once more and allowed them to drift. "I will let the current take us from here," she said. "Otherwise we might crash into the rocks."

They sat in silence as the canoe rocked and the water stirred around them, barely visible through the billowing grey.

"Do you hate me?" she asked suddenly.

The mist swirling past her shoulders made her look ghostlike, as if she were apparating before him. The intense green of her eyes pierced through the vapour and he could see that her cheeks were wet with tears.

He took her hands in his. "Of course not. Why would I hate you?"

"For bringing you out here when you should be safe on the ship. Now you are lost and in trouble."

He squeezed her still-clenched knuckles and smiled what he hoped was a reassuring smile. "Look, I don't know where I am at the best of times and I'm always in trouble."

Her fists began to loosen. "You are always joking."

"If only people found me funny."

"Can you be serious for a second?"

He pretended to think about it. "No."

Her hands slipped fully into his. He watched as she smoothed her thumbs over the top of his knuckles, then he looked back up into her eyes. "I—"

There was a sudden impact. The canoe shook as the prow ground against rock.

Callum dipped his paddle into the water. It felt thick, more like soup than brine, but as he moved the oar around he realised that it was strands of kelp tangling around the blade. He pushed down through them and hit the underlying shingle.

"It's the shoreline." He lowered a leg carefully over the side, feeling the bite of the icy water at his shin. Then he waited as Darya clambered after him, and together they dragged the canoe back out of the surf.

The scattering of pebbles underfoot, and the crackle of driftwood, told him that they were on a beach. Otherwise, they might have been anywhere on earth. The world beyond was nothing but a ghostly glow.

"Should we call for help?" Darya asked. "I am wearing my wristband." She pulled back the sleeve on her jacket and exposed her emergency locator.

Callum's gut reaction was to say: *Yes, for God's sake press the button and get us the hell out of here!* But his feet were back on dry land and his initial sense of panic was beginning to wane. "If you want to call then that's okay."

"But *you* do not?"

"The way I see it, we're both okay, we know where we are... sort of. I don't think we actually qualify as needing help. Not just yet. Do we?"

She smiled. "I see. You mean you would prefer that nobody knows you ignore the rules and go for midnight boat trip without an escort?"

He cleared his throat. "If possible."

"This is fine. I would prefer it this way also."

"Then we wait it out," Callum said. "Me and Lungkaju have been caught out a couple of times. You just have to sit tight and wait."

"So you are pro then?"

"I wouldn't say *pro* exactly. But I know there's no need to panic. If we're lucky, we'll be out of here in a couple of hours."

"In this case follow me. I know a place where we can shelter."

"You know where we are?"

She bent down and stroked her fingers across a patch of yellow-green moss. "There is only one place on Harmsworth where I have seen this species in this colour. This is Konrad

134

Cove. There is a ledge not far away, where I have seal hide. Come on, we will be safe there."

She set off inland at her usual athletic pace.

"Konrad Cove, of course it is," Callum whispered to himself. Then he crunched after her up the shore.

3

The observation room was cluttered and dark. As anticipated, it was also empty. Two high-backed chairs faced a wall crammed with security camera screens and protruding wires, below which sat a large console. Rows of recordable laser disc drives topped with blinking red lights, one for each on-board camera, flanked a central control unit.

Ptarmigan wasted no time tapping into the operating programme and resetting the record parameters as planned. He also inserted a data stick into the main drive and uploaded two new programmes. One of them had been agreed with Finback. He smiled. The other... that was a *little* something that he'd cooked up himself.

He checked his watch. He had four minutes, five max, before he could expect the belated guard change. A bleep sounded from the console as it accepted his alterations. Next he searched out the cameras that had tracked his movements already that evening. One by one, fingers working furiously, he searched back to the relevant sections and deleted his Oscar-winning performances. Using the first of the uploaded software programmes, he then stitched the footage back together as best he could. Finished, he reset the screen the way it had been left and made his way to the door.

It was a rush job. The crudeness of it was already busting his balls. But he consoled himself with the knowledge that it would serve. By the time any eagle-eyed jobsworth had picked up on the rough edges, the whole vessel would be on the bottom of the ocean anyhow. With this thought, he cracked open the door and exited.

Retracing his steps around the side of the deckhouse, he could hear the sound of low conversation as the two replacement guards approached the room from the other direction. Moving as fast as he could, he now made his way along the deck, past the funnel to another restricted entrance.

He listened for company.

Nothing.

He punched in the code and slipped inside.

The ship's engine room was arranged around three inter-dependent platforms. Ptarmigan entered onto the upper platform. Though he knew the layout by heart, he was still taken aback by the sheer scale of the room. It was cavernous. To his right, stretching off into the distance, were a row of workshops and spare-part repositories stacked with tools, workbenches and crates filled with metal components. Beyond this sat the enormous electrical main motherboard and control panel. To his left he scanned his eyes across the central exhaust manifold, the oil settling, service and storage tanks, and the mind-boggling array of pipes that formed the hydrophore pump system for supplying the ship's water. In the far corner sat the sewage plant, next to which were the incinerator and a spare propeller and tail shaft, poised like monumental works of modern art sculpture.

The first cluster of security cameras was mounted high up, besides the ceiling crane terminus. Even though nearly all of them seemed to be pointing directly at him, Ptarmigan was confident that he was out of shot. His security programme updates had turned his entire route into a temporary blind spot. To avoid suspicion he had needed to keep the camera coverage as comprehensive as possible, meaning that, as blind spots went, it was pretty narrow. More of a periphery spot. Not a toe could stray from the carefully planned route. There was also a rigid schedule to stick to, with the cameras programmed to resume full coverage behind him.

Having oriented himself, he followed around the hot well and expansion tanks, careful to stick as close to the railings as possible, and descended the next staircase. Before setting foot from the bottom step he waited, watching as the seconds ticked away on his wrist. Then, precisely on schedule, he stepped onto the walkway.

The central platform was as crowded with machinery as the upper and just as silent at this hour. The main generators loomed large at the far end. In the gloom, Ptarmigan could also pick out the auxiliary alternators, the oil heater and purifier system, and the row of large, vertical canisters that comprised the main, auxiliary and emergency air bottles. It was all exactly as it had been on the plans. Growing in confidence, he slipped between the dehumidifier system and the fresh water generator, kept towards the edge of the room and descended the next staircase.

On the lower platform, he checked his watch once more. He took a deep breath. His hands were clammy and shaking. Sweat lined his brow in the humidity. But so far, so good. And he was on schedule.

In the centre of the platform was the main engine, a mass of pipes, cylinders and cables, surrounded by a moat-like cofferdam. The rest of the far end of the platform was taken up with the seawater, oil, lube, bilge and sludge pumps. To his left, the entire aft area was beset with rows of tanks.

"Bin-fucking-go!" he whispered to himself, already searching out the bunker fuel tanks. The three large metal containers were painted green and their sides were adorned with international warning symbols above lists of white-painted bunkering instructions translated into numerous languages.

Ptarmigan dropped the rucksack from his shoulders and unzipped it. To an outsider, the charges would have looked like everyday bathroom items: two toothpaste tubes, two shaving foam cans and two deodorant bottles. Of course, they were just casings. The six canisters no longer contained toothpaste, shaving foam or deodorant spray, but enough concentrated explosive to blast through the lining of the tanks, ignite the considerable quantities of diesel within them, create an atomic particle explosion and blow the *Albanov* clean in half. Ptarmigan's heart raced at the thought of the raw, concentrated power in his hands.

Nam Myoho Renge Kyo, Nam Myoho Renge Kyo, Nam Myoho...

The explosives drop had been at the exact coordinates supplied by Finback, and he had retrieved it no problem only the day after the inductions. God knows how the guy had got it there in the first place. The going rate for somebody to fly to Franz Josef Land just to make a drop-off must have been astronomical. But still, there it had been. And now here it was, signed, sealed and about to be decisively delivered.

Having worked quickly to attach the charges, two to the base of each tank, he made a final check then stood back and checked his watch. He counted exactly seventeen seconds and then set off back the way he'd come. Everything was now in place. In a few hours' time that bastard Volkov and his cronies, the G&S Corporation, every other thieving, raping gas conglomerate in the world would get the wake-up call of a lifetime. If they wanted to sink their teeth into the Arctic so bad, then they'd better be ready. Because, with a little help from Ptarmigan, this was one ecosystem that would sure as hell bite back.

Chapter 6

CAVES

1

Koikov flicked the end of his papirosa and watched it disappear into the mist. Just being back on the island was bad enough. A search and rescue in zero visibility was the last thing he needed.

The emergency locator signal had been picked up early that morning. It belonged to one of the science club, the Einstein lookalike Doctor Semyonov. God knew how long it had been transmitting for, but it had quickly been established that nobody had seen old Einstein or his guide now for over twenty-four hours.

He rubbed at his scar. "Marchenko! What's the story?"

Marchenko peered at the GPS tracker. A red dot flashed in arrhythmic pulses across the screen. "Signal keeps cutting out and shifting."

"What the hell does that mean? More interference?"

"No, Starshyna. My other sat signals are unaffected at present."

"What then?"

"I'd say that unless Doctor Semyonov's invented himself a teleporter, then he's taken shelter in a cave."

A cave. Koikov's pulse quickened.

"It's the worst thing he could've done," Marchenko continued.

"There's no line of sight between him and the satellite."

"Shit!" Koikov reaffirmed his low-visibility visor to reveal a landscape of contrasting shades. It was undoubtedly a useful piece of kit, giving him exceptional visibility through the murk. But the weight of it was distracting, and the constant fading in and out of the combined heat and ambient light signatures made him feel queasy.

"That's our boy," Marchenko said, his voice tinged with excitement.

Koikov looked over to see Marchenko's gangly aura standing right next to him and pointing ahead. Through the visor, he looked like some kind of computer game character. Koikov hated computer games. He wasn't that keen on Marchenko. He was a pussy. Not a hard bone in his body.

Koikov followed the line of his outstretched arm. A hundred metres up ahead there did appear to be the mouth of a large cave. His pulse picked up again. He scanned back to see the rest of the rescue team advancing up the incline, their colour signatures growing bolder against the barren rock.

"Old Einstein better be in serious trouble," he said, striding on towards the cave. "Let's get him and get the hell out of here."

Standing at the mouth of the cave, Marchenko turned to Koikov. "That's one hell of a stench. I reckon the doctor could be dead already."

Koikov nodded. "Or it could be something else."

"Like what?"

Koikov held a hand to his radio collar. "Private Yudina."

"Starshyna?"

"On me."

Koikov turned to Marchenko. "Sergeant, hand me that tracker."

Marchenko went to protest, then unstrapped the tracker from around his neck and handed it over.

"Now fall back and take charge of the others," Koikov ordered. "Advance them to the mouth of the cave then wait outside until I give the all clear."

Marchenko fell back, and seconds later Private Yudina arrived at the mouth of the cave.

"You smell that?" Koikov asked.

The towering private took a lungful of air and nodded.

"You recognise it?"

Silence.

"Yudina?"

"Of course I do. How could I forget it?"

Koikov grunted in agreement. Though he knew that he was not directly to blame, he had still taken Dolgonosov's death personally. How dare that *creature* think that it could fuck with his team! He should have reported the tragedy immediately. He knew full well. But instead he had finished his papirosa, slid Dolgonosov's eyelids shut and set off in pursuit. It had been a serious error of judgement.

After repeated tours in the Northern Caucasus, Koikov knew a thing or two about taking things personally. He had witnessed some of the vilest injuries affronted men could inflict on innocent others. The attack on a nursery school in Nazran. The revenge massacre of an entire mujahedeen unit. The merciless show-decapitation of young Russian conscripts. The list went on. Yet he had dealt with it, just as he had dealt with the many other atrocities that he had witnessed in that sorry region.

But there was something about the attack on Junior Sergeant Sharova that Koikov knew would be altogether harder for him to deal with. It wasn't the injuries. Sharova had been mauled almost as badly as Dolgonosov, for sure. But all Koikov could think about were the screech, the curled-back lips, the teeth. When he closed his eyes he saw only the hellish pair that had peered back at him out of the cave after he and Private Yudina had responded to Sharova's screams and opened fire on the thing standing over their comrade's body. And all the while, the air had been rife with its gut-wrenching stink. He swallowed hard. It was the same stench that was wafting over him now.

Koikov hung the tracker cord around his neck, and he and Yudina cocked their assault rifles. The crunch and slide of the metal working parts echoed around the cave. Glancing down at the tracker, Koikov could see a blinking red dot approximately thirty metres up ahead. As he watched, it disappeared suddenly, then reappeared several metres to the west.

"Why's it doing that?" Yudina asked.

"The satellite signal's weak in here," Koikov replied. "The tracker can't get a proper fix."

"Can't it pick up the signal direct at this range?"

Koikov raised his hand to his throat. "Marchenko?"

"Starshyna?"

"Is it possible to pick up the locator signal direct?"

"I already switched it over, Starshyna."

Koikov studied the screen. Nothing had changed. The red dot flashed in roughly the location it had before. Then it disappeared and relocated a short distance away.

His brow furrowed. Something wasn't right.

2

The seal hide stood on a ledge set back from the edge of the cliff. It was a small canvas lean-to, braced against an overhang and camouflaged with dumps of scree. Callum reached out and shook one of the struts. The canvas scrunched between his fingers, but the structure held firm.

"We have built many of these along this coast because this is where the seals are mating," Darya said, pulling back the flap. "Let us get inside before it gets colder."

The hide's interior was cosy and mist-free, and the pale grey-green canvas glowed with absorbed light. The overhang recessed steeply where it met the ledge. Darya reached into it, unfurled a roll of material and arranged it as a floor covering. "This will stop the cold from coming up."

Callum secured the entrance as best he could, then he turned and slumped back against the rock. Having rummaged around inside her rucksack, Darya sat next to him, mimicking his position.

Callum looked over at her. She was silhouetted against the canvas. A bluish-white light fell across her face as she turned her camera on and began scrolling through her digital images.

"It's a shame," he said, as her shots of the bear flicked past. "Are you okay?"

"I just don't understand how anybody could do this. I told you it was the bears who needed protection."

"Perhaps whoever shot it was defending themselves."

"This is not likely." She looked up at him, her eyes focussed. "And do you not think that we would have heard about this? Do you think that if somebody was attacked by bear they would still let us onto this island?"

"I don't know," Callum answered. "I admit they seem big on health and safety, but how much do you know about this Volkov character? It's him calling the shots, after all."

She snorted. "You are right, this man is ignorant pig. He is not interested in the bears or Harmsworth, or even people. He is interested in money and power."

"You knew him before?"

She nodded. "He is one of the richest men in Russia, very high up executive with state-run oil company. I have worked with him before on Sakhalin."

"Sakhalin?"

"It is very beautiful island in the Sea of Okhotsk off east coast of Russia. They find oil and gas there few years ago and build two onshore processing plants, one in the north and one in the south. It is very similar project to Harmsworth. I was part of the assessment team for this also."

"So what did he do wrong?"

She rolled her lips. "It is what he did not do right. He did not listen to what we recommend and now the beautiful nature on Sakhalin suffers. Many of the rivers are polluted, with eroding banks, and the sea life is being driven away from the coast by the seismic testing of the seabed. Can you believe that Mr Volkov tries to pin this on us! He tells the environment minister that our assessment is unprofessional, that we are not doing a good enough job even though we are very thorough while he tries to make it as difficult as possible for us." She took a deep breath. "I just wait for him to do the same here."

The guy had seemed a bit intimidating perhaps, creepy even with his skull-like face. But there had been nothing in his conduct to suggest that he was hostile towards the EIA process. If anything, his attitude was accommodating, more so than Callum had expected from a man in his position. Perhaps Darya's perception of him was more a reflection of her sensitive nature.

"I can tell what you are thinking," she said suddenly, looking deep into his eyes, seeming to read his thoughts. "You are thinking, *What is she talking about?* You are thinking that Mr Volkov has sympathy with the Harmsworth assessment. But I promise you, this man does not know the meaning of this word. Do not be fooled by him, Callum. He acts this way because of money."

"Money?"

"Friends of mine in the Academy of Sciences made sure that the damage done to Sakhalin is big news in Russia, and in Scandinavia where the partner companies are based. There was then a lot of pressure on the Federal Service for Natural Resources to fine the company and to make sure that they clean up their mess."

"You don't think he's learnt his lesson then?"

"Yes, but I think that he is learn the *wrong* lesson. He does not want to lose more money here on Harmsworth. This is perhaps why you do not see the real Mr Volkov. It is not because he cares." She paused then added, "He is also very clever man. Before Sakhalin he was in politics, and before this it is thought that he was member of the KGB. It is well known that he still has many friends high up in the State Duma. He is what is wrong with the new Russia. He is old Russia." She turned off the camera, throwing her face back into shadow. "His eyes are closed and dishonest. They are not like yours, *solnishko*. You have good, caring eyes and good, caring heart. This is why you try to defend him."

"I'm not defending him, Darya. I just don't know him."

She placed a hand on his cheek. He could feel the coolness of her palm against his stubble. Her eyes lightened and a faint smile parted her lips. "You need to shave."

He looked into her eyes. Bags had begun to form under them. "You should take a rest," he said, pulling her rucksack around. "Use this as a pillow."

"Maybe just a short time."

He moved over so that she could lie down facing the overhang. Then he took the bag and positioned it under her head.

"Are you not tired also?" she asked. "You have been awake a long time."

"I couldn't sleep just yet," he replied. "Besides, we should probably take it in turns to stay awake, just to be safe."

"Still frightened of the big bad bears?"

Callum said nothing but stroked the hair from her cheek.

She closed her eyes. "Wake me when it is my turn on guard."

He lay down next to her, hands folded on his chest. Then he took the white pebble from his pocket and flipped it through his fingers as the day's events churned over in his mind. The hide creaked in the wind. The canvas sucked against his arm, and he couldn't help imagining that the world outside was feeding on him. He pulled his arm away. No sooner had he done so than he felt something fold over his other wrist, not canvas but skin. Now familiar soft fingers slipped in-between his own.

He turned his head slowly. Darya was on her back, facing towards him. Her eyes were open wide and looking deep into his. He could feel the press of her knee against his thigh, making the muscle tense.

"On the canoe, you would say something before—"

Heart racing, he leant forward and kissed her gently. Her lips tasted sweet and exotic, and the warmth of her skin made him forget all about the island and its cloak of mist, the cold, hard rock beneath his shoulders.

When he moved his head away he could see that her eyes were closed once more and she was smiling. As her knee rolled from the outside to the inside of his thigh, he kissed her again.

This time she wrapped her arms around him and pulled him close.

3

"There's something on the ground."

"It's shit."

"How do you know?"

Koikov spat on the floor. "I've stepped in enough."

The cave was strewn with rocks, and water dripped from the stalactites hanging tooth-like from the ceiling. Up ahead, something lay heaped against the foot of a rock-pile. It wouldn't have been worth a second thought if it hadn't been giving off a heat signal.

As they approached it took on form, until it was clearly identifiable as a jumble of clothing. The relief that Koikov felt at finding clothes rather than a dead doctor was fleeting. By now the temperature on Harmsworth was consistently a degree or two above freezing. But even so, why the hell would anybody shed their clothing like this? Something wasn't right.

The two men pushed back their visors and engaged their rifle lamps. At their feet was a blue, fur-lined jacket, torn and covered in dark stains.

"Blood," Yudina said.

Koikov nodded.

Curving round from the base of the jacket was a pair of

shredded trousers. One of the legs ended in a black leather boot, while the other boot and a glove lay propped against each other a short distance away.

"Do you think these are Semyonov's things?"

Koikov brought his hand to his throat. "Marchenko."

"Starshyna?"

"What was Semyonov wearing?"

"White jacket, blue trousers... brown boots. Have you located him?"

"No. What about his guide?"

There was a commotion at the other end of the line. Then, "Starshyna Koikov, this is Lungkaju."

"What is it?"

"Lambie was with the doctor. He was wearing dark clothes. Dark blue jacket with a hood and dark blue—"

"Jesus Christ!"

Koikov turned to see that Yudina had picked up the glove and was staring into the wrist-hole.

"What is it?" he demanded.

Slowly Yudina turned the glove.

What was left of the wrist itself, splinters of bone and rags of gnarled flesh, dribbled out of the opening. Yudina tossed it back to the floor.

"Starshyna?" came Marchenko's voice. "Starshyna, what's your status?"

Koikov thought about ignoring him then grunted, "Hold your position."

He moved past Yudina and peered inside the removed boot. Chunks of ankle bone and shredded tendon flowered up at him, and he backed away again.

"Is it..."

Koikov nodded. Beads of sweat forming on his brow, he panned his rifle around the cave. Yudina followed suit. The light from their rifle lamps reflected off the moisture on the rock and caused the walls to glisten. It looked as if a million beady eyes were watching them from the shadows. But there was nothing. No movement. No sound, besides their breathing. Nothing.

Koikov brought his weapon back to bear on the heap of clothing. His mind was racing, and the more it raced the more certain he became. He swallowed back the bile in his throat, leant forward, poked the muzzle of his rifle into the main body of the jacket and lifted.

The clothes were arranged around a remnant skeleton. Shattered fingers of rib seemed to burst up out of the chest area, beyond which the partially articulated spinal column curved its way along the back of the jacket and down into the trousers. The pelvis lobes peered up over the belt-line, and the shoulder and collar bones clamoured at the neck area. The internal organs were nowhere to be seen. The bones had been picked entirely clean of flesh.

There was a sudden shrieking sound at the back of the cave, and neither Koikov nor Yudina hesitated. In an instant, the stale air erupted. The sound of automatic fire, of undirected rounds ricocheting off the walls, created a deafening explosion of sound as both men reacted on reflex. Shoulder to shoulder, they strafed the darkness repeatedly, stopping only to change magazines: one, two, three, four... The muzzle flashes illuminated the interior of the cave like an orange and white strobe, animating every rock and shadow and creating more and more fictive targets to draw their aim.

As they fired on, something tore past Private Yudina, causing him to stumble backwards. Koikov ceased fire and turned towards him. The cave fell back into silence.

"Yudina?"

Yudina's eyes were racked open with shock. His arms dangled loosely at his sides. His rifle, steaming and toy-like as ever in his enormous grip, slid loose and clattered to the floor.

"Yudina! What is it?"

Silence. Yudina stood and stared, a thin line of saliva spilling from the corner of his mouth.

"Private Yudi—"

Without warning, Yudina's stomach opened horizontally. Like a gaping mouth, his body parted just above the hips, and his intestines teetered, swollen, on the lower lip. Then they rushed out onto the floor, a tongue of red, yellow and grey billowing from the massive laceration. His knees began to tremble before he sagged down onto them, gasping with shock.

Koikov rushed forward to try and catch him. As he did so, Yudina's expression changed. For a split second, Koikov wondered whether it was because he was kneeling on the man's guts; at the back of his mind he was conscious of the swollen mass warm against his groin. But Yudina's gaze no longer met with his. Instead he was staring back across Koikov's shoulder.

His eyes opened wider. His entire face began to shake.

4

Koikov turned his head.

The creature was behind him. It was the same impossible, stinking creature that had killed Dolgonosov and Sharova. Silent, still, it had craned its neck down until its face was within an inch of Koikov's. The reek of its breath was like nothing he could describe. It vocalised a sequence of alien clicks and gurgles that would not have been audible were its snout not so horrifyingly close. It sniffed gently at his collar. Then it cocked its head and stared at him through enormous empty eyes.

Koikov froze. He had come face to face with death many times before, but this was an encounter like no other. His mind read like a military training manual. His saving grace had often been his ability to flick straight to the relevant page. But there was no page for this. The closest thing that he could draw on now was his instruction on surviving shark attacks... deliver a hard blow to the nose... attempt to crush the eyes... insert your hand(s) into the gills and damage the internal organs... manoeuvre on top of the shark, hold tight around the body and bear-hug... But punching *that* nose would be pointless and crushing *those* eyes would be impossible and it had no gills and a bear-hug was out of the question and anyway it wasn't a motherfucking shark! It was a… a thing. It was a…

Still the creature stood motionless, staring. A frenzy of new thoughts crowded Koikov's mind: *Why doesn't it attack? Why am I still in one piece? Could it be scared as well? Is it waiting for me to make the next move?*

The creature jerked its head downwards suddenly and sniffed at the tracker dangling around Koikov's neck. Only now did he realise that it was emitting a frantic beep, the red dot reflecting directly in the centre of the creature's eye.

It nuzzled at the handset until its breath had fogged up the screen. Then it took a step backwards. It raised its head and threw it forward again as if choking. Strings of thick yellow mucus stretched from its jaws to the floor as it retched, and it chomped its teeth together, breaking them off.

When it eventually reared back up, Koikov could see that it had regurgitated something, and even through the coating of sputum it was clear what that something was. It was a partially digested hand. Attached to the wrist, still blinking, was Doctor Semyonov's emergency locator.

The creature bobbed its head as if satisfied and made a low, rasping sound. In that moment, something frighteningly like a grin emerged on its face. In blind terror, Koikov flung his rifle around and aimed it at the creature. But before he could fire off a shot, it had lashed out with one of its hind legs and knocked him to the ground.

Through his new delirium Koikov could feel a crushing pain in his chest. Perhaps it was the heart attack that would put him out of his misery. But as the cave swam back into focus, he could see that it was the creature's hind foot stamped across his sternum. It was pinning him, helpless, onto his back; just as it had pinned Sharova as he and Yudina had watched on in stunned disbelief, unable to fire off a single shot before it was too late. It reared its head once again, this time opening its beak-like mouth to display its teeth.

This is it, Koikov thought. *My turn.*

He held his breath.

As the creature brought its head back down, there was a loud bang and its bottom jaw exploded. It crowed out in surprise. Another bang sounded, and this time a large chunk of its neck disintegrated, throwing a shower of vermillion droplets up into the air and across Koikov's face. The intermittent bangs then became a frenzy of rattling as the creature appeared to self-destruct before him.

It staggered backwards. The feathers covering its body seemed to shimmer from white to black and back again, over and over. Its legs and torso were now riddled with holes oozing blood, and the eye that had stared so hard at Koikov had disappeared back into its skull.

With a final screech, it slumped down onto the floor, hammering its tail at the rock.

Koikov pulled himself to his feet, still disoriented, and felt hands reach out to steady him.

"Are you okay, Starshyna?" It was Marchenko.

"I'm fine," Koikov replied, "but Private Yudina—"

"He's dead," a different voice called out.

Koikov looked over to see two medics and Lungkaju knelt down beside Yudina's body. Yudina was on his back now, his face pale. His eyes closed.

"I am sorry," the older of the two medics said, "but there is nothing anybody can do for him."

"Starshyna Koikov, we are all in great danger," Lungkaju said, rising to his feet. Trails of smoke spiralled from the barrels of the shotgun in his hands. "We should leave now."

"We'll leave when I say we leave!" Koikov bellowed.

"No, he's right," Marchenko said. "I don't know how many more of those things there are in here and I'm fucked if we're hanging around to find out!"

"Look, Marchenko—"

A loud screech emanated from deep within the cave. It was followed by another, then by several more in quick succession, until the interior of the cave was alive with screeches and other terrifying echoes.

Koikov snatched up his rifle. "Okay, everybody back to the Kamov now!"

As the team obeyed his order and fled, he unloaded a final magazine towards the back of the cave, then turned and raced after them.

Chapter 7

SEA CENTAUR

1

Callum awoke to find himself alone in the shelter. He checked his watch. It was mid-morning. *Christ!* By now Lungkaju would know that he was missing and may well have raised the alarm. If he had then Volkov would know that he had disobeyed the safety regs and that meant that he was in deep shit. If the guy was as bad as Darya suggested, he might even be kicked off the project. Then what about the ice mummy?

The potential seriousness of the situation dawned suddenly, and he dropped his head into his hands. "Why do I drink that stuff?"

Jonas. Jonas is dead, that's why! And then Darya had set out to distract him, and man alive had she done a good job! So where the hell was she now?

He crawled out of the hide and scanned around. The air was still and the temperature just above freezing. The mist had cleared and he could see the ledge on which the seal hide stood. It was nestled along the face of a low cliff overlooking the cove. From here he could make out the up-ended canoe, part-way up the beach. The view inland was blocked by the rising relief, but it was unbroken along the coast to the south and beyond to the *Albanov*. Suddenly the ship looked a hell of a long way away.

"Callum!"

He spun around.

Darya looked weary and dishevelled, and there was an odd look on her face, somewhere between excitement and fear. "You must come and see this!" She grabbed him by the hand and went to take off again, but he pulled her back.

"Are you crazy? We need to get back to the ship or they'll be sending out a search party. We'll be off the project."

Smiling, she squeezed his hand and replied, "Relax. We will go back to the ship and everything will be fine, but first you *must* see this. Trust me, you will not believe!"

Ten minutes later, they were standing on top of a headland, looking north towards the heights of Svayataya in the distance. Callum recognised the beach immediately below the promontory. It was where they had landed the night before; there in the far corner was the polar bear carcass, unchanged from when he'd seen it last.

Darya crouched behind a rock and pulled him down beside her.

"What exactly am I looking at?"

"Just wait, you will see."

Callum settled onto his stomach and watched. They passed a few minutes in silence before he said, "About last night—"

"Yes, it was very good," she replied, pecking him on the cheek, "but look."

His eyes wandered back towards the carcass. Its pose looked about as undignified as possible, splayed out on its back with its neck twisted around and one forearm draped across its chest. It looked drunk rather than dead. But today there was no riot of gulls fighting to get their beaks into it. Instead it lay eerily still and undisturbed and... Callum removed his sunglasses and blinked.

Its paw had moved. He looked across at Darya. She was

watching intently through her binoculars, wearing the same bemused smile. As he squinted back down, the paw seemed to move again. He was about to speak when he felt the binoculars tap against his cheek. He took them and looked back. No sooner had he refocussed than something appeared out of the bear's armpit. It was a head, small and white, with an elongated snout and two large eyes. It was like no creature he had ever seen before. "What is it?"

She shrugged. "I have been watching them for the last hour and I am starting to think that nobody would know."

The creature emerged fully from the carcass. It stood for a moment, perched on the side of the bear's arm, a chunk of meat in its mouth. Then it bounded with great agility down onto the shingle, followed by another two identical animals. With the bear for scale, they only appeared to be half a metre or so in height, and their white coats were murky with dried blood.

"They look like birds," Callum said. "Ugly ones."

"This is what I thought," Darya replied. "They are bipedal, two-legged, like birds. Their coats look more like feathers, though I cannot be sure of this from so far away, and their snouts are long like beaks, but…" She hesitated. "I do not think that they are birds. They do not behave like birds."

"And they have no wings," Callum added. "They have little forearms."

"And the tail is actual tail and not just feathers."

"You think this might be a new species?"

"I think yes," she answered. "This might be true."

They watched as the little creatures leapt in and out of the hole that they had burrowed into the carcass, squabbling over morsels of flesh. Then one of them froze suddenly and sniffed at the air. Its body was held parallel to the ground, its neck and its tail both long and outstretched, its forearms bent at the elbows beneath its chest. It bobbed its head as it strutted a few paces on its muscular hind legs.

"We must get closer," Darya said suddenly, setting off back towards the hide.

Callum went to argue, then closed his mouth and followed after her.

2

"We must be very quiet now," Darya whispered, as the canoe approached the far end of the cove. "I do not want to scare them away or I will maybe not see them again."

Callum dug his paddle in and brought them to a stop twenty metres or so from shore. The current was weaker than it had been the day before, and he was able to keep the craft still while Darya attached a telephoto lens to her camera and began taking shots.

Almost immediately, one of the creatures noticed them and scampered to the water's edge to inspect. It was quickly joined by the others, and the three stood shoulder to shoulder, staring out towards the canoe.

"I don't think there's much danger of them running away," Callum said.

"No, they seem to be very interested in us. It could be because they have never seen human beings before."

"Shouldn't they be scared?"

"Sometimes it is the other way. Some new species are completely unafraid of humans, because they had never seen one. Their ecosystem is isolated."

Callum nodded back towards the shore. "Do you think I should try and get closer?"

"Yes, but not too close… and still be gentle."

He raised his paddle and manoeuvred them forward another few metres.

The creatures remained as they were, silent, their eyes fixed on the canoe's every movement. From this distance, it was clear that their coats were feathered. The hind feet were taloned, and the slender fore-fingers were tipped with claws.

"Do you recognise them now?"

"No," Darya replied. "At first I think that they were rodents of some kind, but I can see now that they are very different."

Callum noted the streaks of dried blood on their chest plumage. "Whatever they are, they're carnivorous."

"This could be island adaptation," she replied, continuing to photograph.

"Island adaptation?"

"Because they are isolated population they may have developed different to the parent group because of very different environment.

"Like the woolly mammoth on Wrangel Island," Callum said. "They grew to be much smaller than the mainland group because of the limited food supply."

"This is true, and Franz Josef Land is maybe similar situation. Remote island with limited terrestrial food supply."

Time ticked over as they continued to observe. The creatures' eyes were enormous, disproportionate against their tiny cocked heads. Their expressions made Callum uncomfortable; it was as if they were seeing something he wasn't.

The creature on the right broke its vigil suddenly and turned its head. In an instant it had launched forward and latched on to the side of its neighbour's neck, causing it to squeal out. Now the third creature turned and joined in, grabbing onto the victim's tail. The two attackers began a tug of war, before their prey struggled free and pounced on the original attacker, pinning it to the floor with its hind legs.

Again the third creature joined in, barging indiscriminately into the scuffle and causing the others to leap to their feet and scatter. Moments later, having seemingly expended their burst of energy, the three were back shoulder to shoulder, peering across at Callum.

There was something strange about this behaviour. It was boisterous and naïve. "Could they be youngsters?" Callum asked.

Darya stopped photographing and turned to him. "You are very observant," she said. "I cannot be certain, but yes, this is not typical adult behaviour. They act like juveniles."

Callum watched her raise the camera once again. But before she had taken any more photographs, she relowered it, a look of confusion spreading across her face.

"What is it?"

"Look at the water."

Several metres ahead of them, the surface had begun to foam.

"It is a shoal of fish," she said.

"What are they doing?"

She made no reply, watching as the shoal formed a frenzied arc around the prow.

"They are panicking," she said at last. "Something has scared them."

The words had barely left her lips when a large shadow darted through the centre of the shoal, causing it to splinter.

"What was that?"

She shook her head. "The narwhal would not come this close to shore."

"Then what?"

"I do not know," she replied. "It could be seals, but I do not like it. Something is wrong."

There was a sudden crash and the canoe rocked as something collided with the underside. Darya screamed, and they both grabbed tightly on to the gunwales. Gradually, the craft shook itself steady and the water stilled.

Callum peered over into the calm grey-blue. The panicking fish had disappeared. All movement had stopped. Even the strands of kelp stood still and erect, barely rustling in the gentle current.

His gaze came to rest on something only an inch or so below the surface. He couldn't make it out. It was dark and circular and…

…then it blinked.

3

The massive eye blinked again then disappeared into the shadows.

Callum jerked his head back from the edge just as a mouthful of teeth exploded up out of the water. He toppled backwards into the body of the canoe. When he opened his eyes, he was looking up across Darya's face towards the sky. Both were pale. Darya was screaming out in terror, and he followed her gaze towards the stern.

Beside the aft seat, three clawed fingers were clamped over the side of the canoe like a grappling hook. They were followed by three more, and then by the unmistakable face of one of the creatures. It threw its head backwards and swallowed down the writhing fish that was speared onto its front teeth.

This was no juvenile. The snout was weathered and scarred. The eyes were ten times larger than those of the scrappers on the beach, and the grey-blue feathers along the back of the neck were thick and full. There was no mistaking that this thing, whatever it was, was a fully grown adult.

Callum grabbed the paddle and rammed it as hard as he could into the creature's face. It screeched out as the wood splintered against its skull. Straight away Darya brought the other paddle down onto the back of its head, leaving it stunned, and Callum wasted no time landing a final blow to the side of its neck, sending it crashing backwards.

"Start the motor up!" he yelled.

Darya pushed past him, slung the outboard propeller over the stern and tore at the pull-cord. The engine spluttered then lapsed back into silence. She tugged at it again. This time the splutter was replaced by a low metallic whine.

"Let me," he said, taking the handle and yanking it as hard as he could. Nothing. He tried again and again. But it was no use.

"Seawater must have mixed with the fuel," Darya said.

At that moment there was another crash and they were both thrown onto their backs.

"Watch out!" Callum pulled Darya's head out of the way just as a clawed foot shot over the side of the canoe and smashed into the inside of the prow. A sabre-like claw arced down and punctured deep into the timber, then the leg retracted and whipped over the gunwale a second time. The heel crashed down in between their heads. Callum watched as the calf tendon contracted and fired the toe claw down into the timber once again. This time it did not retract but remained lodged only inches from his face. He fumbled for what remained of the oar and speared it into the foot muscle. There was a loud screech and the leg disappeared once more.

Callum and Darya lay still.

"What the hell is that thing?" Callum whispered, barely daring to make a sound.

"I do not know, but it does not want us here."

"You can say that again."

Callum began climbing to his feet.

She grasped at his elbow. "What are you doing?"

"I've got to try and start the engine. We're sitting ducks."

"Yes, but be careful!"

On his knees, Callum cast a glance around the canoe. The water was calm. Nothing stared up at him from below the surface. He got to his feet and approached the motor. His face was soaked in sweat. At any moment that thing could reappear, burst up out of the water and into the canoe.

He reached out and grasped the pull-cord toggle. "Please, for the love of God, please work," he whispered to himself. Then he yanked at the cord. The engine spluttered. He tried it again, then again. "Come on, you rusty piece of shit!"

Finally, the splutter deepened into a roar as the engine fired up.

"Now get us out of here!" Darya shouted.

Callum turned the craft around and steered it south towards the *Albanov*.

"Here, let me," she said, taking the rudder control back from him.

As the canoe accelerated, Callum scanned the shoreline. The little creatures were still there. They were no longer still. Instead they appeared to be jumping up and down in agitation. As he looked on, something else, much closer, caught his eye.

"Oh, shit!"

"What is it?"

He pointed behind her. Below the surface of the water, two dark shadows were following in the wake of the canoe.

"Can this thing go any faster?"

The two shadows coursed through the water. Propelled by their muscular tails, they burst forward, criss-crossing each other's paths and easily outpacing the canoe.

"They're closing!" Callum shouted.

"We are going top speed!" Darya yelled back. "It is not meant to be racing boat!"

Searching desperately around, he grabbed her survival rucksack and spilt the contents out onto the deck. "There must be something…" He kicked her emergency tent out of the way and scooped up the bolt gun and a handful of bolts, before noticing the emergency flares. He stuffed the bolt gun into his pocket and snatched up a flare from the bundle. He held it at arm's length, removed the safety guard and smashed his palm up into the base. It fizzed and spewed out a gust of smoke, but the charge failed to ignite.

There was a sudden shriek as one of the creatures burst out of the water, launching itself at the side of the canoe. It landed half-in half-out, causing it to tilt perilously. As it scrabbled for a hold, Callum ignited another flare, reached forward and stabbed it at the creature's face.

With a shower of sparks, the flare went off, thumping into its jaws. It screamed, choking as coloured smoke poured from between its teeth. Then it released the side of the canoe and crashed back into the water, clawing at its snout.

Callum's gaze searched out the other creature. Using its partner as a distraction, it had drawn level with the side of the canoe. It was keeping pace with Darya as she fought to control the vessel, its head turned, water slicing underneath its eye as it watched her.

"It's stalking you!" he shouted.

"What?"

Before he could speak again, the creature had dived out of sight.

"Get down!"

He lunged forward and wrenched her out of her seat just as the creature exploded up out of the water and smashed into the stern. The outboard's wooden mount shattered with the force of the impact, and with nobody at the rudder the canoe was thrown into a spin.

The creature clung to the rear of the spiralling vessel as the centrifugal force pinned Callum and Darya into the prow. They could only watch as it battled for grip, clawing at the timber with all four limbs before being flung back into the whirlpool.

The relief that Callum felt was short-lived. Next second the canoe bucked, the prow dug down into the waves and he was catapulted out into darkness.

4

Callum resurfaced, gasping for air as the cold beat it from his lungs, punch after freezing punch. What was left of the canoe was scattered around him, and the air was sour with the smell of fuel. Splinters of wood swirled past. The outboard propeller floated upside down on the buoyancy of its half-empty tank, the blades still churning into the air.

There was a sudden rush as Darya resurfaced next to him. He swam towards her and brushed the clumps of hair from her face. "Are you hurt?"

"Not badly," she replied, gasping for air. "But if we do not get out of this w-water quickly…"

"How long do we have?"

"When the water is this cold, n-not long."

"It's okay," he replied on instinct, "somebody must've seen that flare. They'll be on their way to rescue us."

Darya's eyes widened. "*Der'mo!*"

He sculled around. A short distance away, the two creatures were side by side, watching them. Only the tops of their heads were visible, their eyes focussed, their snouts protruding out in front of them. Their plumage now appeared the same grey-blue as the water.

Slowly, they started forward.

"Come on!" Callum raced over towards the propeller. Heart pounding, he took a hold of the residual wood attached to the rudder and turned back towards the island.

"Get behind me!" he yelled. "If these things want a meal, they're gonna h-have to work for it." He watched as the two creatures advanced, Darya's hands clinging to the back of his jacket.

The creatures shared the briefest of glances, then they left one another's side; the slighter creature swam around to the left, as the larger broke to the right.

Callum swallowed hard. "They're gonna come at us from both sides," he shouted above the growl of the motor. "Do you have anything you can use as a weapon?"

"Everything was in the bag!"

At that moment, the larger of the creatures burst forward. Callum dashed the propeller blades into the water and sliced them in an arc towards its head. At the last instant it dived. The blades tripped along its back as it bolted past, churning up a slick of blood and feathers. It resurfaced a short distance away, thrashing in agitation. Then it charged again.

Once more, Callum dragged the propeller into its path. This time it dived sooner and then burst up from below. He could feel it collide with his legs and he braced himself for pain. But there was nothing.

It re-emerged suddenly beside him. A piece of wood was protruding from its chest. He turned to see that Darya had grabbed one of the splintered oars and speared it into the creature's armpit. Now she was fighting to hold it at bay as it raged at her, swiping for her throat with its hind claws.

"Where is the other one?" she yelled.

Callum scanned around for it, but he could see nothing, only the bobbing wreckage of the boat and the distant shoreline. As he turned back towards her, something clamped on to his foot. He kicked out with his other leg, but it was no use. He was dragged under.

The creature pulled Callum along feet first, deeper and deeper. The world was a freezing blur as the silty water rushed past his face. He stamped on the side of the creature's head, and it reacted by shaking him and jarring its body from side to side. Already his lungs were screaming out for air. All he could think about was Jamie and Darya.

Fighting against the rush of water, he dug his hand into his pocket and forced two, three, four numbing fingers around the bolt gun. He withdrew it, pressed it into his other hand and drew back on the rear portion to open the chamber. He grabbed a bolt and attempted to load it, but the feeling had drained from his hands and he fumbled the shaft of metal against the handle.

He reached for another. This time it slid home, and he slammed the chamber back into position. He leant forward and scrabbled around. His fingers clawed over his ankle and along his boot before they met with the creature's teeth, a dozen solid rungs protruding from the leather. He continued to scratch his way across its gum, along its snout and all the way to its eyeball, where the protective membrane twitched against his fingertips.

Sensing his intentions, the creature accelerated, dipping and rising, doing everything it could to try and throw him off balance. But Callum dug his free hand into the feathers along its nape and held on tight. Then, with one jerk of his hand, he pressed the barrel of the gun up to its eyeball and fired.

The jaws cramped. He could feel its bite crushing into his foot and pain forced the last of the fading breath from his body. Then, just as quickly, the jaws relaxed and he was free to make for the surface.

He burst up out of the surf. The air hitting the back of his throat was pure ecstasy and the world went on hold as he drank in lungful after precious lungful. As he worked to regain himself, there was a splash beside him and the creature bobbed to the surface, blood pouring from its eye.

Callum backed away in horror, as the creature turned towards him before rolling over onto its back, thrashing weakly. It called out in a series of pitiful wails, which lapsed into clicks and then, finally, into silence.

"Callum!"

He could see Darya a hundred metres away, waving an oar frantically above her.

His mind raced. The other creature must have grabbed her. The image of its teeth sinking into the soft flesh of her ankles overtook him and he set off swimming towards her.

He had taken his first few strokes when he became conscious of her calls once more. His brain was sluggish with cold, but it was telling him that they weren't the screams of somebody in pain. They were warnings. Warning screams. He stopped and strained to make out her words.

"It comes to you! Please, Callum! It comes to you!"

Halfway between the two of them, the second creature broke the surface of the water and bellowed into the air. Responding to the calls of its dying sibling, it was heading his way fast, tearing through the water like a shark about to breach. There was no chance that he could outswim it or make the shore. In his scrabble for air he had dropped the bolt gun, leaving him defenceless, and he could feel the extreme cold sapping the last of his energy. He brushed his hands over his jacket in a vain attempt to find a weapon, something, anything that he could use in a last-ditch defence. But there was nothing.

The creature had closed the gap to only a few metres. Its eyes were milky pale where the membranes had closed, protecting them against the rush of brine. As it bore down on him, Callum did the only thing he could and closed his eyes.

He waited.

Nothing.

When he reopened his eyes he could see that the creature had stopped dead only a couple of metres in front of him, sending a pulse of water slapping into his face. Blood seeped from its back where he had caught it with the propeller. The membranes had retracted from its eyes, replaced by a look of unmistakeable confusion.

As he looked on, it burst back into life, scrabbling and fighting, not against him, but against some invisible enemy. What the hell was it doing? Panic and exhaustion turned suddenly to rage in Callum's chest. "Come on!" he shouted. "I'm right here!"

Then, still writhing, the creature began to rise up out of the water as if levitating. Water dripped from its feathers, which changed colour suddenly, shimmering from the grey-blue of the water to a brilliant white. The sea around it seethed with bubbles and a large shadow began emerging out of the depths.

"For God's sake, w-what now?"

The creature continued its incredible ascent until its entire torso was suspended above the surface of the water. Below it, a huge, dark fin broke through the water's skin, followed by a pointed nose.

Clamped around the base of the creature's neck was a tripartite metal pincer, each of the three fingers speared firmly into its skin. Another identical metal pincer gleamed around the base of its tail. Both were attached to mechanical arms, which trailed off into the now-unmistakable shadow of the *Sea Centaur*.

Callum let out a massive sigh of relief as an equally unmistakable voice boomed out from the loudspeaker: "You sure know how to pick your company, McJones!"

Chapter 8

ATOMIC PARTICLE EXPLOSION

1

"*Your* symptoms are mild, you lucky son of a bitch," Peterson said, resealing the *Centaur*'s hatch. "And your foot wound's nothing but a scratch." He gestured towards Darya. "She's a different story."

She was on her back, head propped up against the wall, fighting to remain conscious. Callum knelt beside her. Her skin was freezing and her lips were blue. "She w-won't stop shivering."

"That's good," Peterson replied. "That tells us she's only moderately hypothermic. If she was still... well, then she'd be in a world of shit."

Callum took her hands, attempting to warm them. But his own were just as cold. "Darya?"

"I'm o-okay," she answered; her voice was low and breathy. "W-what about you? I-I... thought... that thing..."

"I'm fine," he said, stroking her cheek. "But I won't be going swimming again any time soon."

"Help her get her clothes off," Peterson ordered, "yours too. And don't worry, Docs plural, it's nothing I haven't seen before. Come on now, every second counts."

Working as fast as he could with numb fingers, Callum unzipped her thermal jacket and pulled it from her shoulders.

Then he removed her underlying fleece, thermal top and undershirt, followed by her boots, trousers, long johns and several pairs of saturated woollen socks. The previous night, they had laughed at the drawn-out process of removing each other's clothes. "*Does this count as foreplay in the Arctic?*" he had asked. She had laughed and moved on top to straddle him. "*Not a chance!*"

Now she was silent, and as her pale skin emerged before his eyes once more, the atmosphere couldn't have been more different. "Are you sure this isn't going to make her c-colder?"

"Nope," Peterson replied. "Those wet things are preventing heat getting to her skin. Yours too, so quit stalling and strut your stuff."

As Callum stripped himself down, Peterson turned the heating system to max, and a burst of super-heated air flooded the cabin. "I hope you appreciate the sacrifice I'm making here. Any minute now and I'll be sweating like a whore in church." He pushed to the back of the craft and began rooting around in an overhead compartment. "And keep her talking, McJones. Don't you let her sleep now."

Before he could open his mouth, something patted against Callum's head and tumbled to the floor.

"Thermal blankets," Peterson said. "One for each of you. Make sure you wrap 'em round good and tight."

Callum removed the silver blankets from their packets, tucked the first one around Darya and pulled the other around himself. He watched as Peterson now wrestled a bright orange machine with an attached respirator from the back of the compartment. He placed it down beside Darya's head, sloshed some drinking water into one of the inlets and turned it on.

"Here, place this over her mouth and nose."

Callum took the face mask and did as Peterson instructed.

"It's an IRS, an Inhalation Rewarming System," Peterson said, cranking up one of the dials. "A souped-up humidifier.

Hypothermia kills because it decreases the core body temperature. The fastest way to treat it is to reheat the core and not just the outside of the body. Like most things, it's plain old common sense."

Callum held Darya's hand underneath the blanket and watched as the machine ticked away, the transparent plastic mask filling with vapour. Peterson scrutinised the various dials and then sat down next to him.

"Why doesn't she stop shivering?"

"She will," Peterson replied. "Trust me."

After what felt like a lifetime, Darya's hands fell still. The deep blue left her lips and the first traces of pink flushed back into her cheeks. Ten minutes later and they had eased her up into a sitting position.

"How are you feeling?" Callum asked.

She squeezed his hand. "Like I am no longer an ice cube."

"We should get you back to the *Albanov* as quickly as possible so you can get checked out."

"No," she protested, pulling the mask from around her mouth. "I will be fine. I just need drink of water."

Peterson grabbed the bottle of drinking water and handed it to her. "Easy does it, princess. Small sips."

She raised the bottle to her lips and took two enormous gulps.

"Or I guess you could down the whole thing, sure."

Callum eased the bottle from her fingers. "I really think you should get checked out."

"No! I need to get my camera."

"Your camera?"

"Yes, it is the only evidence for those animals." She looked to Peterson. "Will you please help me to find the camera? It fell from my bag, but the water is not deep here and it will be near to where the boat is sinking."

"If it's the animals you're interested in then I can do better than that," Peterson replied with a grin. He pointed out through the curve of the front screen.

Darya climbed to her feet. Confusion turned to wonder on her face as her gaze skipped up over the console and through the window. Callum rushed to support her as she staggered towards the control deck.

Outside, the creature was still struggling to free itself from the pincers. As if sensing the sudden attention, it stopped and slowly turned its neck to stare back in at them. Its mouth cracked open and it let out an ear-piercing screech.

"You have caught him!" Darya said, her voice shrill with disbelief.

Peterson perched himself in the sub operator's seat. "Sure I managed to catch the ugly son of a bitch. Now would one of you care to tell me what the hell it is?"

2

"We've no idea what it is," Callum said, his gaze fixed on the creature. "Darya thinks it might be a new species."

"You have not seen anything like this?" she asked Peterson.

"Not in twenty years of trawling the oceans looking at weird critters." He leant his arms across the control deck and manoeuvred the creature closer to the screen. Darya watched him closely. The arms whirred as they retracted and turned, and the creature hissed back and launched a series of kicks into the air.

"Those clamps are secure, right?" Callum asked.

"Those *pincers* can exert hundreds of pounds of pressure per square inch. Any securer and Mr lizard bird's *cahones* would be stuck in his back teeth."

Callum's eyes widened. "Lizard bird?"

"That's sure what it looks like to me," Peterson said, "unless you know better."

"*Tansu Taibaa.*"

"Tansu what-now?"

Callum surveyed the confusion on the Texan's face. "Tansu Taibaa. It means *lizard bird* in Nganasan."

"Since when do you speak Nganasan?"

"I don't." Callum hesitated. Whether it was the adrenaline controlling his lips, mental exhaustion or something much more basic, the urge to keep on talking was overwhelming. "A couple of days ago I found something."

"Something archaeology?" Darya asked.

"An ice mummy. A man frozen solid, his body preserved for thousands of years."

Peterson let out a loud cat-call. "Sounds like a pretty big deal."

"The mummy on its own would be a big deal. But there are two things which make this one even bigger. For one thing, I'm pretty certain I can identify him. He was called Ngana'bta. He was an ancient Nganasan warrior."

"How can you be sure?" Peterson asked.

Callum told them about his discussion with Lungkaju, about the tooth pendant that he had pulled from beneath the mummy's parka and held in his palm.

"You sure this ain't some kind of messed-up *Candid Camera*?" Peterson asked.

"Out here?"

"Okay, point taken. So what about number two?"

"Number two, whatever killed Ngana'bta tore off both his legs before he could escape into the tunnel."

"And you think that one of these ugly little bastards might have been to blame?"

Callum shrugged. "In the legend, Ngana'bta is sent to hunt the *mythical* Tansu Taibaa, and he never returns. Ngana'bta was supposed to be mythical as well, and against all the odds he's turned out to be real. So why not Tansu Taibaa?"

Peterson leant back in his chair and scratched a hand through his sideburns. "I can see where you're coming from, McJones. But it all sounds just a little far-fetched."

"Of course it sounds far-fetched," Callum retorted. "In fact it sounds bloody ludicrous even to me. The whole thing does.

But just look." He pointed back towards the creature. "You said it yourself. What's that if it isn't a lizard bird? Personally I don't believe in coincidences, especially ones on this scale."

His words hung in the air as all three of them stared at the creature. It was craning its neck forward, straining to assault the pincer at the base of its tail.

"I don't know," Peterson said at last. "You talk a good case, McJones. Sure looks like a goddamn oversized marine iguana with feathers." He swivelled his chair around. "So anyway, what? This Tansu whateymajig just up and attack you?"

Without taking their eyes off the struggling creature, Callum and Darya took him through what had happened that morning, from the moment Darya had first spotted the three youngsters, to the *Centaur*'s arrival on the scene. As the story unfolded, Peterson's eyes widened with undisguised awe. "So let me get this straight, you actually killed one of these things?"

"I guess so," Callum replied. Confronted with the full horror of the creature, he hardly believed it himself. "I promise you it was more luck than judgement."

Peterson laughed out loud and slapped a hand across his thigh. "Bull*shit*! When a monster like that's got you by the tail and you take him out underwater with… with a camping tool, that's nothing but sheer ball-busting heroics. I don't care whether he's a Tansey whatey, a rooster on steroids or what. You're a goddamn hero, McJones!"

Callum felt a hand stroke at the back of his arm. He turned to see Darya staring up at him.

"You *are* hero, *solnishko*," she said. "You are very brave."

"Dan's the real hero. If he hadn't turned up when he did, we'd both be dead for sure."

"I won't argue with you on that one," Peterson replied. "But you folks sure were lucky. It's unusual for me to be out in her so early."

"Why today is different?" Darya asked. But before Peterson

189

could answer she shouted, "Look!"

Outside the creature was no longer struggling. Instead it lay motionless, its body starting to go limp. "He is dying, you must please let him go now!"

"Let him go?" Peterson exclaimed. "Are you crazy? That thing just tried to make mincemeat out of the both of you."

"Yes, but it is living creature. He does not try to eat us for fun – he just does not know better." She grabbed on to Callum's forearm. "Please tell him. We are not in danger from him anymore."

Callum took another look at the creature. By now its head was dangling down, while its other limbs twitched pathetically against its flanks. For a moment it reminded him of a strung-up chicken, albeit an enormous one, waiting to be plucked. Then his eyes passed over the mass of twisted teeth lowering towards its chest, and the razor-like claws still clenching on the ends of its hands and feet. He could feel her grip tighten around his arm. "I'm sorry, but I agree with Dan. I think letting that thing go would be a very bad idea."

Her face tightened with betrayal. Before either of them could stop her, she lunged for the *Centaur*'s arm controls with both hands.

"Forget killing him, you'll rip the sorry son of a bitch in half!" Peterson shouted, grabbing onto her arms and attempting to prise them away.

"What does this matter?" she replied. "You want him to die anyway, so at least it is quick this way. We must let him go. That is why we are different!"

"But you'll damage the goddamn controls. Do you have any idea how much this thing costs? I shouldn't be using it to save ungrateful Russkies in the first damn place." Unable to loosen her grip, he turned to Callum. "Little help here, McJones?"

Callum lowered his hands gently onto Darya's shoulders and spoke as calmly as he could manage. "If we let this thing go it could hurt other people. There could be other members of the team on Harmsworth right now. They could be hurt. Killed. Please, Darya."

Her face softened at his words and gradually the muscles in her arms began to relax.

Peterson slowly removed his hands from hers and sat back. "You gonna listen to the man?"

Darya said nothing in reply. Then she pulled back suddenly on one of the levers, causing the left pincer to release. "But I cannot let him die!"

The creature's head careered down into the water. Before Peterson could lunge back in and secure her other hand, she had released the second pincer, freeing the creature's lower half.

There was silence in the cabin as all three of them held their breath, watching the inert body bobbing up and down below the *Centaur*'s nose.

"Already dead," Darya said in a sorrowful voice.

Peterson shoved her hands away from the controls. "Good thing too! What the hell are you thinking, Lebedev? You don't get to commandeer million-dollar equipment just because you've got a conscience needs calibrating."

"I am sorry," she replied, "but I cannot see animals in pain."

"What about us? We're animals. Can you see us in pain? Because that's what you'd've seen if that thing wasn't dead and it'd decided to rip on through the hull."

Callum noticed the tears welling up in Darya's eyes. "Come on, Dan, she could've died just now, she's obviously not thinking straight, that's all. Besides, it's dead, so no harm done."

"Oh, it's dead, is it?" Peterson replied. He nodded towards the creature. "Not any definition of dead I ever heard of."

Callum looked back just in time to see the creature's tail disappear beneath the water.

"Sneaky little critter was playing possum all along," Peterson shouted. He quickly reclaimed the controls and directed one of the arms down into the water in pursuit. There was a clunk as he brought the pincers together below the surface. Then the three of them watched as he toggled the lever, causing it to retract once more.

Peterson rocked heavily back in his chair. "Damn it!"

Out in front, water dripped rhythmically from the tips of the empty pincer.

He turned to Darya. "You better hope those things don't hold a grudge!"

3

What remained of the Kamov lay on its side, twisted and glinting in the sunlight.

"Three hundred million rubles' worth of military hardware," Marchenko observed, shaking his head in disbelief.

"*Enhanced* military hardware," corrected Koikov.

The two men stood shoulder to shoulder, staring into the burnt-out hulk. Like the other members of the search and rescue team, their faces were stained grey with the thick smoke that had flooded into the cabin after it had crashed into the Svayataya plateau.

"Did you speak to Lungkaju?"

Marchenko nodded. "He says the tail clipped something on take-off. Whatever it was took out the drive shaft and sent us spinning."

"So he lost control."

"It was an emergency take-off, Starshyna. Under normal circumstances he wouldn't even have attempted it."

Koikov pursed his lips. Deep down, he knew Marchenko was right. With the hideous screeching of the creatures close behind them, the team had fled the cave to find the world outside still cloaked in mist. Visibility had been next to nothing and the shared sense of terror amongst the men had resulted in a chaotic scene as they'd scrambled for the aircraft. So as much as he wanted to, Koikov couldn't bring himself to blame Lungkaju for the fucked-up evacuation. Ultimately, the responsibility lay with him.

The two men continued surveying the remains of the Kamov's fuselage in silence. It was buried into marshy ground only metres from the Svayataya precipice. The landing skids lay crumpled a good distance away, and window glass and scraps of metal debris littered the surrounding moss. It was a miracle everybody had made it out alive; even Lungkaju's wolf had escaped uninjured despite being thrown across the cabin and narrowly avoiding Koikov's head.

Koikov looked over at Marchenko. The sergeant's brow was furrowed and his eyes were swollen with the events of the last few hours. "Where the hell are those things?" he asked. "We're sitting ducks out here."

"They're too smart to come at us now," Koikov replied, lighting a papirosa. "Either they've never seen humans before and they're scared, or else they've seen humans before and they're scared." He spat on the floor. "They knew they could get the drop on us inside that cave. Yudina found that out, God rest him. So did Semyonov and his guide. But out here, in the daylight, they're not so sure." He paused to take a long drag. "At least not yet."

Marchenko snorted. "You make them sound educated."

"How long have you been on this shithole, Marchenko?"

"A couple of months."

"Not jerking off in your cabin. I mean actually out *here*, on the island."

"Seven or eight hours, Starshyna."

"And are *you* not finding this place an education?"

"Of course, but—"

"But nothing. Whatever those things are, I'm guessing

they've been here a lot longer than seven or eight hours. What they don't know about this island probably isn't worth knowing, and that's all the education they need."

Marchenko looked hard into Koikov's face. "You respect them."

Koikov's gut reaction was to answer, *Anything that's got the balls to take me on deserves respect!* But he couldn't bring himself to be so flippant with a man that had helped to save his life. "If you'd been as up close and personal with these things as I have, Sergeant, you'd respect them too."

Marchenko was uncharacteristically quiet. It could have been the tail end of shock or exhaustion. But Koikov had operated with him many times before and, as a rule, nothing but the threat of outright apocalypse would've shut him up. "What's on your mind, Marchenko?"

Keeping his eyes on the wreckage, he replied, "It wasn't a bear that attacked Dolgonosov, was it, Starshyna? Or Sharova. It was one of those things."

Koikov took another drag on his papirosa and exhaled the thick grey smoke through his nostrils. His mind moved reflexively to the sight of the fleeing polar bear. It had been innocent. Nothing had been more certain. But Koikov had been in shock. He had lost two men to something he didn't understand, something he couldn't even bring himself to believe. Major Rabinovich had wanted answers. Mr Volkov had wanted answers. Everybody had wanted answers. In the immediate aftermath of the tragedy, a rogue polar bear had been the only plausible explanation, and Koikov had hunted one down, squeezed the trigger and hoped that it would all just go away.

"Yes, it was," he said at last.

The confirmation seemed to stun Marchenko. "You knew about them and you didn't think to warn us?"

Koikov snorted and turned away. Whether the man had helped save his life or not, he didn't know a thing about it.

"You brought us here, me, Gergiev and the others, on that ridiculous bear hunt, and then again to find Einstein, and at no point did you think to point out that there was a horde of bloodthirsty fucking animals!" His voice reached a crescendo. "What the hell were you thinking?"

"Watch your tone, Marchenko."

"It's not my tone you should be worried about. It's my neck. It's all of our necks, because they're on the block thanks to you. Yudina and Einstein are dead *because of you*. Why the fuck didn't you say anything before?"

"I hardly believed it myself for one thing!"

"That's no excuse."

Koikov turned and squared up to him. His extra height cast a shadow over Marchenko's face, but the sergeant stood firm, his narrow features set into a scowl of disbelief. "And what do you think would've happened if I *had* said something? Do you think Rabinovich would've patted me on the head and said, 'Oh, well in that case we'll just have to keep you and the boys all safe here on the boat – why not take the afternoon off?' No, for a start he'd've had me sectioned. Then he'd've sent the rest of you back out here anyway."

"How can you say that about the major? He's already sent the reinforcements we requested this morning, and if he'd known before that there was this kind of threat—"

"Because it's not the major who's in charge," Koikov spat. "It's G&S. The company is in charge. Rabinovich is just a puppet out here, you know that as well as I do. And the company doesn't give a shit about the likes of me and you. It gives a shit about money. There's so much of it riding on this island that the rest of us could disappear one by one without explanation and they'd still go ahead and build their gas plant."

"Well, for what it's worth, I would've believed you, Starshyna. And I'm willing to bet the others would as well."

"Yeah, well, *I* don't gamble," Koikov retorted. He turned and walked the short distance from the site of the wreckage to the edge of the cliff.

"That's exactly what you've done."

Koikov pretended he didn't hear. During impact, the Kamov's swash plate had snapped, allowing the primary rotor to detach and cartwheel off the side. As he peered over the edge of fissured stone, he could see the surf pounding the cruciform blades into the rocks below. The sound of a million gulls nesting along the cliff-face rushed upwards and filled his ears, and the breeze brought him the cool, salty tang of the ocean.

Marchenko arrived at his side. "We're lucky that isn't us down there."

Koikov took a last drag on his papirosa and flicked the end over the edge. "Are we?"

There was no reply.

"What's the situation with the others?" Koikov asked.

"Still no sign of any movement. I've got every man surrounding the cave, just as you ordered. Including the reinforcements from the *Albanov*, that's sixty eyes, twenty-eight rifles and two RPGs pointed at one hole in the earth. So much as an ant pokes its head out and it's World War Three."

"Perfect," Koikov said. "Go and make it twenty-nine rifles."

"Are we really just gonna sit around like this and wait for something to happen?"

"No, Sergeant, we're getting the fuck out of here. I spoke to Major Rabinovich again and he's sending the remaining Kamov back over to start the evacuation. It'll be here any minute, but until then I want every rifle, including yours, trained on that cave. I'm not taking any chances."

4

Gergiev slid his leg across the scree and booted Khabensky in the ankle. "Hey, Khabensky."

Khabensky turned his tiny little pin-head from the cave and stared at him. "Gergiev, you prick, keep your voice down!"

The call had gone out just after 05:00 that Koikov's team needed help. Yudina had been killed, and the whole team, along with a small arsenal of weapons, were being sent over to the island on some kind of killer bear hunt.

"You don't believe this shit, do you?"

"What *shit*?"

"That there's some kind of psycho creature living in this cave."

"No, I think it's fucking crazy," Khabensky said. "But what's new?"

Since arriving on the island, all thirty or so men had spent the entire time in the same position, lying prone on the jagged, ball-chafing rock, rifles shouldered and trained on the mouth of the cave. It wouldn't have been such an ache if they'd had some proper intel. But so far all they knew was that Koikov reckoned creatures of one kind or another were holed up inside. Rumours of what the creatures actually were had stretched from an unnaturally large bear to a flock of killer birds to a colony of dragons! As far as Gergiev was concerned, the whole thing was crazy with a capital C.

"You want to hear something else weird?"

"You're really a woman?"

"Fuck you!" Khabensky tore up a tuft of moss and flung it in Gergiev's face. "No, I was down on R-Deck a couple of days ago."

Gergiev's eyebrows rose and he scanned around for anyone listening. R-Deck was where the G&S technicians carried out the research, testing and technical prep that underpinned the entire project; from assessing the quality of gas samples, to working out the optimum locations for the wellheads, to designing the plant itself. The industrial sensitivity of the activity taking place on R-Deck, and the mind-blowing sums of money riding on it, meant that access was highly restricted. Under no circumstances, Major Rabinovich, flanked by numerous company officials, had told them, was anybody to enter R-Deck unless expressly ordered to do so. "Shit, Khabensky! What the fuck were you thinking? Rabinovich—"

"Yeah, yeah, I could have been discharged, banged up, whatever. I had the same lecture."

Gergiev tossed the clod of moss back at Khabensky and it struck him in the shoulder. "You were fucking lucky. Any one of those researchers could've raised the alarm."

"That's the thing." Khabensky dropped his voice. "There *were* no researchers."

"No researchers?"

He shook his head. "I got lost. You know what it's like on that ship. It's like a fucking maze, that's how I ended up on R-Deck in the first place. Anyway, when I realised where I was I couldn't help snooping in one of the labs."

Gergiev waited. "And?"

"And nothing. No researchers, no equipment, nothing. Just an empty room. I tried the next one and same again. Every single room was empty. Didn't look like they'd been used in decades. Whole place stank like rat piss and rust. It was worse than your mother's bedroom."

Gergiev grinned and cracked his knuckles but didn't rise to it. "Must've been a decoy deck, fool any pin-headed little dumbfucks that manage to break in down there."

Khabensky's lips pursed. "No, I don't buy it. That was R-Deck and there was no-one there. I'm telling you, Gergiev. This whole operation looks legit from the surface, but below decks it's a fucking ghost ship." He moved his attention back to the cave and peered through his rifle sight. "Creatures I can deal with, but ghosts—"

A voice crackled into their earpieces: "Listen up, this is Sergeant Marchenko. The Kamov is heading back to pick us up. We're going back to the ship. Hold your positions until it's on the ground."

From further down the line, Private Tsaritsyn's voice rang out: "All morning staking out this cave, and I don't get to kill one stinking dragon?"

A low ripple of laughter passed along the rank.

"Feel free to head inside and claim your prize, Tsaritsyn," Marchenko retorted. "The rest of you don't know how lucky you are to be getting off this rock. You may not have seen these things, but I have, and once was enough. If the mist comes back, we won't last five minutes out here."

* * *

Koikov raised a pair of binoculars and peered over at the *Albanov*. He could see the remaining Kamov lifting off from the helipad. Perhaps when all this was over and the remainder of the team were safely back at base in Moscow, then it would finally be time for him to leave the department.

As he watched the blur of the Kamov's rotors lift the aircraft further off the deck, he felt a weight lifting from his own shoulders. In twenty minutes time he and his men would be back on board the *Albanov* and the nightmare on Harmsworth would be over—

Without warning, the entire ship was replaced by a gigantic fireball. The roar of an explosion filled his ears. Columns of fire shot up into the air and a cloud of thick black smoke blossomed around the epicentre and rushed outwards in all directions.

"Jesus Christ!" Koikov yelled, ducking down out of pure reflex.

In an instant, every last bird had taken off from the Svayataya cliff-face, hollering in fright. They swooped around in their thousands, forming a cloud that engulfed the cliff-top and blotted out the sun. Hundreds careered into one another in mid-air, plummeting stunned onto the rocks below.

Bleeding from the assault of beaks and talons, Koikov had no choice but to turn and run before the sudden chaos threw him from his feet. He took cover behind a pile of rock, just as a second shockwave hammered into it and caused the ground below to tremor.

Suddenly, Marchenko's voice droned in his ear: "Starshyna, what the hell's going on? We heard an explosion. Starshyna, come in?"

Koikov kept his head down and waited. Then, when all movement had stopped, and the majority of the startled birds had either flown away or resettled themselves on their cliff-side nests, he climbed back to his feet.

Ears ringing, numb with shock, he staggered towards the precipice and raised the binoculars to his face once more.

Where the *Albanov* had been, chunks of burning debris now lay scattered over a huge area. Dark shapes, charred and indefinable, bobbed on the agitated water, which was discoloured with slicks of burning oil. The air around was hung with a dark semi-circular curtain, a decayed rainbow of thick black smoke.

"Starshyna, come in… Koikov! Come in! What's your status?"

Still staring out in disbelief, Koikov searched for the words to reply. In a quiet voice he said, "The *Albanov* is gone. I repeat. The *Albanov* has been destroyed. Rabinovich was on board."

There was a long pause at Marchenko's end before: "What happened?"

Koikov raised a hand to his throat, heart racing, tongue dry. "We just got stranded."

Chapter 9

SURVIVORS

1

It was done.

Despite the miles Ptarmigan had put between himself and the *Albanov* before detonation, the explosion had been so great that it had rocked the *Sea Centaur*. He had fallen and struck the side of his head, leaving him bleeding through his hairline, in a daze. The shockwave had also upset the sub's inertial guidance system and triggered the emergency siren. His nice orderly cabin was now alive with sound and bathed in a chaos of red light. Consciously he fought to get the situation under control. Subconsciously he relished the momentary distraction from the keening of his conscience.

What the hell have I done? He'd always known that this would be the end result of his actions, and he'd tried to prepare himself through meditation and chant. But now that it was finally here, it was a whole new ballgame. He was no longer just a terrorist subversive. He was a mass murderer. An indiscriminate killer.

He felt suddenly very alone.

The siren finally faded out and normal lighting resumed inside the cabin. Forcing himself to focus, Ptarmigan picked up his copy of *Ship of Fools* and turned to the back page. On its reverse, top corner, there were the two eight-digit codes written in pencil. The first was the coordinate he had followed to the explosives drop. It had taken him to a location just north of Nansen Rocks. The explosive had been contained within a weighted capsule deposited on the sea floor. His hands had rung with sweat as he had extended the *Centaur*'s pincers and grasped the gleaming cylinder. As he was well aware at the time, it had been a real turning point. He could have secreted it elsewhere on the seabed, called Finback and claimed that it was missing, gone back to his life. This and a hundred other alternatives had paraded before him in that instant. But instead he had retracted the pincers and brought the capsule into the *Centaur*'s storage chamber just like any other sample.

A trickle of blood made its way from his hairline to the corner of his eye and he removed his spectacles to wipe at it. Without thinking, he then reclaimed his book and winced as he picked up on the bloody finger-marks now skating across the inside of the back cover.

"Ah, Jesus!" He tore the cover off in its entirety, slinging it to the floor. The damn book had served its purpose anyway. All he needed now were directions.

Coordinate number two was for the rendezvous point. He remembered Finback's instruction. *When it is done, make your way there. You may have to wait, but I will have somebody pick you up.* Wiping the ends of his fingers, he typed the code into the *Centaur*'s navigation system and waited while the computer calculated the location. This time the coordinate appeared to lead him to an inland location on the north coast.

He leant forward and scrutinised the digital mapping arrayed on the screen in front. From memory he knew that this was largely an area of steep bluffs and rock-strewn coves, not exactly the sort of place to land a hi-tech submersible. Was Finback expecting him to get out and swim to shore, for God's sake? Why the hell hadn't he done a dummy run? His eyes desperately retraced the lie of the coastline. There must have been something there, a feature that he wasn't seeing, a cave or deep-water inlet to accommodate the *Centaur*.

Without wasting another second, he submerged the sub and set off along the course. He was close. In less than fifteen minutes he would be there, and shortly afterwards one of Finback's associates would be transporting him to safety.

As he manoeuvred the *Centaur* around an underwater shelf, his mind moved on: Ava. Perhaps his one consolation was that he'd managed to transport her off the *Albanov* before it blew. It had taken some doing. Stealing the ketamine sedative from Lebedev's office alone had been a nightmare. In fact the whole thing had represented a substantial alteration to his plan that had driven him almost to distraction. But he had gotten there in the end. And it had been necessary. No matter how hard he had tried to convince himself otherwise, he had fallen for her. There wasn't a chance in hell that he could've gone through with it, any of it, knowing that she was still aboard.

But even that little glimmer of self-redemption had fallen under a shadow. A shadow with teeth, claws and a real bad attitude. He hadn't minded saving McJones earlier that morning. Back when he'd still been plain old Dan Peterson. Back when he'd still had time to reconsider. McJones was a good guy; cool and confident in a way that Ptarmigan could only pretend to be. Lebedev was another matter altogether. That miserable bitch! He wished to high heaven she hadn't let the goddamn creature go. If McJones hadn't been there then Lord knows what he would've done to her if she'd dared touch his controls like that. Yeah, the thing was wounded. Yeah, it was probably none too hot for its run-in with the *Centaur*'s pincers. But there was something about the sly little bastard that had left a seed of unease germinating deep in Ptarmigan's gut.

The on-board processor bleeped suddenly. His destination was only a couple of hundred feet up ahead. He could see the fractured seabed rising up towards the island's northern shores.

As suspected, there didn't appear to be any kind of natural harbour. The *Centaur* could always breach and approach the shore as a surface vessel. Shallow water navigation was one of its major design benefits. But there still had to be somewhere to navigate *to*, other than dry land. And Ptarmigan couldn't see any-such-where. What's more, from the pull of the current and the movement of the seabed silts, it seemed as if the surf above was none too friendly. The last thing he needed was to wreck the craft. If, God forbid, Finback turned out not to be on the level, then it would be his only lifeline.

As he searched the seabed, a winding shadow emerged heading shoreward. A smile of relief passed across his lips. Of course! He'd seen it only once before, pretty much ignoring it as he'd passed by en route to the explosives drop. Now it was everything. It was a fissure in the seabed, a deep trench that appeared to bore straight through the rising bedrock. Probably remnant of some ancient riverbed, it must have led into a concealed deep-water cove.

"Finback, you piece of work!" he whispered.

He retracted the *Centaur*'s fins, allowing her to fit neatly within the narrow confines of the trench, and engaged the deep-dive headlamps. Squadrons of colourful fish broke formation in front of him, shimmering and darting for cover. Multi-coloured flora clinging to the rocks either side billowed around the *Centaur*'s nose like curtains in a gentle fall breeze, their tendrils trailing deftly over the metal panelling. Shoals of much larger fish passed coolly under the vessel, crustaceans scuttled over the upthrusts of exposed rock, and molluscs, anemones and species that must have been new to science clung to whatever they could.

As he watched, the head of something resembling a moray eel shot from a crevice, snatched a fish and disappeared once again, bringing him smack back to reality. Before he knew it, his thoughts were with Ava again. He'd had no choice but to leave her, McJones and Lebedev on Harmsworth. He figured that their chances of running into that thing again were probably slim, and their odds of survival would be infinity times higher than if they'd all been on the *Albanov* at 1300 hours that afternoon. Hell, McJones had already chalked one up, that slick Scottish sonofabitch!

Even so, Ptarmigan had already decided on one final change of plan. He would go ahead and meet with Finback's associate. But instead of being whisked away to begin a new life while the world woke up to the news of his tragic death, he would tell whoever it was that Dan Peterson was not going to have died on board the *Albanov* at all. Instead he was going to have been out researching at the time of the explosion, ending up stranded on the island along with the others. He and the other survivors would await help from the international search and rescue effort, and then he would live out his days with Ava.

Ptarmigan slowed the craft even further as it passed under a bridge of natural stone, a passage through the base of the cliffs above. He could feel his panic response reasserting itself: *What if it's a dead end? What if there's a rock-fall? What if—*

"Enough!" he shouted, holding his course.

Moments later the fissure's floor dropped away and its sides began to widen out into a natural chamber. Light filtered down into the water once again, broken by the shadows of seals swooping around excitedly above.

Seals meant air. Sure enough, when he cast his eyes across the sub's sensors, they were telling him that it was okay to breach.

He took a deep breath and brought the *Centaur* up.

2

Callum blinked his eyes open. The world was a blur of shades and shadows, which gradually began to sharpen. Darya lay next to him, curled up in a foetal position, out cold. Beyond her lay the unmistakable figure of Ava Lee, also unconscious.

He reclosed his eyes and tried to remember what had happened. The last thing he recalled was sitting next to Darya, on the floor at the back of the *Sea Centaur*. Peterson had submerged the sub and they were on their way back to the *Albanov* so that she could get checked out by the ship's medics. Wrapped in their thermal blankets, she had pushed her hand into his and leant her head against his shoulder. He had let his head rest on top of hers, closed his eyes and then... nothing. Darkness.

He reopened his eyes. Pebbles ground together underneath him as he edged himself upright. Surf rolled up the shore towards his feet and a familiar coastline tore away from him in either direction. There was no mistaking where he was, and the growing certainty that it was not a dream brought vomit to the back of his throat.

He placed a hand on Darya's shoulder. Her skin was reassuringly flesh-coloured, her expression serene. She was somehow fully clothed once again, as was he, and he could see that her breathing was deep and regular.

He shook her gently, and she groaned and opened her eyes a crack. Her face took on a look of pure confusion as she attempted to sit up. "What happened?" Her voice was croaky with sleep. "Where are we?"

"Harmsworth."

Her confusion turned to alarm. Her body stiffened. "Harmsworth? Those things—"

"Try and relax," he said. "There aren't any just now, but try and keep your voice down."

"But what if they come back?" she half-whispered.

Callum was about to admit that he had no idea what they would do if one of the creatures suddenly turned up uninvited, when Darya noticed Ava lying beside her.

"Ava?" She looked back to Callum as if for an explanation, then staggered to her feet.

Lying next to Ava on the shingle was a hunting rifle. It was similar to the ones Lungkaju and the other security guides carried. Callum walked around her and picked it up.

"Can you use?" Darya asked.

"I'm no marksman," he replied, running his hand over the wooden stock. He fumbled around, eventually managing to open the breach. "It's loaded."

"How many bullets?"

"A couple, but..." He bent down and seized a handful of loose rounds that had been placed in a pile next to Ava's head. "There are maybe a dozen or so more here." His mind racing with a thousand questions, he stuffed the spare bullets into his pocket and slung the rifle strap over his shoulder.

Darya had knelt down beside Ava and was attempting to rouse her. She responded with the same grogginess and confusion that they'd all experienced. When it had worn off, the two of them helped her slowly to her feet. She squinted in the light and clung to Darya's shoulder. "So you've no idea what in the hell we're doing here either?"

"Afraid not," Callum answered. "Can you remember anything at all?"

"Last thing I remember is talking to Dan."

Callum and Darya exchanged glances. "Peterson?"

"The one and only."

"Can you remember where you were?"

Ava's lips pursed as if she wasn't clear why it was any of Callum's business. "Yeah, sure. He was trying to impress me with that damn submarine of his again. Honestly, the number of times he's tried to get me to go out in it, and I just keep on telling him, 'Dan, some people are seadogs, some people are landlubbers, you're evidently a dog and you're barking up the wrong lubber!'" She laughed at her own joke, then added, "Hell, I haven't felt this spaced out since my freshman year."

It struck Callum that she would have no knowledge of the creatures that had almost killed him and Darya only hours before. To her, being out on Harmsworth was no more or less treacherous than it had been at any other time, regardless of how she got there. She had no idea the danger they were in.

Darya seemed to share his thoughts. "Ava, earlier this morning we were attacked by some kind of animals. I think that they are new species."

The remains of Ava's smile disappeared. "Animals? What animals? Where?"

"Close to here," Callum said.

"Well, that's awful! When… I mean, what happened?"

They recounted the story of their encounter, including their rescue by Peterson. Ava listened intently, her gaze remaining stony throughout. Then, after a long silence, a smile broke across her lips. "Okay, I get it. It's international wind-up-the-Canadian day. Well done you two, you got me! I take it Dan's in on this as well?"

"No," Callum said, more forcibly, "this is no wind-up. I wish to hell that it was, Ava, but it's true. Every word."

Brow furrowed, she looked from Callum to Darya. Both wore the same unyielding expression. She opened her mouth as if to speak, but instead of words, a jet of vomit rushed out and splattered over the shingle. Darya placed an arm around her as she bent over and clasped her knees. "I'm sorry," she said, still hacking. "It's all... I'm just—"

"It's okay," Callum said. "Trust me, if there was anything in my stomach I'd join you." He turned to Darya. "One rifle and a handful of bullets aren't gonna be much use if we run into any more of those things out here."

She nodded, her attention still with Ava.

"We need to get out of the open quickly. Where's the nearest seal hide?"

She threw a glance along the coastline in either direction. "There should be one north of here, about a kilometre."

"Are you certain?"

"I would be," she replied. "I think we are on the east coast, but..." Still with her arm around Ava, she took another look around.

"What is it?" Callum asked.

"Usually I would see the ship, to the south."

Callum turned and scoured the horizon. She was right. The *Albanov* was nowhere to be seen. For as long as they'd been on Harmsworth, it had been anchored off the island's south-east corner, opposite Valerian Cove. Now there was nothing but an expanse of calm, open ocean rippling below the empty sky.

Perhaps it was delirium. He screwed his eyes up, opened them and looked again. Nothing. Then something caught his attention. High up, just below the streaks of white cloud sat a grey band; what looked like a single raincloud in an otherwise tranquil sky. It was getting thinner and thinner, bleeding away into the ether.

"Do you think they might have gone looking for us?" Darya asked.

"No, I'm pretty certain they'd send the helicopters over before upping anchor." He turned back. Ava was upright again, but her face remained grey and she looked unsteady on her feet.

"They won't've gone far without us," he said, doing his best to sound confident. In reality he was more concerned about the absence of the *Albanov* than anything. It was their one and only lifeline, the only reason any of them could expect to survive even twenty-four hours at this latitude, summer or not. He pulled the rifle back into his shoulder. "We'd better get moving towards that hide. We'll be safer there."

Concealed from Ava, Darya cast him an uncertain glance.

* * *

Koikov flicked the end of his papirosa off the edge of the cliff and watched as it spiralled down into the surf. Then he turned to face his team. "The *Albanov* is gone. I've got no idea why or how, so don't ask. But as far as I can tell, we are the only survivors. From now on we have two priorities. Number one. Shelter. Somewhere that we can protect ourselves from the weather and defend ourselves against those things."

A cynical undercurrent of sniggers, looks and comments passed amongst the men, before young Private Tsaritsyn spoke out. "You mean the dragons, Starshyna?"

Koikov kept his cool and held Tsaritsyn's gaze. "I mean the creatures that killed Private Yudina."

"What do they look like?"

"They look like you," Koikov replied. "Ugly. With bad teeth."

A second round of laughter went up, only this time it was rooting for Koikov.

He seized the momentum. "Priority two. Communications. The primary transmitter for long distance and satellite communications went down with the *Albanov*, so our radio communications are limited to short-range field transmissions."

214

He tapped the side of his earpiece. "As of this moment we are cut off from the outside world. Nobody on the mainland knows a thing about what's happening here."

"What about the sudden radio silence?" Private Gergiev called out. "Surely they'll know there's an emergency now that they can't raise the *Albanov*?"

"That's true," Koikov answered. "And they'll send a team to investigate, but it'll take time, perhaps weeks if they send a ship, and whatever else we've got here, we don't have weeks. We need to try and make contact with the mainland so that we can explain the situation and get ourselves off this hellhole as soon as possible. Does anybody disagree?"

Silence.

"There's an old military compound on the other side of the island. The bunkers will do for shelter and defence, and there's an old transmitter that we might be able to resurrect." He shouldered his rifle. "Now let's stop fingering ourselves and move out. The sooner we get there the better." He searched around. "Orlov, Zakrevsky. Grab RPGs and stick behind. The rest of you, I want four- and five-man teams, hundred-metre intervals. Let's move!"

3

The hide was similar to the last, only larger and better concealed. The journey there had been nerve-racking but uneventful. There had been no sign of the creatures.

As they crawled inside, Callum was still battling to understand the situation. How did three sane, intelligent adults end up on a remote beach with a rifle, a handful of shot and not a clue between them as to how or why? It reminded him of some kind of macabre schoolyard brain-teaser. *A hundred people are found dead in a cabin in the woods. They're all sitting down. How did they die?*

Besides the notion that the last few days were a whiskey-induced hallucination, the only common denominator was Dan Peterson. He was the last person any of them could remember being with. But why would a respected professional like Peterson drug three of his colleagues and maroon them on an island? Particularly when he professed undying love for one of them? It just didn't add up.

"Would you look at this!" Ava was sitting opposite him with her back against the rock. The colour had all but returned to her face. In her hand she held a water canister. "This was in the inside flap of my jacket."

"It's not yours?" Callum asked.

She shook her head and raised the neck of the canister to her lips. "But I'm sure glad it's here. My throat feels like sandpaper." She stopped short of drinking. "I don't suppose either of you have water, do you?"

Darya patted her hands across her jacket but found nothing.

Callum did likewise. "Looks like you're the one with the guardian angel," he said. "You know, I'm pretty certain the rifle was meant for you as well?"

She shrugged. "Was it now? Well, you can go ahead and keep a hold of that for us. I wouldn't know which way to point it. As for the water, I guess we're gonna have to ration it until we get rescued. Two sips and pass."

Ava took her sips and passed the container to Darya. When it had made its way back around to her, she reaffirmed the lid and pushed it into a crevice in the rock. "There, that ought to keep it cool. Now let's see if I've inherited anything else."

She emptied all of her pockets out onto the floor of the hide. "Okay, folks, our inventory stands at one fully stocked survival tin, four energy bars, a pocket-sized torch, three emergency glow-sticks, a penknife and a bag of hard-boiled candy. The survival tin's mine. Otherwise I haven't the first idea where any of it came from."

She prised the lid off the tin and checked the contents. "That's interesting." She withdrew a small, black plastic rectangle with a metal hoop through it. "Haven't seen this before."

"What is it?" Darya asked.

"Key ring," she replied, inspecting it. "Maybe it's not my tin after all."

Callum cast his eye over the assemblage. Then he looked to Darya. She met his gaze and he could tell that she was thinking the same thing. "How well do you know Dan?" he asked Ava.

"That's an odd question," she replied, her tone suddenly guarded. "I mean, I know Dan like the rest of you know him. We're colleagues is all."

As tactfully as possible, Callum said, "I thought you might know him a bit better?"

There was silence. Ava's face flushed, "Wha… what's that no-good Lothario wannabe been saying?"

"Nothing really. He just said that you and he were… more than colleagues."

"I can't believe he's gone and shot his mouth off like this. I specifically told him not to say anything!"

"It is okay," Darya said, picking up on her embarrassment. "Me and Callum are also… more than colleagues."

Ava looked between the two of them. Her expression seemed to soften. "You know, I guessed as much. Two good-looking youngsters like yourselves and everything. Just, I'm confused why you want to know about Dan. You can't possibly think he's got anything to do with this? He's a clown, but he's no Pennywise."

"Dan's the last person any of us saw before we blacked out and ended up where we are now," Callum said. "On top of that, only one of us has woken up armed with a whole raft of survival equipment, and that's you."

"The one he has feelings for," Darya said.

"I wouldn't exactly say *feelings*. It's just a thing, you know? For crying out loud, I turn forty-one next year, not sixteen."

Callum shook his head. "I don't think that matters to Dan."

"Besides," Ava went on, "if he does feel for me at all, then I can't imagine for a second why he'd go and do this to me, especially if he knows there are *things* on here. And he saved both of your asses earlier today as well. Why would he do that, huh? Save you then strand you?"

"I've no idea," Callum said. "I just wondered whether he'd said anything to you, that's all. Anything that might've seemed odd."

Ava laughed. "Are we talking about the same guy? Everything he ever says to me sounds kind of odd. It's kind of what I like about him. But no, as far as I'm aware he's never betrayed any desire to strand the three of us on Harmsworth."

There was no point pressing her any further, so Callum let it drop. They shared out one of the energy bars and passed a few moments in silence before Ava said, "Tell me more about these creatures? You say they're a new species?"

"Yes," Darya replied. "They are different from anything I have seen before. They have feathers and they are bipedal, like large birds. But they appear to be flightless. Instead of full wings they have forearms."

"Forearms? Sounds like evolution in reverse," Ava said.

"Plus their eyes are large," Callum added, "and they have a snout instead of a beak. They seem almost reptilian."

"There are no contemporary bipedal reptilians," Ava said.

"Well, whatever they are, I think the Nganasan peoples of northern Siberia might have known about them for a long time—"

"What was that?" Ava whispered suddenly, the blood visibly draining from her face.

"What?"

"There was a noise… from outside."

"Probably a rock falling from the cliff," Darya whispered. "It happens all the time."

They listened in silence, Callum clasping the rifle close to his chest.

And this time they all heard it: the sound of scattered rock.

"Callum," Darya whispered. Her voice trembled as she pointed past him at the side of the hide.

A low shadow was moving along the outside of the fabric, shuffling towards the entrance. The way the light fell left the shadow formless, so that it was impossible to identify. Its movement was divided into a series of slinks; move, stop, rear-up, pause, move, stop, rear-up, pause…

Whatever it was, it wasn't small. Whatever it was, it sure as hell wasn't human.

A cold sweat broke across Callum's brow. "Get behind me," he whispered. "Slowly. Don't make any noise. If we're quiet, maybe it'll move on." He could hear the desperation in his own voice. Perched on his knees, he raised the rifle up and trained the barrel on the entrance.

From behind him came Ava's muffled sobs, and he could feel Darya's fingers digging into the sides of his ribs as the shadow crept closer and closer to the entrance. The sound of his own heart pounding drowned out every other sound in existence.

The shadow stopped suddenly. Its head bowed down and tapped at the base of the fabric, sending ripples radiating up the side. Ava winced and squeaked into his shoulder. Whatever it was jerked its head back up and listened intently.

"It is not going away," Darya whispered, her voice barely audible. "It knows we are here."

Callum fought to hold the rifle in position. Hands shaking, he brought his finger to the trigger just as the shadow reached the entrance flap.

4

The sound of the creature's breathing filled the hide, loud and abrasive. Inside, Callum, Darya and Ava waited, huddled in silence behind the rifle.

A snout pushed through the gap in the fabric. The creature's mouth dropped open, and a long pink tongue unfolded over the teeth of the lower jaw.

Ava and Darya screamed, while Callum dropped his shoulder at the last minute and discharged the bullet into the roof.

As the sound of the gunshot echoed, he let out a massive sigh of relief. "Fenris!"

The dog's ears, which had flattened at the sound of the rifle, sprang back up. He gave a string of excited barks and bounded into the hide. His tail wagged frantically as he barged into Callum, toppling him back into the others. Then he whined and nuzzled the side of his face.

"It's a dog," Ava said, her hand on her chest, her voice matter-of-fact with shock. "It's a dog."

Lying next to her in a heap, Darya broke into relieved laughter. "It is a dog," she echoed.

"You don't know how lucky you are, boy," Callum said,

rubbing behind Fenris's ears. "Now, where's Daddy, huh? Where's Lungkaju?" He noticed a smear of dried blood on the side of Fenris's snout. The dog's coat was matted. It felt slick with some kind of oil and gave off the faint tang of burning rubber. "What's happened to you, boy?"

The dog backed away, casting cursory glances at Darya and Ava. Then he pushed his way back out of the hide.

Without a second's thought, Callum crawled after him. "We've got to follow."

"And leave this place? Are you crazy?" Ava protested.

Callum looked back. "Do you want to sit around and wait for one of those things to turn up for real? Trust me, we're a lot safer with that dog than we are in here."

"But where's he leading us?"

"With any luck, he'll take us to Lungkaju. Then we can get back to the ship and report what we've seen before anybody else gets hurt."

Darya got to her knees and began following on, but Ava remained rooted to the back of the hide, her face twisted with fear.

"Ava, this is our best chance at rescue," Callum said as calmly as he could manage. "But we have to move. Believe me, that dog does not stand on ceremony."

Darya cupped Ava's narrow face in her hands, pushing the strands of dishevelled brown hair back from her forehead. "I know that you are scared, Ava. I am scared too. But Callum is right. We have to move now or they will not find us. I will help you, come on." She wrapped her arms around her colleague and gave her a hug. Then she took her by the hand and moved slowly towards the entrance.

"Why did you have to tell me about those things?" Ava mumbled as she edged forward. "Nobody ever tell you ignorance is bliss?"

Callum emerged from the hide. His attempts at stealth were

undermined by the impatient whinnying of Fenris, but still he kept as quiet as possible and concealed himself behind a stand of rock. The other two clambered after him.

He glanced around. They had the vantage of high ground, and from what he could see there was no immediate threat, either from inland or the coast. There was also no Lungkaju. This wasn't totally unexpected; he recalled the countless hours that Fenris had disappeared for, when he and Lungkaju were carrying out the survey. Humans obviously moved at too deliberate a pace for Fenris.

In his most commanding voice, he called the dog over. To his surprise, Fenris actually came. He quickly removed his belt and tied it as a makeshift leash around the dog's collar. "I'm sorry boy, but we'll lose you otherwise."

Fenris whined and tugged at the restraint. But Callum held firm. The dog was a new lifeline and he wasn't about to let him get away.

As they set off, Fenris pulled so hard against his new lead that he could only breathe in wheezes and grunts, which seemed to echo far and wide.

"Why don't we just fire off a couple of rounds on the rifle?" Ava said.

But despite the noise, Callum felt a quiet confidence, not least because Fenris seemed to know exactly where he was going. He led them a short distance inland away from shore. Then he turned north and took them through a winding valley littered with strange, near-spherical boulders. Some were several metres in diameter, some perfectly round, others oval like gigantic eggs. Some were smooth, others criss-crossed with a web of mineral veins, and together they created a Martian landscape unlike anything Callum had ever seen before.

"I wonder what has caused these rocks to be this way," Darya said.

"They're concretions," Ava replied, her voice low. "They

form within sedimentary strata on the seabed over millions of years. Either a cavity in the sediment in-fills with minerals of a different kind, similar to the fossilisation process, or a sediment nucleus gradually enlarges as minerals accrete to the surface, similar to how a pearl's produced. Either way, when the surrounding sediment erodes away, you're left with these beautiful formations."

"You've seen them before?" Callum asked.

"Not these ones," she replied. "But I've visited formations in Koutu and Moeraki in New Zealand, and a few others in the States. They're interesting because they quite often contain fossils. They sometimes form around them. I know for a fact that some of the concretions on North Island in New Zealand contain the fossilised bones of prehistoric marine reptiles."

Callum stopped suddenly and held his hand up. Ahead of him, Fenris had ground to a halt and was standing with his ears and tail erect, sniffing at the air.

"What is it?" Darya whispered.

Callum shook his head. They were approaching the end of the valley and the land was rising steeply, the trail veering east, back towards the coast. Callum tugged gently at the leash. "What is it, boy? Can you smell something?"

With a sudden growl, Fenris burst forward and tore the end of the belt out of his hand. Before he could regain his grip, the dog had raced off around the corner and out of sight.

There was a scrabbling noise up ahead, and Fenris howled out.

Callum brought the rifle back into his shoulder, but a second later the dog reappeared, Lungkaju by his side.

"Oh, thank God!" Ava shrieked, her voice swollen with relief. She ran over and threw her arms around Lungkaju, almost knocking the rifle from his hands. "You beautiful man!" She smothered the side of his cheek with kisses. "You beautiful, *beautiful* man!"

Darya was close behind her. "I can't believe we find you," she said, throwing her own arms around him.

"Believe it, sister," Ava said. "We're saved! We're gonna go back to the ship, take a shower, get some food and forget that any of this ever happened!"

By now Callum had made his way over, and Darya pulled him into the group hug. For the first time in what seemed like days his chest felt light. His heart wasn't racing with fear any more, but excitement. He glanced at his watch. And there was still an hour until his video link-up with Jamie.

"My friends," Lungkaju said. "You are alive. I cannot believe it—"

"I can't tell you how good it is to see you," Callum said, grasping his hand and shaking it. "My mind ran away with me. I was starting to think that we were stranded here."

"My friends—"

"I thought we were going to die," Ava said.

"It has been like nightmare," Darya added.

"My friends, you—"

"Look, we need to get off this island as soon as possible," Callum said. "There are creatures living here – we had a run-in with them earlier this morning. We've got to get out of here before somebody gets killed." Before he could stop himself he continued, "I've arranged to speak to Jamie in an hour's time. Do you think we can be back on the *Albanov* in an hour? Where's the Kamov?"

Darya squeezed the back of Callum's arm suddenly. She was staring at Lungkaju, her expression changed from delight to puzzlement. "Lungkaju, what is wrong?"

Lungkaju's smile had disappeared. His eyes were closed, and his face looked so much more haggard than Callum remembered; he wasn't certain, but he thought that he could smell the same tang of smoke on the man's clothing as he'd smelt on Fenris.

Looking hard into Callum's face Lungkaju said, "I am sorry, my friend. But the *Albanov* is gone."

There was a brief silence before Ava said, "Gone? What do you mean, gone? Where the hell would it go?"

"No, Doctor Lee, I am sorry, but you do not understand." He passed his sunken gaze across each of their faces, before returning it to Callum's. "I am sorry, but the *Albanov* has been destroyed. We cannot leave the island."

5

"This is a joke, right?"

Looking as if he hardly believed it himself, Lungkaju replied, "I am sorry, Doctor Ross, but no. We do not know what has happened, but there was an explosion, and the ship has been destroyed."

For an instant all that Callum could think about was Jamie. He'd been making progress, slow but sure, winning back the boy's trust one video call at a time. They were becoming friends again. And now... in an hour's time it would all have been for nothing. Lost. He could see the look of disappointment on his son's face as he gave up waiting. He could see the excitement leave his lips once more and the dullness creep back into his eyes.

Deep inside his pocket, his hand clenched around the quartz pebble. "What about everybody on board?"

Lungkaju shook his head. "The five of us and the soldiers are the only survivors." He recounted what had happened to himself and the soldiers that day, starting with the failed rescue of Doctor Semyonov.

In disbelief, Callum looked to Darya. She and Ava were crouched together at the base of a rock formation. Ava's face was drained of all colour. Darya's was pale but stoical as she continued to comfort her.

"What about the other helicopter?"

"It is also gone. It was on the *Albanov*."

"So, what? We're really stranded here?"

"For now," Lungkaju said. "But now that communication has been lost with the mainland they will know that there is an emergency and they will send a rescue team."

"And how long will that take? Hours? Days?"

"I do not know." He closed his eyes and let out a long sigh. "Starshyna Koikov says that it could be weeks."

Ava screamed out suddenly and dropped her face into her hands. Her pale skin had turned a disturbing shade of grey and her tears bled out through the gaps between her fingers.

Lungkaju walked across to her. "Please, Doctor Lee," he said, placing a hand gently on top of her head, "I know that this is a shock, but you must try and be quiet."

She knocked his arm away. "No, to hell with being quiet! What the hell's the point of being quiet? We're all dead anyway! We're trapped on here with no way off and there are things and oh, Jesus, *Jesus*, what the hell are we going to do now?"

"It is okay, Doctor Lee," Lungkaju persisted. "We will meet up with Starshyna Koikov's team. They have weapons and ammunition. We will be safe with them."

"And where do we meet up with them?" Darya asked.

"There is the old military compound in the south-west of the island. Starshyna Koikov told me to meet him there. We will have shelter. There might be an old radio and together we will be safe."

"The south-west?" Darya said. "But, Lungkaju, we are in the east. It will take us a day just to walk there."

Having surveyed much of the southern part of the island himself, Callum knew that she was right. It would take them a day's walking at a good pace to reach the compound, and the state Ava was in, a good pace would be asking a lot.

"I know this," Lungkaju replied. "But there is nothing else for us. We must try."

For several minutes the only sound was that of Ava's continued sobbing, as the four of them tried to get their heads around the situation and contemplate the task ahead. On his haunches beside Lungkaju, even Fenris seemed to sense the gravity of their circumstances, and he kept quiet and still.

The silence was broken suddenly by the sound of Ava pulling herself to her feet. With Darya steadying her, she wiped at her eyes and took a deep breath. "So what are we waiting for? The sooner we get there, the sooner we get safe, right? So let's get the hell out of here."

The others stared at her briefly, as if waiting for a punchline. Her skin retained its pallor, her eyes were red and her cheeks still wet. But her jaw was set firmly and it was clear she meant business.

"She is right," Lungkaju said, seizing the new momentum. "We should begin. I still have my emergency equipment, so we can pitch a tent when we need to rest." He turned to Callum. "We have the only rifles, so one of us should go first, the other at the back."

"I'd rather go ahead," Callum replied. "But you're the one who knows where we're going, so it should probably be you."

Lungkaju nodded. "You will need to be very careful at the back, because there is nobody to watch for you."

"Tail end Charlie, I know." Callum rolled his lips. "Let's do it. I'm not sure whether my life expectancy could get any lower anyway."

Lungkaju reached out his hand and the two men shook.

Callum went to release his grip, then retightened it at the last second. "Just one question."

Lungkaju waited, reasserting his own grip.

"How did you know that we were out here in the first place?"

"I did not," he beamed. "It was Fenris that knew you were alive, my friend. I just followed his nose."

* * *

Ptarmigan threw open the *Centaur*'s main hatch and looked around. He was inside a large, natural inlet, concealed from the coast by a barrier of rock. An opening had eroded some fifty feet or so up, allowing daylight to pour down into the interior. A substantial seal colony was sprawled around the rocks lining the cavern's walls. Their cacophony of barks merged into one deafening echo, and their stink hung thick in the unexpectedly warm air.

Something glimmered towards the back of the cavern. Ptarmigan could see that it was a small, white vessel of some kind, moored up next to a stone ledge. As he ran his eye up and along the ledge, something else caught his attention. From amongst the shadows, a tiny spec of red appeared, darting upwards and intensifying briefly before returning to its original position. He could tell immediately that it was the end of a cigarette.

Without bothering to resecure the hatch, Ptarmigan dropped back into the cabin and manoeuvred the *Centaur* to rest beside the other craft. It was a second submersible. It was smaller than the *Centaur*, probably only one, two-occupant capacity tops. He knew that technologically it was unlikely to be the *Centaur*'s equal, or anywhere close. But it looked otherwise sleek and advanced.

He used the pincers to anchor the *Centaur* loosely to the natural harbour wall, powered down and climbed out. The tumble of rocks which greeted him formed a convenient, if unstable, stairway up to the ledge.

"Thank God you're here," he said, scrabbling to the top. "I'd been kidding myself that you were gonna stand me up."

The contact said nothing but remained in the shadows and

took another drag on his cigarette. Unnerved but not deterred by the silence, Ptarmigan tried again. "So Finback sent you to meet me, huh?"

This time the man shifted and replied in a well-spoken Russian accent, "Not exactly."

"What do you mean, *not exactly*?" Ptarmigan said. "Unless by some gazillion-to-one chance you're just caving in the wrong place at the wrong time buddy, then you're Finback's man." He paused. "Say, have we met before? You sound awful familiar."

The man took a commanding step forward into the light.

Chapter 10

FINBACK

1

The man in front of Ptarmigan was imperiously tall. He wore a dark woollen hat pulled down over his ears, a navy-blue jacket and a pair of highly polished black boots.

"Mr Peterson," Volkov said, his eyes piercing in the gloom. "How nice that you could make it."

Peterson attempted to speak, but the sides of his throat felt as if they were glued together.

"Congratulations are in order," Volkov continued. "You have done very well. Please excuse me."

There was a sudden flash, accompanied by a loud bang. Peterson jumped at the sound of the gunshot, while around the cavern every last seal dived from its perch and disappeared from view. Silence descended.

"Apologies," Volkov said, reholstering his pistol. "But I do not like to shout."

Still tongue-tied with shock, Peterson could only nod.

"Now, where were we? Oh, yes. Congratulations. You have carried out your task with dedication and professionalism, and I thank you."

"You... you thank me?" Peterson stammered, slowly regaining his voice. "But... I destroyed your ship. All of your equipment, your research…"

Volkov laughed out loud. It was a coarse, braying laugh that tore into Peterson's ears. It was a laugh that made the former seal chorus sound like the tittering of a new-born. "Nonsense," Volkov said. "You destroyed exactly what I wanted you to destroy. An old ship that should have been decommissioned years ago, a bunch of foreign meddlers and very little else."

Peterson shook his head. "An old ship? I took the tour, remember? That ship was state of the art."

"Correction," Volkov replied. "The parts of it that you were allowed to see *appeared* state of the art. But there was no equipment of any real value on board, and I assure you, the restricted areas were clear of valuable restricted activity and personnel. In reality, your target was only a shell. A floating hotel, and a small price to pay." A menacing grin cut across his cheeks, and his pale, emaciated face glowed in the gloom like a fresh skull. "You would do well to learn that all that glitters really is not gold."

Peterson fought to reconcile the flood of new information. "I don't understand. Do *you* work for Finback too?"

Volkov's grin disappeared. He drew himself up and raked a finger through his neatly trimmed moustache. "According to *Forbes* magazine, I am currently the ninth richest man in Russia, with a net personal fortune of some ten billion of your American dollars. Of course this is an oversimplification of my circumstances, but suffice it to say that I own hundreds of companies across the globe and have substantial shareholdings in everything from office stationery to space technology."

Peterson's jaw dropped. "You mean… you're Finback?"

Volkov nodded then raised a small voice distortion box to his lips. "It is a pleasure to meet you at last, Ptarmigan."

Sure enough, it was the same robotic drawl that had so raised Peterson's hackles over the phone. Just the sound of it again was enough to jolt him out of his stupor. "But I still don't get it. I mean, are you nuts or something? Why the hell would you authorise an attack against your own venture? Your own damn ship?"

Volkov tossed the voice distorter carelessly into the sea. "It may not surprise you to learn that one of my principal shareholdings is in the Russian partner company in the G&S Consortium." He indicated the G&S emblem on the shoulder of his dark-blue jacket.

"But—"

Volkov held up a gloved hand.

Peterson thought about carrying on and having his say regardless. Then he closed his mouth. The one fact staring him straight between the eyes was that Mr ninth-in-*Forbes* didn't really have to tell him anything at all. In fact, he hadn't even had to turn up for their little rendezvous. He could have said to hell with it, and there wouldn't've been a damn thing Peterson could've done. But he had turned up. So far he was keeping his end of the bargain, sort of. And if he was willing to spill a few beans, then it would be well worth keeping schtum.

Volkov: "As I mentioned during our little show-and-tell hour back on the *Albanov*, Russia continues to lead the world in the production of natural gas. What I did not mention is that we have been spoilt by our vast inland reserves." He began pacing slowly back and forth, his eyes trained on Peterson's. "Until recently there has been little incentive for investment in our off-shore Arctic drilling capabilities and we have been forced to turn to our international neighbours. Our Norwegian partner company has been invaluable in passing on hard-earned experience, some of it knowingly, some of it not so knowingly." He paused to take a last drag on his cigarette, before dropping the nub to the floor.

"But Russians have always been fast learners, Mr Peterson, and our need for foreign input is over. My associates and I are now confident that we have the knowledge and techniques to allow us to benefit from our off-shore Arctic resources without the need for further international assistance."

"So you're cutting them loose?" Peterson said.

Volkov's eyes met with his. "As we speak, a buy-out is being finalised by a consortium of other interested parties."

"Let me guess. Volkov Associates Limited?"

Volkov smiled. "You can be very insightful, Mr Peterson. That is one reason why I selected you for this project."

Peterson scoffed. "Dare I ask the others?"

"Your passion for the environment, your experience of clandestine eco-terrorism—"

"Cut the crap!" Peterson spat. "This has got nothing to do with the environment or eco-terrorism. It's about getting your Norwegian partners to hand you control of the entire company. You're hoping they'll baulk at the failure of your sham little operation out here and cut their losses, right?"

"A bonus, nothing more."

Peterson found himself speechless once again.

Volkov: "I see that your insight stretches only so far."

Given the circumstances, the remark packed a disproportionate sting. If Volkov hadn't had ten billion gees and a loaded pistol, Peterson was certain he would've swung for him. Instead he swallowed his anger. "So, what? You just needed a little extra excitement in your life or something? Where the hell do I fit in to all of this?"

"You are the reason why I no longer have to worry about the interference of the Arctic Council in my affairs," Volkov replied. "You are the reason that the truly state-of-the-art *Albanov II* will arrive from my dockyard near Murmansk, fully equipped and fully staffed within the month. You are the reason why construction of the Harmsworth Gas Processing Plant will begin *this* year, rather than in ten years' time when every little fish and flower has been removed to safety." He paused then added, "You do not merely *fit* into all of this. You are the reason for it, and I thank you."

"What the hell are you talking about?"

A shadow seemed to pass over Volkov's face. "Did it not strike you as odd that an American citizen was allowed to get within a thousand miles of this project?"

"No, it didn't," Peterson responded. "The Cold War's over, Volkov. Wake up and smell the concord, would you? Your scientists and ours have been collaborating peacefully for years. The world's moved on."

Volkov dragged out a sigh. "The roots of political enmity run deep, Mr Peterson, and the peace between our nations remains fragile as ever. Just look at the recent unpleasantries in Ukraine."

Peterson rolled his eyes. "So what's your point? That superpowers don't trust each other? Tell me something I don't know."

"The point is that by allowing foreigners of any nationality, let alone an American, onto one of our most sensitive installations, Russia has made a massive concession to the will of both the Arctic Council and the United Nations, and a progressive leap in terms of Russian-US relations. We have demonstrated our openness and willingness to engage in international cooperation in the responsible exploitation of the Arctic. The Harmsworth project was to be a united flagship, spearheaded by tolerance, the first step in a peaceful partnership that would have seen harmony in the Arctic, rather than a hostile smash-and-grab." He levelled the full weight of his gaze at Peterson, that hideous grin reblossoming. "And you, my American friend, have quite literally blown it."

Peterson's heart sank as Volkov's words hit home. But before he could protest, Volkov went on in that same stomach-churning tone. "Following this unprovoked attack on our national infrastructure, G&S will, of course, be withdrawing our participation from all international initiatives concerning energy procurement in the Arctic. A Russian team will be commissioned to complete the Harmsworth assessment to the satisfaction of my associates at the internal energy ministry.

Russia's affairs will be firmly back in Russian hands, and the company will enjoy an estimated cost saving in excess of twenty billion rubles."

"And how exactly are you going to prove what happened?" Peterson asked, trying to steady his voice. "What evidence have you got that the explosion wasn't caused by a systems failure? Sabotage by one of your own? Hell, how could you possibly prove that it wasn't somebody smoking where they shouldn't've been?"

"A sensible question," Volkov sneered. "Not that a Federation commission would need much convincing of a foreign terror plot, but several hours of incriminating CCTV footage, starring no less than yourself, has already been uploaded to a secure server awaiting submission to the inquiry. This should satisfy the curiosity of the international community. Your own government will, of course, deny any involvement, and they will no doubt enjoy popular support. Yet they will face some awkward questions when your previous *terrorist* activities – your assault on your own government's Barranquitas nuclear facility, for example – are also publicly disclosed and they are reminded that the vetting process for the Harmsworth assessment was largely an internal affair."

Peterson couldn't control himself any longer. On impulse, he strode towards Volkov. "You crazy son of a bitch! Are you trying to start World War Three?" He felt a crushing pain radiating through his chest as a kick landed in his sternum. He stumbled backwards and dropped to the floor, winded.

"Don't be so dramatic, Mr Peterson," Volkov snorted, advancing on him. "You are doing a very good job of lowering yourself in my estimations." He peered down, his eyes wide and emotionless. "Besides, Cold War Two would seem the more likely outcome, wouldn't you say?"

2

Peterson closed his eyes. How could things have gone so wrong
and so quickly? How could he have been so stupid?

The pain in his chest was nothing compared to the guilt
and despair that he felt in that moment. There was no Finback.
There was no cause. There had only ever been Ptarmigan, the
misguided puppet. He had been one hundred goddamn per
cent duped! Manipulated into committing an act so heinous for
a cause so offensive to his own convictions. And that was the
pit that he really couldn't swallow; far from helping to prevent
the ruin of the Arctic, his gullibility had actually kicked it
into overdrive. Not to mention the damage it could do to the
spiralling relations between Russia and the west. The more he
thought about it, the faster his sense of self-loathing turned to
indignation, and then to fury.

Struggling for breath, he pulled himself up into a kneeling
position. Volkov's pistol was aimed directly at his face, but in
that moment it might as well have been a steak sandwich. "You
piece of shit, Volkov. You talk about Russia as if you're it. As
if you somehow embody a nation of hundreds of millions of
free-thinking souls. But that's not what this is about. Russia's
got nothing to do with it. You've got nothing to do with Russia.

This is about *you* and *your* greed. Do you honestly think it's in Russia's interest to promote the neglect of the Arctic? To promote conflict? You short-sighted sonofabitch!"

"Mr Peterson—"

"Save it!" Peterson shouted. "You may kick-start your bankroll on this one, but this is only the start. What about the next project ten years from now, and the one after that, and the one after that, when it's not you, but your children in the driving seat? You're just plain deluded, you know that? You're a power-mongering criminal, nothing more. And you're certainly not a goddamn patriot!" He broke off, shocked at the vehemence of his own outburst. Then, just as suddenly, he started to laugh. Within seconds he was beside himself, his roars of hysteria echoing around the cavern. He removed his spectacles and wiped the tears from his eyes. "And you need me."

"Excuse me?"

As quickly as it had started, Peterson's laughter subsided. "I said, you need me."

It was Volkov's turn to laugh. "Well, now I am intrigued."

A cocktail of fear, anger and loathing surged through Peterson's veins, across his tongue and out over his lips. "One word, one letter. Stuxnet D."

Volkov's expression froze. For the first time since their encounter had begun, a quiver of uncertainty sounded in his voice. To most it would have been barely detectable. But to Peterson, it was as if somebody had smashed a gong over the bastard's head. "You are lying."

"Oh yeah? Check your goddamn footage!" Peterson began climbing slowly to his feet. "When I was in the security room on the *Albanov*, I uploaded the CCTV editor programme just as we discussed. But you'll see I also uploaded something else from the data stick. A little something I left off the table."

"And you expect me to believe that it was the Stuxnet programme?"

242

"No," Peterson replied. "I expect you to believe that it was version five of the Stuxnet programme. Ten times more powerful than the previous version. Ten times harder to detect. Virtually impossible to eradicate without causing permanent, irreparable damage to the host system. It would've been transmitted straight back to your Unified Gas Supply System primary control centre on the mainland via your own security control signal. By now it will've spread to each and every one of your installations' operating systems, nationwide."

The two men stared at each other. Both knew that the original Stuxnet virus had been the most powerful computer worm of all time, specifically designed to attack SCADA systems operating national infrastructure, electrical grids, oil and gas installations and pipelines. It targeted specific critical sub-processes, altering them and cloaking those alterations from the relevant monitoring programmes, leaving critical errors undetected. The result? Catastrophic system failures.

What both men also knew was that Stuxnet D represented a massive advance in the potency of the virus, by allowing it to attack multiple sub-processes simultaneously at predefined intervals. It was the stuff of national security nightmares.

"You could not have obtained this."

"Oh yeah?" Peterson's eyes flashed. "You selected me, Volkov. What were your reasons again? My passion for the environment? My experience of clandestine eco-terrorism? But that's not the half of it, is it? You've been funding my ventures for some time now, trying to woo me over and building up your goddamn evidence case file on me at the same time. Think about it. You know damn well that in me you've got a whole lot more than some jacked up, banner-waving hippy! You look at me like a piece of dog shit on your boot, but in me you've got the best. You think I'm not plugged in to the subversive underworld? I'm at the goddamn heart! You think I don't have global contacts? I got a whole fucking international empire of contacts! I'm not the kind of person who can obtain Stuxnet on the black market? I'm exactly the sonofabitch who can obtain it. And if you weren't so busy underestimating me, you smug fuck, you might've known all about it."

Volkov stood quietly, just listening, his eyes searching Peterson's for any sign of deception and evidently finding none.

"We're both big players in our own separate little worlds," Peterson continued. "Only me and *my* associates and our little global empire, aren't in it for the money. We're in it for the good of the planet, something the likes of you will never understand." He watched as Volkov's adamant expression finally wilted.

"And you know what clinches it? I did it for you, *Finback*. I did it for you, for God's sake." He was unable to stifle another full-on belch of laughter. "I thought it would impress you, you greedy, psychotic asshole! And now, well…" He moved his face closer, until their noses were almost touching. "I'd be interested to hear what *Russia* has to say when it emerges that the entire national gas infrastructure went bye bye on your watch."

Volkov's hand collided with Peterson's throat. His fingers clamped into a vice-like grip as he shoved him back into the cavern wall and rammed the end of the pistol into his cheek. "How do I remove it?" he growled, composure a distant memory on his face.

"You don't," Peterson choked.

"Don't fuck with me! Tell me how I remove it, now!"

"I'm telling you, you can't!"

Volkov yelled out in fury, his pale cheeks flushed red with rage. He lifted Peterson from his feet and slammed him face-down onto the floor. No sooner had Peterson's body hit the rock than Volkov was on top of him, his free hand moving feverishly through his pockets, around his person, searching. "Where is it?" he demanded.

"Where's what?" Peterson replied, his voice muffled by the cold stone.

"The data stick. Where is it?"

"I destroyed it."

"Bullshit!"

"Even if I hadn't, you think I'd have it on me?"

Pain erupted in his back as Volkov drove a fist into his kidney.

"I'm telling you it's not on me!"

"We shall see."

Having patted him down and found nothing, Volkov thrust a gloved hand between his legs. Peterson screamed out as Volkov's fingers searched around, crushing his testicles and digging into his anus. The search ended suddenly and Volkov sat back on Peterson's thighs. Now came the sound of a buckle unfastening, and the next thing Peterson knew, a long, black blade was pressed against his cheek. As the blade rocked back and forth against his skin, he could feel his own condensed breath moistening the steel.

"One last chance, Mr Peterson," Volkov snarled, turning the narrowed point of the blade in towards his eye, "or I will start with your eyeball."

Having kept his cool for so long, now Peterson began to panic. Sweat broke out across his brow. It wasn't the pain, but the darkness that terrified him. As a child he had suffered temporary blindness after watching a solar eclipse with his naked eyes. His vision had not dimmed immediately, but suddenly and traumatically. For over a week, until sight had limped back to him, irreparably damaged, the world he had taken for granted the previous decade had simply disappeared, leaving him alone and scared and screaming.

He struggled weakly, in the grip of the memory. "Please, I don't have it. You've got to believe me. I don't have it—"

The blade teetered at the edge of his eyeball, the sharpened steel scratching at the lid.

"Have you destroyed it?"

"No," Peterson whispered. And it was true. He was no longer making any attempt to lie.

Volkov seemed to sense this, and the control returned to his movements. He leant patiently forward until his face hovered beside Peterson's cheek. "Where is it?"

"I gave it to… to…"

Volkov's face crept even closer. "Who?"

Peterson bit his lip. His mind flailed desperately around, searching for something, anything that would keep him from making the admission on the tip of his tongue. Through his fear, he could feel that Volkov had relaxed his grip. Was he off balance? Not entirely, but maybe just enough. His heart pounded. It was now or never.

He bucked suddenly, as if a ten thousand-volt shock had cramped his spine up into an arch. With a growl of surprise, Volkov toppled over onto his back and Peterson rolled the other way and lashed out with his foot, catching him square in the groin. As the Russian doubled up in pain, Peterson sprang to his feet.

Adrenaline had full control of his functions. Without any sense of a plan, he bolted for the *Centaur*. He arrived at the open hatch and reached for the rim. His palms were slick with sweat as he seized his fingers around the edge of the cold metal panelling and went to haul himself into the cabin.

There was a loud bang. The strength left his arms, and he turned around just as another gunshot sounded. This time he felt a dull thump, followed by a pain radiating throughout his torso. His hands pressed against the flood of warmth welling up through his jacket, and his legs began to buckle.

The last thing he saw as his vision faltered to the top of the slope was Volkov, his pistol smoking and aimed towards him, his face like hell warmed up.

"You overestimate yourself, Mr Peterson."

With a groan Peterson stumbled back towards the *Centaur*

and then collapsed onto the edge of the harbour. Half sitting, half sprawled, his body teetered.

Volkov raised his pistol once more, but before he could fire off another round, Peterson folded like a ragdoll and tumbled backwards on an avalanche of rock.

3

Volkov lowered his pistol. Rage tore through him like never before. That American bastard! How dare he create such an obstacle! Why couldn't he just do as instructed? Did he not understand what a delicate game Volkov was embroiled in? Did he have any idea how far up this thing went? Of the calibre of the players involved?

It was all supposed to have gone smoothly!

Unused to being defied, he threw his head back and roared out with frustration. The sound took off like a banshee around the cavern, echoing from wall to wall and back. With the taste of blood on his tongue, he strode towards the water's edge. The American's body was nowhere to be seen, buried under the fall of dislodged rock that had followed him into the water.

He took aim at one of half a dozen seals that had hung around in the inlet, curiosity getting the better of their instinct to flee. It had probably never seen a human before. Only its eyes and nose were visible above the surface as it stared up in evident confusion.

Volkov blew its brains out with a single shot.

He knew it was petulant and pointless, but he didn't care. He craved catharsis. He needed to vent what he was fast accepting to be fear rather than simple anger. If seals were all there were to take it out on, then seals it would have to be. He took aim at another, firing off a medley of shots, all of which missed as the frantic creature dove for cover.

The American's words chased round and round inside his head: *the entire national gas infrastructure... bye bye on your watch! ...entire national gas infrastructure... bye bye on your watch! ...bye bye on your watch... bye bye...*

And the bastard was right. Volkov couldn't have cared less about the effect on Russia, not the sorry, spineless excuse for a nation that it had come to be. Soviet corpse. Europe's energy fence. In truth, there was nothing left there to love but the pursuit of wealth, nothing to take pride in but power.

What he did care about was the effect of Mr Peterson's meddling on the interests of his *associates*. He had promised them a minimum twenty billion-ruble saving, not a share in the worst national systems failure the country had ever seen. At this level, these were the sort of people that even he, Andrei Vyacheslav Volkov, was reluctant to disappoint. If the Harmsworth project went sour, the consequences would go way beyond his bank balance.

He reached into his pocket and removed the chrome-plated pill dispenser. He dropped four red and white pills into his hand, threw them into his mouth and dry swallowed them. Then he lit a cigarette and inhaled deeply, fighting to regain his composure. This was a business venture. Business ventures encountered problems. Blips. Granted, this blip was of a greater order of magnitude than usual, but it was not insoluble. All was not lost. He just needed to calm down and think it through.

His mind flitted to the data stick. It was the key. Its recovery was paramount. He was no technology expert, but then he had fiscal involvement with some serious players in the European and Asian technology markets, including systems security. If he could deliver the raw virus to one of them, they could unlock the programme's base coding just like any other. They could then formulate a solution. An anti-virus. Stuxnet would lie dormant for a period before becoming active, in order to adapt to the specific operating parameters of the host system. With any luck, he could cleanse the entire national delivery system before anybody even knew it was infected.

That just left the small matter of locating the data stick itself.

The obvious first port of call was the submarine. The late Mr Peterson had proven himself an unexpectedly adroit opponent, and while Volkov believed his terrified confession that he had entrusted it to somebody else, he wasted no time ransacking the submarine anyway. Finding nothing, he then disabled its systems with his last two bullets and made his way back to his own vessel.

He seated himself in the leather operator's chair and began to think. Where would it be? *If I were an impudent, Yankee tree-hugger, who would I have entrusted it to?*

As a former *illegal resident* KGB operative, the ability to accurately profile a target had often proven the difference between success and failure. So critical a skill was it, that it had developed into an intuitive, almost mechanical, response that had served Volkov equally well in business. Even now his mind had begun picking apart Mr Peterson's. What were his weaknesses? He cared about things, people, places. Why did he care about them? Because he ascribed meaning to them. Why? Because they elicited an emotional response from him. Did he cross the fine line between the emotional and the sentimental? Yes. He was clearly sentimental. So how did sentimental people act? They pined and they regretted and they pitied and they loved and they... *loved.*

Volkov's lips tightened into a self-satisfied grin. *Love.* People entrusted their most valuable possessions to loved ones – secrets, dreams, memories, fears – often without even realising. Physical items were only the logical next step. He'd seen it more times than he could remember. Passwords in lockets. Keys on charm bracelets. Was it possible that Mr Peterson had done the same?

His affair with the Canadian, Doctor Lee, was no secret. Indeed, after his source had first brought it to light, Volkov had monitored the romance closely, fearing that it would distract *Ptarmigan* from his mission. Could the American really have entrusted the virus to his unsuspecting paramour?

The more he thought about it, the more it made sense, until he was quite certain. The data stick was in the possession of Doctor Ava Lee. And where was she? According to his man on the ground, she was stranded on Harmsworth along with an awkward number of other survivors: Doctors Lebedev and Ross, either of whom might also have had the data stick, and a sizeable Spetsnaz contingent. Despite his grin, Volkov felt a genuine sense of remorse that none of them would be making it off the island alive. He wasn't a monster. He was a businessman.

Newly focussed, he slid his knife from its sheath, flipped it from one hand to the other and back, and then examined his hazy reflection in the blade. He dragged it across the back of his hand to test the sharpness. It was razor.

So the survivors were heading for the old military outpost. He resheathed the blade. If he wanted to be there to meet them, then he would need to move quickly.

Chapter 11

POSSUM

1

Koikov took one last look into the mouth of the cave. "Rest in peace," he uttered. Then he turned around, spat on the floor and signalled to the two privates.

Jets of smoke erupted from their RPG housings and the explosive-tipped projectiles streaked forward side by side, scoring their trails into the air. With a roar, they careered into the ceiling of the cave and sent a torrent of rock cascading down.

Back on their feet, Privates Zakrevsky and Orlov fell in at Koikov's side, and the three men watched together as the rumble of tumbling stone petered out and the smoke gradually cleared. Where the cave mouth had been, there was now an almighty pile of scorched rock.

"Good work," Koikov said. "That should give those fuckers something to think about."

He ran his gaze across the faces of the two younger men. He'd never expected them to share his sentiment, but neither had he expected the conflict betrayed in their expressions to cut so deep.

It was understandable. They hadn't been part of the original rescue team, so they'd seen no evidence of the mysterious creatures that they were supposed to be afraid of. They were going through the motions all the same, accepting what they were told and obeying orders because they were soldiers, highly trained soldiers, and that's what they were trained to do. But clearly there was still a part of them that wondered whether Koikov had lost his mind.

They'll learn soon enough, he thought to himself, hoping beyond hope that he was wrong. "Let's catch up with the others before they get too far ahead. Orlov, you man the tower."

Koikov wove the Czilim expertly in between the outcrops of rock, and after half a kilometre or so they caught up with the rest of the team. Zakrevsky fell back in. Orlov stuck with the gun, as Koikov continued shadowing the staggered rank of troops at a distance.

As he drove, he traced his eyes across the surrounding landscape. The place looked less hospitable than ever, barren, hostile and eerily still. The glare from the midnight sun was blinding. Even the darkest stone seemed to reflect the rays directly up into his face. With a sigh, he pushed his shades firmly back against the bridge of his nose. If it wasn't shades, then it was LVV. If it wasn't LVV, then it was shades. Sun glare, mist, sun glare, mist… *And then the rest of the year it's pitch fucking black!*

"If ever a place didn't want to be seen," he mumbled to himself.

"Starshyna?"

He looked around and saw Orlov staring over at him. He was an ugly one. Big nose. Buck-teeth. Ridiculous mousy sideburns. "I said we should never have come here." Orlov pursed his lips; they were cracked and bulbous. "I thought that the moment we arrived, Starshyna."

"What are you talking about?"

"A feeling I had. Something isn't right."

"Not right? I'll tell you what isn't right, Orlov, the *Albanov's* gone and the creatures living on this island keep eating members of my team."

Orlov turned his attention back to the mounted gun. "There's something else, Starshyna. Something bigger. I can't put my finger on it, but—"

"You keep your finger on that trigger, Private." In truth, Koikov sensed it too; this place was making puppets of them all. But there was no time for daydreaming.

Bringing the Czilim to a halt on high ground, he raised his binoculars. From here, he could pick out most of the team as they disappeared off along the winding valley that arced towards the island's heart. They were progressing just as he'd ordered, in a series of four- and five-man teams at hundred-metre intervals. With few exceptions, they looked alert and battle-ready. Still he was uneasy. Clustered, linear movement was inadvisable in hostile situations; it presented a soft underbelly just crying out to be assaulted. And the image of what could happen to soft underbellies was still fresh in his mind.

The reinforcement team had brought considerable firepower over with them that morning, but he wasn't about to let his guard down. All the weapons in the world wouldn't be worth dick if Harmsworth turned on them. And he still didn't have any clear idea how many of those things there were. He prayed not many, but deep down he feared the worst.

He lit a papirosa and scratched at his scar; the cold had caused it to swell and he could feel his pulse, hard but steady, beneath the scabrous tissue. Inadvisable or not, the situation was what it was. There was no alternative. They needed to get to the compound and get there fast.

A sudden burst of static flared up in his ear. It was Marchenko: "Starshyna, you should check out Hjalmar."

Koikov cast his gaze up over the Hjalmar Ridge. The ever-present spine of rock towered to his right. Banks of scree, tinged green with lichen growth, were piled against its flanks, and pats of remnant snow and ice clung to cavities in the shadows of the rockface.

"What is it, Starshyna?" Orlov asked.

"Shit!" Koikov raised a hand to his throat. "Spread the word. From the looks of it we don't have long."

"Starshyna?"

Koikov spun around. "Goddamnit, Orlov, would you use your eyes!" He pointed up towards the top of the ridge, beyond the glacier. But it was no longer visible. A dense blanket of mist that had been teetering on the edge had now tipped over the side and was flooding towards them like fumes spilling from a volcano.

"Marchenko, get the men to find cover, now! Something tells me we're gonna have company."

2

"Did he say anything else?"

Zakrevsky slotted the remaining rounds into his magazine and clipped it back into his rifle. "Koikov? No. Just got me and Orlov to take out the roof."

"Waste of grenades if you ask me," Tsaritsyn replied.

"Keep your voice down, Private," Corporal Yevtushenko snapped. "The mist amplifies your voice. They can probably hear your whining back on the mainland."

Tsaritsyn went to reply. Then he closed his mouth. He looked around. The three of them and Private Ilyn had taken cover beneath an overhang. They were in the middle of the caravan, and they had been passing over a low rise when the mist had flooded over them. The call had gone out from Sergeant Marchenko and within seconds the world had become a very different place. The vast, sweeping landscape that they had been traversing had vanished from sight, and a new and claustrophobic one had squatted. It felt heavy, drizzly, like millions of tiny raindrops prickling at his skin. And it was freezing. He could feel it heavy in his throat and lungs with every breath, and when he exhaled, the same oily grey cloud escaped his lips.

Through the haze, he could barely make out Yevtushenko's

features, though the man was perched right next to him. The others, sitting with their backs to the rock opposite, were visible in outline only. In truth, it was the closest thing to a thrill that Tsaritsyn had felt since being posted to Harmsworth: a foreign location, near-zero visibility, a state of high alert and the threat of ambush, no matter how far-fetched the supposed enemy.

"So you think the Starshyna is imagining these creatures?" Ilyn asked.

"Of course he's imagining them," Tsaritsyn replied. "Lizard monsters with feathers and killer claws? I never heard such fucking nonsense."

Yevtushenko grunted. "So what killed Dolgonosov then? And Sharova? And Yudina?"

"Either it was a polar bear, or..."

"Or what?"

Tsaritsyn pulled his hat down over his ears and scratched at his patchy stubble. "Or it's not a question of *what* killed them."

"What are you suggesting?"

"I'm not *suggesting* anything," he replied. "I'm just saying that something really fucked up is going on. First people start getting killed, then the *Albanov* explodes and we're stranded. Then we're on a monster hunt. I'm telling you, something's going on and we're being kept in the dark about it. It's a conspiracy."

"Well, I'm with Koikov," Ilyn said. "He's straight up. Always has been. Plus Marchenko backs his story up." He drew his knees in to his chest. "Anyway, your conspiracy theory sounds just about as crazy as theirs."

"We may not have seen anything in that cave," Yevtushenko added, "but I sure as hell feel like something's with us on this island. I've felt it since the moment I first got here."

"I'm just not sure it's *here* we should be worried about," Tsaritsyn said.

"Meaning?"

"For a start, whoever blew up the *Albanov* must've had

inside help. There's no way they would've got their explosive on board and beat security without it."

"You think it was intentional?"

"I'd bet my sorry excuse for a pension on it. I was demolitions for four years before I joined Department V, and I'm telling you it'd take more than a haphazard explosion to take out a ship that size. It'd take a real expert, and it would take them time and resources." He banged the butt of his rifle down. "Either this is an inside job, or I'm the next president of the Federation."

"So what's your point, President, Sir?"

Tsaritsyn grinned. "Blowing up an icebreaker is a big deal, especially if it belongs to G&S. Whoever masterminded it must have a fucking good reason, and that scares me."

"Why?"

"Because what if *we* don't form part of the plan?"

At that moment a burst of gunfire rang out in the distance, followed by the familiar percussive booming of grenades.

A voice crackled into their earpieces: "This is Corporal Fermanov on point. We're under attack. Private Rykov is down and we need help out here!"

Yevtushenko's voice rang out in response: "This is Corporal Yevtushenko. I read you and we're on our way." He turned to Tsaritsyn. "I guess it's time to test your theory."

3

There was no doubt in Callum's mind about the source of the distant cracks and rattles. It was the sound of machine gun fire. He glanced at Lungkaju, who nodded.

"They have found Tansu Taibaa."

With everything that had happened over the last few hours, Callum had forgotten. "You think so?"

"I am certain of this." Lungkaju repeated his words from the tunnel: "*The only difference between myth and history, Doctor Ross, is that we choose to believe history.*"

A louder explosion sounded off in the distance. Fenris sat bolt upright in the middle of the emergency shelter and growled. His enormous ears were pricked, and the hairs along his back had tensed up into a ridge. Lungkaju stroked his side and spoke to him softly in Nganasan. The dog's ears flattened once more and, with a yawn, he turned and lay back down again with his head in Callum's lap.

"Remarkable," Callum said. "What did you say to him?"

"I told him it is only bad dreams."

"I wish that worked for me."

"That was a grenade, right?" Ava broke in. "That explosion. They've found the monsters."

Sensing her panic starting to build, Darya reached out a comforting hand and placed it over hers. But it was no use.

"They're Special Forces, though, right? If they've found the monsters they should be able to kill them? Shouldn't they?"

"Starshyna Koikov is a very good soldier," Lungkaju said, his voice calm. "We can trust him." He shuffled up onto his knees and checked his rifle.

"Where are you going?" she demanded.

"I must go and look around. I must make sure that we are still safe here."

"You're going out there? But why don't you just wait here with us until the mist goes? It's safe in here. Surely it's safer in here? You won't be able to see anything anyway—"

"It is okay," he replied. He fished around in his pack, producing what looked like a pair of very narrow sunglasses. There was a distinct silvery sheen to the single lens, which gave it a holographic appearance. "I have this."

"Oh, well, that's okay then," Ava replied. "As long as you've got your X-men costume we're all saved."

"What is it?" Callum asked.

"It is LVV, a low-visibility visor. It is a new technology to help soldiers to see in bad weather." He pulled the rifle strap up onto his shoulder and unzipped the tent.

Through the open flap, Callum could see the mist billowing around them. If it was possible, then it felt even colder than usual. It seemed to have developed a faint purple tinge, and it glowed with an eerie half-light. "Are you sure this is sensible?"

Lungkaju grinned and slipped the visor on. "It is actually a very beautiful day, Doctor Ross." He crawled out. "I will not be long. Come, Fenris."

The dog sprang to his paws and raced out of the tent after him.

Callum watched as Lungkaju refastened the entrance zip, then he sat silently for a while, he, Darya and Ava just listening to the distant chorus of rifle fire. "It sounds like all hell's breaking loose."

There was no response. The others probably felt the same sense of conflict that he did: relief not to be in the thick of it, but a biting sense of guilt at not being able to help. He was no soldier; the closest he'd ever come was the cadet force at school, and even then his participation had been grudging. But neither had he ever been a spectator. And he could fire a rifle, couldn't he? Doing nothing felt wrong.

"I hope that the soldiers are okay," Darya said. The calm, self-assured expression that she had worn when Callum first met her was long gone. Instead she looked exhausted, distracted, and the once-vibrant green of her eyes had dimmed. "I cannot believe that I am letting one of those creatures go," she continued. "I am such an idiot!"

Callum reached out and gently leant her head over onto his shoulder. "You're not an idiot," he said, kissing her forehead. "And there's nothing wrong with being compassionate. You said it yourself. It's what makes us different."

"I always thought it was a sense of reason," Ava said.

Callum's eyes opened. Despite his fear and the sound of the gun battle, exhaustion had overcome him. He wasn't the only one. Darya's head was pressed into his chest, her dark hair draped over the side of her cheek. She was breathing loudly and her hand was clamped tightly onto his jacket as if, in her dreams, she was clinging to a rockface. Ava was also asleep, slumped over onto her side with Lungkaju's pack propped awkwardly under her head.

Lungkaju himself was still not back. Callum checked his watch. He had been gone almost twenty minutes. Given the circumstances, that was a long time. But if there was one person who seemed to know exactly what they were doing at all times, it was Lungkaju.

Having to unpeel his tongue like a strip of Velcro from the roof of his mouth was a new experience for Callum. His throat was parched. He was dehydrating in the warm, dry atmosphere inside the tent. Thankfully, Lungkaju had brought another canteen of water with him for the group to share, so they were no longer solely reliant on Ava's. As he went to retrieve it from the tent pocket, he heard the door zip begin to unfasten.

"I was starting to worry," he said, turning towards it.

A pair of large, black eyes was staring across at him.

4

Callum froze.

A narrow snout, over-crowded with teeth, cracked open and vented a cloud of reeking breath into the tent space. Three clawed digits crept calmly around the doorway and held back the fabric as a long neck extended towards him, into the interior.

At that moment, Ava awoke. Still lying on her side, she took one look at the face peering down at her, before sitting bolt upright. Her eyelids seized open in terror and she screamed out, startling Darya from sleep. Darya also screamed, and the creature looked from her to Ava, before unleashing its own high-pitched bray into the tent.

It burst forward suddenly, attempting to force its way in through the doorway but failing as its shoulders caught behind two of the struts. Callum scrabbled for the rifle. In the chaos it had been kicked out of reach and it was now lying on the other side of the tent. With no other option, he lashed out with his feet, kicking repeatedly at the side of the creature's head. Beside him, Darya joined in.

"Get the rifle!" he shouted to Ava.

Still hysterical with fear, she was screaming out and clinging so hard to his arm that he could feel her cutting off the blood supply.

"Ava!" he shouted again, snatching his arm away. "This thing is going to kill us if you don't get the rifle and shoot it, now!"

Kicking against the creature's jaw felt like kicking against marble. It must have been doing some good, though, as blood was now pouring from its nose and gums. Undeterred, it was still forcing itself ferociously towards them, and with every charge it bent the tensile struts further inwards.

"For Christ's sake, Ava!"

Responding at last, Ava extended her leg and caught her heel over the edge of the rifle. Her eyes were fixed on the creature's face as she dragged the rifle within reach of her hand. Then she stretched down and took hold of it.

"Shoot it!" Callum yelled.

She fumbled the heavy weapon until it was aimed loosely in the direction of the doorway. Then she snatched at the trigger.

Nothing happened.

"I-i-it's n-not working," she stammered.

"You need to switch the safety off!" Callum yelled. "It's the catch beside the trigger guard!"

One of the creature's hind legs shot suddenly in through the doorway. It passed between Callum and Darya, shaving the side of Callum's neck, and tearing a gash in the back of the tent.

For a split second they were left staring at each other in disbelief, before coming round. "Ava!" they chorused.

"I'm trying!" Hands shaking, tears streaming from her eyes, she ran her fingers over the rifle's stock until she found the safety catch. It depressed with a clunk.

By now, gusts of mist were spilling into the interior, giving it the same opacity as the world outside.

Ava raised the rifle once again. This time the creature shrieked and made a determined charge towards her. Finally breaking through one of the tent ribs, it seemed to get caught up on the fabric and slumped to its knees.

"Come on!" Callum shouted, taking the opportunity to turn

and drag Darya through the tear at the back of the tent.

"Ava!" she screamed. "What about Ava!"

Callum left her outside and pushed his way back in through the half-collapsed structure. After several lungfuls of fresh air, the creature's impounded stink turned his stomach. He could no longer see it, but he could feel its bulge pressing into him through the fabric as virtually its entire weight pulled at the roof's apex. Strong as they were, the remaining poles creaked loudly. Any second and the whole thing was coming down.

Callum could just make out Ava's legs from the shadow. His hands fell upon her ankles, and he dragged her clear, heaving her from the ailing tent just as it folded in on itself.

She fell to the ground next to Darya, the rifle still clamped in her hands. Callum wrenched it from her, shouldered it and aimed it at the fabric now entangling the creature. As he brought his finger to the trigger, the creature's head burst up out of the tear and it lunged for him, letting out a frustrated screech.

He fired two well-aimed shots into the top of its crown, watching as the back of its skull exploded into pulp, and its face dropped down onto the cold rock. He stared at it. His memory of the creature supposedly dead in the *Centaur*'s pincers was fresh in his mind. He was convinced that if he looked away, this one would also reanimate, fresh and ready to pounce. But it was still.

All the same, he edged forward and prodded its snout with the muzzle. Only when he saw the rest of its brains slop from the back of its cranium did he allow his shoulders to relax. Then he walked back over to the others. They were huddled together, and he knelt down and held them both.

Darya placed her hand on the back of his head and squeezed his face into hers.

"I'm sorry I had to kill it," he said.

She pulled her face away and looked deep into his eyes. "So am I," she replied. "But I am not sorry that you did."

"Me either," Ava added, her voice breathless.

"We should not wait around here," Darya said. "We should go somewhere."

"Go where?" Ava asked. "What about Lungkaju?"

"I do not know," Darya answered. "But I think that we should find somewhere quickly." Her voice took on a new undertone. "I cannot be sure, but I think that these animals might be hunting in pairs."

5

The hairs rose on the back of Callum's neck. He brought the rifle back into his shoulder and scanned around. The mist definitely seemed to be thinning. Rather than a blanket, it had fractured into discrete banks, still frequent enough to impair vision beyond a three- or four-metre radius. It was camouflage enough. Beneath his jacket, Callum could feel his arms break out into sudden gooseflesh. "I think you could be right—"

A shadow leapt from the haze, knocking him down and sending the rifle clattering to the floor. He landed on his back and immediately a second creature was on top of him.

His hands fastened around its throat as it lunged for him. Even with his arms locked, its jaw snapped shut just millimetres from his cheek. Beads of saliva rained onto him, and he could feel its foreclaws digging through his jacket into the flesh of his upper arms.

The frantic screams of Darya and Ava tore into his ears. Out of the corner of his eye he could see that they were pelting the creature with rocks. As one connected with its eye, it turned its head to snarl at them, its body tensing as if to leap in their direction.

With no time to lose, Callum grasped for one of the scree

missiles that had fallen beside him, picked it up and swung it with all his force into the side of creature's head.

"Run!" he shouted to the others, as the chunk of rock split against its target. "Go now! Find Lungkaju!"

With a high-pitched scream, the creature turned its attention back to Callum. The ferocity of its attack seemed to double with its rage. Callum's arms, which he had locked, his hands clamped around its neck, began to buckle under the weight of its lunges.

One of its hind claws shredded at his boot, before shooting up and pinning itself into his thigh muscle. He screamed out in pain, bracing himself for a strike to the body as the claw uncoupled itself and reared back.

Instead, from beside him, there was a sudden growling, followed by a deep roar. The creature was knocked sideways away from him, and he felt himself dragged clear. He scrambled to his feet.

Fenris was on top of the creature, his mouth clamped just below its jaw, tearing at the exposed neck muscle. The creature was on its back, fighting furiously to right itself but unable to rotate its knees and claw at the dog's underbelly. Its hind legs could only flail uselessly, yet its foreclaws were still free to burrow at his flanks. Tufts of fur drifted to the moss below and a criss-cross of red striations were beginning to blossom up though Fenris's coat.

Callum looked around to see Darya sprinting in the direction of the tent. She grabbed the rifle. "We must help him! It is too strong! It will kill him!"

He took the rifle from her. There were no rounds left in the chamber, so he pulled a handful from his pocket, spilling most of them on the floor in haste, but managing to reload. He cocked the weapon and pointed it towards the creature.

"Do not hit Fenris!" she pleaded with him.

Before he could do another thing, shots from a different rifle rang out beside him. The creature's stomach burst open and it fell limp in Fenris's jaws.

Next thing, Lungkaju came sprinting past Callum towards it, calling the dog away as he went. Fenris obediently dropped the creature's neck and backed off, chewing the loose feathers from his mouth. Lungkaju placed the barrel square against the side of the creature's head as if to dispatch it once and for all. But there was no final shot. Instead he waited. Watched.

"It is gone," he said, eventually turning from the dead creature. He noticed the wound on Callum's leg and his face dropped. He began walking over. "My friend, you are injured."

"Never mind me," Callum shouted to him. "Are you sure it's dead? Those things play possum."

"Fenris!" Darya screamed.

Their eyes moved to where the dog stood panting beside the creature's body.

The eye had reopened.

In an instant, the dying creature lurched forward and plunged its toe claw deep into the side of the unsuspecting dog's chest. Fenris jumped with the impact and yelped in pain. Then he stumbled forward, whining, and collapsed onto his front.

The creature's leg retracted slowly, mechanically, and a lid slid shut across its eye.

A scream of anguish ripped through the air as Lungkaju raised his rifle and fired shot after shot into the creature's body. It twitched with the impact of each round. Then it lapsed back into stillness, the clicking of the trigger signalling that all rounds were spent.

Lungkaju dropped the weapon and knelt beside Fenris. The others watched in silence as he examined the wound. Fenris had rolled over onto his side. Having licked at the gash in confusion, he was now quiet and barely moving. He stared ahead, only the faint twitching of his muzzle betraying that he was still alive.

Lungkaju pushed a glove over the wound to try and stem the bleeding. But it was no use. The puddle had already swollen out around his knees, staining the moss and draining in-between the rocks. "I cannot save him," he said, his rage turned to disbelief. "I cannot save him."

Slowly, he pulled the glove away from the wound. The gush of blood was now a trickle. He wrapped his arms tightly around Fenris's body. Burying his face into the side of his friend's neck, he spoke softly to him in Nganasan until the flow stopped altogether.

Callum hugged onto Darya as she wept against his shoulder. Ava slumped to the floor beside them and dropped her face into her hands.

The minutes ticked by before Lungkaju's head rose up and he took a deep breath. By now the sun's rays were beating their way through the mist, carving the remaining vapour into pockets around him.

He turned from Fenris to face the others. His eyes were red, his bronze skin streaked with blood. He reached a shaking hand inside his parka, withdrew his flask and took a deep draught.

"I told him it was just bad dreams."

Chapter 12

LAZARUS TAXON

1

Peterson burst up out of the swell. Before he could take stock, the current had thrust him against the side of the natural harbour. He scrabbled for a hold. His fingers dug in and he clung on as a second swell tried to grate his body like a lump of mozzarella up against the rock. As it receded, he took his chance and hauled himself up the side.

His sense of déjà vu was immediate; he half-expected Volkov to be stood smoking in the shadows once again, to step, laughing, from the gloom and finish him off with a voice-distorted cackle and a bullet to the head. But this time there was no cigarette end. He was alone and the white sub was nowhere to be seen.

After blacking out and falling into the water, the freezing temperature had shocked him back to consciousness. His instinct had been to resurface immediately for air. But he had fought it. The last thing he'd wanted was to be fished, defenceless, out of the swell by that monster Volkov and tortured into complicity. He'd rather have drowned. Fuelled by a mixture of panic and rage, his mind had worked quickly. He had propelled himself under the *Centaur*, feeling his way towards the anchor point. Then he had slid between the nose of the craft and the natural harbour.

He didn't have long. That much was obvious. He was bleeding, freezing and drowning all at the same time. Without a chance in hell of seeing anything through the dark water, he began a desperate clawing around the *Centaur's* hull. He knew exactly what he was looking for, but unless he found it soon, it would all be over.

His lungs clamoured for air as his hands scrabbled across the metal panelling. His fingers searched and searched, finally catching against a shallow indent. He tugged at it, and it pulled down to form a handle. His heart leapt. He searched out the second handle. It too pulled down and he grabbed both, twisted them and forced the hatch open. He felt the rush of the water as it flooded into the cavity, urging him with it, and he squeezed himself in through the gap.

As long as the *Centaur* was upright, the chamber had been designed to only partially submerge in the event of a breach. In true scientific fashion, it was less an issue of buoyancy for the sake of the crew, and more one of preserving the delicate internal systems; research first, people second. As his head burst up into the pocket of air, Peterson couldn't have cared less why it was there. He just gulped it down, lungful after heavenly lungful. All the while he clung to the upper of three wide storage ledges, the same one, he noted darkly, on which he had stored the explosive all those weeks ago.

He mustered what strength he could and dragged himself clear of the water. The image of Doctor Lebedev's shivering, hypothermic body still fresh in his mind, he began removing his wet clothes. The proximity of the engine meant that the air inside the chamber was warm against his skin. He was lucky. Ordinarily, the temperature would have been artificially lowered in order to preserve whatever samples had been taken.

No longer drowning or freezing, he turned his attention to the bullet wound. It was pitch dark inside the compartment, but he could feel that the bullet had passed through the strait of flesh between the bottom of his ribcage and the top of his pelvis. His grasp of human anatomy was pretty damn weak. He knew that one of his kidneys was probably somewhere in that area. The side of his guts too. But to what extent either had been damaged, he had no idea. He started by using his undershirt as a compress. God only knew how much blood he'd lost already.

There was a sudden thud above him and he froze. As he listened in silence, the sound was followed by a series of lighter thuds that could only have been one thing. Footsteps.

Peterson could feel his already pounding heart beat faster at the thought of that psychopath Volkov boarding *his* sub and dicking with *his* controls. He needed to calm down or he would quickly bleed out. He took a deep breath and fought to clear his mind. *Nam Myoho Renge Kyo, Nam Myoho Renge Kyo, Nam Myoho Renge Kyo...*

There was a burst of hammering, no doubt as Volkov began ransacking the place. It was clear what he was looking for: the data stick from which the virus had been uploaded. He'd want it so that he could get his people to design him an anti-virus. If the pain in Peterson's side hadn't been busy reaching climax, he'd have laughed. The thought of him leaving something like that just lying around in the sub was plain ridiculous. It may have looked like a shitty little hunk of plastic, but it was anything but. What its circuitry contained was just about priceless.

The noises got louder and louder as the futility of the search seemed to dawn on Volkov. The clanging culminated in a series of loud bangs as he kicked out at various parts of the interior and launched into a tirade. Despite it being in Russian, Peterson got the gist of it loud and clear: *I'm the richest most powerful asshole in the world and I AM PISSED!*

Two gunshots rang out. No doubt the crazy sonofabitch was trying to disable the sub's operating systems. With a final enraged growl, he pounded his way up the ladder and slammed the exit hatch behind him. The impact vibrated throughout the craft's framework and Peterson found himself shuddering, not with the sensation, but with anger.

There was another sound, this time a low rumble. It was an engine and it wasn't the *Centaur*'s. Volkov must have been leaving in his own sub. Peterson listened to the noise increase and then peter out, as the craft submerged and passed towards the cavern's exit. Then silence.

He remained where he was. Having somehow kept alive this long, he didn't want to blow it all by risking a move too soon. He was smart, but so far Volkov had proven himself a hell of a lot smarter. What if the sound of him leaving was all just a ploy designed to flush him out? What if he left the safety of the specimen chamber now and resurfaced in the inlet only to see the white sub anchored up next to the exit tunnel and the end of Volkov's pistol pointed at his face once again?

And what if his injury was worse than he realised? For all he knew, he might not even have the energy to pull himself up out of the damn water. Say he did. What then? From the sounds of it the *Centaur* was going nowhere fast, and without it neither was he.

He looked at his watch. The pale glow of the twelve increments and two hands was the only source of illumination in the whole chamber. *One hour.* An hour from then, and whether or not he'd managed to formulate a plan, if there was still breath in his body then he would make his move. Sure, it was a gamble. He'd have more chance of treating his wound with the first aid equipment in the cabin. But he was still conscious, wasn't he? And the bleeding had seemed to be under control. It was a gamble he'd been willing to take.

The inside of the *Centaur* was as he'd expected. Her storage compartments had been turned out and several of the doors had been ripped from their hinges, their contents spread around the cabin floor. He could also make out the two bullet holes, one in the heart of the instrument panel, the other in the centre of the navigation screen.

He set about dressing his wound properly. It was the first time he'd been able to see it and it was clear just what a lucky sonofabitch he'd been. Having dressed it as best he could, he bolted a double dose of painkillers and turned his attention to patching up the *Centaur*.

"Your turn, old girl," he whispered, unscrewing the top of the console. "Here's hoping you're in a better way than yours truly."

The sight that greeted him was bittersweet. Volkov had obviously known what he was doing. The bullet had scored a direct hit on the primary control system. But Peterson could also see that the damage was far from irreparable. He checked for the emergency repair kit in the narrow compartment beneath the console, and found it unmolested. Having been drilled in the finer points of emergency sub surgery, he was confident that the console would be no problem. A few replacement parts here, a touch of solder there, and he'd have her up and running again in no time.

The navigation screen was a different matter. On inspection, the circuitry was ruined beyond repair, and that was a genuine handicap. He would have no instrumentation readouts, no GPS or mapping capabilities, no proximity sensor or statistical information display. Yet as lousy as it was, none of those things were show-stoppers. As long as the *Centaur* was up and running, he would just have to handle her the old-fashioned way. Instinct.

He set to work. Time ticked by as he focussed himself on the task at hand, stripping out the damaged components, fixing in the replacements, rewiring and testing his connections, just as he'd been taught. Just as he'd practised, again and again and again…

When he next checked his watch he could see that nearly two hours had passed. Another half an hour and he had reaffixed the top of the console and seated himself back in the operator's chair. It was the moment of truth. With a cursory prayer, he flicked the primary control switch.

The standby lights on the instrument panel lit up as one, accompanied by a soft whirr. It was music to Peterson's ears. Not even the blank navigation screen could dampen his sense of achievement. He was one step closer to catching up with Volkov and then... well, then he'd have to improvise. The asshole was armed, dangerous and clearly insane. What he planned to do next, Peterson had no idea. But one thing was clear as piss in snow. He would be after the data stick. And that landed the surviving EIA team members in a whole world of shit. Why the hell had he left the damn thing with Ava in the first place? The answer was there, somewhere between his stomach and his brain, but it was beyond his ability to articulate. All he knew now was that the thought of her in danger because of his foolishness, left him sub-zero.

He turned the dial to prime the engine. The little semicircle of LED striations lit up a vibrant green one after another, indicating a full charge. He reached out, grabbed the power-up handle and slid it forward until the engine burst into life. The cabin shook with the sudden power surge. Then it stilled, leaving only the familiar hum of the electrical systems as the power switched from auxiliary to main.

Slowly, carefully, he retracted the mechanical arms and took the *Centaur* down.

2

The mist had lifted. As far as Callum was concerned, whatever beauty he may once have seen in the glacier, the ridge and the rugged valleys and foothills had lifted with it. The swathes of red and yellow moss along the distant coastlines made him think of blood and bile. The green moss, which was much more frequent inland, looked like rot on the face of a blackened corpse. The air smelt stale, and the retreating mist had left behind a crust of rime, which crunched like brittle bone underfoot.

With Darya's help, he had used a wodge of undershirt and his belt to make a temporary tourniquet for his leg. It was a deep puncture midway up on his thigh. But despite all the blood, it seemed to have missed his major arteries.

When they had rescued what kit they could from the emergency tent, Lungkaju removed the tourniquet, disinfected the wound and began to apply a proper field dressing.

"I'm sorry," Callum said. "I should've warned you sooner about those things."

"It is not your fault," Lungkaju replied, taking a swig from his flask. "It is my fault for not killing it."

For a time, neither man spoke.

Callum: "Fenris saved my life."

Lungkaju sighed deeply and forced a smile. "I told you he liked you, Doctor Ross." He paused to begin wrapping the bandage. "He was a good dog. A good friend."

Callum placed a hand on his shoulder.

"I do not want those things to eat him," Lungkaju said suddenly.

Callum stared at him. "I'm not sure I understand."

Lungkaju's voice had regained its natural command, but his eyes were still swollen with grief. "We cannot bury him in this rock and there is no wood to make a fire. But I cannot just leave him here... for them."

"We can build a cairn," Callum said.

"A cairn?"

"A tomb. Out of rocks." He picked up a nearby boulder. "Last time I checked, we're not short on these."

Lungkaju seemed to consider it for a moment as he wrapped the final length of bandage and fastened it above the knee. "Will you help me, Doctor Ross?"

Callum and Lungkaju carried Fenris from where he lay and, with the help of the others, wrapped him up in a length of tent fabric. They lowered him into a natural hollow at the base of a promontory. Lungkaju removed his pendant bearing the carving of Ngana'bta, placed it on top of his friend's body and said goodbye. Then, taking it in turns to stand guard, they began collecting boulders and packing them into the hollow around the body. When the ground was level, they began building up.

As the last of the tent fabric disappeared, Lungkaju started to sing. It was a haunting melody, sombre, beautiful. Though Callum couldn't understand the meaning, the sound itself spoke to him.

They worked tirelessly, packing stone after stone onto the mound. All four of them threw themselves into the activity, slotting the chunks of broken stone together to create something lasting. Even Ava seemed to lose her fear temporarily, finding focus in the raising of the cairn.

When it was somewhere between knee and waist height, Lungkaju stopped singing. The sudden absence of his song was deafening and it brought the others to a standstill. Their muscles ached and their breath steamed into the air.

"Thank you, my friends," he announced. "But that is enough."

After passing around the water canteen, they stood silently before the grave.

It was Lungkaju who eventually broke the silence. In a low tone, he said, "Just promise me one thing, Doctor Ross."

Callum waited.

"If you ever come back here, please do not dig up my dog."

Callum had no idea whether he was serious or not, until the shade of a grin broke out across his face and he let out a chuckle.

As much with relief as anything, Callum joined in. "You have my word," he said.

After resting briefly the group gathered up what provisions they could. "The compound is only three or four hours' walk from here," Lungkaju said, shouldering his pack. He turned to Callum. "How is your leg?"

"Nothing a handful of painkillers won't fix."

"If it gets worse then you must tell me," Lungkaju said. "I may need to change the dressing or it could get infected."

"Where is Ava?" Darya asked suddenly.

"I'm over here."

The three of them turned to see that she had wandered away unnoticed and was now on her knees, pouring over one of the dead creatures.

"Ava, *solnishko*, we need to leave," Darya called.

"Sure thing," she replied. "Only, if anyone's interested, I think I can put a name to these damn ugly faces."

The three exchanged a glance, then hurried to her side.

285

"You know what they are?" Darya asked.

"I think I might just do. Though I hardly believe it."

Callum was shocked to see that she had her hands virtually inside the dead creature's mouth. It rang of that same academic tenacity he'd witnessed in Darya when she'd examined the polar bear. "So what's the story?"

She prised its jaws open wider and began examining its teeth. She placed the thumb and forefinger of her hand around one of them to form a frame. "Do you recognise that?" she asked, looking up at him.

"Do I recognise it? Of course I recognise it. Over the last twenty-four hours, we've become rather well acquainted."

"No," she said, scowling. "Do you recognise the shape of it? The shape of the tooth?"

Callum made up his mind to humour her. He knelt down and stared at the selected tooth. Viewing it up close, it did look familiar. But where had he seen it before? His eyes followed the shark fin-like outline, with the apically oriented serrations…

"It looks like one of those fossilised teeth," he said, suddenly. "Like the one you gave me back on the *Albanov*. Only bigger."

She smiled at him. "I knew you'd remember."

He laughed reflexively. "So what are you saying? That this is a dinosaur?"

"Not *per se*," she replied. "You probably wouldn't've seen these exact same creatures walking around back in the Cretaceous, but I reckon you'd've seen their direct ancestors alright. And my guess is they'd've looked pretty similar."

There was a silence. Not for the first time, Callum, Darya and Lungkaju stared at Ava as if waiting for a punchline. When none came, Callum asked, "A type of evolved dinosaur?"

She nodded. "That's one way of putting it."

3

Callum turned to the others. Their expressions looked the way he imagined his did: a cocktail of wonder, concern and outright disbelief.

"An evolved dinosaur? And you're basing this entirely on the shape of the teeth?"

"Don't be ridiculous," Ava replied. Just as when she'd spoken about the concretions earlier that day, all trace of fear had vanished from her voice. She talked plainly and passionately, as if presenting a lecture. "I know how this probably sounds, and trust me, if I was you I'd be thinking exactly the same thing. Hell, part of me's thinking it right now. *What a fruit cake! She must be delusional with fear or hunger or thirst or whatever the hell you're thinking! Am I right?"*

For a while nobody spoke. Then Callum said, "Ava, nobody thinks—"

"Ah, of course you do! But just remember that I was chosen for this project because I'm one of the best in my field. There are few people that know prehistoric fauna like I do. And I'm also an academic. Credibility is everything to me. I trade on it, same as you, Doctor Ross. I don't go around making claims that I don't *one*, believe in and *two*, have at least a reasonable evidential basis for."

"I know that you are very good scientist, Ava," Darya said. "But what you suggest is that these creatures survived extinction event and lived in small isolated community for tens of millions of years after this. I'm sorry, but I do not think that this is possible."

"I agree it's hard to swallow," Ava replied. "But it's actually entirely possible. Look. I think this creature may have evolved from a very specific late Cretaceous therapod known as Troodon. We've found plenty of troodontid fossils. I've pieced many of them together myself, so I'm pretty familiar with their anatomy. They seem to share the attributes of two different genera, the ornithomimids and the dromaeosaurs."

She ran her hand along the top of the creature's pale grey snout. "The ornithomimids were anatomically very similar to modern-day flightless birds, African ostriches and emus, Australian cassowaries, and South American rheas. They had long, slender beaks rather than snouts. Their skeletons were lightly built. Their bodies were compact and their legs were long, allowing them to move with incredible speed."

"Not bad jumpers either," Callum said.

She pursed her lips in agreement. "They also had long necks and a comparatively small skull."

Callum frowned. "I wouldn't call that a small skull."

"I agree," Ava replied, patting the side of the dead creature's cranium. "That's where the dromaeosaur characteristics take over. Dromaeosaur anatomy was similar to that of the ornithomimids – gracile body, long necks, long legs – but their skulls were much more in proportion, allowing for increased brain size and intelligence."

She turned from the creature's head and dragged her hand slowly down the line of the hind leg. Stopping at the ankle, she now placed her fingers over the retracted toe claw. With her hand for scale, it was clear that the formidable-looking weapon was at least seven or eight curved inches. She eased it cautiously forward and released it, letting it spring back into position. "Troodontids can also thank their dromaeosaur heritage for this little beauty."

She went to continue, then noticed the uncomfortable look on Lungkaju's face and moved her attention to the creature's forearms. She stretched one out and straightened it at the elbow. "Both ornithomimids and dromaeosaurs had long arms, but dromaeosaurs in particular had these long, slender fingers, tipped with curving claws. They were certainly capable of grasping objects palm to palm, and they were arguably even more dexterous."

"And the massive eyes?" Callum asked, trying not to think about those dextrous claws digging into his shoulders. "Do we have dromaeosaurs to thank for those as well?"

"No," Ava replied. "Those are all Troodon's. They're what allowed him to hunt so effectively in the dark and probably to out-compete his dromaeosaur cousins. If you notice, they're forward-facing as well. This would've given another big advantage. Stereoscopic vision."

"And the feathers?" Darya said. "This is new development?"

"Feathers are just highly developed scales," Ava replied. "With advances in technology over the last decade or so, we've been able to discern that lots of later therapods had them. With feathers, some species of oviraptor now look so similar to birds that there are calls for them to be reclassified *as* birds."

"Could they fly?" Darya asked.

"No." Ava plucked a couple of longer plumes from the underside of the creature's arm and handed them to her. "Some species evolved to fly, of course, eventually surviving on the wing. But for the non-avian dinosauria, they served a number of different purposes; almost certainly display, increased thermo-regulatory capability, perhaps, and in the case of Troodon, plain old aerodynamics. His long tail gave him an exceptional sense of balance whilst moving, but he could also use those underarm feathers in particular to give him increased manoeuvrability when running down prey at high speed. For example, he could manipulate them to help him make rapid adjustments in speed and direction, to corner more sharply."

"So kind of like the flaps on a modern aircraft wing."

"Pretty much," she replied. "They were really a wonder of predator evolution. Only sharks come anywhere close in terms of streamlined predatory potential, hence their success."

After fanning through the individual fibres, Darya passed the creature's feathers to Callum. He looked them over then went to pass them to Lungkaju, who just shook his head.

Ava continued, "As I've already explained to Doctor Ross, we know that a northern troodontid population emerged here in the high Arctic and it grew to be genetically distinct from the main genus. It grew even bigger, faster, stronger and more intelligent. Its visual acuity seems to have increased dramatically, and its teeth and jaws developed to allow it to exploit a wider range of foodstuffs."

"I'm pretty sure the creatures that attacked me and Darya this morning were chasing fish before they were chasing us," Callum said.

"That's entirely plausible. Probable even," she replied. "As Doctor Lebedev will know, if there's one food source which remains abundant year-round in the Arctic, it's marine life. If I'm not mistaken, the polar bear, the known apex Arctic predator, subsists almost entirely on seal meat. At any rate, all of these adaptations allowed Troodon not only to survive but to thrive in harsh Arctic conditions." She laughed. "It's remarkable when you think about it. This is one of the harshest environments on earth – adverse climate, limited food supply, long periods of complete darkness. But it was nothing evolution couldn't handle."

"This is true," Darya said. "And what you say makes lot of

sense. But surviving in the Arctic is very different to surviving mass extinction that kills almost every living thing."

Ava smiled. "You'd think so. But it's not necessarily all that different. Whichever version of the extinction event you subscribe to, in all likelihood the thing that finished off those remnant dinosaur populations – the animals that weren't killed immediately, that is – was a long volcanic winter. The huge quantities of ash thrown up into the atmosphere, be it from volcanoes, a meteor, whatever, would've blocked out the sun, plunging the earth into darkness and cold. It would've been like one long polar night, one that would've lasted years, maybe even decades. Without light, most florae would've died away. Herbivorous fauna would have perished, and with no fresh meat on the menu, the carnivores were next, unless—"

"They'd already adapted to similarly harsh conditions," Callum said.

"Precisely. It's like I was telling you before, Doctor Ross. The idea that some species of dinosauria may have slipped through the Cretaceous-Tertiary boundary is nothing new. I've been advocating it most of my career. But I'll admit, I never would've expected *that* species, or any derived from it, to have survived all the way through to present."

"Sixty-five million years is a hell of an innings," Callum said.

Ava nodded. "Damn straight. If it's true, then it'd make this creature a member of a very exclusive club: one of the most successful faunal species known to man." While talking, she had manoeuvred herself around to face the others, perching herself on the creature's torso as if it were now no more than a beanbag. Her eyes were alive with discovery, her cheeks flushed with colour. "It's not unprecedented, though. It's what's known as a Lazarus Taxon."

"A Lazarus Taxon?"

"After Lazarus in the bible, the guy Christ was supposed to have resurrected. Palaeontologists use the term to refer to groups of animals, taxa, that go AWOL from the fossil record only to reappear alive and well." She looked to Darya. "You've heard of the coelacanth?"

She nodded. "It is type of fish found in only two places in the world, the east coast of Africa and the north coast of Sulawesi, Indonesia. I know it is very old order of fish."

"Cretaceous old," Ava said. "And it's a classic Lazarus Taxon. The coelacanth turned up frequently in the Mesozoic fossil record, just like troodontids, and everybody assumed that it subsequently went extinct. Then a museum curator observed one caught in a fisherman's net back in the 1930s. Turned out local peoples had been fishing coelacanth out of the water for generations. Anyway, the point is they survived."

"I wonder how did they manage this," Darya said.

"A combination of being hardy and just plain managing to go unnoticed is my guess," Ava replied. "Food and temperature requirements have continued to restrict their range, which in turn has limited their numbers, keeping them rare. They're extremely long-lived, up to a hundred years, and they're also reclusive by nature. They spend most of their lives hiding out in deep underwater caves. The life of a coelacanth is so well camouflaged, even time itself overlooked them."

"You think these Troodon successors have evolved along the same lines?" Callum asked.

"Isn't it obvious? This island is the ideal place for a species like this to have carved out their own successful little niche. Its remoteness means that it was the last landmass on earth to be discovered by modern man, and as far as we know," she looked to him, "the place has never been properly settled by humans."

"As far as we know," he agreed.

A satisfied smile appeared on her face. "It's remarkable. All the elements have come together to preserve these creatures. A remote wilderness, virtually untouched by humans precisely because of the hostility of the environment, and a creature perfectly evolved to exploit those conditions in self-sufficient isolation."

"Until now, Doctor Lee," Lungkaju said. "Until now."

He had been quiet for so long, just listening to Ava speaking, that the sudden sound of his voice, like the end of his singing, made an impact. He cocked his rifle. "But I think that whatever these creatures are, we should not wait here for them any longer."

Chapter 13

THE COMPOUND

1

The ice had melted. The ground had thawed. The compound itself was unchanged. It was just as Koikov had left it when he, Sharova and Yudina had first raced to Dolgonosov's aid.

Koikov shuddered and reached for a papirosa. *Shit!* Only two left in the carton. He lit up, inhaled deeply and began refamiliarising himself with the layout. The remaining buildings were arranged in a grid pattern to the west of the partially constructed runway. There were seven in total: four dilapidated huts and three Nissen-style hangars, rusted semi-cylinders beaten into disrepair by the extreme conditions.

The three concrete heads of the interconnected bunker system sat to the east. The forklift was still parked out front, forks lowered towards the entrance, a snapshot of the moment Koikov had first heard Dolgonosov's screams. In the background, the remains of the fixed crane towered over the northern end of the runway, its cross arm drooping down at around forty-five degrees. The surrounding area was still strewn with chemical drums.

He revved the hovercraft and descended towards the compound. It may not have been much, but it was shelter.

Sitting next to him, Marchenko said, "The men are exhausted."

"Me too," Koikov replied, surprised at his own openness. "My nerves are as close to being shot as I can remember." He spat over his shoulder. "What's the ammunition situation?"

"Depleted."

"Check the numbers. I want to know exactly what we're playing with."

He pulled up next to the bunkers, dismounted and watched as his team jumped out the back and formed up. To a man, they were wide-eyed and pale, their white combat uniforms daubed with streaks and swirls of dried blood. He did a quick headcount. Fourteen. Only fourteen of them had survived the mist, including himself and Marchenko. Fourteen men. A day on Harmsworth and over half his team were already dead.

Koikov's mind replayed the horror of the last few hours. It had been a fucked-up scene, carnage cloaked in white. The creatures had encircled them. There might have been twenty, two hundred or two thousand. Even with LVV there was no telling. They had moved too fast, bolting in through the circle of men and inflicting what wounds they could before disappearing again. It was classic hit and run. If he hadn't been on the receiving end, Koikov would've felt nothing but admiration. But he had been. And after the longest hour of his life, the enemy had simply melted away with the mist.

He addressed what remained of his team. "Home sweet home."

No reaction. Just the same rank of sunken faces. He thought about trying to reassure them, but they were way past it. "Okay, this is how it's going to work. Marchenko. Take Khabensky and two others. Go search for a radio transmitter. There must be one here. Without reliable external communications, they'd all have gone nuts."

"Yes, Starshyna. Turov, Dubrovsky, with me."

"Corporal Voronkov. I want you and Zyryonov up on top of that ridge over there." He pointed to the moraine where Private

Dolgonosov should've stayed put. "Regular comms, you hear me? And don't you even think about moving from that post. Dragons and mist are what you're looking for. You see so much as a flash of white that isn't clearly a seagull and I want to know about it."

"Yes, Starshyna."

"Ivanov. We need a medic and you're it. I want you to take care of Private Tsaritsyn."

Tsaritsyn was laid out in the back of the hovercraft, his stomach crudely bandaged, barely conscious. Koikov removed his glove and placed a hand over the young man's forehead. It was cold and clammy. He was no expert, but he could see that the abdominal wounds were serious, probably mortal. Tsaritsyn's condition was deteriorating fast. "Do what you can for him. If all you can do is keep him warm and comfortable, then that's what you do. Private Koshkin. You assist."

He turned back to face the remainder of the team. "The rest of you, I know you're tired and I know you're hungry, but I want the drums removed from these bunkers," he gestured to the semi-subterranean structure, "and sorted into two stacks, empty and full."

"What about the half-empties?" Corporal Aliyev asked.

"You mean the half-fulls," Koikov replied. "Positive is all we've got out here, Corporal, so do me a favour and suck its dick. Count them with the full ones. And Aliyev, you take charge here while I'm gone."

"Gone where, Starshyna?"

"Recruitment drive," Koikov replied. "Private Gergiev, with me."

2

While Turov and Dubrovsky were checking out the other Nissen shelters, Marchenko and Khabensky had searched three of the four huts and found precisely fuck all. Hastily constructed out of breeze block and corrugated iron sheeting, the remnant barrack blocks were sparsely furnished with rows of wall-mounted wooden bunks. Construction debris and other oddments cluttered their interiors – abandoned items of clothing, cigarette packets, even the remains of a broken dartboard. Something large, hopefully a bear, had made a nest in the back corner of one. But so far there was no sign of any radio equipment.

"This place looks more like a prison colony," Khabensky said. His blond hair was smeared with grime, and his eyes were pale and bloodshot.

"My thoughts exactly," Marchenko replied. He approached the door to the fourth building and kicked it in. The sound of the timber splintering echoed around the compound. Once inside, he could see that the internal layout was different. A large table was positioned centrally and desks were pushed up against the walls. The door to the rear partition was still in place and it led through into a narrow back room.

"Bingo!" Marchenko said. "It's the comms room."

"But there's nothing here, Sergeant."

Khabensky was right. The long, wall-mounted wooden surface in front of them bore nothing but a few scraps of old timber and the fingerprints of former items thrown into relief by the dust.

"It looks like they've taken most of the portable comms equipment," Marchenko said. "But I doubt they bothered with the antenna."

"What antenna?"

Marchenko turned his attention to a room-height timber unit jutting from the wall to the right. He pounded at one side of it until it shifted and creaked open on a concealed hinge, exposing a transmitter mast.

"It's retractable," he said. "The conditions out here get too bad for a fixed mast."

"Does it still extend?"

Marchenko fiddled with the control toggle. "It was meant to be electronic, but there must be a manual override here somewhere." He felt around the back of the mast and his fingers fell upon a handle that had seized up with cold. "Khabensky, see if you can shift this while I give Koikov the news."

Khabensky started work loosening the handle.

"Starshyna, this is Marchenko. Over."

There was a pause before: "Give me good news, Sergeant."

"I've located the comms room."

"Does the equipment still function?"

"The equipment's gone, Starshyna."

There was another pause, before: "I said give me *good* news!"

"The good news is that the transmitter mast is still in place. If we can get it extended then I can try and adapt a tactical radio and transmit over an extended range."

"The tactical radio signal is weak as fly piss."

"But we only need to reach the base at Nagurskoye. It's 250 kilometres as the crow flies and I'm pretty certain I can boost the signal. Then it's just a matter of finding the right frequency."

There was silence before: "If you think it's doable then do it. If it doesn't work then gather your team and rejoin the others at the bunker. Out."

* * *

When Koikov returned he could see that the rest of the team had made a good start at removing the chemical drums from the bunker and stacking them as ordered.

"The majority are either full or *half full*, Starshyna," Corporal Aliyev reported.

"Good, that's how I remember it," Koikov replied. "We need to gather up any others that are lying around as well."

Aliyev's brow furrowed. "Why? The bunkers are nearly clear. We've got shelter."

"True," Koikov replied. "But then what? I'm not about to just sit in there and wait for the mist to come back. Are you?"

Aliyev said nothing.

"We need to make what's left of our ammunition count. I say we use the empty drums as a defensive barricade and set the full drums up at regular stations to form a series of perimeters. Concentric perimeters." He mimed taking a shot with his rifle and then brought his hands apart to signal an exploding drum. "If those things want another fight, then this time it's on our terms."

Aliyev's expression remained stolid. "You realise shifting all these things around is going to take time and manpower? Perhaps more than we've got."

"Marchenko's sending Turov and Dubrovsky back to help, and I'm here as well. Also—"

There was a sudden rumbling noise behind them, followed by the screech of metal on metal. Both men turned and watched as first the bucket, then the arm and then the body of an enormous mechanical excavator appeared over the head of the bunker. The roof of the cabin was easily three or four metres off the ground and the massive arm was laced with vein-like wires, pipes and pistons.

"I clocked her when I was out here before, cleaning the place up," Koikov said. "Must've been left behind when the whole project went to shit."

The corporal's face flushed with wonder as the machine's chest-height tracks clunked and rattled their way around the side of the concrete and came to a stop. The arm lowered down, pressing the teeth of the metal bucket into the permafrost. The cabin door swung open and Private Gergiev poked his beefy, oil-smeared face around the side and cracked his knuckles. "Anybody call for backup?"

Koikov turned to Aliyev. "This should speed things up, Corporal. We can balance two, maybe three drums in the bucket with each run and we can lash another two or three to the cabin. We can fit at least another three in the Czilim and another on the forklift."

Gergiev left the machine idling and climbed down from the cabin to join them.

"Are you confident you can operate that thing?" Koikov asked him.

He grinned and cracked his knuckles again. "The controls are simple enough. The pedals work the tracks, the handles control the arm and bucket. It's not rocket science."

"So let's get the fuck on with it," Koikov said.

3

"The thing that really amazes me," Ava was saying, "is their ability to change colour. Just like a chameleon. It's a startling adaptation, I can't think of any other parallels in nature. Contemporary nature, that is."

Two hours had passed since they had left the remains of the campsite and she had talked about the creatures more or less continuously the whole time. Under the circumstances that was a good thing. Her obsessive scientific focus was probably all that was keeping her from seizing up with panic. In complete contrast, Lungkaju had kept himself to himself, walking ahead of the others, sipping at regular intervals from his hipflask. Without a word, he had navigated them around the southern edge of the Hjalmar Ridge and into the south-west of the island.

"There are no parallels for this in modern birds, or mammals," Darya said. "Only in reptiles, amphibians and marine cephalopods. Chameleons are obvious example, but also some species of cuttlefish, squid and the mimic octopus, are changing their skin colour by manipulating their chromatophores, the cells that contain the pigment."

"Why not birds and mammals?" Callum asked.

"This is because fur and feathers are made of dead cells,

like human hair and fingernails," she replied. "Their properties cannot be changed. To change colour, birds and mammals must produce whole new coat. It is why they moult."

Ava looked confused. "So how do *they* do it then?"

Darya shook her head. "I am not sure of this, but I know that it is not the feathers that are changing. I think it is probably the skin. The feathers from the dead creature were without colour."

Callum remembered the dull translucent fibres that Ava had handed him, like lengths of frayed fibre-optic cable.

"I think the feathers act only like magnifying glass," Darya continued, "reflecting underlying skin colour."

"Fascinating," Ava said. "It's the sort of thing that our current scientific techniques could never pick up on in fossils. Things have advanced so quickly over the last few years that it's now possible to detect trace colour signatures in fossilised material. So we can say, for example, what colour triceratops was. Isn't that crazy? But, I mean, even that technique is still in its nascency. The ability to detect a colour-shifting capacity simply doesn't exist yet."

"It makes you wonder," Callum said.

"Wonder what?"

"What other basic assumptions we've got wrong."

"You bet it does," Ava replied. "If there's going to be one beneficiary of all this, it's going to be science. Science is going to learn a hell of a lot from Harmsworth. And I don't just mean in terms of palaeontology." She paused then added, "That is, if we ever make it out of here."

Her words lingered in the cold. Then, to everyone's surprise, she began to laugh.

"What is funny?" Darya asked.

"I'm sorry," she said. "It's just that the more I think about these creatures, the less surprised I am that they've survived, you know?"

Callum hummed agreement. "Such a versatile species, it's strange that they've never made it off the island."

"Who's to say they haven't?"

There was silence once more.

"You think they have?"

"I think it's entirely possible. But no, as it happens, I don't think they have."

"If it's possible for them to leave then what's stopping them?"

"Perhaps nothing's stopping them," she replied. "There's nothing stopping me from stripping down naked and doing a handstand right here and now." She smiled wryly. "But you'll agree that there's a big difference between what's possible and what's desirable."

Callum thought about replying, but in the end he just smiled back.

"Of course it's possible for these creatures to have left Harmsworth," she continued. "You said that you'd observed them swimming."

"You make it sound as if they weren't trying to kill me at the time."

"You know what I mean."

"Okay, yes, Darya and I observed them in the water."

"So even without the pack-ice land bridge, the fact is they could've left anytime." She paused then added, "But the real question, Doctor Ross, isn't why *wouldn't* they leave, it's why *would* they? They've evolved to exploit this very particular environment. They've got everything they need to survive here."

"You think they're territorial?"

"I don't think it's as simple as passive genetic attachment to a home range. I think it's based on active decision-making."

"You give them great intelligence," Darya said.

Ava nodded. "I think they're probably incredibly smart. Smarter than some people I've known, that's for sure."

Darya looked as unconvinced as ever. "Do you get this from the size of the brain? Because this is not always reliable."

"It's not just that," she replied. "I mean, let's look at the evidence. The creature that attacked us in the tent came in through the door. But Lungkaju closed it after he left."

Callum shuddered at the memory of turning to see those bottomless eyes staring across at him, appearing to read and reread his thoughts. "It undid the zip."

"It unfastened the zipper," Ava repeated. "It could've slashed its way in, but it was smart enough to know that it could get the drop on us better if it entered the same way we did."

"So it is work out how to operate the zip," Darya said, unimpressed. "But many animal species are problem-solving: primates, chimps, orangutans, gorillas. Also dolphins and the octopus are very intelligent problem-solvers."

"Am I right thinking that all of those creatures learn by mimicry?"

"This is true," Darya said. "It is the same for human beings when they do not have direct instruction from another. They copy those around them."

"I don't think it was trial and error," Callum said. "The zip slid open nice and smooth. At first I thought it was Lungkaju."

"So that leaves mimicry," Ava said. "*Mimesis.* The creature must have seen the zip being operated, learnt the process and remembered it."

"How could this be?" Darya asked. "This is the first time anybody uses their tent on the island."

Ava's silence brought a chill to Callum's chest. "You think it was watching us, don't you? Studying our behaviour."

"I think it saw Lungkaju leave, yes. And I think it saw how he operated the zip."

Darya frowned. "If it saw Lungkaju leave, why did it not attack him? Why would it just let him walk away?"

"Precisely," she answered. "It *discerned*. And that's the one thing above all else that convinces me we're dealing with a highly intelligent animal here. It didn't just savage the first one of us that it saw. It watched. It waited. It selected a target. Again, that would require an active, decision-making intelligence. Much like ours."

"It reacted when you pointed the rifle at it as well," Callum said. "It knew that the rifle represented danger."

"Perhaps this is why it is not attack Lungkaju in the first place," Darya added, "because he carries rifle."

"And the fact that it saw the rifle as a threat suggests that it must've seen one before," Callum said. "It must already have had a run-in with the soldiers."

"Or maybe it is watching when the polar bear was killed."

"Either way, it's learning," Ava said.

Darya cast her eyes around the undulating rock that stretched up the valley-side in either direction. "Do you think that they are watching us now?"

Ava: "It's possible. But by now I think it's pretty clear that they only attack when our vision's impaired."

"You mean when there is mist."

"Since it's cleared, we haven't seen a single one, have we? Again, it's the most intelligent behaviour. Exploit our species weaknesses, in this case our over-reliance on sight."

"They attacked me and Darya in broad daylight," Callum said.

"Yes," Ava admitted, "but on that occasion, I think it was *you* who took *them* by surprise. They weren't actively hunting you, they were fishing."

"You think that they were just protecting their young?"

"Makes sense."

Lungkaju had stopped on a ridge of high ground. As the others arrived at his side, he was busy surveying the route ahead, rifle draped across his forearm, hood fastened tightly around his face. "The compound is only two hours from here."

Callum was surprised at the familiarity of the way ahead. From the gradient, to the meandering channel gouged into the valley bottom, the landscape triggered something. "Why do I remember this place?"

Lungkaju looked thoughtful, as if trying to remember something very specific. Then he replied triumphantly, "*Palaeochannel!* Doctor Ross, it is the old riverbed."

Before Callum could say anything else, Darya asked, "This is the channel that leads to the tunnel? To the ice mummy?"

He nodded.

Ava looked confused. "What in the hell are you all talking about?"

With everything that had happened, she still hadn't heard the story; the discovery of Ngana'bta; the link they'd made between the mummy and the creatures.

Together, he and Darya filled her in.

"You think this guy was killed by the same creatures?" she said. "What, thousands of years ago?"

"All the pieces seem to fit," Callum answered. "In the myth, Ngana'bta was sent to hunt Tansu Taibaa, the lizard bird. To anyone without an exhaustive knowledge of extinct palaeofauna, that's exactly what one of these things would look like. A lizard bird. Then there's the matter of Ngana'bta's legs. Both completely removed above the knee before he was able to escape. These things are clearly more than capable of inflicting that kind of trauma."

Ava seemed to think long and hard before saying, "Can we see it… him? Can we see the mummy?"

Lungkaju frowned. "No, Doctor Lee, we must get to the compound." His words were metered. His expression spoke volumes. Callum was certain that it was only because the gentle Nganasan was so well-mannered that he hadn't replied: *Are you out of your mind, you crazy bitch? Our lives hang in the balance and you want to go sight-seeing!*

"I agree," Darya said. "It would be stupid not to keep going."

Callum could feel their gazes urging him to add his voice to theirs. He opened his mouth to do so. It was a foregone conclusion that he would agree with them, after all. Wasn't it?

Indulging Ava's academic curiosity to keep her moving was one thing. But now was not the time to go straying off course, no matter what…

…but there was another voice inside him. One that he couldn't quiet. A part of him found it not just hard, but impossible to resist the opportunity to see the ice mummy one more time. Was it because he wanted to relive the discovery? Possibly. Or was it to prove that it wasn't all just a figment of his exhausted imagination?

He looked to Lungkaju. "How far is the tunnel?"

"Ten minutes, but Doctor Ross—"

"I know. I know," he said. "But look, we've been walking for a long time. I think that we could all use a rest. Mummy or no mummy, that tunnel is somewhere close by and convenient that we can shelter in."

"My friend, I really do not think that this is sensible," Lungkaju protested. "Doctor Lebedev?"

There was a long silence before Darya replied, "We are all tired. Let us just go and rest in this tunnel for half an hour. No more. Then we go from there straight to the compound with no more stops."

Lungkaju nodded, then stalked away in silence along the valley.

As he followed on, Callum felt a hand press into his.

"I think that you owe me, *solnishko*," Darya said.

He smiled at her. The last few days had taken its toll on all of them, but though her skin was sallow and her eyes heavy with exhaustion, she was as beautiful as ever.

He squeezed her hand. "More than you know."

4

"Marchenko. How long till we're in contact with Nagurskoye?"

"One hour, Starshyna. Two, tops."

"As soon as you're up and running, make the call. Don't fuck around. Don't mention anything about the dragons."

"Starshyna?"

"Repeat. Not a word about the creatures. I don't want them thinking it's all a hoax. Just tell them the *Albanov* went down. All survivors stranded on Harmsworth. Request rescue vehicles to this location immediately and tell them to prepare for casualties."

"Request contact with the mainland, Starshyna?"

"Negative, Marchenko. Keep it simple. Out."

* * *

The entrance to the tunnel did bring the excitement of its first discovery rushing back. Only this time the experience was marred by apprehension. Callum had forgotten how cold the interior was, and he shivered as the chilled fingers of air picked their way into his neckline. That same smell of ancient rock seemed to burn inside his nostrils and the emergency glow stick dangling from his neck emitted a brilliant but eerie green light that cast a whirlpool of shadow around the walls.

"It's a helluva tight squeeze," Ava said, crawling her way in after him.

"It opens out a little up ahead."

With Lungkaju determined to keep a vigil at the entrance, the three of them crawled along the passage, the sound of their every movement amplified. Before long Callum could make out the dark outline of Ngana'bta slumped against the right-hand wall.

"It's just ahead," he called back. "Are you squeamish?"

"After the last couple of days, it'd take a lot to make any of us *squeam*," Ava replied.

Stopping at the head of the mummy, Callum manoeuvred himself around to allow the others to see. Its upturned face was as fascinating and grotesque as he remembered, the vacant glare of the eye cavities both repulsive and mesmerising in the gloom. He watched as the others drew round. "Ladies, meet Ngana'bta."

Ava gasped and held a hand to her mouth as Callum brought the light of the glow stick down over the mummy's face. She spoke through her fingers. "The millennia have not been kind."

"Actually they've been incredibly kind," he said. "Such a superficial level of soft tissue decay after such a long time is remarkable."

"Of course." Her gaze passed from the mummy's face to his torso and down towards his tattered legs. She held her hand out for the glow stick. "May I?"

Callum passed it to her and she began inspecting what remained of the mummy's legs.

"Were these his things?" Darya asked. She was pointing towards the dead bird and pottery shards that had spilt from the fibre bag.

"They must have been," Callum said. "The shards are all the same material, probably from the same broken vessel."

She moved towards the scatter. "And the bird skeleton? Why would he have this?"

"I've no idea," Callum replied. "My guess is it's something to do with shamanism."

"Black magic?"

"Not necessarily evil," he replied. "But something like that."

Darya inspected the skeleton. After a few moments she said, "It was young. I cannot tell species, though. I do not recognise."

Ava's voice rang out suddenly: "Check this out."

Callum and Darya looked over. She was running her fingers over the mummy's frozen leg flesh. "This is interesting."

"You're telling me," Callum said. He moved back to her side. "If we weren't next on the menu, I'm pretty certain he'd be one of the biggest archaeological sensations of our time. In fact—"

"Very interesting indeed," she repeated, completely ignoring him. "This injury was inflicted by an animal alright." She looked up slowly, her face half in lime, half in shadow. "Only it wasn't Troodon."

Callum stared at her. "Are you sure?"

"Absolutely," Ava replied. "For one thing the tooth marks left in the thigh don't match."

He examined the mummy's legs. She was right. The edges of the flesh were stippled with slit-like gouges. *Tooth marks.* He wasn't surprised that they were there, just that he'd missed them when he'd first examined the corpse. "I'll be damned."

"You didn't notice them before?"

He shook his head.

Ava prodded at the frozen flesh, then said, "You got that fossil by any chance?"

Callum unzipped his jacket, reached into his inside pocket and withdrew the small, brown tooth. "I promised Jamie I wouldn't let it out of my sight."

Ava took the serrated triangle and held it against one of the marks in the thigh muscle.

The tooth was smaller. It was also clearly a different shape, thinner and more angular. She handed it back. "You've heard of the principal of bite radius identification?"

Callum shook his head.

"In cases of animal attack, you can typically work out the size of the animal's jaw from its bite radius."

"This is correct," Darya said. "From the size of the jaw you can then work out the size of the animal itself."

"Look." Ava ran her finger across a number of consecutive tooth marks. "You can see an imprint of the arc of the upper jaw here."

Callum looked to where she was pointing at the left-hand thigh. "But there are only four tooth marks," he said, "and they hardly seem to arc at all."

He watched as Ava ran a resolute finger across the marks. But she didn't stop at the edge of the thigh as he'd expected. Instead she crossed over the gap between the two legs and continued along a further line of tooth marks spanning the right-hand thigh. They matched up, forming a much larger arc.

Callum swallowed hard. "I see."

"Whatever made this mark had a large mouth," Ava said, "much bigger than that of Troodon, ergo it was larger."

"So what could it have been?" Callum asked.

In a moment of rare deference, Ava said nothing. She looked to Darya.

"These are not the tooth marks of polar bear," Darya said, "and even if he is giant, the bite is still too large and there is no bigger land carnivore known in the Arctic today." Resignation rang in her voice. "I do not recognise this bite. The only carnivore with bite radius this big would be marine, a large shark. Maybe even orca, killer whale."

Through pursed lips, Ava said, "But we're much too far inland."

"We are now," Callum said, "but sea levels change. Maybe the level was that much higher at the time."

"Could be, though surely such a dramatic change in landform would take longer than a few millennia?"

"Typically, yes," Callum replied. "Still, it's a possibility. Personally, I wouldn't rule anything out in this place."

"No," Darya said. "This you *can* rule out. Only the Greenland shark is living this far north. He is large, but he is not man-eater. Neither is orca, and these are not teeth marks of either. Also this bite is too clean." She examined the bite marks once again, tripping the ends of her fingers across the rank of gouges. "It is mystery."

There followed a brief silence as Ava's gaze left the mummy and she swept a hand back through her matted brown hair. Her brow was furrowed, her expression troubled but sharp in the ghoulish light. "With respect, Doctor Lebedev," she said at last, "we may not be able to name the exact species responsible, but this is no mystery."

Both Callum and Darya looked to her to continue, but she kept quiet. It was typical academic self-indulgence. She was waiting for an invite.

"So?" Callum prompted.

Ava looked from him to Darya. "Isn't it obvious? Even Troodon isn't the apex predator here on Harmsworth."

"Not the apex predator?" Callum repeated.

"There's something else here," she continued. "Something bigger. Something new."

Callum's gut clenched. "You mean something old, don't you?"

Darya's eyes met with his.

"Whatever it is," Ava said, "we just haven't seen it yet."

5

Ava's words echoed round the tunnel.

"You know, I'm really starting to hate this place," Callum said. He was about to speak again when Lungkaju's voice ricocheted towards them. "My friends, it has been long enough. We should be moving on now, please."

"He is right," Darya said. "This is what we agreed." She called out to Lungkaju to let him know that they were heading back.

"I guess we should all be thankful of the distraction," Ava said, setting off after her.

Callum snorted. "Amen to that."

He took one last look at Ngana'bta. A strange feeling washed over him. For a moment, the question of what had killed the ancient warrior was forgotten. Instead it was the idea that he might never be rediscovered, that this might be the last time anybody looked upon his immaculately preserved features that sent the shiver down Callum's spine. And he could hardly bear it. Why the hell hadn't he emailed the photographs he'd taken to the department? If only he'd had a camera now, he could have preserved some kind of record. But he didn't. If by some miracle he survived all this, there would be nothing to take with him but his memories and his word. "I guess some myths are meant to be just that," he whispered. Then he turned to follow the fading corona of light down the tunnel.

But perhaps something more *could* be preserved. Before he could think better of it, he turned back and began carefully peeling the cord bearing the pendant from around the mummy's neck. He placed it around his own and tucked it into his jacket. The teeth and intermittent silver spacers felt freezing against his chest, and the cord itself felt like a snare of ice. Reaching under the mummy's parka, he then eased the sheathed flint blade from the belt and slipped it into his pocket.

"Doctor Ross, are you okay?" came Lungkaju's voice.

With a last glance down at Ngana'bta, Callum turned and set off back along the tunnel.

* * *

Even with the drums removed, the inside of the bunker still stank to hell and back of diesel. The temperature was a degree or two colder than it was outside and the only light came through the narrow, shoulder-height rifle slits on either side.

Koikov walked over to the east-facing slit and peered through. It was meant to be tight, designed to allow for defensive fire should the base ever come under attack. Could the dragons fit through it? He leant forward and pushed his head and one arm between the two tapering concrete lips. Maybe. But it would be a tight squeeze. That was fine. A tight squeeze would give plenty of time for a traditional Department V greeting.

Koikov pulled his collar up and paced the ten metres or so across the chamber. *What a grim place this would be to die.* He heaved open the door to the next chamber and walked through.

Central Chamber 2 lacked rifle slits. It was gloomy, dank and totally enclosed. In the corner lay the butt-end of a papirosa that he'd ditched last time he'd inspected the place. On that occasion, all he'd given a shit about had been how many barrels he could stack within its reinforced walls before heading back to the *Albanov* for a shower. This time couldn't have been more different. He picked up the butt-end and pocketed it; where Koikov came from, you didn't shit in your own bed.

He turned his attention to the escape hatch mounted centrally within the roof. A ladder was fixed to the wall of the cylindrical shaft, accessing the cap. He jumped up and grabbed the bottom rung of the ladder. He half-expected the fittings to pull loose from the wall, but they held, and he heaved himself up, hand over hand.

The release handle for the cap was stiff with disuse. After a struggle it juddered round and Koikov forced open the mushroom-like slab of iron, which squealed on its hinge before crashing back onto the rooftop. The smell of diesel was replaced by fresh air. The dark by light. Uncertain which he preferred, Koikov pushed his head up through the hatch and looked around.

A few hundred metres away, Privates Gergiev, Nazarov and Reznikoff were unloading barrels from the roof of the mechanical excavator. They were arranging them at approximate twenty-metre intervals, creating an outer perimeter, just as Koikov had ordered. Lifting his rifle, he peered through the sight and brought the crosshairs to rest over one of the barrels. With vision unhindered it was un-fucking-missable. But in the mist… He lowered the sight from his eye. Half of him hoped that they would never have to find out. The other half wanted nothing more than to fuck some dragons up.

He reclosed the hatch and continued through into Chamber 3.

6

The slope stretched ahead for several hundred metres before rounding into the coastal plain below. It would have been an awe-inspiring sight: the sub-oval basin of low ground ringed by a batter of foothills, the ocean lapping at its western edge. But there was no getting away from it. It looked like a monumental bite mark, as if a gigantic sea monster had risen up and bitten a chunk out of the island's flank.

A number of other islands loomed on the far horizon. Callum held a hand above his eyes and squinted through the blinding sunlight. He could just make out the strokes of snow and ice on their peaks, their necks hung with wreaths of mist. He shivered.

In the centre of the plain below was the same ill-fitting arrangement of grey concrete that he had first spotted from the Kamov. He remembered the feeling of intense dislike, disappointment that the island wasn't quite the virgin wilderness he'd envisaged. Then he laughed. Virtually overnight, the compound had transformed from eyesore to oasis.

Since leaving the tunnel, the group had walked in silence. Exhausted and overwhelmed, they had moved as quickly as Callum's leg would allow them, fuelled by the thought that when they reached the compound they would be safe at last. It was an illusion; there was no such thing as *safe* here. But it was necessary nonetheless.

"I can't believe we've made it," he said.

"Almost, my friend," Lungkaju replied cautiously. "We are almost there. Now we must be careful moving downslope. The rock is uneven. Let us go north to where it is more gentle."

A short distance along the ridge, the gradient eased and Lungkaju began a painstaking descent. Callum followed on, keeping his body sideways and carefully testing the scree-strewn slope with every step.

A voice called out suddenly, "Do you wait?"

They turned around to see that Darya and Ava had stopped at the top of the slope. Ava was slumped on the ground, her head between her legs, Darya's hands on her shoulders. The two men shared a look of patient resignation, before clambering back to the top.

"This has got to be a joke," Ava was repeating between muffled sobs. "This is a setup, right? A great big, steep-sided setup!"

"Let me guess," Callum said, remembering back to their tour of the *Albanov*'s bridge. "Heights?"

Darya scowled at him, while Ava nodded. She took several loud, exaggerated breaths. "Stairs are bad enough."

"The slope is gradual here," Callum said, trying hard to comfort her.

"I know, but I can't help it. It's because I can see so far into the distance. When I even look at it, I feel light-headed. What if I black out and fall? What if I slip over? I… I just can't do it. I'm sorry, I'm so sorry. I feel so weak." She burst back into tears.

Lungkaju knelt down beside her and spoke softly. "Doctor Lee, please do not be sorry. You have done nothing wrong. And you are not weak."

Ava wiped at her eyes.

"But you know that we must go to the compound," he continued. "It is not possible for us to stay here."

She nodded. "I know. I just… I just need time… to get my head straight."

Lungkaju smiled and took her hand. "Then I will stay with you and wait." He turned to Callum. "My friend, you and Doctor Lebedev should go ahead."

"And leave you two here?" Darya protested. "No, we cannot."

"You are not leaving us," Lungkaju answered, maintaining his air of calm command. "You must get to the compound as soon as possible and let them know that we are still alive. They probably think…" He trailed off, then added, "We will follow you down, yes, Doctor Lee?"

She nodded.

"But—"

"He's right," Ava said, cutting her off. "You two go on ahead. I'm just being silly. Making a big deal out of nothing." She punched herself in the thigh. "I've been up the CN Tower before, for God's sake. Twice! I just need a few moments, that's all, and then we'll follow you down."

Darya was still protesting as Callum took her hand. Exchanging a nod with Lungkaju, he set off down the slope.

* * *

In the middle of the floor in Chamber 3, Ivanov and Koshkin knelt either side of Private Tsaritsyn. They had made him a makeshift mattress out of jackets and other spare bits of clothing and were attempting to tend his wounds with the meagre contents of the field first aid kit.

Tsaritsyn's narrow, youthful face looked even paler than before. His eyes were closed. Blood was soaking through his chest dressing and his trembling was continuous.

Ivanov looked up. "He won't stop shaking, Starshyna."

For a moment Koikov was silent. He knew a dying man when he saw one. "How much morphine do we have?"

Koshkin eyed him suspiciously, then he rooted through the first aid kit and produced a vial of liquid. Reading off the label he said, "Six hundred milligrams, Starshyna."

Koikov took a deep breath. "One hour."

"One hour, what?"

"One hour, and if we've had nothing from Nagurskoye, then dose him up."

"Starshyna, are you suggesting—"

"This man is beyond our help, Koshkin. He's not beyond our compassion. One hour. And move him into Chamber 2. From now on that's your theatre."

He went to exit the bunker, but as he approached the stairs he drew to a sudden halt. His gaze was fixed above the doorway. "Son of a…"

"What is it, Starshyna?" Ivanov asked.

Attached to the ceiling, directly above the doorway, was a detonator. It was strapped to a sizeable block of C4.

"My charges!" Koikov's mind raced back to when Dolgonosov's screams had signalled the start of the living nightmare. The charges he'd been setting in order to collapse the bunker system had been left in place. The wiring was unfinished, but it was nothing half an hour's attention wouldn't solve.

Ignoring the continued questioning of Ivanov and Koshkin, he paced back through to Chamber 1. Above the external doorway, the second of the two charges also remained. A smile had just enough time to break across his lips before his radio crackled.

"Starshyna, this is Corporal Voronkov. Come in."

"What is it, Corporal?"

Voronkov seemed to hesitate. "Mist, Starshyna. Coming in from the east."

Koikov's heart sank. He strode over to the rifle slit and stared out. Another thick bank of grey-white was already obscuring the high ground; Hjalmar Ridge was completely shrouded. He watched, mesmerised, as the heart of the island disappeared, the front of the vapour cloud splitting into five thick fingers, feeling their way down into the basin. "What is it with this fucking place!" he shouted. "Okay, Voronkov, I need you to be my eyes up there, you understand? Keep me up on what's happening around this bunker? I know it's not ideal, but there's no other option."

There was a long pause, then, "Understood. Out."

Koikov peered over at the small cache of weapons that had made it this far. Stacked like a shrine against the wall of Chamber 1 were five or six ammo crates, two RPGs and a flame unit. He took small comfort in them, but comfort nonetheless.

He turned his attention back to the mist. By now it was cascading down over the Hjalmar foothills, devouring the island from the top down. He could smell its sour tang already. He wanted to spit, but his mouth was already as dry as sun-bleached bone.

"Shit!" He brought a hand to his radio collar and made an open transmission: "All personnel, this is Starshyna Koikov. Brace yourselves."

Chapter 14

GRUDGE

1

The narwhals were agitated. The larger males had taken up wide positions, flexing their tusks and chaperoning their families' flanks. In the centre, the dark blue calves stuck close to their mothers. They swam huddled, barging forward, careless with angst.

Out of curiosity, Peterson switched on the sub's hydrophone. The cabin came alive with clicks, frequency-modulated whistles and pulse-like bursts of sonar as the thirty or so animals broke around the *Centaur* and left it rocking in their wake.

Maybe it was the presence of the sub? Peterson doubted it. They were skittish by nature, but there was something else. He switched off the hydrophone. Had the circumstances been different, he would have taken a much keener interest, perhaps even followed the pod as they made for deeper water. Instead, with the cabin plunged back into silence, he refocussed his attention on the grey-blue waters off Valerian Cove.

Several hours had passed since Peterson had relocated the beach where he'd left Ava, McJones and Lebedev stranded. They had long gone. He'd suspected as much. But that had been little consolation as he'd searched his way to the top of the scree-slope surrounding the beach and scanned in vain over Harmsworth's interior. For someone who had barely set foot on the island before, it was a new kind of desolation that had confronted him. Vast and unforgiving. Ridges and valleys. Rock and more rock. It looked about as welcoming as a mound of fire ants.

The idea that the three of them had made for the old military base was by no means a certainty. Peterson knew its location well enough – he'd earmarked it as a possible contingency shelter – and it was all the way on the other side of the island. Getting there on foot would be no mean feat, and he was willing to bet that there would be plenty of rock shelters nearby, where they could've camped down to await rescue. Hadn't Lebedev rambled on about animal hides at dinner one time?

But heading for the base would also make a whole lot of sense. From what he recalled, there were a handful of standing structures around the runway, which would make decent enough shelter, plus there would probably be enough leftover crap to make fire with. There might even be other useful equipment, perhaps a radio. More than anything, it would be the obvious place for a rescue party to look. Ava was sharp. Ditto McJones. That's where he'd find them alright.

He'd left the little cove and headed south. Navigation hadn't been an issue. Visibility had been good, perhaps as much as thirty feet in places. Hugging the coast had allowed him to keep tabs on the shoreline, so for the most part the island's underskirt had dictated his movements. He'd made sure to breach the *Centaur* every so often, raise the hatch and check his location to make sure that he was on course. It was slow and it was painfully old-school for a man with the pinnacle of modern submersible technology teasing his fingertips. But it was working.

As he negotiated the rock formations off the island's south-western tip, the clarity of the water diminished rapidly. Soon visibility was halved on what it had been, no more than ten, fifteen feet. He slowed and crept the *Centaur* to the surface. Flipping open the hatch, he climbed up and peered across at western Harmsworth.

At first he wasn't sure what he was seeing. He lifted his spectacles – he'd lost the first pair back when he fell into the water, so they were ill-fitting spares that he hated wearing – and rubbed at his tired eyes. Vast swathes of the island seemed to have disappeared. It was as if an enormous eraser had been to work; all that remained were a ghostly outline, a few scattered strokes of rock and a smear or two of sky. The rest was white, thick, oily white that seemed to shimmer and pulsate.

It was shocking how quickly the mist had descended this time. Even as he looked on, it continued its spread, swollen tendrils abandoning the shore and flowing out to sea. He watched, mesmerised, until the surge was too close for comfort. Then he dropped back into the cabin and took the *Centaur* down.

What little ambient sunlight the water had held was now filtered from existence as the shroud settled overhead. Peterson sighed. It was disconcerting, but it was no show-stopper. He would just have to be careful not to lose sight of the submerged shoreline. Besides, the military base was now only a few more kilometres to the north. He just needed to keep his nerve.

Ahead, something loomed out of the murk and into the *Centaur's* lamps. It was a shadow, an elongated shadow, with an angular protrusion at one end. It looked inanimate, bobbing close to the seabed and churning up flurries of sand. If he'd been south of the tundra, he would've put money on it being a sunken tree trunk, such was its size and shape. But then the nearest living tree was a thousand miles south of his location.

Warily, he edged the *Centaur* forward.

2

The carcass belonged to an adult male narwhal, a real old sonofabitch judging by the size and pale colouration. It looked fresh. Its death must have been what had freaked the rest of the pod out earlier. Like dolphins, narwhals were intelligent, highly emotional creatures. The younger animals relied on the older for their knowledge of hunting grounds, migration routes, everything. The death of such an old member would have been traumatic.

Peterson reversed the *Centaur* out of range of the animal's giant tusk. "*Remember, there's always life in a dead critter,*" his uncle's voice reminded him. Face stern, he had brandished his three-fingered hand before his eight-year-old nephew. "*I got a coyote to thank for this, and that was after I shot him dead.*"

As Peterson performed the manoeuvre, the current dragged the narwhal around, revealing an enormous laceration across the side of its head. Fingers of brain emerged like a deep-sea anemone from its pulverised cranium, and a cloud of blood and tissue spewed from the gash.

Peterson had seen similar injuries on seals that had been dragged through ships' propeller blades in the busy shipping lanes off Greenland. But there sure as shit weren't any shipping lanes around Harmsworth. Leastways, not yet.

There was only one other explanation, and it spurred Peterson to take off—

Something bolted past the *Centaur*'s nose. It could have been a seal, but it moved too fast for him to be certain. As he peered out into the murk, something darted the other way. Missed it again!

Then, from nowhere, a slender creature, with the same dark colouration as the surrounding water, torpedoed into the carcass. Definitely not a seal, the creature tore a strip of blubber from the narwhal's flank, the gouge pumping out blood and clouding up the surrounding brine. There was no longer any doubt in Peterson's mind. It was another one of those weird lizard birds, a Tansey whatey.

It didn't seem bothered by the presence of the *Sea Centaur*. In any case it was obviously no match. Tonnes of cutting-edge machinery versus three hundred pounds or so of chicken lizard. No contest. Yet even just the sight of the creature made him feel strangely vulnerable. "Goddamn things," he growled. "It's a goddamn infestation."

The sensible move would've been to get the hell away while it was busy feeding. But this time Peterson couldn't shift his science brain. He was safe enough, wasn't he? And the opportunity to watch this new species engaged in its natural feeding behaviour had him tethered to his seat.

Just then, a second creature streaked into the carcass and stripped away another ribbon of flesh. Then came two, three, four more, one after another, each performing exactly the same action: strike-tear-away, strike-tear-away.

Peterson watched them, wide-eyed, silent. Over the next few minutes, both the number of animals and the frequency of the strikes increased dramatically. It was as if the first few mouthfuls had just been testers, clearing the way for an all-out feeding frenzy. Soon virtually the whole of the narwhal's ribcage lay exposed, arcs of off-white bone clamped around a sausage bag of internal organs. Then, just as suddenly as they had appeared, the creatures faded back into the gloom. What remained of the carcass lay unmolested, bobbing on the current.

Peterson had seen enough. He began to back the *Centaur* away. This close to the seabed, the lack of a guidance system forced him to focus all of his attention on the controls. He needed eyes in the back of his head.

There was a subtle thump. Had he hit something? He looked back up.

One of the creatures had its face pressed up against the screen.

Peterson cried out as fear clenched like a giant fist inside his chest. The creature didn't move, didn't react. It stared in at him, eyes wide, each covered over with a fine milky membrane. Its claws were steadying its face against the glass. A chain of bubbles leaked from its nostrils, and its blue-black feathers rustled in the undertow. It seemed to hang, motionless, in the water, just studying him. Then it broke away and disappeared beneath the sub.

Peterson sat frozen in his chair as silence gave way to a faint tapping noise, then to the unmistakable sound of claws raking across the hull and a series of much louder, more concerted bangs.

Peterson accelerated suddenly, forcefully, skidding over the top of the narwhal carcass. In his panic he almost lost control of the *Centaur* as it veered and plunged towards the seabed. At the last moment he managed to regain control and bring it back level. Maintaining his bearing north, he scoured ahead. In all probability the creatures would choose to stay and finish off the carcass. Wouldn't they? It wasn't like the *Centaur* was edible. They were just curious. Surely they didn't see him as prey?

There was a crash as something collided with the sub's flank. Glancing through the porthole, Peterson could make out one of the creatures clinging to the right pelvic fin. Its hind claws were tearing at the slit into which the fin retracted, and already he could see thin slivers of the Kevlar-reinforced epoxy resin being shredded away. Bad news. Just like a fish, the sub's manoeuvrability relied on the integrity of its fins. Without them, it would flounder.

He secured his seat restraint and reached for the throttle. "Okay, old gal, time to move out."

The engine roared, and the *Centaur* careered upwards. The force of the acceleration crushed Peterson back into his chair. As the sub's nose broke the surface, he turned hard right, trying to fling the creature off. Loose items shot from one side of the cabin to the other as the sub arced sharply around on its side, before righting once more.

Peterson glanced through the porthole. It had worked. No more parasite. But as he scanned ahead, he could make out two more of the creatures in front of the craft, one either side, like spectral wingmen in the murk. And there were more. At least another half dozen stalked just beyond either flank. He supposed that there would be a similar number to his rear, leaving the *Centaur* surrounded.

Realisation dawned, and dawned hard.

Hell yeah these things saw him as prey.

He was being hunted.

3

On top of the moraine, drenched in mist, Voronkov wiped the sweat from his brow. The rifle scope creaked into his LVV as he peered towards the compound.

Private Zyryonov, Voronkov's junior by ten years, was lying prone next to him. "Anything?" His high-pitched voice was croaky with exhaustion.

"Nothing," Voronkov replied, his own tone as deep and as smooth as ever, despite his fear. "Only Gergiev."

"Gergiev? What the hell's he doing out there?"

"Still dropping barrels along the perimeter."

From the vantage of high ground, Voronkov had watched the mist roll down from the ridge, flooding the coastal basin. Koikov and the others had quickly retreated into the bunker, their outlines vanishing from sight. For a time the top of the moraine had pierced through the mist, like an island in a vast white swell. But soon it too had fallen under the cloak.

"This is fucked up!" Zyryonov whined.

The man's continual bitching had quickly neutralised Voronkov's sympathy for him. "Which bit?"

"The bit where everybody else gets to hide out in the shelter and we get to sit up here just waiting to get killed."

"Shelter? Have you even seen it in there?"

"Yes, and it beats the shit out of being up here."

"I'm not so sure it's gonna make any difference," Voronkov answered coolly. He adjusted his sight. "Personally I'd rather be up here than trapped inside that concrete coffin."

"It's okay for you, you've got the LVV. I can't see shit!"

"Shut up!" Voronkov ordered. "I think I might have something."

Zyryonov's rifle clanked as he pulled it tight into his shoulder. "What is it?"

"Shh!"

Something was flitting down the slope from the foot of Hjalmar. It was heading in Gergiev's direction.

"What is it?" Zyryonov demanded.

Voronkov ignored him and engaged his tactical radio. "This is Corporal Voronkov. Starshyna, come in."

Static, then, "What is it, Voronkov?"

"I've got movement. Half a kilometre from your position, up on the ridge. Heading for Gergiev's machine."

"Can you make it out?"

"Negative. Definition is limited at this range. Whatever it is it looks like a red blur. It's fast, though. Moves in bursts. Outcrop to outcrop."

"It's one of them," Koikov said, without hesitation. "Maintain visual. If it gets to the perimeter, light it up. I'll contact Gergiev. Out."

By now the red blur had made its way to within fifty metres or so of Gergiev's machine. As it ducked behind another outcrop, a second flicker caught Voronkov's eye. With a sinking sense, he saw that several more had now emerged on the side of the slope. All looked the same. All moved the same. All were heading in the same direction.

He knocked the safety off his rifle and brought his finger to the trigger.

"What the hell's going on?" Zyryonov demanded.

Voronkov turned to him. "They're coming."

"Coming? What's coming? The dragons?"

"No, the strippers I ordered."

"For fuck's sake, talk to me, Corporal!"

Voronkov resolved not to talk to him anymore. He was in no mood to hold another man's hand. If Zyryonov pulled himself together and did what he was told, he'd be okay. Otherwise… He brought his eye back to the rifle sight and blocked out the private's continued protests.

The first of the blurs was now within thirty metres of Gergiev. It had slowed down and was approaching him cautiously, stalking him from the north. Voronkov took a deep breath. Any second and it would pass by one of the perimeter barrels. He brought the crosshair over it and exhaled.

Light her up, Koikov had said.

"With pleasure," Voronkov whispered.

Then he squeezed the trigger.

* * *

Gergiev's immense biceps pumped as he extended the arm of the mechanical excavator and placed the last of the barrels onto the ground. He had been so caught up in his task of reinforcing the outer perimeter that he had completely ignored the closing mist. The world outside the cabin was now a murky swirl, but he had simply stuck his LVV on and continued.

Now that he had full control of the machine, he felt safe. Mist or not, any of those things tried to mess with him and they were going to regret it. All the same, he tried not to think about them; his memory of their last encounter was still fresh in his mind, his helplessness as they'd dragged Orlov screaming from beside him and torn him limb from limb.

He dug the teeth of the bucket under the last barrel and

raised it upright. It was incredible how tender you could be with such a powerful machine—

At that moment there was an explosion. Gergiev ducked as a ball of flame erupted up into the air a short distance away. The effect was like a flame tornado, the intense blast seeming to incinerate a funnel of mist at least twenty metres across. Everywhere, grey became orange as ribbons of flame sprayed out and burnt on across the barren rock.

There was little doubt what had happened. Some asshole had sniped one of the perimeter barrels. But why the fuck didn't they wait for him to get clear?

As if in answer, something came racing out of the blast epicentre. He watched open-mouthed as one of the dragons raced past the front of his machine. Its entire body was on fire. Its feathers had been incinerated, revealing its full musculature, charred black and streaked with flame. It sprinted around wildly, screeching in torment before disappearing into the mist.

"Gergiev, come in."

Gergiev's muscles had tensed with shock, clamping his arms painfully against his chest and crushing his hands around the machine controls. He rolled his shoulders, loosened his grip and cracked his knuckles, watching in a daze as the blood flowed back into his fingers.

"Gergiev!"

"Here, Starshyna."

"Are you hurt?"

"I don't think so."

"Then get back to the bunker now, you hear me? They're coming."

They're coming.

Gergiev panned around. He couldn't see any other creatures, but there was something. To his amazement, fifty metres east of his location, were two definite outlines. Human outlines. But who did they belong to? Everybody else was supposed to be back at the compound.

The two people stood up out of their crouched positions and looked around. They couldn't be Department V, but Harmsworth was uninhabited, and as far as Gergiev was aware no civilians had made it off the *Albanov*.

Was he making it up? He scrunched his eyes closed and then reopened them.

The two outlines remained.

* * *

Darya clung to Callum's arm. "What was that?"

The shock of the sudden explosion had stopped them in their tracks. "Just keep moving!" he shouted. He had no idea what had caused the explosion, or where exactly they were moving to. All he knew was that they had descended onto the coastal plain and had been making good time towards the compound when the mist had smothered them. Lungkaju and Ava were lost. The world had turned grey again and now all hell was breaking loose.

Another explosion went off nearby. He flung his arms around Darya once again, protecting her as best he could. The rattle of automatic gunfire rang out in the distance. "They must be attacking the compound."

"Do we still head there?"

"It'll still be safer than being out here."

As if to confirm his suspicion, a screech tore through the air behind them, and they spun around.

"Can you see it?"

Rifle shouldered, Callum squinted into the mist. It broke over them in waves. Visibility was only a metre or two at most. "I can't see anything. Nothing at all."

"I cannot see it either," she whispered.

At that moment, a shadow bolted past, and Callum fired off a round.

"Did you hit?"

His legs wanted to buckle beneath him. "I don't know."

Another screech sounded off to the right. He turned and fired again.

"They are all around," Darya screamed.

"Just stay behind me," he ordered, fumbling to reload the rifle. But before he'd had time, the scene around them seemed to still. A strange clicking noise echoed out, and one of the creatures emerged from the mist.

The creature was only metres away. Callum's breath froze in his chest. Behind him, Darya was silent, completely still. The creature was also still. Only its head moved slightly as it looked from his face down to the rifle in his quivering hands. *It knows*, he thought. *It knows the rifle is no good like this. It knows that we're defenceless.*

Their eyes locked. Jets of breath tore from the creature's nostrils. Its eyes bored into his. Then, to Callum's surprise, it removed its gaze and bowed its head down, as if in supplication.

"What does it do?" Darya asked.

"I've no idea, but look!"

Running along the creature's back was a criss-cross laceration. The surrounding feathers were clotted with dried blood. The wound looked infected. It looked recent.

Callum swallowed hard. Was it possible? *You just better hope those things don't hold a grudge…*

The creature raised its head back up to let out a screech.

Darya's grip tightened. She could see what he could: the chafe marks around the base of its neck, where the *Centaur*'s pincer had bitten down.

There was no mistaking it.

"It remembers," Callum hissed.

4

Peterson flinched as another thud rang out above him. Through the periscope, he could see that two of the creatures were now attacking the sub's dorsal fin. Already one of them had torn a gouge into the base, while the other had near as dammit gnawed the tip off.

He increased speed again and jerked the craft from side to side as sharply as he could without losing control. Whatever he did, the two creatures clung on tight with all four limbs, their combined body weight wrenching the fin back and forth.

One of the wingmen broke formation suddenly, veered in and kicked out at the windscreen. As the crunch of the collision sounded, Peterson threw his arms over his face. When he looked back up, he could see that the blow had chipped away only a tiny fragment, no bigger than half a centimetre from the six centimetre-thick screen. But his sense of relief was fleeting, as the creature then dug the tip of its hind claw into the chink and began to pick it open.

The second wingman now side-winded towards the screen. Peterson's mind blanked with fear, and it was only at the last second that he thought to deploy the sub's pincer. The three prongs had barely emerged from their housing before they speared into the front of the creature's chest, bringing its charge to an abrupt halt. Peterson forced the arm out further and further as the pincer tips clamped down harder. Blood streamed from the creature's mouth as it scrabbled to escape. The pincer tips bore though the skin and deep into its flesh, gradually sliding in-between its lower ribs and closing firm around its sternum.

"Still reckon on messing with me, you ugly piece of shit!" Peterson bellowed.

With its talon still embedded in the *Centaur*'s windscreen, the other creature looked across at its mate. Then it plunged over and joined in the attack. Peterson seized the opportunity to deploy the second arm, and by the time the free creature realised what was happening, it was too late. The pincer had dug into its neck, just below the jaw, and begun to constrict.

He roared with success. "Too damn easy!"

Outside, the creature fought against its restraint, jerking the mechanism from side to side. But as the pincer grip tightened, its movements grew softer and softer. Finally, its eyes bulged and its tongue dribbled out of its mouth, flapping like a blood-red eel in the current.

Remembering the two creatures on the roof, Peterson raised the angle of both arms until the pincers were level with the sub's dorsal fin. Then he released the dead creatures simultaneously. The slipstream overhead pulled their corpses towards the rear of the vessel, flinging them into their live counterparts and dislodging both from the roof.

The initial despair Peterson had felt was transformed to jubilation. He was half-dead, goddammit, but no matter what tricks these goggle-eyed, fuck-faced little critters tried to pull, he was kicking their reptilian ass!

"Any more takers?" he screamed out, drunk with adrenaline. "*Centaur*, five! Overgrown iguanas, nothing! How does that feel?"

No sooner had he spoken than the sub lurched to the left.

Speed was reducing, and keeping her level was like wrestling a bull. Peterson watched in renewed horror as another of the creatures took a final swipe at the pelvic fin. As the remaining thread snapped, it leapt clear with the fin caught between its teeth.

Peterson tugged the throttle back, attempting to bring the *Centaur* to a stop. But it was no use. No matter what he did, he just couldn't hold her steady. The next thing he knew, the world was thrown into a spin. He was tossed around, and the only thing stopping him from braining himself on the *Centaur's* interior was his seat restraint.

Then came the inevitable. With a terrifying groan, the roof of the submarine smashed into the seabed, ricocheted off and came crashing back down. The internal lighting shorted out and the emergency warning sirens burst into life. There were more impacts to both sides of the sub, before the tail caught and the nose flipped upwards. Then the whole craft tumbled forward again and again, eventually grinding to a stop along the jagged bedrock.

Peterson opened his eyes. He was delirious. So much so that it took him several minutes to realise that he was hanging upside down. Sparks leapt from the control panel and narrow jets of gas vented into the cabin around him. It was the last sight any submariner wanted to see.

He unfastened his seat restraint and slumped awkwardly down onto the roof. His side was an ecstasy of pain. The rest of his body ached like hell. As he surveyed the wreckage of his cabin, the system supporting the emergency siren faltered and then stalled, the whine giving way to the sound of leaking gas.

The situation was dire. If he wasn't imminently burnt alive or poisoned by the build-up of stray gases, then before long the cabin's damaged atmospheric regulator would give out and he would be left drowning in his own CO_2.

To Peterson's surprise, his first response was: *So what?* There wasn't a chance in hell that he was making it out of there alive anyway. For one thing he was trapped. The *Centaur* was upside down, which meant that the hatch was wedged against the seabed. Even if he could get out, with no idea where he was, he'd get lost and the temperature of the water would finish him off in minutes. That was if he wasn't immediately ripped to shreds by those things.

He lay his head back down. It was time to accept that it was game over.

"*Nam Myoho Renge Kyo, Nam Myoho Renge Kyo, Nam Myoho Renge Kyo…*"

Chapter 15

CHAMBER 2

1

The creature took a step towards Callum, stopped and cocked its head. With deliberate poise, it leant forward as if in mid-bow, then parted its arms and puffed out its feathers. The long plumes on the undersides of its arms, and those remaining along its nape, stood erect. Its tail lifted until visible above its shoulder, and the feathers adorning the tip fanned out and quivered. The shorter plumes across the rest of its body seemed to shimmer, creating a silvery white blur that mirrored the surrounding mist.

There was something mesmerising about the display. It was the first time that the creature's eyes, mouth and claws hadn't been the focus of Callum's attention. For the briefest of moments, he felt his panic recede. He was looking through his fear, seeing something as vulnerable as it was fearsome.

But his feelings were short-lived, as the creature's head began to bob rhythmically, its jaws chomping together in time. Seconds crept by, and the creature maintained its stance. It appeared to be in a trance; head bobbing, teeth grinding, harp-strings of saliva now trailing from its chin. Why did it not attack?

Callum took a tentative step backwards. At this, the creature stopped its posturing. Its feathers flattened out and it raised itself back up to full height. Vocalising a series of loud clicks, it advanced another step.

"What does it do?" Darya whispered over his shoulder.

"I think it's playing with us."

She peered up just as the creature bowed once again, brought its arms apart and raised its plumage. This time its feathers flushed with colour. The white became an amber glow, spreading in veins from the base follicles to the very tips of its erect feathers. The amber then intensified, becoming a deep red inflammation that seemed to scorch the surrounding mist.

On impulse, Callum retreated another step.

Again the creature was sensitive to his movement. With an agitated bray it followed.

One step.

Darya's voice drifted through to him. "You are wrong."

"What?"

"You are wrong," she repeated. "It is not playing with us."

"Then what?"

"I think it is challenge you."

On cue, the creature bowed its head and repeated its colourful display: white, silver, amber, red.

"Challenging me?"

"To fight. It sees you as rival male."

Callum's mind raced at the suggestion. As unlikely as it sounded, it actually made sense. If the creature could remember him, then it would remember that he had won their last encounter. He had proven himself a worthy adversary, and now... now it wanted a rematch, complete with formalities.

"What do I do?"

"There is only one thing," she replied. "You must win."

"Win? Win how? That thing could tear me to shreds!"

"Yes," Darya replied. "But this is not physical fight. Not yet."

There was a silence, as Callum searched desperately for a solution.

Then something dug into the side of his ribs. "Take these."

He reached backwards and took hold of the objects in Darya's hand. Without looking he could tell that they were the two remaining glow sticks.

"But…" His mind skipped back to their first encounter with the three little creatures back on the foreshore, when their untempered aggression had marked them out as youngsters; Darya's words repeated themselves: *In the wild, the adult animals will avoid conflict, because of the risk of injury. The adult is more likely to use posture and vocalisation than physical force…*

He brought the glow sticks out in front of him, and the creature ceased its display. All colour bleached from its feathers and it stared at the two dull tubes. Its mouth cracked open and it watched intently as Callum brought his shaking hands together and snapped them.

The same high-intensity luminous green light that had illuminated Ngana'bta's face burst from one of the sticks, while the other produced an intense iridescent blue. Their glow was scattered and reflected in the mist. The suspended water particles enhanced their lustre and produced two wide penumbras of colour that increased their luminosity ten-fold.

The creature snorted at the sight and let out a high-pitched crow. It hopped in agitation from foot to foot, its talons shredding strips of moss from the rock.

"It is working," Darya said, unable to conceal the surprise in her voice. "You intimidate him."

Without any semblance of a plan, Callum raised the glow sticks. Despite the cold, his palms were slick as he began to move them slowly, forming sweeping S shapes before him. The pressure was exhausting. His trembling arms felt stiff and his movement uncoordinated. Any second and he was certain that he would drop the sticks, leaving himself and Darya defenceless once more.

The creature looked in confusion from one light to the other, tracing the progress of each as they cut through the moist air. It stood silent and still, hypnotised.

Adrenaline surged through Callum's veins. He took a deep breath and stepped forward.

The creature crowed out in alarm but held its ground.

"Move back!" Callum shouted, his voice deep but breathy.

There followed a tense pause. Then the creature moved backwards. One step.

"Move back!" he shouted again, advancing another pace.

This time the creature did not retreat but stood firm and retaliated. With a screech, it rebowed its head, parted its arms and puffed out its plumage. Instead of red, its feathers now turned the same neon green as the one glow-stick, before flushing the blue of the other. The two colours pulsed effortlessly into being, one after the other, as the creature's head bobbed and the sound of its teeth grating shredded the air.

Callum's heart sank. Did he really think a couple of glow sticks could intimidate such a lethal prehistoric predator? Maybe. Maybe not. But what option did he have?

Summoning all of his courage, he stepped forward once again. Speeding up the flailing of his arms, and roaring from the bottom of his gut, "Move back! Move back now!"

Less than four or five paces now separated the two of them in their stand-off. At this range even the mist had lost its grip. Callum could make out every detail of the creature, from the bunched folds of purple-grey gooseflesh below its eyes, to the thread-like blood vessels pulsing in its bared gums. At this range its musk was as overpowering as the reflected colour still coursing through its plumes.

The world was thrown into deep silence. All that existed now were himself, Darya, the creature and something else. It was nothing visible. It was a contract. An understanding, older than the creature itself, which kept it from simply lashing out with its hind claws and tearing his throat out.

As Callum went to take another step forward, it stopped displaying suddenly and turned its head upwards. There was a new look on its face. The colour shed from its feathers. Was he winning? Had he won? Was he about to die?

Callum was desperate for reassurance from Darya, but speech left him at the sight of the creature's whole body bathed in a mysterious light. The light intensified, spreading out into a halo until he could barely see the creature for the glare.

As a low rumbling sound grew louder and louder, his voice returned at last: "What the hell?"

There was a crunch followed by a piercing shriek as a large mechanical arm appeared out of the mist and came crashing down in front of Callum's face. The bucket-fist pounded the creature into the ground like a child crushing an ant, and the force of the impact vibrated through the rock under Callum's feet.

In that moment, as Darya's grip tightened around his shoulder, he wasn't sure what scared him the most: the creature, the sound of gunfire, explosions and screeching that rushed to fill the air once more, or the towering mechanical beast now emerging from the mist.

The arm reared upwards, the blood-stained bucket clanking at its hinge. Beneath it, the creature's lifeless body shook violently. Blood and bone burst up through its now-dull plumage. Bathed in the light streaming from the machine's headlamps, its entire upper torso was pulped. Its legs twitched and a startled look lay splattered across what remained of its face.

"I do not think that he plays possum this time," Darya said.

Callum said nothing. There were no words for how he felt in that moment.

2

Peterson had never given up before. It was weird. Kind of comforting. He'd always figured he would be racked with panic when his time finally came. But if anything he felt a deep sense of calm.

"*Nam Myoho Renge Kyo, Nam Myoho Renge Kyo, Nam Myoho Renge Kyo...*"

Only, where was his film reel? Weren't a lifetime's worth of memories meant to be flashing past his eyes in one big cognitive chunder? There were enough of them for sure. Good and bad. But now that it came to it, there was only one thing on his mind.

Stupid! he scolded himself. *You've known toenails longer than you've known her. How can you even pretend to be in love with her? Just look what you're risking.*

"Oh yeah, and what's that then?" he slurred.

No reply.

What was that Robert Burns claptrap McJones had spouted back on the ship? *But t'see her was t'love her, love but her and love forever.*

"But to see her was to love her," he repeated. Perhaps it could be just that simple. He had no real clue. Robert Burns obviously thought so, and so did McJones. All Peterson knew was that *she* was what he was thinking about now, as he drew his last breaths. Ava, and the knowledge that because of him she was in deep shit.

His desire to succumb was waning. He fought to regain it. Death – nice, responsibility-free death – would be so much easier. Wouldn't it? But, sprawled out in the carnage of the upturned cabin, his sense of acceptance was being replaced by a strange, very much alive kind of restlessness.

Perhaps he was looking at it all wrong. Did it really matter what he felt for Ava or not? Whether it was love or delusion or just plain old animal lust? No. What mattered – at least, what he figured to matter – was that he didn't bail on her without a fight. As a human being, he owed her that. As a human being suffering *his* consequences, he owed her those last breaths of his. And that went for McJones as well and any other sorry sons of bitches that were suffering because of his stupidity. Hell, it even went for Lebedev.

He pushed himself up off the ceiling. The decaying atmosphere was starting to make him feel sick, light-headed. He shook it off. He'd wasted enough time already. If he was serious about not bailing on anybody but Davy Jones, then it was now or never.

He wrestled the tool kit from beneath the upturned console and grabbed a screwdriver. He prised up the flooring and got to work on the reinforced panel secured across the top of the specimen chamber. The screws were structural and not intended to be removed. He had to score away the anti-corrosion paint before using every last ounce of his strength to unfasten them, all the while supporting the weighty metal panel on his shoulders like some kind of twenty-first century Atlas.

At last, hands and shoulders numb, he allowed the panel, and the better part of the underlying refrigeration module, to clatter down beside him. He wiped the condensation from the inside of his glasses and stared through into the chamber.

A deep sigh escaped him. "Here we go again."

The gap was just big enough for him to squeeze his shoulders through. Having pulled on his Arctic wetsuit and diver's utility belt, he tucked the IRS inhalator into a waterproof bag and fed it up into the chamber, along with his face mask and a single-use respirator. He clipped his diver's knife and an underwater lamp to his belt and then grabbed his harpoon gun.

As he stood up and prepared to squeeze himself through, he made the mistake of glancing through the screen. The creatures were out there. Five or six of them at least. They hung, wraith-like, in the water, their collective gaze glued to the *Centaur*. They were expecting him, he could tell. They looked like dark angels, waiting to escort him into the next world. Only problem was, he wasn't ready yet. His grip tightened around the shaft of the harpoon gun.

As he moved to pull himself up into the chamber, his foot kicked into the side of the console, and the cabin came alive with the clicks and whistles of the fleeing narwhal pod that he'd encountered earlier; the hydrophone was programmed to make an automatic recording whenever it was engaged, and he must have kicked it into playback.

An idea clicked and whistled into his head. If the internal hydrophone speaker was still active, then perhaps there were other residual electrical functions. It was a long shot, but it might just work.

He lowered himself back down into the cabin and hit the button for the external speakers.

Outside, the creatures began searching around frantically. Thrown into confusion by the sudden explosion of sound, they abandoned their harrying positions and formed a defensive huddle, only metres from the *Centaur*'s nose. Panicked by the invisible pod, they then scattered into the murk.

Peterson's elation was tempered by the possibility that they could return at any moment. Sure, they were gone. High five. *But for how long?* He dragged himself up into the specimen chamber, grabbed his equipment, and affixed his mask and respirator. Not wasting another second, he took hold of the internal door handles, braced himself and cracked open the chamber door.

The trickle of water became a torrent as he edged the door open wider. The power of the deluge forced him back against the wall. It was deafening, and he could do nothing but hold on tight and wait. In less than a minute, the cabin below was entirely flooded and the water had begun filling the chamber cavity. There was no going back.

He closed his eyes.

The sting of icy water on his face, Peterson forced the door all the way open and wriggled through.

Outside, he scanned around. The water had quickly shorted out the hydrophone. But still the creatures were nowhere to be seen. He looked to the seabed. It was subtle, but beyond the impact scar left by the sub as it touched down, there was an obvious gradient; both his experience and his instinct were telling him that if he followed it, it would lead him ashore.

He checked the respirator gauge. Ten minutes of air remaining.

With his bag tethered to his waist, and the harpoon gun in hand, he kicked off from the *Sea Centaur* and swam like hell for Harmsworth.

3

The machine's horn tore through the air. The front hatch creaked open and a man's voice called out in Russian. Other than the frequent expletives, Callum had no idea what it was saying. But the gist was loud and clear: *Get in the cabin now!*

He helped Darya up onto the machine's track, then hoisted himself up and leapt into the cabin after her. The screen slammed down behind them, and there was more shouting in Russian before a hand grabbed him by the shoulder and began pulling at him.

"You stop him operating the control!"

Callum could see that his leg was blocking the joystick-like handle mounted at the front of the driver's armrest. He clambered out of the way and perched himself on the narrow ledge behind the chair, back-to-back with Darya.

The cabin sat a good couple of metres off the ground. As the three of them peered out through the windscreen, a shadow stalked from the mist. It was followed by three others.

One by one, the creatures stopped before the machine. Their heads seemed to cock in unison as they assessed their super-sized quarry. One of them dipped its neck and sniffed at the pulverised remains of its companion. Then it turned to the others and let out a loud rasp. Screeching in reply, they rushed over to see for themselves, dipping their snouts into the mush of blood and feathers.

"What do they do?" Darya said.

"I'm not sure," Callum replied. "I don't think they know what to make of us."

"Do you think they are afraid?"

"No," he said. "I think they're angry."

There was a sudden whirring sound as the soldier flexed the mechanical arm, attempting to ward the creatures off. With incredible agility, they bounded backwards out of reach. But rather than turning to flee, they split up and charged the machine from multiple directions.

Callum was thrown over as the cabin span clockwise. The outstretched arm collided with one of the creatures mid-leap and batted it from view. The driver shouted out in triumph as the cabin then swung back the other way. This time the arm shaved past its three remaining targets, two of which leapt up onto the tracks, while the third bolted underneath.

The driver slammed his foot into the pedal and the machine bucked and then rolled forward. It felt painfully slow, but while the creature on the right-hand track jumped clear, the other lost its footing and crashed to the ground. With a roar, the machine accelerated and Callum felt the cabin tilt as the track drove straight over its body. Its screeches were audible even over the engine. Then they stopped, replaced by the crunching of its bones.

Three down, Callum thought. He shared a look with Darya. After feeling so vulnerable for so long, he could tell that she too was revelling in the sudden sense of power as they ploughed over the uneven ground.

"Does he know where we're going?"

Darya spoke to the driver then relayed, "He thinks so."

"He *thinks* so?"

"Yes, he thinks so." She pointed ahead. "This way is the compound. You have better idea?"

There was a sudden crash overhead, and the next thing Callum knew they were spinning again. Only this time they weren't doing 180-degree arcs. They were spinning round and round, continually, as the driver fought to shake the creature from the roof.

The cabin felt like a G-force chamber and Callum was thrown up against the side window. As he tried to right himself, an eye appeared on the other side of the Perspex. It peered through at him and a pair of jaws ground menacingly below it.

He ducked as the creature's leg snapped towards him. The hind foot collided with the Perspex and left a deep gouge in front of his face, but the material didn't shatter.

The soldier's voice sounded and Callum felt something cold thrust into his hands. He looked down to see a machine gun. The soldier was repeating the same instruction again and again in Russian.

"He says to shoot!" Darya said.

"What about the window?"

"Through the window," she shouted. "Just shoot!"

The creature was clinging to the side of the cabin with its foreclaws tucked around the handle. As Callum raised the rifle barrel and took aim, it reached upwards and tried to slide back the window.

Callum pressed his finger down and unleashed a burst of automatic fire. The rounds peppered the little pane, blowing the centre out and propelling the creature from the side of the machine. Trails of warm blood lashed against his face and streaked what remained of the acrylic screen.

It was Callum's turn to yell out in triumph. But all celebrations were quickly off as another two thuds sounded on the roof.

The soldier shouted something to Darya.

"He says to take the controls."

Before Callum could protest, the machine jerked to a halt. The hulking soldier turned and shot him a glance. His dark eyes were narrowed, his lips crushed together in a determined half-grin-half-grimace. He cracked his knuckles, seized the rifle from Callum and shoved past.

On reflex Callum slipped into the driving seat. His feet fell naturally onto the pedals and his hands clasped on to the two control sticks mounted at the end of either armrest. The seat was warm and the controls clammy. "But… what does what?" he shouted over his shoulder.

There was no reply as the soldier's boots disappeared through the shattered window.

4

Callum slammed his foot onto the pedal. To his relief the machine bucked and trundled forward as before, the engine roaring, the tracks squealing below. He had no idea where he was going and he didn't dare mess with any of the other controls, so he simply held the control sticks steady and ploughed blindly ahead.

The mist flowed past in a torrent, thick and unrelenting as the minutes ticked by. The growling of the machine's engine filled his ears. His leg wound pulsated with the frantic beating of his heart, and Darya's fingers dug into his already-aching shoulders.

Gunshots rang out suddenly from above. Then, before either of them could react, the machine slammed to a halt. Callum was thrown forward over the controls, while Darya was hurled from her perch behind the seat. The smell of burning metal filled the cabin, and the machine's engine shuddered and gave out.

Callum looked up, dazed. Piercing through the shattered screen was a corner of grey concrete. "I think we've found the compound."

There was no reply.

He looked around to see Darya draped over the floor of the

cabin. She looked like a ragdoll. Her arms were twisted beneath her and blood dripped from a gash on her head. Callum ignored the ringing inside his own skull and dragged her up into a sitting position. The wound above her eye was only small, but it was bleeding profusely, and he bunched his sleeve up and stemmed the flow.

"Darya? Can you hear me?"

She said nothing. When he drew his hand away to check her pulse, her body slumped back down against him. She was alive, but she was out cold. He tore a strip of fabric from his undershirt and fastened it around her head. As he fumbled to secure the knot, a loud thunk rang out beside him, and a boot came smashing through the windscreen. It was followed by a forearm, which forced its way through the cleft and levered the screen open.

Callum expected to see the soldier who had been driving the machine. But it was a different man who clambered up into the cabin. He was taller, and his face looked as if it had been chiselled out of solid granite. A large, hook-shaped scar ran the length of his cheek and the dense surrounding stubble looked more like iron filings than hair.

His white uniform drenched in blood, the soldier wasted no time scooping Darya up into his arms and backing out of the windscreen.

Without a word, Callum followed on.

5

The bunker was a reinforced concrete shell set around a ribcage of steel girders. Soldiers were stationed at intervals along the rifle slits on either wall. Their steaming rifles were shouldered and a vomit of spent cartridges lay scattered around their knees. Some were still firing, prompting more explosions off in the distance.

The scar-faced soldier passed into a second chamber. It was danker, and the lack of rifle slits on either wall heightened the gloom. In the middle of the floor, a wounded man was being tended to by one of his comrades. Barely out of his teens by the look of him, the young man's injuries looked horrific. There were clear puncture marks across his shoulder and chest, and a deep gouge ran just below his ribcage.

The soldier stopped and lay Darya gently down next to the dying soldier. The older-looking medic set to work examining her, as Scar-face addressed him in a commanding tone.

"What is it?" Callum asked. "She'll be okay, right?"

The two soldiers stopped their conversation and stared at him. The medic then spoke to Scar-face, who nodded, grunted and spat on the floor.

Callum went to speak again, when another voice cut him off:

"Doctor Lebedev will be okay, my friend. She is unconscious, but she is not badly injured."

Lungkaju was kneeling down in the corner of the room. His arm was wrapped around Ava Lee as she rocked back and forth, the same look of silent hysteria on her face that she'd had back in the emergency shelter.

"Lungkaju! Ava!" Callum flew across the room and threw his arms around them both. Lungkaju responded with his free arm, while Ava continued her rocking. "I didn't think you'd make it… not before the mist…"

"We did not," Lungkaju replied. "We were only half-way down the ridge when it came."

"He carried me," Ava piped up suddenly. Her voice was manic, her eyes fixed on middle distance. "He carried me," she repeated. "Carried me…" She went silent once again and continued rocking.

"She is in shock," Lungkaju said.

Callum knelt beside her and placed a hand on hers. She was in a bad way. Her face was smeared with grime. Her once neat, brown hair was now matted, dark with sweat, and her eyes were swollen with exhaustion and fear. Every one of the survivors was in the same boat. But he identified most with Ava. Like him, her life was one of middle-class comfort: hot showers at the end of a day in the field, financial security and intellectual gratification. Her greatest challenges were deciding between Claret and Beaujolais of an evening, deciding which journal to publish her latest paper in. Now here they were at war.

He squeezed her hand and spoke softly. "Ava?"

No reply.

"Ava, they display just like birds."

For a while she carried on rocking, knees drawn up tightly to her chest, lips trembling. Then her eyes stumbled around to meet his. "They… they do?"

He nodded. "It's beautiful. They mimic each other's colouring."

The faintest of smiles flickered across her lips. "You saw it?"

"First-hand."

There was a sudden commotion at the other end of the bunker, and Starshyna Koikov marched over and threw open the door. A soldier, his body steaming, his face flushed red with exertion, fell through it into his arms. Koikov steadied him, and the two men engaged in an intense exchange.

"What's going on?" Callum asked Lungkaju.

"That is Sergeant Marchenko. He says that the rescue helicopter will be here in half an hour."

Callum let out a huge sigh of relief. "Thank Christ for that!"

"Thank the sergeant," Lungkaju replied with a grin. "Without him we would not make contact."

Callum reached out and stroked Darya's cheek. Her skin felt freezing, so he removed his scarf and tucked it around her neck. "Did you hear that?" he whispered. "They're coming for us. We're going home."

She made no response.

Through in Chamber 1, Starshyna Koikov brought his conversation with Marchenko to an end. He slapped the exhausted-looking sergeant on the back, almost sending him over. Then he turned and bellowed out an order. His words immediately upset what little routine had been established. All three chambers buzzed with renewed energy as the troopers began raking their equipment together.

Callum looked to Lungkaju. His hood drawn tightly around his chin, he appeared composed, still maintaining his vigil over Ava. She had now stopped rocking and her head rested on his shoulder. "We must get ready to leave," Lungkaju said. "I will take care of Doctor Lee. You must take care of Doctor Lebedev. Can you do this?"

"Of course," Callum replied. In fact, it was the only thing he was still certain of. Until they were dead or rescued, he would not be leaving Darya's side. "Where's the helicopter landing?"

"There is high ground to the west."

"How far to the west?"

"A kilometre, no more."

"A kilometre? But what about the creatures?"

"There is no choice, my friend. It is the safest place for the helicopter to land. We must trust Starshyna Koikov."

Callum said nothing, just watched as Lungkaju removed his vodka canteen from his jacket and took a swig. His gaze traced the line of the brown, gently curving leather rectangle that he had first encountered in the Kamov on the journey from the mainland. The memory of the liquid's burn at the back of his throat rushed back to him. He held his hand out. "May I?"

Lungkaju did not offer it up. Instead he slowly turned it upside down.

Nothing came out. Not a single droplet. Lungkaju looked slowly from the empty, upturned canteen to Callum. With a mournful look in his eyes he said, "I am sorry, my friend. There has been nothing for days. It is only..." He searched for the right word.

"Habit," Callum said.

"Yes, but there is another word also."

"Comfort?"

Lungkaju seemed to think about it. Then he closed his eyes and nodded.

Inside his pocket, Callum's hand tightened around the quartz pebble. He went to speak, when a sudden hail of gunfire erupted through in Chamber 3, and both men rushed to the doorway.

One of the creatures had snaked its head through the east-facing rifle slit and seized onto a soldier's arm. The man's rifle had fallen to the floor and he was flailing his free arm against the creature's face, screaming in pain.

"We've got to help him!" Callum shouted. He went to rush forward, but Lungkaju grabbed his shoulder.

"No, my friend. We will only be in the way."

As he spoke, two other soldiers rushed to his aid. Seizing the creature around the neck, one of them stabbed his knife into the side of its skull, while the other pounded the bridge of its snout with his rifle butt.

Then another creature speared its head into the chamber and clamped its jaws around the knife-wielder's throat. In one quick motion, it ripped its head back, tearing away the entire front half of his neck. Eyes wide with shock, the soldier slumped to his knees, jets of blood drenching his killer's face.

The first creature still had a hold, and the second now tossed the lump of throat flesh aside and lunged for the captive soldier's other arm. Working together, the two pulled backwards, attempting to drag him outside.

Koikov barged past Callum into the room, an inhuman rage twisting his features. Running straight past the carnage, he rammed a flamethrower out through the rifle slit. Seconds later the bunker's interior was thrown into blinding relief as a flash of light poured in from outside accompanied by a tremendous wave of heat. Both creatures released their hold on the soldier and wrenched their heads back through the gap, braying in agony.

The soldier collapsed back into the room, and Koikov paced by him, unleashing a second tongue of bright orange flame out through the rifle slit. With a roar of his own, he strode up and down the length of the bunker, blasting a stream of liquid fire out into the mist, incinerating whatever was unlucky enough to be within a twenty-foot arc.

At last, he released the trigger and bellowed out an order. Then he dragged the injured soldier through into Chamber 2. The soldiers grabbed whatever they could carry and retreated after him, heaving the door behind them.

"Look!" Lungkaju shouted, pointing back through the remaining sliver of doorway. One creature after another had begun clawing its way in through the undefended rifle slits into the abandoned chamber, some with scorched feathers, others unharmed. With an indignant grunt, Koikov joined in with the others, and together they slammed the door shut and bolted it.

* * *

Corporal Voronkov was having a field day. So far he'd chalked up twenty-seven of the little bastards. One for every year of his life. He'd even allowed Zyryonov to make a couple of kills, which had shut him up for a few precious minutes.

His radio crackled. "Voronkov!"

"Yes, Starshyna?"

"How's it looking down here?"

The truth was Voronkov hadn't checked the state of the bunker for some time. He'd been far too busy picking off the creatures that had picked up his scent and massed at the base of the moraine. They were sly, he'd give them that much. They hadn't just herded towards him. Instead they'd dispersed, each individual creature flitting its way from cover to cover towards him. But he was now confident that he had the remaining handful pinned down behind various outcrops, leaving him free to take pot shots.

"Voronkov, answer me!"

Voronkov threw a glance over at the bunker. His stomach turned. "Shit! They're all over your position!"

"Tell me something I don't know, you useless prick! We've abandoned Chambers 1 and 3 already. We're holed up in 2 for now, but we're about to break out and move to your position. What I need to know is whether they're on the roof?"

Voronkov surveyed the scene. Ground level at either end of the bunker was squirming with red forms. Through the LVV they looked like some kind of bacterial infection laying waste to a shred of tissue. Dozens more were flocking in from the east, rivulets of red carving up the basin.

"They're concentrated at either end, Starshyna. No more than a couple currently visible on the roof. Take them out?"

"When I give you the word," Koikov replied. "Then I want you to take out those on the roof *only*. And Voronkov, you wait for my order, you hear me? These things are smart. I don't want to risk alerting them until the last minute. Are we clear?"

"Just give me the word."

6

The last of the soldiers made their way from Chamber 1 to Chamber 2 and secured the door behind them. Chamber 3 was already teeming with creatures. The sound of them screeching and clawing at the other side of the door was impossible to ignore. And now Chamber 1 was filling up as well. So far the doors were holding, but for how long?

Kneeling beside Darya, Callum looked around at the other survivors. Aside from Ava and Lungkaju, he counted only nine remaining soldiers, soon to be seven by the looks of the two men laid out beside him on the blood-stained floor. His mind flicked back to the *Albanov* and the hundred or so people he must have seen on the first day alone. It was hard to believe that this was all that was left. It was even harder to believe that *he* was left.

As Koikov's voice rang out, all other conversation died away; his only accompaniment now was the screeching and scratching of the creatures to either side, and the moans of the two dying soldiers.

"We will go through the roof hatch," Lungkaju translated. "There is a hovercraft behind the bunker to take us to the extraction point. Corporal Voronkov and Private Zyryonov are on the high ground. They will clear the roof for us and give us cover."

Koikov cast his gaze around.

"The starshyna wants to know if there are any questions," Lungkaju said.

Nobody spoke as the scraping of talons on concrete continued its disembodied assault to either side. Screeches and clicks wafted in through the ventilation ports, which Callum now noticed in the upper corners of the chamber. His eyes narrowed at the sight of a couple of lengths of wire poking in through the grills and dribbling down onto the floor.

Lungkaju: "Starshyna Koikov says that if we stay here, the creatures will very soon break through these doors. They are old and no longer strong enough."

Callum dragged a finger along the top of one of the hinges. A film of beige dust coated his fingertip.

"We must go quickly now," Lungkaju said. "The helicopter will be here soon. Ten minutes."

There was a sudden groan and all eyes moved to the centre of the room. The younger man, whom the medic had been treating when Callum first arrived in the bunker, was still somehow clinging to life. But the soldier whose arms had been savaged in Chamber 3 was now staring blankly upwards, his lips parted, his face still and grey. A lake of blood had seeped through his bandages and pooled around him on the floor. The medic reached out and pushed his eyelids closed.

For a moment the survivors were still and silent, the same horror bold on each of their faces. There could have been no more graphic an example of what was at stake for all of them the second that hatch opened.

Sergeant Marchenko knelt down beside the man, settled a hand onto his chest and bent his head in prayer. Only then did Callum recognise Marchenko. **Антон** was tattooed on the back of his knuckles in black Cyrillic font. It was Gavriil. Gavriil

Marchenko, father of Anton and Natalya. The gentle features and intelligent gaze that had become so familiar to Callum during his visits to the comms centre were now so masked by blood, dirt and fatigue that he looked like a different person. He spoke a few soft words before climbing back to his feet.

"Gavriil," Callum said.

Marchenko looked over at him. It was clear from his look of surprise that the last few days on Harmsworth had also done a number on Callum's face. "Callum," he said with a smile. "You..." he held his hands out to indicate Callum standing there, "...for Jamie."

Callum nodded. "You, for Anton and Natalya."

Marchenko reached out and shook his hand.

Koikov eyed them both with undisguised suspicion, then he leapt up, grabbed the bottom rung of the escape ladder and began hauling himself up. At the top, he spoke into his radio collar, waited for a response and then flung the hatch open to reveal a disc of swirling grey-white. Rifle shouldered, he scanned across the roof before climbing out and signalling to the others.

One by one, the survivors made their way up the ladder. As he emerged, Callum was greeted by the reassuring sight of two dead creatures, both with single bullet wounds to the head. Beyond, he could just make out the rest of the group crouched in a huddle a few paces away, and he crept over and joined them.

Marchenko was cradling Darya, and Callum knelt next to him and took her hand.

"She is will be okay," Marchenko whispered, in his familiar broken English. "The heart," he spasmed his fist in front of Darya's chest to indicate a strong heartbeat, "and the breath, is good." He gave a reassuring smile. "This I promise."

"What about the other soldier?" Ava said. "Are we just going to leave him?"

Marchenko seemed to understand her question, and he shuffled restlessly.

"Private Tsaritsyn is dying," Lungkaju replied. "We cannot help him. Starshyna Koikov has given him some drugs to help."

They watched as Koikov emerged from the bunker and peered back down through the hatch. He was tall, but the supernatural shadow cast around him in the mist gave him another two or three feet in height as he turned and signalled to Sergeant Marchenko to move out. He then dropped his legs back down onto the ladder.

With a final nod towards Marchenko, he disappeared back into the bunker and heaved the hatch closed after him.

Chapter 16

GUNSHIP

1

With the others on their way to meet the chopper, Koikov wasted no time finding the fuse wires. Earlier that day he'd run them from the two wads positioned above the opposing external doorways and threaded them through the ventilation grills into Chamber 2. He now produced the manual detonator and began stringing the wires to the two nodes.

He had never planned on being a hero. In a perfect world he would have escaped with the rest of the team and detonated the charges remotely. But the world was far from perfect – Koikov knew that as well as anybody – and the remote detonator had been aboard the other hovercraft when the *Albanov* had blown. Once again, the island had decided it would take no prisoners.

Still, it was no big deal. Things got fucked up when you relied on remote technology. Here on the ground, he could more or less guarantee an explosion. And what an explosion! That amount of C4 was meant to reduce the bunker and everything in it to dust. Even better, the sheer number of dragons that had taken the bait was beyond anything he could have hoped for. With one twist of the trigger, he was going to take out half the colony.

He had just finished wiring up the detonator, when he became conscious of a low groan. Private Tsaritsyn was stirring.

His face was colourless, his skin and clothing slick with sweat. Shit! Why hadn't Ivanov done as he was ordered and put the poor bastard out of his misery?

Tsaritsyn's body shook violently, as if he'd been dowsed in freezing water. Then his eyes flickered open until he was staring up into Koikov's. In obvious agony, he reached a shaking hand out.

Koikov hesitated. The youth reminded him of Dolgonosov: the same narrow, babyish face and dark features, the same look of innocent confusion, even the same grotesque bulge to his dying eyes. He took the private's hand.

With surprising strength, Tsaritsyn pulled his hand away before reaching back out.

This time Koikov could see that he was gesturing not towards his hand, but towards the detonator. The private's lips peeled apart. His voice was barely audible: "M-my turn."

Koikov stared down at him.

"My turn," Tsaritsyn repeated. "Not yours, Starshyna."

Kneeling down, Koikov picked up the blood-streaked rag from beside Tsaritsyn and mopped the sweat from his brow. His mind raced. This wasn't what he'd imagined as he'd reclosed the escape hatch behind him, prepared to never have to open it again. The emotion was beyond his ability to define. Was it relief that he might not have to die? Was it disappointment? Was it guilt that his leadership had brought Tsaritsyn and so many of the others to such a hideous end? Or was it shame that he was now considering allowing a young man to die for him? Perhaps it was all of them.

He dropped the rag back down and took Tsaritsyn's hand once more, holding it firmly. He hesitated again, disgusted at his own indecision. Then, at last, he pushed the detonator into the soldier's palm and folded his fingers around it. Tsaritsyn brought his hand back and clutched the detonator to his chest.

For what seemed like an eternity, the two men said nothing.

The clamouring of the creatures had grown louder and louder around them, and their collective stink was wafting through the vents and poisoning the already stale air.

"You know how to work it?" Koikov said at last.

Tsaritsyn nodded.

Koikov placed a hand on his forehead. Then he climbed slowly back to his feet and stared down at the young private. He brought his hand up in a salute.

Tsaritsyn's arm twitched and he nodded again. "H-hurry."

2

With Sergeant Marchenko at the controls and the two snipers from the ridge safely aboard, the hovercraft roared across the runway towards the extraction point. All Callum could see were the backs of the soldiers' heads and the gusts of grey-white rushing in between them. Darya was draped across his lap on the back row, still unconscious. Behind them, Corporal Aliyev manned the rear-mounted machine gun.

Nobody seemed to know what the hell had happened to Starshyna Koikov. Was it a breakdown? Was it all just part of the plan? Either way, his absence had been felt by every last one of them as they'd lowered themselves from the roof of the bunker and silently boarded the hovercraft.

Marchenko called back over his shoulder.

"Two minutes," Lungkaju translated. "Then we must climb on foot."

A screech sounded, and Corporal Aliyev swung the machine gun around and unleashed a volley into the murk. Callum flinched at the sound of the barrage, watching as the muzzle flashes pulsed through the mist like sheet lightning.

The other soldiers joined in, putting down small arms fire and slinging grenades out into the hovercraft's wake. Angular shadows broke the haze to either side. Shrieks sounded left and right as rounds found their targets.

Lungkaju: "One minute more, my friend. Just be brave."

Callum glanced back over his shoulder just as the mist lit up. A tremendous explosion ripped through the air and a tidal wave of light, sound and heat rolled over the hovercraft, sending it into a spin. Callum was thrown to the floor as the craft swept around out of control. It skidded in a huge arc, the air cushion deflating, grinding the hovercraft's chassis along the bedrock. It skidded along, sparks erupting where the metal frame ground against rock. Then it shaved past an outcrop and spiralled to a halt.

"The bunker," Lungkaju shouted, jumping down from the craft. "Koikov has destroyed it!"

Ears ringing, Callum clambered back to his feet. "Was he still in there?"

"I do not know," Lungkaju said. "But we must hurry now, Doctor Ross. The helicopter will arrive soon. We are nearly there."

As the two men dragged Darya down from the hovercraft, Sergeant Marchenko and the remainder of the troopers maintained a defensive formation around them.

"You are okay?" Marchenko called out.

"I think so," Callum replied. Still partially deaf, he bent down and scooped Darya up into his arms, then they set off at a blistering pace up the side of the moraine.

By the time they reached the summit, Callum was panting with exhaustion. His lungs burnt, his muscles ached and his leg wound felt fresh again, as if the claw was still embedded. But as he peered up into the swirling mist, all exhaustion, all pain, all negativity was swept aside in one magnificent downdraft.

3

The rescue helicopter was landing. First to emerge was the glare from its headlamps and under-carriage lighting, weak at first but intensifying as it made its cautious descent. Then came the line of its landing rails, followed by its nose and cabin, and finally its tail. The noise from the rotors drowned out everything as they whipped the surrounding mist up into a funnel.

Callum hugged onto Darya and yelled out with joy. After everything they'd been through, he could hardly believe that it was here. "We're going home," he whispered, kissing the side of her cheek. "*We're going home!*"

As the lights from the helicopter penetrated the mist and bathed the cracked and bloody skin of his face, he could feel the weight that had been squatting inside his chest leave him in a sudden rush. In the glow of those lights, with the rotor-whipped mist buffeted and beaten into submission around him, Darya felt weightless in his arms; he could have carried her forever. The pain in his leg was a distant memory. *What pain? What creatures? What island?*

He looked across to see the soldiers cheering, some jumping up and down despite their exhaustion, others collapsed on their knees with a mixture of gratitude and disbelief, just watching the descent. Corporal Aliyev and the medic who had cared for Darya were locked in an embrace, while two new faces, presumably the two snipers, shared the same ear-to-ear grin as they punched the air and waved their arms triumphantly at the descending helicopter.

Callum caught Marchenko's eye. The gentle soldier smiled across at him and held his thumb up. Callum smiled back, and they watched together as the helicopter finally touched down.

It was smaller than Callum had expected, more like a gunship than a troop carrier, its white-painted exterior dripping with armaments. It appeared to have two sets of rotor blades, mounted one directly above the other, no tail rotor and its windows were blacked out. Still, in that moment nothing could have mattered less. It could have been a microlight, a hot air balloon, a magic carpet for all it counted. If it was airborne and it could bring this nightmare to an end, then it was the greatest thing in creation.

With Darya draped in his arms, Callum staggered towards it. With every step he could imagine himself back home. He was sat with Jamie. What were they doing? They were doing nothing, beautiful nothing. Just sitting, just being father and son… television on… half-eaten tubs of Ben and Jerry's ice-cream – they both agreed Cookie Dough was best – in each of their laps… he was watching Jamie read his comic books… he was watching as Jamie skipped a stone from one side of Loch Ness to the other…

It's just a stone, Dad.

A few more steps. A few more steps and he was on his way home.

He was on his way home as the side-mounted machine gun swivelled towards them.

He was on his way home as the side-mounted machine gun opened fire.

4

A hail of bullets sprayed in an arc across Callum's shoulder.

But... the killing was over... I was on my way home...

As reality hit, he flung himself and Darya to the ground. From the shadow of the helicopter, he looked back and saw the first bullets tear into Sergeant Marchenko's chest. The smile on the gentle soldier's face became an open gasp of shock as the bullets peppered his flesh. The force lifted him off his feet and sent him reeling backwards, his back arched, his chest coughing up a cloud of blood.

With a hideous polyphonic rasp, the bullets sliced through Corporal Aliyev's back and shoulders, unzipping the flesh and passing through into the medic. The man's throat opened up as the bullets pulverised the top of his chest, almost severing his head. The snipers' stomachs turned to red pulp as they waved frantically, then collapsed against each other in a heap, their bodies seizing, seeming to throb under the continued strafe.

A bullet passed through one of the soldiers' eyes, another through his ear, then the centre of his forehead, leaving his grin unchanged as he toppled onto his face. As the others turned to run, the bullets found their legs, blowing out their ankles, shredding the meat from their thighs and ripping into their backs. As they stumbled down, the bullets criss-crossed their shoulders, necks and heads, and one by one, in quick succession, their faces hit the freezing rock.

The universe crawled. Sound vanished. Callum could only watch as the men that had saved his life lay crumpled over one another, their limbs twitching, their remaining eyes wide with shock. He closed his own eyes in disbelief; when he reopened them, the team would be clambering up into the helicopter, alive and well. It was all just a figment of his exhausted imagination.

But as his lids crept back open, the scene of carnage was unchanged. The only people left standing were Lungkaju and Ava, who had gone to ground just behind him, both unharmed. Lungkaju wore that same look of intense pain and anguish that he had at the death of Fenris, while Ava's tear-streaked face bore dumb incomprehension.

Instinctively, Callum ran his hands across Darya's body. Not a scratch.

With a final, sadistic pass over the mangled corpses, the gunfire ended. The machine gun barrel was now silent and smoking, pointed directly at Lungkaju. With his eyes glued to the twin-muzzle, he took Ava by the hand and climbed slowly to his feet. "Doctor Ross. Are you hurt?"

Callum grunted and shook his head. The world had fallen out from under him.

The helicopter's side door opened and a Russian voice boomed out over the PA system.

"He tells us to get on board," Lungkaju said. "We should do what he says."

The cabin was cramped, much smaller than that of the Kamovs. Like a robot, his mind still clouded with shock, Callum lay Darya on the floor between the two opposed rows of seating and slumped down next to Ava.

The door slid shut.

The images of what he had just witnessed played over in front of him, and he watched them, powerless to turn away, barely conscious of where he was or what was happening around him.

Opposite him sat another man. He was tall and dressed in a neatly pressed navy-blue uniform. His back was turned as he leant in-between the two front seats and spoke loudly to the pilot, but Callum recognised him even through his daze, and the realisation brought him crashing back to earth.

"Doctor Ross. Doctor Lee." Volkov beamed, turning to face them. "It is so wonderful to see you both again."

Chapter 17

DATA STICK

1

Wonderful was not the adjective Callum would have chosen. *Disturbing,* maybe. *Confusing,* for sure. He went to speak, but he was unable to. His brain cried out for answers, but his tongue felt like a lead weight.

"Come now, Doctor Ross," Volkov teased. "If this is truly the limit of your communicative abilities then I am afraid I must cancel my application to the University of Aberdeen." He sniggered.

"You... you murdered those soldiers," Callum said, regaining the ghost of speech. His tone was so naturally hate filled that he could hardly recognise it as his own. "Marchenko and his team, you just... gunned them down... in cold blood."

Volkov sneered, "As an educated man, Doctor Ross, you do surprise me. You must surely understand that there are no rights or wrongs in this fairy-tale world of ours. Faith. Fact. Fiction. Reality itself. They are all determined by one thing, are they not? Perspective. These were not saints. These were professional killers. *Mercenaries.* They had blood on their hands, each and every one."

"They saved my life."

"Do you imagine that the families of the many young

mujahedeen fighters that these soldiers have brutally cleansed from the Caucasus would share your appreciation? Tell me, what makes your horror any more relevant than their elation?"

"But why, Mr Volkov?" The voice was Lungkaju's. "Why did the soldiers have to die?"

"Everybody must go down with the *Albanov*," Volkov snarled. "Otherwise it is… awkward."

This made no sense. *Go down with the* Albanov?

"What the hell are you talking about?" Callum said. "Do you know what happened to the ship?"

Volkov waved his hand dismissively. "I know rather a lot about what happened to it, Doctor Ross. It was me that gave the order to destroy it."

Callum gasped. "*You* did it?"

"It was my design," Volkov replied. His tone was conversational, as if he were chatting over coffee. "Not to force the issue of perspective, but the deed itself was carried out by none other than your friend and colleague Mr Daniel Peterson." He shot a glance in Ava's direction.

Callum felt her twitch beside him. As if awakening from a dream, she eased her grip from Lungkaju's arm and stared at Volkov. Her look of torment sent a shiver creeping along Callum's spine. Dark crescents hung beneath her eyes as she peered through a veil of matted hair. "You're saying it was Dan's fault what happened on the *Albanov*?"

Volkov's eyes lit up. "Ah, Doctor Lee. I was hoping that you would join in the conversation. It may shock you to learn that your paramour Mr Peterson was an *eco-terrorist*. Membership of the EIA team was his cover. His objective was always to destroy the *Albanov*."

"I don't believe you," Ava said. "Dan may have been a lot of things, but he was no murderer."

"The purity of his intentions is beyond doubt," Volkov replied. "He is a misguided fool, but his motives were noble enough. He wanted to save the Arctic from exploitation. The problem is that this is impossible. Naïve idealists like Mr Peterson are just too blinded by sentiment to see it. Commercial exploitation of the Arctic is inevitable." He grinned. "Thanks to his own actions, it is now closer than ever."

Callum kept quiet. The last thing he wanted was to believe a word Volkov said. Yet there was a ring of truth. He remembered when Darya, Ava and he had first awoken on Harmsworth. His own words repeated on him: *Dan's the last person any of us saw... one of us has woken up armed with a whole raft of survival equipment... the one he has feelings for...*

The conundrum had been why Peterson would drug three of his colleagues and strand them on Harmsworth? Now, in the surreal confines of Volkov's assault helicopter, the answer seemed to slug him hard around the face. And the pieces kept on fitting. Peterson was a true nature lover. He was passionate about the Arctic. The submarine would have given him the ideal means of operation and escape...

But what Ava said was also true. Peterson was not a ruthless killer. Of that, Callum was certain. He was a nice guy, quirky and highly strung, but a decent human being.

Suddenly it all made perfect sense.

Why would Peterson drug three of his colleagues and maroon them on Harmsworth?

Because he was trying to save their lives.

2

The mist was clearing. The grey blanket had fractured into a 3D jigsaw puzzle, its pieces thinning and warping, billowing past Koikov as he sprinted to the top of the moraine.

Until now, his only indication that the rescue helicopter had arrived at the extraction point had been the thumping of the rotors as he'd scrambled up the slope. Now that he could see the craft, he could tell instantly that there was something wrong.

Marchenko had been told to expect an Mi-26, a troop-carrier with a hundred-person capacity, perfectly suited to severe weather conditions. The co-axial, heavily armoured assault helicopter now heading away from him was no Mi-26. It was more similar to a Black Shark, a Kamov 50, only slightly larger. And why would the craft be painted white rather than regulation military shades? *A White Shark.*

As he cast around for an explanation, his gaze fell upon the jumble of blood-stained corpses. His eyes widened in disbelief and he sprinted over. Dropping to his knees, he rolled the nearest man onto his back.

"Marchenko!" The damage to his body was extensive. But his eyes were open and the tiniest shred of life clung on within him. Koikov raised his head up, supporting the back of his neck.

"Marchenko? Marchenko, what happened?"

Blood spilt from the sergeant's mouth as he tried to speak. "They... must have... intercepted... my transmission..."

"Intercepted your transmission? Who? Marchenko? Who's *they*? Who the fuck did this?"

This time there was no response. Marchenko's gentle eyes took on that sudden dimness that Koikov had seen too many times before. In vain, he crouched over the corpse and began chest compressions. He'd performed no more than three before his hands cracked through Marchenko's shattered sternum and disappeared into his chest cavity.

He tore his hands away and retched violently. It was no use. Marchenko was gone. He checked the others for signs of life. All of them were gone.

Koikov's breathing spiralled; his head spun. The scene before him was more gut-wrenching than anything he had witnessed so far on Harmsworth. It was not the work of dragons. His team's wounds were not the result of claws or teeth. They were bullet holes, the result of man-made metal rounds fired at close quarters.

Something cold stung at Koikov's cheek and he wiped away at it. His fingertips were moist. A single tear had escaped him. He couldn't remember the last time he'd shed a tear. They were useless. They solved nothing. But, on this occasion, they just happened.

As the helicopter made away, he buried his face into Marchenko's shoulder and wept.

* * *

"You used him," Callum spat. "You used Peterson. And for what? What's this all about, Volkov? Money?"

Volkov pursed his lips. "I did not *use* Mr Peterson; he volunteered his services readily. And I much prefer to think in terms of economy, not *money.*" He grinned. "My reasons for involving Mr Peterson are none of your concern. But let's just say that the Harmsworth Project is going to be much more *economical* when his transgressions are brought to light."

"Darya told me you were a greedy, manipulative bastard, but this…"

Volkov threw a glance in Darya's direction. His eyes narrowed. "Yes, our paths have unfortunately crossed before. She and her kind have cost me a great deal in the past, but not this time."

Ava turned to Callum. "Doctor Ross, surely you don't believe this bullshit about Dan?"

"Of course not," he lied; he needed Ava's help more than ever and the last thing he wanted was to isolate her feelings.

"What is it you want, Volkov? If everyone was supposed to go down with the *Albanov* then why are *we* still alive?"

A dark smile crossed Volkov's lips. "I have kept you alive because I would like to play a little game with you, Doctor Ross."

"A game?" Ava said. "Are you serious?"

"Deadly," he replied, reaching into his belt and removing a handgun. "I call it *Mr Peterson's Data Stick*, and it works like this." He pulled back on the top of the weapon, cocking it. Then he pointed it at Callum's face. "Round one. I point this gun at each player in turn. I then ask, 'Do you have Mr Peterson's data stick?' If the player answers no, then unfortunately they are no longer in the game. If they answer, 'Yes, I have Mr Peterson's data stick,' then congratulations, they are through to round two."

Callum frowned. "What data stick?"

"I cannot tell whether you are bluffing, Doctor Ross." Volkov paused, eyeing Callum coldly. "The data stick in question belonged to Mr Peterson, and it is now of *considerable* value to myself and my associates."

"So what happens in round two?" Ava asked.

"Round two is where the game starts to get interesting.

In round two, I say, 'Give me Mr Peterson's data stick.' The remaining player then has only to hand me the data stick and they win the game. If the player is unwilling to hand it over immediately, then unfortunately they are also out of the game." He sat back in his chair. "Are we all clear on the rules?"

Callum went to speak, but he was drowned out by the pilot yelling back into the cabin. Volkov's expression soured and he rushed over to peer through the side window.

Heart racing, Callum also stole a glance. By now the mist had largely disappeared. Through the glass he could see back towards south-western Harmsworth. The moraine rose from the centre of the basin, the abandoned hovercraft glinting at its base. To the east, there was now a smoking scatter of rubble where the bunker had once stood.

His gaze moved to the top of the moraine. A dark blotch was spread across the rock where Marchenko and his team had fallen. From this distance, their individual bodies had merged into a single, lifeless heap that brought the image of their massacre flashing back through Callum's mind.

As he looked on, something else caught his attention. Movement. Next to the bodies, something was moving around, subtle but unmistakable. Was it one of the creatures? Could one of the soldiers really have survived?

His face cut with a sudden rage, Volkov bellowed something through to the pilot, and the helicopter began to turn.

"Bind their hands!" he ordered, leaping through into the co-pilot seat.

Confused, Callum looked across at Ava. Who the hell was he talking to?

His heart skipped a beat.

With one hand clamped around her wrist and the other brandishing a pistol, Lungkaju met his gaze. "I am sorry, my friends. But you must put your hands behind your back."

3

Callum could hardly believe his eyes as Lungkaju uncoiled a
length of rope and began coolly binding Ava's wrist.

"What are you doing?"

"I am doing what I have to do, my friend."

"Don't call me that!"

"Doctor Ross—"

"How could you? How could you help that... that murderer?
Did you even see what he just did?"

"Yes, I saw, and I am very sorry that this had to happen. I
hoped that nobody else would have to die."

"Nobody *else*?"

Ava offered no resistance as Lungkaju pulled her other
arm gently but firmly behind her back and secured her hands
together. He then approached Callum and took hold of his wrist.

Callum wrenched his arm away.

"Please do not make this more difficult, Doctor Ross,"
Lungkaju said. His tone was soft, apologetic. It was also
accompanied by a metallic snap as he cocked the pistol. "I have
no choice."

Callum stared into the face of the man he had considered a
friend, the gentle Nganasan who had dressed and redressed his

leg wound and grieved so hard at the death of his pet dog. His eyes moved back to the gun aimed at his chest, and he turned and put his hands behind his back.

"Do you remember when I told you about my daughter, Doctor Ross?"

Callum did remember, but he made no reply. All he could think was: *Marchenko had a daughter too, and a son. And thanks to your boss they'll never see each other again.* But he said nothing. As the rope snaked around his skin, he felt numb with betrayal.

"She is everything to me. Like your son, Jamie, is to you."

The name was like a kick to the stomach. "Don't you dare talk about my son!"

Lungkaju steadied himself as the helicopter banked. Then he sat down opposite Callum. "We are very different people."

"You can say that again."

Lungkaju sighed. He lacked the poise with which Volkov wielded his own pistol. His movements were controlled but pensive, his eyes heavy with conflict.

"In Russia, the Nganasan, my people, are..." he searched for the right words, "...not equal. Life is hard for them, Doctor Ross, harder than I have ever seen it before. The melting ice makes hunting less predictable and more dangerous for those who try to live the old way. Because of this there are less and less of them, and it is harder for them to support their families."

He leant forward. "The old way is dying, and for those who move into the towns to find work, there are other problems. Education and healthcare are very poor. Unemployment, crime, and drug and alcohol addiction are high. I have friends who have drunk themselves to death, others who have tried to kill themselves because they see no future. This is not unusual now, and it is very sad when I go back and see what is happening to my people." He paused, a look of resolution in his eyes. "I do not want this for my daughter."

"I can sympathise with the plight of your people," Callum

said. "But poverty and social deprivation are not an excuse to go around pointing guns in people's faces. You must know that?"

"It is okay for you to say this, Doctor Ross. You are a good man, but you are also very fortunate. You do not know what it is like to be unequal. You do not know hopelessness."

"I know right from wrong," Callum replied. "I know that I wouldn't want my son to grow up knowing that his father was a criminal. That he'd stood there and watched as innocent men were murdered and others taken hostage, and all for the sake of money."

"It is very easy to look down on those who envy wealth, Doctor Ross, when you yourself are wealthy."

Callum threw a glance at the others. Darya's eyes were still closed, but she was stirring slightly, in the early stages of coming round. He hoped to God she didn't wake up now. Beside him, Ava sat still and quiet, just listening to Lungkaju.

"Mr Volkov was working in Ust Avam in Taymyr many years ago. He was caught in a blizzard and was freezing to death. My father and grandfather were out hunting, and they found him. They cared for him. They saved his life. I can still remember walking in and seeing him, the white man sleeping in my father's bed.

"He promised that he would help them however he could. My grandfather was far too proud to ask him for anything. But before he passed away, my father wrote to him and asked if he could help me to find work. He said that I could go and work directly for him. That I would earn good money to support my family."

The helicopter dropped down suddenly and accelerated. Callum could see that they were fast approaching the coastline. Now that they were closer, it was clear that there was still somebody alive on top of the moraine. Whoever it was, the helicopter was heading straight for them.

"What are we doing?" Ava asked.

"There can be no survivors now," Lungkaju replied. "Not now." He stood up and fastened both hers and Callum's seat belts, before fastening his own.

"So we're going back to chalk another one up, are we?" Callum said. "Another innocent life. It must be some package Volkov's offering you, *my friend.*"

"Mr Volkov takes very good care of me. He allows me to take very good care of my family. When my wife was dying, I could afford the best medical care for her, so that she could spend her last days with dignity, in comfort and not in pain. I can afford to send my daughter to the best schools and provide for her everything she needs to be safe and happy. None of this would be possible without Mr Volkov." He paused, before adding, "Tell me, Doctor Ross, what would you do if you were me?"

Before Callum could answer, a mechanical whirring noise rang out beside him. He had never been in a helicopter gunship before in his life, but he knew with grim certainty exactly what it was.

He watched as the front, side-mounted machine gun rotated into position.

4

It wasn't an illusion. The sound of the helicopter was growing louder. Koikov lifted his head from Marchenko's shoulder, his face streaked with the man's blood, and searched the sky. The helicopter was returning to Harmsworth. He watched as its shadow passed low over the coastline. The White Shark was bearing straight for his position.

The next thing he knew, two parallel bursts of automatic gunfire hammered into the slope and ripped towards him.

In an instant, he was on his toes, bolting in the opposite direction. As he leapt from the plateau onto the side of the slope, the White Shark tore overhead. Bullets strafed past him to the left, peppering the scree and throwing up mini-mushroom clouds of dust and rock.

He kept on running, arriving at the bottom of the slope just as the Shark turned around and came back for another pass. The automatic fire flared up once again, and Koikov flung himself behind a stand of rock.

He hit the deck only to find a dragon, its brains blown out, slumped awkwardly beside him. He rolled forward into it and then backwards, heaving the stinking carcass up in front of him just in time. The stench was horrendous, but the line of bullets beat into the creature's flank just as he'd hoped, their force absorbed within the barrier of muscle and bone. He shoved the dragon shield to one side and leapt to his feet. Then he ran like hell.

In seconds the White Shark was back on him. Rounds ricocheted to either side as he dove for cover behind another outcrop. As it passed overhead once more, he sprinted on and finally made it to the hovercraft. He threw open the weapon store. He knew full well what should be in there, but still he prayed out loud. His eyes lit up as his fingers fell against one of the two remaining RPGs, and he snatched it out and primed it.

With only seconds to spare before the Shark came in for another skirmish, he knelt down and prepared to launch.

The craft had now turned fully. It was bearing down on Koikov with immense speed. Any moment and he would see the tell-tale flowering of smoke from the side-mounted guns, before the rounds bit into him.

It was all about nerve. In its determination to take him out, the craft was flying so low that a hit with the RPG was almost guaranteed, so long as he didn't fuck up. He took a deep breath. The only question was where to put the grenade. He wanted to plant it square in the pilot's ball-sack. But something was stopping him. Where were the scientists? He hadn't seen their bodies on top of the moraine, and this left the possibility that they were hostages on board.

He had to think quickly. The military training manual in his brain kicked in, and his eyes came to focus on the twin rotors. One of the main military advantages of the co-axial rotor system was that it negated the need for a tail rotor. This was significant because a high percentage of artillery attacks on assault helicopters took out the tail, leaving normal single-rotor machines in a spin, fatally compromised. With the co-axial models, blasting out the tail would still take them out. But it wouldn't necessarily cause them to crash. If he played it right, he could bring the Shark down, but bring it down safe. His jaw clenched and his grip tightened around the RPG housing. That would have the added advantage of allowing him to wring the neck of the motherfucker responsible for wiping out his team.

With only a split second on the clock, Koikov took final aim and fired. The rocket screamed from the launcher, spewing a thick trail of smoke behind it as it curved up and around. He held his breath.

As the first few rounds pummelled into the side of the adjacent outcrop, the rocket found its target. With a loud explosion, the tail shaft was obliterated. Red-hot shrapnel rained down onto the rock below, and the entire craft was engulfed in thick, black smoke.

Koikov slammed the launcher into the floor and let out a victorious roar. Above him, the Shark shuddered with the impact. Then it headed inland, its altitude reducing by the second.

Koikov leapt up into the hovercraft and set off in pursuit.

* * *

Ava's screams filled the cabin as the helicopter lurched downwards. Smoke rushed past the windows, blacking out the view. Between gusts, Callum could see that they were hurtling towards the bluffs at the foot of the Hjalmar Ridge.

In all the chaos he had managed to manoeuvre his hands around and into his jacket pocket. He now searched around until he found what he was looking for. He withdrew the flint blade that he had taken from Ngana'bta and worked it carefully from its sheath.

He began sawing at his lashings. The blade was cold and the action of sawing with bound hands was awkward, but it was working. One by one he could feel the fibres unpick.

Lungkaju turned from the window. "Do not worry, Doctor Ross. I will make sure that you get off the helicopter. You, Doctor

Lee and Doctor Lebedev." He was panicked and gabbling, forced to shout over the whine of the emergency siren.

"What difference does it make?" Callum shouted back. "If we don't burn to death on this thing, we're just going to get killed as part of your boss's depraved game anyway. And that's if the creatures don't get to us first. All of us!"

They were now less than ten metres off the ground.

Callum arched his back, allowing him to get a better purchase on the blade. "What the hell's on this data stick that's so important anyway?" He couldn't have cared less. He just needed to keep Lungkaju distracted.

"It is a computer virus."

"Is that it?"

"It is a very powerful virus. Mr Peterson has infected the computers which control the gas supply in Russia."

One by one the fibres unpicked. The flint blade hadn't dulled with age. As Callum had hoped, it was as sharp today as it had been when it was first knapped. He laughed out loud as he attacked the few remaining strands. "So your friend Mr Volkov got more than he bargained for in old Dan Peterson! Though why the hell he'd think Peterson would give the stick to us is beyond me." With one final jerk of his wrist he sliced through the remaining fibres. "None of us have ever seen it, Lungkaju. I've no idea what it even looks like."

"It is a small black key ring."

Callum's mind raced. *Ava!*

"Brace!" Lungkaju shouted suddenly, throwing his arms up over his head.

A split second later and the helicopter hit the ground. The entire craft shook. Sparks erupted overhead and Callum could hear screams emanating from the flight deck.

The landing rails skidded across the rocky plateau. The battered craft tipped, teetered on one rail and then, with a hideous groan, crashed over onto its side.

5

Smoke filled the cabin.

In the first moments after impact, Callum's only concern was Darya. She had not been restrained and her body had been flung into the far window. He brought his hands out from behind his back and quickly unfastened his belt. Then he dropped down past Ava and helped her free.

The two of them crouched beside Darya. She appeared uninjured and the shock of the collision had finally roused her. She stared around in confusion. "Wh-where…"

Callum held her face in his hands and kissed her. "There's no time to explain. We just need to get out of here."

"Where is here?"

"Volkov's helicopter."

"Volkov?"

Callum cast around. To his right, Lungkaju was still struggling to escape from his restraints. The crash landing had thrown the pistol from his hand and his body dangled awkwardly, reducing the movement of his arms. He'd managed to manoeuvre his hands up onto the belt clasp, but before he could undo it, Callum punched him as hard as he could in the side of the face.

It was the first time since he was a schoolboy that Callum had thrown a punch in anger, and he was surprised at how natural it felt. Sometimes, he realised, there was just nothing else for it. His knuckles stung with the impact, but it had the desired effect. Lungkaju now hung limp, not unconscious, but stunned. His limbs dangled down through the harness straps once again, as if he was caught in a net, a thin trickle of blood weeping from his cheek.

The fumes within the cabin were making it difficult to breathe, and Callum and Ava prised open the side door above their heads. Callum lifted her and Darya up, and fed them out through the doorway. As he went to hoist himself free, his gaze fell upon Lungkaju. Still delirious, the Nganasan was squirming against the seat harness, straining for breath.

Callum turned away and went to lift himself out again. The sense of betrayal that he felt was still as raw as the smoke burning his lungs. His fingers fastened around the rim of the upturned doorway and he hauled himself up. He wanted nothing more than to leave Lungkaju to the death that he deserved. But as his head broke up into the open, he let out a growl of anguish and dropped back down.

With his mouth and nose dug into the crook of his arm, he reached across and undid Lungkaju's belt clasp. The straps retracted and Lungkaju tumbled forward into his arms.

"What are you doing?"

Callum glanced up to see both Darya and Ava, their faces twisted with panic, peering down at him through the smoke.

"You need to get out of there! The tail is on fire, it is spreading!"

"Just grab his arms," Callum shouted, lifting Lungkaju's body up as high as he could. "I'm not leaving him to die." He struggled to support the man's dead weight. Then at last the strain began to lift, as Darya and Ava helped drag him from the cabin.

Remembering the pistol, Callum scrabbled around at his

feet, found it and stuffed it into his jacket pocket. Then he finally hauled himself up out of the smoke.

Callum emerged from the helicopter, lungs heavy, eyes stinging. Gasping for air, he and the others slid down the exterior panelling onto the ground and hurried from the craft. They stopped at a safe distance and looked back towards the wreckage. It was concealed in great swathes of smoke, the cloud swelling out towards them.

Lungkaju looked up at Callum. "You saved me."

Callum said nothing. He was still struggling to breathe.

"Why?"

He coughed up a lungful of black phlegm. "I didn't do it for you!"

"Then why, Doctor Ross? After what I have done—"

"Because I didn't want your little girl to have to grow up without a father, that's why. I didn't want that on my conscience."

"How very touching."

The group turned around to see Mr Volkov emerging from the smoke, his pistol drawn and aimed towards them. His face and uniform were smeared black, but his eyes were the only thing aflame.

"Mr Volkov? Is that you?" Darya asked.

"It's him alright," Callum said, looking Volkov straight in the eye. "And you were right about him too. This man is pure evil. He's the one who ordered the *Albanov* to be destroyed."

"He murdered Sergeant Marchenko and the rest of his team as well," Ava said. "He took us hostage, and Lungkaju... well, Lungkaju's just his stooge."

"Lungkaju?"

Lungkaju met Darya's gaze and then looked away.

"Thank you, Doctors," Volkov said, "for such a colourful summary." He gestured towards Lungkaju. "Now release him at once."

"They are only helping, Mr Volkov—"

"Be quiet and come here."

Lungkaju staggered forward.

"Wait." Volkov's eyes narrowed. "I want you to search all three of them. One of them has the data stick and I want it now. Playtime is over."

"Mr Volkov—"

"There's no need," Callum said.

"Oh, really, Doctor Ross, and why is that?"

"Because I know where it is."

A triumphant smile broke across Volkov's face. "I knew it! I knew that Yankee imbecile had entrusted it to one of you." He brought the pistol to bear on Callum. "You will hand it over now."

Callum turned to Ava. "Do you have your survival tin?"

She looked at him in obvious confusion. Then she dug a hand into her inside pocket and removed the gold tin. Callum took it. He unhitched the lid and rifled through the contents until his fingers fell upon the small, black, rectangular key ring. He removed it and pressed at the centre. The concealed USB connector emerged from the tip.

"I'll be damned!" Ava said.

Callum held the key ring up. "Is this what you're looking for?"

Volkov's eyes widened. "Hand it to Lungkaju."

Lungkaju held his hand out, and Callum dropped the data stick into his palm.

"Bring it here. Quickly!"

Lungkaju hesitated. "You must promise to let them go."

Volkov's face contorted as he bawled at Lungkaju.

"Mr Volkov, please. Nobody else has to die."

Volkov's pistol panned around to aim at him. "I wouldn't be so sure," he sneered. "Now bring me the data stick!"

"Just give it to him," Callum urged.

"If I do this, Doctor Ross, then he will kill you all. He cannot risk leaving you alive."

Volkov cocked the pistol. "Lungkaju, it sounds suspiciously as if you are betraying *me*. You know how very dangerous that would be, and not just for yourself." He paused, then dropped his voice, adding, "I owe my life to your father. It is for this reason *only* that I am giving you one last chance to prove yourself to me." He spoke slowly. "Bring me the data stick now."

With Volkov distracted, Callum seized Lungkaju's pistol from his belt and trained it on Volkov. "Drop the gun."

With his own pistol still pointing at Lungkaju, Volkov's eyes moved slowly back across to Callum. He took one look at the gun in his hand and then laughed out loud. "Ah, Doctor Ross. Come now. You are a thinker, not a killer. Besides which, you do not reach where I have reached by arming your enemies."

"What the hell are you talking about? Drop the gun or I *will* shoot you."

"Of course you will."

"Don't push me, Volkov!" Not for the first time, Callum was shaken by the venom in his own voice. "A month ago, if anybody had told me I'd be stood here now pointing a gun at another man, perfectly prepared to kill him, I'd have called them crazy. But not now. If Harmsworth's taught me one thing, it's kill or be killed. Now this is *your* last chance. So drop the gun!"

Volkov shifted slightly.

Callum squeezed the trigger.

6

There was an impotent clicking noise, but no bullet.

"How unfortunate," Volkov beamed. He withdrew a small silver container from his pocket and tipped whatever the contents were into his mouth.

As he did so, Callum snatched at the trigger again and again. But still nothing happened.

"It was clear to me that Lungkaju's loyalties may have been misplaced," Volkov said, placing the container back into his pocket. "He is not a man of business."

Callum dropped the pistol to the ground.

"As I said," Volkov continued, "you do not reach where I have reached by arming your enemies. Or by letting them live."

He fired a single shot.

With a gasp of shock, Lungkaju stumbled backwards into Ava's arms and collapsed. Callum and Darya rushed to help support him. The bullet had passed through the side of his neck and the wound was spewing out blood. It was fatal, that much was clear to all of them, but Darya attempted to stem the flow, while Callum grabbed his hand and tried to comfort him.

Lungkaju's face was drained of colour. He dug a trembling hand into his pocket and produced a letter. "Give this to my daughter, Doctor Ross. Will you do this? Please? It is my next letter to her. My last letter."

Callum nodded and squeezed his hand.

"Perhaps one day she can meet your son," he whispered. "I hope for this."

His eyelids fluttered shut, and a last breath gurgled from his ruptured throat.

"Enough!" Volkov shouted. "Now, Ms Lebedev, *you* will bring me the data stick. You have seen what happens when this request is denied."

Callum could only watch as, sobbing, Darya peeled open Lungkaju's lifeless hand and removed the data stick. His blood still warm on her fingertips, she walked across and gave the stick to Volkov.

"Finally!" he said, snatching it away and slipping it into his top pocket. He brought his pistol back up and pointed it at Darya. "And now, I am afraid Lungkaju was quite correct. It is time for us all to part company—"

Volkov lurched backwards as a bullet ricocheted off the rock at his feet. He threw his arm around Darya's neck, digging the pistol into her side, and turned.

The hovercraft was racing towards them. Starshyna Koikov was at the helm, and he clearly had no intention of slowing down.

Volkov bellowed out in Russian. Then he took off, herding Darya ahead of him.

It was only now that Callum noticed where they were. If the helicopter had continued just another few metres, they would've smashed straight into the rockface at the southern tip of the ridge. The pilot had brought them down in the nick of time, landing on a wide plateau in the shadow of the cliffs.

Ahead, he could see out over the coastal basin, the faint wisps of smoke still rising from the remains of the bunker, the blotch on the moraine still clear. A short distance behind them, the ridge itself rose steeply, riven towards its summit by the crystal blue cusps of the ancient ice cap, riddled at its base with a wood-worm of caves. He watched with horror as Volkov urged Darya towards them.

The hovercraft screamed to a halt suddenly next to Callum, and Koikov leapt down, rifle poised. His gaze was stony with hate and the heat of his body steamed into the cold air.

Volkov stopped at the base of the ridge, holstered his pistol and pulled out an ornate combat knife with a savage-looking black blade. With incredible deftness, he spun it through his fingers and then pressed it against Darya's throat. "I will make this simple. *You* follow, *she* dies a slow and painful death."

"You carry on, you both die!" Callum shouted back. "The creatures... those caves will be crawling with them."

Volkov looked confused. "Nonsense!"

"Volkov!"

"You follow, she dies." He dragged Darya the last few paces towards the nearest cave. Then, with a final hate-filled glare at the three survivors, he and Darya melted away into the darkness.

Callum, Koikov and Ava stood in silence as the smoke from the grounded helicopter billowed around them. Then, without a word, Callum started forward.

"What are you doing?" Ava said.

"I don't know," he replied, "but I'm not leaving her."

"But... the creatures... you'll be killed as well, Doctor Ross... you've got nothing, no weapons... nothing..."

Callum felt something thrust against his arm. He looked down to see a machine gun. Koikov nodded at him and grunted. His face was streaked with blood. The scar on his cheek was flushed purple, surrounded by the start of a dense, dark brown beard.

Callum took the rifle and watched as Koikov marched over to the hovercraft. After rooting around in the hold, he produced another rifle and what looked like a bazooka cannon, then marched back over to Callum's side.

"Ava, you stay here with the hovercraft," Callum said. "If we're not back in an hour then you can assume we're dead. There might be enough fuel for you to make it to Nagurskoye."

"Assume you're dead? Nagurskoye? Are you kidding me?"

Callum pushed a hand back through his hair. Matted with grease, the curls caught around his fingers. "I don't know what else to say."

She took a deep breath. "Look, I'm coming with you, alright. You're not the only stupid, impulsive jerk on this island."

Eyes focussed, she took his hand. "Nobody would ever believe me about this place anyway. And besides," she gestured towards Koikov as he slammed a magazine into his rifle, "we're packing Special Forces."

Callum reached out and hugged her.

Koikov snorted and spat on the floor.

Chapter 18

THE HIVE

1

A few paces in and the cave narrowed into a tunnel. Callum, Koikov and Ava walked in silence. Koikov, the only one with LVV, took the lead. The bazooka was slung across his back. His rifle was shouldered. Callum and Ava followed on, using Callum's rifle lamp to light their way.

As they walked, the temperature increased until sweat lined each of their brows. There was no breeze. No through-draught. Barely any air. What there was hung still and stale. Beyond the echo of their footsteps, the only sound was a low hiss, as if the rock itself was whispering a faint warning.

After a while, the tunnel began to widen out. The combination of heat and the stink of musk was overpowering, and Callum had to fight to control his gag reflex. Beetles scurried amongst the faeces underfoot, while pale cave spiders and other creatures that would never see the midnight sun picked their way overhead.

Callum had never felt more out of place. The sights, the sounds, the smells were all so alien. Only, it wasn't they that were unwelcome, not here, where they had survived the eons undisturbed. It was him. Himself, Koikov and Ava. They were the intruders into this ancient world.

Another few metres and a glow emerged. As they moved forward, it intensified until the tunnel was largely illuminated. Callum stopped and turned off his rifle lamp. He wiped the sweat from his face, watching as Koikov removed his LVV. The survivors shared a brief exchange of glances, all three of them well beyond fear.

The creatures... Volkov...

Volkov... The creatures...

The two had become one in all three minds. They had merged into the same threat, a single faceless monster lurking somewhere in this forgotten place.

They edged onwards.

Soon the tunnel ended. The rock that had grazed their elbows now recessed sharply to either side, and the ground ahead sloped away for a distance, before levelling off into the floor of an enormous sub-circular chamber. It had to be three or four hundred metres across. The walls were riddled with openings and ledges, and they rose upwards and inwards to form a dome-shaped ceiling high above.

Rather than an unbroken expanse, the chamber floor was carved into a series of islands. Some were connected to one another and to the walls of the cavern, by narrow stone aisles, umbilical cords of rock that meandered from one to the other. A few of the islands seemed to be entirely isolated, appearing to float, but no doubt rooted to the others lower down.

"My God!" Ava exclaimed.

"Mine too," Callum said.

The bases of the deep fissures contained rivers of magma. Red-hot and steaming, the molten stone snaked its way beneath them, crackling and sending up clouds of scalding vapour, before flowing out of the chamber through a lower system of tunnels. The overall effect was like a stone web strung across a basin of fire, both awe-inspiring and terrifying.

The first thing to cross Callum's mind as he beheld the sight was Doctor Semyonov. He had been convinced that there would be substantial geothermal activity on Harmsworth, much to the derision of his peers, not least Ava. He may have got the exact location wrong, but now, standing in the heart of this ancient magma chamber, there was no denying that he'd been right all along.

"Rest in peace, Nikolai," Ava whispered, evidently sharing his thoughts.

As Callum's eyes adjusted to the glare, the source of the overpowering stink also became apparent. His pulse picked up. The creatures were everywhere. Hundreds of them. They were not unexpected, but their numbers were. Wherever there was space, he was suddenly aware of them twitching, huddled around the edges of the chamber, clustered in the tunnel mouths, perched on the ledges that jutted from the walls. Most seemed to be curled up in small groups, their heads resting on each other's backs as they dozed in the heat. Others clung to the walls of the cavern, claws pinned into the rock, arms and legs splayed, just like the birds that would sun themselves on the walls of his house during summer.

Without exception, their feathers were flushed with the same grey-brown as the surrounding rock. It was a triumph of camouflage. If Callum's senses hadn't been honed by fear, he was certain the entire colony would have been invisible.

"What is this place?" he whispered to Ava.

"Isn't it obvious?" she replied. "Volkov's led us right into the hive."

Hive. Just the word made Callum's skin crawl.

Koikov stirred suddenly and pointed out into the chamber.

It was Volkov. Oblivious to the danger that he and Darya were in, he was standing at the end of one of the rock bridges. Darya was in front. She looked dazed, terrified as she peered over the edge of the precipice at the good thirty-metre drop down into the flame. The sight of Volkov's knife around her throat as he pushed her ahead turned Callum's stomach, and in that moment he knew that he would not be leaving this cave without her.

Koikov raised his rifle as if to take a shot, but Callum shoved it back down. Even if he was the best shot in the world, he still wouldn't have risked a bullet in Darya's direction. Not only that, but it would wake the hive. Just about the only thing in their favour right now was the fact that the creatures appeared to be roosting and had yet to notice them. He tried to communicate this to Koikov, who looked indignant but seemed to understand.

By now Volkov had walked Darya across the stone walkway and out onto one of the islands. The three watched on, each seeming to understand that their best option was to see where he went next, then to follow quietly, without risking a chase across the precarious splinters of rock.

"That's weird," Callum whispered. "There's not a single creature out on the islands."

"Probably keeping a safe distance from the lake of fire," Ava replied.

"I don't buy it. If they were scared of the magma then why congregate here in the first place?"

She shrugged. "Perhaps the islands are reserved."

"Reserved?"

"For something other than sleeping."

Possible, Callum thought. *But reserved for what?* Through the haze, he could make out clusters of pale rocks at each of their centres, but they were otherwise empty.

2

Volkov couldn't shake his fury. He had the data stick, but once again people had obstructed what should have been a very simple operation and made the whole thing unnecessarily taxing. His own, very expensive, modified helicopter had been destroyed. The man he'd trusted more than any other had turned on him, forcing Volkov to kill him. And now he'd had no option but to take refuge in the stifling, labyrinthine bowels of what appeared to be a volcano. The whole thing was intolerable.

His finger itched against the knife handle. What he really wanted to do was slit the throat of this infernal ecologist woman, to send her the way of all the other irritations and inconveniences that he had dispatched with it over the years. But then he needed her alive. For now at least.

He stopped and threw a glance around the cavern. Koikov and Doctor Ross would undoubtedly be in pursuit, but they were yet to make it this far. He would hide out in one of the tunnels up ahead, wait for them to pass through and then double back. Then, and only then, would he allow himself the pleasure of carving up the troublesome Miss Lebedev and making his way back to the submarine.

The craft was concealed in a nearby cove, with just enough

power left to make it to the base on Nagurskoye. He would have to alter his story somewhat, in order to account for recent developments. But there would be plenty of time for him to contact his associates and formulate something suitable en route to the base. He would also need to get a reliable clean-up team to Harmsworth ASAP. All dead bodies and helicopter wreckage would have to be removed quickly, restoring the deceit that all hands, save his, had gone down with the *Albanov*. Again, it could all be arranged. The most important thing now, he reminded himself, was that he had the data stick.

"We shouldn't be here," Darya whispered, her voice trembling.

"Shut up and keep moving." He urged her forward, digging the side of the knife blade into her neck. She had been raving on about some fairy-tale creature or other ever since they'd entered the cavern, and it was starting to grate.

"You fool! Can you not see them? They are everywhere."

His mind ticked over. Hadn't Lungkaju mentioned something about strange animals on the island? Something about a lizard bird? Volkov had paid little attention to his babbling at the time, though, in hindsight, it was unusual for the level-headed Lungkaju to have been quite so excited by an idea. Perhaps there might have been something in it after all.

Out of curiosity, he cast his eyes around the walls and up over the ceiling. Nothing. He couldn't see anything at all, because there was clearly nothing *to* see. This was surely proof enough that it was all madness. Doctor Lebedev said that they were there right now, all around him. Yet there was plainly nothing but rock and flame. She was delusional.

"What exactly should I be looking at?" he growled. "These supposed prehistoric beasts?"

"Talk quietly," she urged him, her voice a breathy whisper. "They are everywhere."

"They are nonsense! I have seen nothing of the sort on this

island because they do not exist, Miss Lebedev. You are delirious. Now keep moving!"

He took another stride forward. As he did so, he kicked against a dump of pale rocks, and a single one dislodged itself and rolled towards his foot. It was oval, with an uneven, cream-coloured surface. Intrigued, Volkov extended his boot and gave it a kick. To his surprise, the exterior shattered and a viscous fluid glooped out, followed by the head of a baby bird.

Volkov found himself repulsed by the look of the creature's face as it writhed, fighting to free the rest of its under-developed body from what he now realised to be a shell. Eggs. What he'd considered to be a spread of rocks was actually a clutch of large bird eggs, perhaps thirty or forty strong. He cast a glance around. There were similar clutches on each of the adjacent islands. Perhaps twenty in total, making as many as eight hundred eggs.

He searched the roof of the cavern. Not a single bird.

"It's one of *them*," Darya whispered. Her eyes were wide as she gazed with evident horror at the remains of the shattered egg. "This must be the nest."

He scoffed.

"Mr Volkov, please listen to me. This is not a trick. We need to leave here right now!"

"Nonsense," he replied. Sweating profusely in the intense heat, he pushed the head of the baby bird to one side with his toe and watched as it squirmed. It was a pink, veiny blob. Its limbs were flushed purple and dripping with albumen. Its beak was dark and globular, and its eyes were fastened tightly shut, as if glued. "You may be the ecologist, Doctor Lebedev. But *that* is a bird. I'll grant you it is rather larger and uglier than most, but it is clearly just a bird of some description. Now enough of this! I do not want to hear another word about fictitious creatures!"

"Mr Volkov, no!"

It was too late. In one quick motion, he curled his foot around the back end of the broken egg and scooped it over the edge of the island. As it fell, the chick's varicose body broke free from its shell. It pumped its arms in vain. Its large eyes unbonded and opened wide. Its still-forming beak gaped with panic, and it let out its first and last scream.

3

Around the chamber, the walls erupted into life as the sound of the doomed chick awoke the rest of the colony. Koikov dragged the other two down onto their fronts and they watched as the creatures unfurled themselves from their huddles, scurried down from their perches and leapt to their feet.

A cacophony of screeching, braying and clicks tore through the air. All eyes, Troodon and human alike, were now locked upon the island of stone and the two intruders at its heart. Volkov and Darya stood side by side, throwing glances in all directions. Any second and Callum was certain that the thousands of enraged creatures would swarm out onto the platform. If they weren't barged over into the magma, Volkov and Darya would be torn to shreds.

He threw a panicked glance at Koikov. Then he raised his rifle, preparing to take out as many of the creatures as he could. The soldier also shifted. He thrust his rifle at Ava, who didn't hesitate to accept it. Then he pulled the bazooka from behind his back and pointed it down into the chamber.

All three held their breath and waited for the attack to begin.

But nothing happened. Around the edges of the magma pit, the swarm of creatures continued their vocal assault. They paced up and down in agitation, bowing their heads, grinding their teeth and erecting their plumages in display.

Their feathers flushed as only Callum and Darya had seen them before, with vibrant reds and oranges, ambers and whites, until it looked as if the magma had seeped up and around the walls of the cavern. But still they maintained their position around the perimeter, posturing, jostling, but refusing to approach the nests.

"Why aren't they attacking?" Callum asked at last.

"I've no idea," Ava replied. "They're acting more nervous than aggressive. They look... scared."

Callum's brow furrowed. What the hell could scare these things? As his finger tapped against the rifle trigger, the entire chamber lapsed into sudden silence. The unexpected and complete cessation of sound was one of the eeriest noises Callum had ever heard, and a shiver passed through him.

All movement had stopped. The cavern stilled. As one, the creatures shed their colour, the effect like a ring of light going out around the room. Shadows now, a sea of bared gums and dilated eyes, they stared over at the intruders, waiting.

* * *

"What do we do?" Volkov demanded, his voice echoing out around the newly silent cavern.

"Perhaps you should tell them that you don't believe in them!" Darya replied. "Why not offer them a bribe?"

Volkov went to slap her around her insolent face. But as he raised his hand back, a breeze blew across his neck. It was warm and rhythmic. It reeked of stale meat and left an oily trace on his skin.

Doctor Lebedev obviously felt it too, and her expression froze.

Together they turned towards it.

Volkov gasped.

Darya's jaw dropped.

There was something staring at them across the top of the egg pile.

Chapter 19

TANSU TAIBAA

1

Callum, Koikov and Ava looked on, open-mouthed, as two large forearms, slender but rippling with muscle, emerged from behind the nest. Each hand forked into three fingers, tipped with claws. At the other end, the two shoulder blades resembled upturned axe-heads, the skin sucked taut around them. And attached to the backs of the elbows were membranous flaps, finely feathered wings, running all the way along the underside of the arms and out of sight along the concealed torso.

When the arms had reached forward, up over the edge of the island, and the claws had picked into the rock either side of the clutch, the creature raised its head to peer at Volkov and Darya.

In contrast to the others, its movements were not brash or aggressive. They were slow, almost timid, and spider-like. At first, its enormous black eyes barely crept above the eggs' pinnacles, as it scoped out the two intruders. Then they rose up to reveal a much stubbier but still beak-like snout, lined with rows of jagged teeth. It shuddered as it sucked in a series of breaths, tasting the air.

"What the hell is that thing?" Callum managed at last.

"It's a Troodon," Ava replied bluntly.

"What are you talking about? It's three times bigger... and

it's got wings, not just feathers, but actual, real wings!"

"Yeah," Ava said. "But look what else it's got. A mix of reptilian *and* avian traits, the same enormous eyes, the same teeth, the same claws, plus it's resident in the same hive." She indicated the horde of creatures massed around the room. "You telling me these things would tolerate a different species in here?"

As Darya and Volkov stood rooted to the spot, the creature clambered fully up onto the island before them. The more Callum saw of it, the more he suspected that Ava was right. Its lower half was much more Troodon-like. Its hind legs were long and muscular, and it carried the same sickle-like toe claws, only the size of scimitars. Its tail, still dangling down over the edge as it perched behind its clutch, was tipped similarly with large, decorative plumes.

"They must be polymorphs," Ava said. "A polymorphic species of dinosaur. Who'd've thought it!" Even under the circumstances, she couldn't keep the wonder from her voice.

"Polymorphs?"

"A species with more than one phenotype. Like with ants, where you've got workers, soldiers and queens. Each phenotype or caste is physically distinct, either because of gender variation or because it's designed to perform a specific social role. *Workers* forage and build. They're male and they tend to be small, your basic model ant. *Soldiers* are also male. They protect the workers and they tend to be bigger, often with increased body armour and weaponry such as large mandibles. *Queens* found colonies and lay eggs. They tend to be much bigger, with bigger abdomens and they're often flyers. They're all still ants, just different manifestations of the same animal."

"So you reckon that's some kind of Troodon queen?"

"Uh-uh. The carcasses I've seen so far have *all* been female. The genitalia's clear. Also," she pointed forward, "if I'm not mistaken then that thing's got a penis."

Callum looked on as the creature continued to sniff around

its nest, its massive ribcage expanding and contracting with each breath. Sure enough, there did appear to be a red-tipped protrusion between its legs.

"I'd imagine it wouldn't usually be so prominent," Ava said. "Either he's displaying because he feels threatened, or he might be subconsciously sexually aroused by the scent of all the females."

"Funny," Callum replied. "They're having precisely the opposite effect on me."

"Cute."

"So he's a king then? Some kind of emperor?"

"Probably, but he's something else as well. Something much worse."

With care not to disturb the remainder of the clutch, the creature now leant forward and sniffed at the remains of the shattered egg at Volkov's feet. Then it froze. Slowly, it raised its face back up, the full intensity of its gaze coming to rest on him.

"How the hell could it be any worse?" Callum whispered, pulling the rifle firmly into his shoulder. Beside him, he could hear Koikov making ready with the bazooka.

The creature's beak curled back suddenly, exposing its blood-red gums and rows of jagged canines. Then, in one swift movement, it spread its wings protectively around the remaining eggs. Its eyes narrowed and it hissed at Volkov, its fore claws scraping at the rock to either side with renewed agitation.

"Oh, it's a helluva lot worse," Ava said. "He's a father."

2

Volkov felt the warm flood of urine soaking through his underwear.

He had been frozen to the spot ever since the creature had emerged from its hidden roost below the stone island, barely able to breathe for fear. Oddly, it was this final humiliating loss of bodily function that had spurred him back to life.

On impulse, he flipped his knife over, grabbed the back of the blade and flung it with all his might. It spun through the air, heading straight for the centre of the creature's chest. *Any second and the blade would pierce through its ribcage and puncture its heart...*

The black birch handle struck the creature's torso and bounced pathetically backwards. Without stirring, the creature watched with interest as the tiny object tripped down onto the rock, where the blade snapped off with a resounding clunk. Both blade and handle then clattered over the edge of the island and down into the magma.

Slowly, the creature moved its gaze back to Volkov.

He turned and fled. The harrowing sound of the creature's hiss pursued him, filling his ears as he sprinted back along the bridge of rock. On the perimeter of the magma pit, he could see a huddle of the smaller, less fearsome-looking creatures. Their heads were bowed combatively, their mouths were open and they were screaming out at his approach.

His every instinct was to turn from them, but turn where? They were everywhere, and the nearest tunnel was directly behind the dozen or so ahead of him now. If he wanted out of the nightmare, then this was his best option.

Uncertain how many rounds he had remaining, he grabbed his pistol and prepared to blaze a way through. But before he'd had to fire a shot, a series of staccato roars sounded out behind him and the clot of creatures simply parted to allow him through. The stinking beasts must have thought better of assailing him after all. He allowed himself a smile of relief as he passed between them and bolted on towards the tunnel.

No sooner had he passed the creatures than his smile disappeared. A flash of pain bolted down his right thigh and he felt himself disabled. No longer able to run for the agony, he had no choice but to pull up.

As he turned around, one of the creatures was lowering its hind leg. Blood, his blood, stained its retracted toe claw. He felt a deep sense of horror, which turned quickly to nausea. There was a gash across his buttock, and blood flowed out over his hand and down his trouser leg to join the urine.

In a fit of rage, he took aim at the offending creature and fired. The bullet missed by a mile. The creature didn't even flinch. By now, his hands were shaking so violently that he knew another shot would be pointless. The creature seemed to know this; it cocked its head and eyed him with something close to pity. Then, to his surprise, it turned its back on him, as did all the others.

Holding a hand over his wound, Volkov limped off into the tunnel.

Darya looked suddenly very alone.

Still hissing, the creature now reached out and took hold of one of its eggs. With incredible dexterity, it lifted it up, reached across its body and fed it straight into a pouch of skin on the opposite side of its chest. No sooner had it done this than the other arm had reached forward and repeated exactly the same action, sliding a second egg into an opposing pouch.

The effect of its wings, along with its extra bulk, made the creature's actions appear cumbersome. But it carried out the process of gathering up its clutch with ease. It was a crab-like motion, one arm after another performed in quick succession, the result of millions of years of instinct to protect its unborn offspring. And it took only seconds for all of the eggs to be concealed, spread evenly between the two pouches.

The creature now turned its attention to Darya. Drawing itself up to full height, it dwarfed her. It was at least twice her size, and with its young out of the equation, its behaviour had changed. It was no longer cautious but openly aggressive, its jaws grinding together, leaking drool, its hind claws tapping impatiently at the rock.

Around the cavern, the screeching of the females reached a zenith.

"I think we know what killed your ice mummy," Ava whispered.

Callum's mind raced. *Tansu Taibaa.*

Suddenly it all made sense. The myth *was* true. The ancient champion *had* made it to the Land of White Death, and he *had* hunted down Tansu Taibaa, the lizard bird, now towering over Darya. Armed only with his ski-pole spears, the champion of the Twelve Clans had failed to make good on his boast of killing the creature. But instead of fleeing in terror, he had chosen another course. In some respects a brave one. In other respects much more foolish. And it had sealed his grizzly fate.

Callum's mind moved to the final pieces of the millennia-old puzzle: the scatter of white fragments, which he had taken for broken pottery, and the little skeleton, which he had taken for that of a bird. How had he not seen it before? They rose up from the floor of the tunnel now, a timeless 3D jigsaw, and repieced themselves before his eyes.

An egg.

Ngana'bta had stolen a Troodon egg. Whether to lure the creature, whether as proof of his journey, whether on pure impulse. His motive was lost to time. But he had paid for it: first with his legs and then with his life, as he'd dragged his mutilated body into the tunnel in a last futile bid to escape.

Callum's thoughts were interrupted by the creature's sudden roar. There was now nothing between it and Darya on the island of rock. No eggs. No barrier. Only a few metres of flat, open space.

As it raised its arms and advanced on her, Callum couldn't wait any longer. Ignoring Ava's pleas, he jumped to his feet, raced down the slope and out onto the bridge of stone. The silence shattered as the females spotted him and let up a deafening howl. The male saw him too and added its own resounding bellow to the chorus.

3

The male brought its hands down either side of Darya, knocking her from her feet. It then swiped at her with its claws, attempting to swat her. She rolled just out of reach as it struck again, but this time its claws found her forearm, smashing her wrist. She screamed out in pain as her bones shattered, then again as a follow-up swipe sent her tumbling towards the edge of the island.

As her body slipped over, she dug the fingers of her uninjured hand into the surface of the rock and clung on with every last ounce of her strength. She screamed for help, as the muscles in her arm strained and her legs kicked frantically against the sheer rockface for purchase that wasn't there.

The creature crouched down beside the edge and extended its head towards her. Mouth gaping, it hissed and raised its arm.

On the edge of the island, Callum dropped to his knee and went to fire. As his finger closed over the trigger, a hail of bullets streaked above his head and into the creature's back. The accuracy of the hits meant only one thing: Koikov.

The creature dropped its arm and howled in surprise. Then it turned from Darya to face Callum. Mistaking him for the source of its pain, it narrowed its eyes and charged.

Callum opened fire. The bullets tore into the male's flanks, stopping it momentarily in its tracks. It scratched at the bullet holes as if they were nothing more than insect bites, before leaping forward and lunging at him with its hind leg.

He dropped to the floor, feeling the rush of air as the scythe-like claw sliced just above his head. As the creature then raised its leg to stomp on him, he fired again. He was aiming for its chest, but the bullets flew past and stung into its shoulder muscle. It was enough to send it stumbling backwards, but still not enough to stop it.

Darya's voice rang out suddenly: "The sacks!" she screamed. "Where he puts the eggs!"

Callum clambered back to his feet and brought the rifle to bear on one of the pouches bulging from the creature's chest. He fired three rounds into it, watching as it shrivelled slightly, and a viscous sap of blood and yoke oozed from the bullet holes.

The creature bellowed with rage as he unloaded the rest of his magazine into the same pouch. It turned its body to protect the remaining eggs, but it was too late. Koikov had identified its weakness too, and another volley of rounds thudded into the opposite pouch. This one burst open like the head of a pustule, spilling a soup of blood, yoke and shell down the creature's abdomen.

At this, it spun around and leapt from the platform. Arms clamped tightly to its sides, it looked for a second as if it might dive straight down into the magma. Then its arms opened with a rush, spreading its wings, and it soared upwards, its body lifted on the super-heated air.

"My fingers, they are slipping…"

"Darya!" Callum raced over to the edge of the island, as she finally slid free, and made a diving grab for her hand.

4

Landing on his chest, Callum skidded over the edge, until only his waist and legs remained on the platform. His upper body was now dangling over the precipice and he was staring down into the magma as its breath rushed upwards to scorch his face.

He closed his eyes and scooped his arms downwards in a desperate arc.

Time stood still.

He reopened his eyes to see that his hands were clamped around Darya's wrist as she swung over the fire. Her beautiful green eyes were wide with terror, her skin tear-streaked and pale.

"Please," she begged him, her voice barely breaking through her sobs. "Please, Callum, do not let me go! Please!"

His heart was pounding. His palms were slick. He was certain that she was sliding from his grip. "Hold on to me!"

He felt her shaking fingers close tight around his wrist. Then, he unclamped one of his hands, grabbed on to her jacket and heaved with all his might.

As his biceps curled, the thought that he might not be strong enough to lift her raced through Callum's mind. But he blocked it out and, with a determined scream, he hauled her up into his arms. She clung tightly around his neck with her good arm, and he worked his way back up onto the island, dragging her with him.

Time had yet to restart. For what seemed like hours, but passed like seconds, they sat there, immobilised with adrenaline, panting with exertion, locked in each other's embrace. With her arm still wrapped around his neck, Darya finally peeled away and kissed him. He kissed her back, pushing his forehead against hers. "Remind me to never let you distract me ever again."

Time. A screech rang out behind them. One of the bullets had obviously damaged part of the male's wing and it was struggling to keep itself aloft. It careered into a cluster of female creatures along the perimeter, knocking several of them off into the magma and causing the rest to scatter.

It scrabbled a distance up the side of the wall and then propelled itself away again. Its damaged wings spread, but once more they faltered. Blood raining from its various bullet wounds, it swerved out of control back over the magma pit and made another landing, this time on a different clutch. Struggling to balance, it stumbled on the eggs, crushing most of them, sweeping others aside.

"The eggs…" Darya panted.

Callum knew exactly what she meant. Something was wrong. It didn't make sense that the male could be so concerned about his eggs one minute, and then so careless about them the next… "They're not his," he announced suddenly.

"What?"

"They're not his eggs!"

At that moment a roar sounded and a second male scurried up from below the nest. Bigger still, it hissed furiously and faced off against the intruder. The injured male lowered its head, eyes narrowed, teeth bared, and brayed back.

Callum had seen enough. As the two males lunged for one another across the remaining eggs, he took Darya's hand and ran.

They hadn't gone far when the bellowing of the Troodon males was amplified. Looking back, Callum could see that more and more were now emerging, one for each island, clambering up onto their nests from their hiding places below. They were in a state of panic. Some were harvesting up their clutches, others were restless, taking to the wing and searching out the source of the threat.

As they approached the incline before the exit tunnel, he could see Koikov and Ava standing shoulder to shoulder at the top. They were gesturing wildly to either side, towards the horde of female creatures flooding towards them in a pincer movement.

"They're going to cut us off!" he shouted, tightening his grip on Darya's hand and going full pelt. "Run!"

As they got closer, Koikov raised the bazooka, aiming it up above their heads. His intentions were clear.

Ten metres away and the missile streaked over them, a thick gouge of smoke trailing in its wake. Koikov shouted to Darya.

"He says to keep going," she said. "He will hold them off."

The missile powered into the roof of the cavern. The sound of the explosion engulfed the chamber, followed by a loud rumble and a groaning sound from deep within the ridge. Next moment, the ceiling began to cave in behind them, colossal chunks of rock hailing onto the nests below.

As they arrived at the top of the incline, the two flocks of females were almost upon them. Ava took straight off into the tunnel, her rifle lamp lighting the way. Koikov swung his arm towards her, gesturing for the others to keep running and follow on.

As they bolted past him, he hollered something after them.

"What did he say?" Callum shouted.

"He says to keep going," Darya said, as they plunged into the tunnel. "Whatever happens, just keep going!"

Chapter 20

HARPOON

1

The survivors burst into the open as a great cloud of debris blasted from the tunnel mouth. The chamber had finally collapsed, expelling whatever it could at them in one last bellow.

"Keep going!" Callum shouted. "Don't look back!"

They ran for as long as they could see the world ahead, then they threw themselves to the ground and covered their heads as Hjalmar's breath engulfed them. The air filled with dust and the island was greyed out yet again.

They clung to one another as a deafening follow-up crash sounded and a rumble passed beneath them like an earthquake. Then, eventually, the last of the stone fragments rained to earth, the cloud began to settle and silence descended.

Callum reopened his eyes to see an altered landscape. The plateau was strewn with stone and ice, blanketed with grey dust. He looked over at the others. Their faces and clothing were stained, their bodies covered in shards of rock.

Slowly, he got to his feet and brushed himself down. "Anybody hurt?"

"I'll live," Ava said.

"By Harmsworth standards, that's pretty good." He moved his gaze to Darya.

"I am okay," she said. She sounded sincere. But the way she nursed her left arm betrayed that she was lying.

"Let me see."

She held out her arm. The hand hung limp.

"Can you move your fingers?"

She winced then shook her head.

He carefully peeled back her sleeve to reveal that the entire top half of her forearm was bruised and swollen. It was a serious injury, not one break but many. Without medical treatment he was pretty certain she would lose her hand, and Ava's glance told him she thought likewise.

He began removing the dressing from his leg wound.

"What are you doing, *solnishko*?" Darya asked. "The bandage is for your leg."

"Not anymore." He took her arm and fashioned a makeshift sling.

She stifled a yelp of pain as he brought her forearm into her chest and finished securing the dressing. Then he fished around in his pocket, withdrew the last of his painkillers and handed them to her.

"Poor Koikov," Ava said. She was staring back towards the tunnel. The tunnel mouth, the rockface, everything had been replaced by an enormous slab of ice. Freed by the vibration of the rock-fall, the entire end of the Hjalmar ice cap had dropped like a colossal show curtain across the front of the ridge, burying it.

Darya: "Do you think…"

Callum shook his head. "Even if he survived the creatures, there's no getting out of that tunnel."

"He gave his life," Ava said.

"He was very brave man," Darya added.

They stood before the glacier, bathed in silence and the reflected glare of the sun.

"So what do we do now?"

"I say we get the hell out of here before it turns out there's more than one hive," Callum said. "We can take the hovercraft back to the compound and see if we can salvage some more fuel. Then we need to try and make it to the base at Nagurskoye."

"Do you know where this is?" Darya said.

"That's the tricky part. We're going to have to figure it out somehow."

"Figure it out *somehow*?" Ava scoffed. "That's the best you've got, Troodon-slayer?"

"I'm all open to suggestions?"

Ava kept quiet.

"We'll have to check the bodies for GPS, or at least a map," he said at last. "I know it's grim, but for now we just need to keep moving. Darya needs medical attention as soon as possible. More importantly, as long as we're on Harmsworth we're bottom of the food chain, and I don't know about you, but I much prefer being at the top."

They made their way back to the hovercraft. The only damage appeared to be superficial, and they removed the debris from the interior and clambered aboard.

"Anyone driven this thing before?" Ava asked.

"Uh-uh."

"I have not."

"Great, me neither."

There was a brief silence before Callum perched himself behind the wheel and examined the control panel. It looked reasonably straightforward. Besides the steering column, there was a throttle control, presumably regulating the speed of rotation of the fan blades, a braking mechanism, pedals which seemed to control the rudders, and a whole number of other controls and gauges.

He located what appeared to be the ignition key and turned it. To his relief, the fans roared into life and the craft rose up on its air cushion. "I'd buckle up," he called out, bringing the craft around. "Here goes nothing."

He cranked the throttle and the hovercraft burst forward.

2

Volkov limped along the tunnel. Besides the pain in his buttock, he felt exhausted. Weak. Humiliated. His world was now composed of two states: dark and less dark. In some ways it was a very simple place. Frighteningly simple. *Dark* he took to be space; *less dark* he took to be rock. He carried on a few more paces through the dark, hands outstretched, testing out his theory. Was the tunnel opening out? Possibly. Only time would tell.

He took another step. This time his heel did not connect with anything. Instead it dropped down into a void, taking the rest of him with it. He cried out as his body tumbled down a slope and came to rest.

Things scattered before him. Inanimate things, he hoped. They clacked and rattled across the floor. They crunched underneath him; plates of something hard, which bit into his flesh.

The thought that he may have damaged his spine took over and he stayed down, forcing himself to breathe shallowly. Paralysis would be a death sentence. As he lay there, he could hear creeping sounds. Gnawing sounds. The percussive crunch of whatever lay beneath him.

He blocked out all noise and focussed on the stars floating before him. Too late. They were extinguishing, one after another, until they had vanished. All except for one.

He narrowed his eyes and stared towards the remaining dot of light. But it was no imaginary star. It was real. Could it be? His heart leapt. Daylight! Perhaps this was all just a blip after all. Perhaps he would still come out on top.

He felt at his top pocket. He still had the data stick.

He began testing out the movement in his limbs. There seemed to be no obvious new impairments. As smoothly as he could manage, he climbed back to his feet and limped towards the light. He waved his hands ahead of him to avoid being sucker-punched by a hidden fist of rock and tested the ground underfoot.

As he moved, the room morphed from a place of darkness to a place of mere gloom. The walls became visible in outline. They were ribbed, uneven and further apart than he'd imagined. The ceiling was lower, only just above head height, and the floor—

He stopped. The objects covering the floor were now visible, more as shadows than anything. But there was no mistaking what they were. Skulls. A sea of skulls was peering up at him, their sockets yawning, their jaws either absent or clenched. They weren't human, he could tell that much. But precisely what they were eluded him. And the fact that they were animal was meagre consolation as they sprang at him from the shadows.

As his eyes adjusted further, he realised that the skulls were not alone. They were only the most prominent parts of the several hundred skeletons that he could now see piled around the chamber. Most were only partially articulated – a spine here, a ribcage there. But a number of those that were lying on top of the jumble appeared full. Volkov could recognise the tusked crania of walruses, as well as a number of more gracile seal skeletons, their segmented flipper bones poised like unnaturally long fingers.

Did walruses and seals journey to ancestral graveyards to die? He wasn't certain. But even if they did, it struck him as unlikely that the two species would share such a place.

Warning bolts of pain flashed behind his eyes. He reached a shaky hand into his pocket and removed his pill dispenser. The chrome flashed in the dim light as he tipped what he knew to be the last two pills into his mouth. It was an odd sensation. For the first time, his mouth was bone dry, and he actually missed the bitterness of the pills beginning to dissolve on his tongue.

As he struggled to swallow them, the light ahead flickered. Then again. He stared towards the opening just as something leapt onto the lip of the crevice. It held its position briefly, before bounding into the chamber.

He kept perfectly still as a train of little creatures followed on, one after the other. They weren't clear to him, but he was relieved that they didn't resemble the monsters in the magma chamber. They were way too small for one thing. Even so, he reached down and selected a large shaft of bone to use as a club, and he also took a smaller dagger of splintered rib and secured it in his belt. It was a far cry from his beautiful combat knife, which had slit so many throats with such precision. But it would do.

There was no longer any sign of the little creatures. A few more paces and he would arrive at the crevice. The blip would be over.

His leg wound flared up suddenly and he spun around to see a chicken-sized version of the monster that had slashed him before. It was standing boldly in front of him. Its head was cocked and it was chewing on a mouthful of flesh. The sudden realisation that it was *his* flesh caused him to vomit.

Before he had time to collect his thoughts, he felt another stab of pain. This time the sensation was accompanied by a ripping sound. He turned back to see a second creature, blood staining its jaws, feasting on another mouthful of his buttock meat. He reached back and felt the blood spilling out over his fingers again from the reopened gash. To his horror, he could even hear the profuse bleeding as it rained down onto the carpet of bones beneath him.

Bones. His grip tightened around the long bone club and he brought it down towards the creature. With a chirrup, it leapt clear and the club collided with the floor.

More meat was shredded from the top of his thigh. His heart raced. Screaming, he swung the club backwards and it thumped into the latest creature, sending it crashing into a bone pile. He charged towards it, overcome with rage, and hacked the pointed rib into its gut. Then he brained it with his club.

Disoriented with blood loss, he threw his head back and roared with laughter before his legs gave way and he crashed down onto the dead creature.

In an instant, another one was on his chest. Another on his groin. Then his face.

They were all over him. But Volkov didn't have the strength left to fight them off, or even to care. He felt a burrowing in his stomach.

Soon his tongue was gone. Then his eyelids.

The last thing he saw was one of the creatures scampering past with something in its mouth. It was small, black, rectangular, with a silver ring piercing one end.

He recognised it, but only dimly, as the darkness finally reached inside his skull.

3

None of the soldiers' GPS tablets were still functioning and none had any useful mapping. Sergeant Marchenko had the same basic plans of Harmsworth that Callum had been issued for his survey, barely legible for blood stains. But there was nothing showing the rest of Franz Josef Land, beyond the outlines of the few immediately surrounding isles.

Part of Callum wished that he hadn't insisted on checking the bodies himself. Perhaps if one of the others had been there to fumble around the cold, lifeless limbs, unable to feel sympathy for disgust, then it would have been a trouble shared. But this would be *his* nightmare.

They were waiting at the bottom of the moraine as he descended. Earlier, the three of them had managed to locate a drum of unexploded diesel and Callum had left the others, within shouting distance, to refill the hovercraft's tank.

"Did you find?" Darya asked.

He shook his head and her hopeful expression faded. "We've got a choice. Either we stay here, take our chances with the creatures and hope that a real rescue turns up, or... we take the hovercraft and whatever supplies we can and move on."

"Move on?" Ava said. "You mean search blindly for the base?

That's like looking for a needle in a whole field full of haystacks!"

"I agree with Ava," Darya said. "There are nearly two hundred islands. We would search forever."

"Not necessarily," he replied. "Look at it this way. They *will* send a search party here eventually. The question is when and whether we're prepared to wait around for it. I'm not. I reckon we decide which way we're going and leave a note here so that when they do turn up they'll be able to trace us. We can do the same at each place we visit, and in the meantime we may just avoid getting eaten."

There was silence as the other two considered his words; either they took their chances with the creatures or they took their chances with the sea.

Then the silence shattered: "How about Option C?"

They spun around to see a bedraggled figure hobbling towards them. The man was shoeless and shaking. His feet, cut to ribbons on the rock, left a trail of bloody footprints behind him. He was wearing a wetsuit and carrying a loaded harpoon gun.

Ava could hardly speak. "Dan?"

Half-dead, Peterson smiled weakly. Then he collapsed where he stood.

Peterson was alive, though his breathing was shallow and his pulse weak. The three of them lifted him up and lay him in the back of the hovercraft. Using a salvaged first aid kit, Callum bandaged up his feet, while the other two placed their jackets over him and attempted to bring him round.

Eventually, his eyes reopened and he mumbled something incomprehensible.

"Dan? What happened to you?" Ava asked, stroking a hand across his cheek.

He beamed up at her. "Ava?"

"What have you done?"

Peterson described what had happened to him since the

449

Albanov had blown, from his confrontation with Volkov and the bullet grazing his side, to his escape from the wreckage of the *Sea Centaur*. He looked uncomfortable, embarrassed, particularly as he described how he'd been duped by Volkov. His voice was low and broken throughout, and shortly after beginning to speak he started to sweat profusely.

"…when I made it back to shore, I couldn't believe it. I was near as damn it hypothermic, even with the suit. Had to curl up between a couple of rocks and warm myself back up with the inhalator. Had no option but to use brine, so the damn thing's good as busted now, all clogged up with salt. Still, it kept me going long enough to realise I'd have more chance of getting hitched to the pope than finding you guys in the mist. So I waited for it to clear. Saw the helicopter go down and figured that's where I'd find you." He paused then added, "Been walking ever since."

"So it's true then," Ava said at last. "About the *Albanov*. It *was* you."

Peterson's eyes seemed to dim and he nodded.

"But… how could you do such a thing?"

"I've been carrying out attacks on corporate installations for years," he replied, the softness of his voice at odds with his frankness. "This was my biggest project to date, but the way I figure it, the threat that companies like G&S pose to the planet is also the biggest to date. *Every action will have an equal and opposite reaction.* In this case, that reaction just so happened to be me."

He surveyed their disbelieving faces. "The Arctic's like a vital organ. We keep it healthy, we live long and prosper. We abuse it and, well… there are worse things than lizard birds in store for us. Anyhow, I know it's not an excuse, but that piece of shit Volkov played me like a prize idiot. For what it's worth, I'm sorry. I'd do anything to take it back, believe me I would." He looked around. "Whatever happened to that piece of shit anyway?"

It was Callum's turn to tell Peterson what had happened since he had stranded the three of them on Harmsworth. Where Peterson had given a plain narrative account, Callum's was more like a list of charges for which he held the Texan accountable. As he spoke, he tried his hardest to exaggerate the sense of horror and loss that they had all experienced, to give Peterson both barrels. But he couldn't. There was simply no exaggerating what they had been through.

Peterson took a while to digest what Callum had told him. Then he said, "So you're the only ones left, huh?"

"Unless Volkov somehow managed to find his way out of the caves," Callum replied. "But I doubt that."

"I wouldn't put it past him," Peterson said. "And he's got the data stick. Shit! With his contacts, he'll have an anti-virus developed faster than a whore can drop her panties. Sonofabitch! He'll probably sell the virus to his mafia friends and then… Shit!"

"I'm sorry if we've disappointed you, Dan," Callum said. "If I'd only known how upset you'd be, I would've tried harder to disarm the maniac."

His surprise at finding Peterson alive had all but vanished and with it any sympathy. In its place was raw anger. "Talk about disappointment. I don't care what your intentions were, what you've done turns my stomach!"

Peterson went to respond. Then he evidently thought better of it and closed his mouth.

"All those people on board the *Albanov*," Callum went on, "everyone that's died on Harmsworth since, they owe their miserable deaths to you. Their blood is on your hands. All three of us have nearly been killed and we still might be. Do you even understand that?" He paused, his eyes locked on Peterson's. "As far as I'm concerned, you're little better than Volkov, and not your high-minded motive or your half-arsed apology redeem you. In fact, the more I think about it, the more I feel like finishing you off myself!"

Darya took Callum's clenched fist and squeezed it gently.

Peterson let out a long sigh. "Like I said before, that's what I like about you, McJones. You're a straight shooter. Everything you've said is true. No matter how many times I say I'm sorry, it's not gonna make up for what I've done to you, not to anyone. It's not gonna make a damn bit of difference. I understand that you want me in a box. Hell, I'd climb on in myself if I had the strength."

Darya spoke up. "You said that there was Option C, for getting away from here?"

With Ava's help, Peterson pulled himself up into a sitting position. "That's right, there is."

"Well, what is it then?" Callum snarled.

"You can use the submarine to navigate directly to Nagurskoye."

"I thought you said the *Centaur* was a wreck."

"It is. But who said anything about the *Centaur*?"

"What then?"

"I mean *Volkov's* sub. It's moored up in a cove a bit further up the coast from here. It's where I came ashore."

"I'm surprised you didn't just climb on board and get yourself to safety."

Darya squeezed Callum's hand again. "Dan tries to help us now."

"So why didn't you?" Ava asked. "Why didn't you leave us?"

Peterson was quiet for a long time. Then at last he said, "Guilty conscience, I guess." His eyes moved quickly back to Callum. "Look, I'm not after forgiveness here, McJones."

"It's Doctor Ross."

"Okay, well, I'm not after forgiveness here, Doctor Ross. I'm not even after sympathy. All I wanna do now is get you folks to safety." He paused. "You gonna let me do that?"

4

The cove was only a few kilometres north of the compound, just as Peterson had said. Sure enough, the submarine was moored up offshore. It was smaller than the *Centaur*, sleek and white, in kind with Volkov's other toy, and it was secured by two retractable anchors to a talon of rock jutting into the swell.

Darya read the name off the submarine's flank. "*White Squall.*"

Callum brought the hovercraft to a halt on the beach and killed the engine. The noise of the fans faded out, leaving only the lapping of ocean on stone.

Peterson's voice was croaky. "You remember when I showed you the *Centaur* controls?"

"Just about," Callum replied.

"Good. Well, when you get inside the sub, the console looks pretty much the same, just smaller." Pre-empting Callum's question, he added, "Yeah, I took a look when I came ashore. Now, it may seem complicated, but don't let it fool you, it ain't rocket science. Smart fella like you'll figure it out in no time." He began running through the basic operating procedures: power, anchor, dive…

"Why don't you just show me when we're on board?" Callum asked eventually.

Peterson was quiet.

"Dan?" Ava prompted.

He looked up at her. "Because I'm not going with you."

"What are you talking about? Of course you are. We're not leaving you here."

Peterson gestured towards the submarine. "That's Volkov's personal, one-man sub. I've seen inside it, and just getting the three of you in there is gonna be pushing it some. Even if I could squeeze in, which I couldn't, it'd be asking for trouble. The extra weight would stress the system, the life support would be inadequate, manoeuvrability would be all shot to hell—"

"Nonsense, you're just delirious!"

"I'm not delirious, Ava…" he hesitated, "…I'm dying."

Though he practically whispered them, the two words seemed to echo around the cove.

"Dying?" She laughed. "Oh, honey, don't be so dramatic. You're just exhausted and beat up like the rest of us. Now come on, let's get out of here."

Peterson said nothing. Tears were welling up in his eyes.

Ava's smile was replaced by a look of panic. "Dan? You're not dying." In exasperation, she looked to Callum. "Doctor Ross, tell him. Tell him he's not dying. He's got to come with us!"

Callum stared long and hard at Peterson. Was he really the only one who had noticed the hand-shaped stain on the side of the man's wetsuit? It seemed so. In a low voice he said, "Volkov's bullet didn't just graze you, did it, Dan?"

Slowly, Peterson yanked the top half of his wetsuit down, struggling against the skin-tight material. A heavily blood-stained bandage was wrapped around his waist.

As he lifted the dressing, Ava gasped and held her hands to her mouth.

The bullet hole itself was purple, black and oozing, and the whole of his mid-section had turned a deep burgundy, as if somebody had punched him repeatedly in the stomach.

"It's infected," Peterson said. "Truth be told, it's a miracle I'm still breathing."

"Dan, this must be so painful," Darya said, dropping to his side.

He waved his hand weakly. "Can't really feel it anymore. Whole body's pretty numb."

Ava knelt next to Darya and began trying to tend the wound. "You told us it was nothing!"

"It *is* nothing," he replied. "You're gonna be safe. That's all that matters." He grabbed her hands in his. "There's nothing more you can do."

She ripped her hands away and kept going, wiping at the crust of dried blood around his stomach with her sleeve. Patiently, Peterson took her hands again and held them tightly. "Like I said, I don't want sympathy or forgiveness, Ava. I've done wrong and now I'm gonna pay the price. This is the right thing."

"What if we take both vehicles?" she said, ignoring him and looking to Callum once more. "We can use the submarine to navigate and follow on in the hovercraft." She pushed a hand through Peterson's hair. "We can take you with us. You can get treated—"

"I wish it was that simple," he said. "Thing is, the only doctors can help me are on the mainland, over a thousand miles away. Besides which, Nagurskoye's about two hundred miles west, and that's if you don't have to dodge any ice floes along the way."

"So?"

"So," he motioned towards the hovercraft, "I doubt whether you'll get any more than forty knots out of that thing, that's forty-six miles per hour, give or take. And that means that if we left now *and* made full speed the whole time, it would still take us what? Four hours?"

"So what's wrong with that?" Ava said. "Let's stop talking about it and do it!"

Callum couldn't take it any longer. He stepped forward and

placed his hand gently on Ava's shoulder. "Ava, Dan doesn't have four hours. Even if he did, there's nothing the medics at Nagurskoye could do for him."

There was silence as the truth of his words sank in.

"What then?" she shouted. "We're gonna just leave him here and save our own skins? You may hate him, Doctor Ross, but he saved us, remember? He got the three of us off that ship before it blew. He's sorry for what he did, okay? We need to help him! Doctor Ross? Doctor Lebedev?"

"I started this whole thing," Peterson told her. "No matter what monsters live in this place, Harmsworth is my creation. Doctor Ross is right. Everything you've suffered here is down to me. I need to see this one through."

As if in response, a loud screech emanated from inland. Darya and Ava jumped to their feet as a chorus rang out in reply, and all four of the survivors stared back towards the top of the low bluffs around the cove.

"They sound far away."

Another, louder chorus went up.

"Not anymore," Callum said. "They're getting closer. They must have our scent."

Peterson: "You need to leave, now."

"Dan!" Ava screamed, latching on to his hand.

He pulled her towards him and kissed her. Their lips lingered together, before another even closer bellow tore them apart.

"Ava, please, you've got to go."

"We're not leaving you!"

Darya took her arm. "Ava—"

"No!" She shrugged her off.

"Ava…"

"*Nam Myoho Renge Kyo, Nam Myoho Renge Kyo, Nam Myoho Renge Kyo, Nam Myoho Renge Ky—*"

There was a loud cracking sound.

5

Ava screamed and stumbled backwards. Her eyes wide with shock, she held her hands to her face. At her feet, Peterson went into spasm. His whole body tensed and shook violently. His jaw clenched and his eyes bulged. His hands were clamped tightly around the discharged harpoon gun, still aimed up under his chin.

When the sight finally registered, Callum could see that the bolt had pierced straight through the arc of flesh beneath Peterson's jaw. It had travelled up through his tongue, through the thin stretch of bone forming the roof of his mouth and into his brain.

His paroxysm continued. The last of his blood coursed from the wound, spreading out over his chest in thick lobes; it trickled from the corners of his mouth as his body stole a last few breaths. Then he was still.

Ava screamed and threw herself down onto his body. The bottom of the harpoon still projected from beneath his chin, and in desperation she tugged at it. But it was lodged firmly, right where he had intended it, deep inside his skull.

Ava dry retched. Then she placed her head on his chest and wept.

"Ava, we've got to go," Callum said. "I'm sorry, but we've got to leave him."

When she still didn't move, he had no option but to reach down and drag her up onto her feet. She screamed and struggled, elbowing him in the ribs. But he held on to her.

"Ava!"

She stopped fighting at last and looked around at him.

"Don't let it be for nothing."

Gradually, Callum loosened his grip on her, until she stood next to him, shaking but unaided. Then he bent down, removed Dan's glasses and placed them on his chest, before gently sliding his eyelids shut.

6

There was no time to dwell on Peterson's suicide. His sacrifice had been for them and now they needed to make the most of it. With the baying of the creatures in their ears once more, the survivors hurried out along the narrow spit of rock and clambered over into the submarine.

Callum slipped into the operator's chair and quickly took stock of the controls. The console looked ten times more daunting than that of the hovercraft: a chaos of switches, dials, gauges, lights and levers, all centred on an angular steering wheel, like that of a race car. With the other two crushed into the storage space behind the seat, he fought to recall Peterson's instructions.

"First you'll need power. This ain't no go-kart we're talking about, so there's nothing as basic as an ignition key. What there is is a lever, right of the steering wheel…"

With several to choose from, Callum took hold of the most conspicuous lever, depressed the thumb-button and eased it forward. To his relief, there was a whirring sound as the sub powered up. Lights came on around the control panel and the on-board computer screen initiated. It flashed up a number of status bars at regular intervals, presumably relating to fuel, battery, compressed oxygen and other finite reserves. Though the annotations were in Russian, all of the levels looked comfortably high.

An electronic voice boomed into the cabin.

"What did it say?" he asked Darya.

"He says that the life support systems are on standby. Temperature is set to fifteen degrees."

The electronic voice sounded again and the screen turned into a numeric keypad.

"Now he says to enter destination coordinates."

"Shit, I've no idea. Isn't there a map search function?"

Darya leant forward and tapped at the touch screen with her good hand. After a few tries, a map flashed up and zoomed in on what Callum recognised as the Franz Josef Land archipelago. As she continued typing, a crosshair appeared over Alexandra Land, an island to the west. The Nagurskoye outpost was located at the northern tip.

"That's it!" he shouted.

"Next you'll wanna unhitch yourself from the rock. Near as I could tell, there's a lever, bottom left of the console…"

"There should be a lever that releases the anchors." Callum pointed to the row of switches bottom left. "I think it's one of these. Can you read the labels?"

Darya scanned across them, mouthing the words written in small black letters beneath each. Her hand came to rest beside the one furthest left. "Anchor engage, disengage," she read, lifting the guard flap and flipping the revealed switch. There was a crunching sound as the two anchor arms detached themselves from the rock and retracted back within the body of the sub.

They were floating. No longer stabilised, the craft began swaying on the surface of the water.

"Look!" Ava shouted, pointing back towards the beach.

The three of them stared towards shore. A single female creature peered back from on top of the bluffs. Eyeing the craft with interest, she raised her head and called out. Her heated breath beat into the air, and within seconds an entire horde had flocked to her side.

"This thing's hi-tech, so there's no dive function. Way I figure it, you'll just take her down using the steering. The air supply, CO_2 filter and dehumidifier systems must be sensor-activated. Soon as the ballast tanks start to flood I'll wager they come on automatic..."

"Let's hope you're right," Callum whispered.

The first of the Troodons had leapt the five or six metres from the top of the rocks and smashed into the shingle. Regaining its balance, the creature shook its feathers and called out once again. One by one, the others followed, raining down like meteors onto the shore beside her.

Callum nudged the throttle forward. The side fins extended and the sub began to move.

"You must hurry!" Darya shouted.

Ignoring Peterson's corpse, the creatures raced straight to the edge of the water. One after another they dived in, their streamlined bodies coursing towards the sub.

Callum lifted the steering wheel and the nose dipped down into the water.

"It's working!" Within seconds the craft was fully submerged, and there was a loud hiss as the life support systems kicked in. The world ahead was clear for a distance of ten metres or so, after which it was a murky blur.

Callum eased the throttle up another few increments and they began to gather speed: ten... fifteen... twenty knots...

Something collided with the stern.

Ava screamed out.

…thirty knots…

The craft shook as another impact sounded. Claws scraped against the exterior panelling and a warning siren went off, sending the cabin into chaos.

"Go!" Darya leant forward, grasped Callum's hand in hers and shoved the throttle to maximum.

The sub's engine roared. Its thrusters flared and the craft burst forward.

Chapter 21

LOCH NESS

1

Callum was forced back into his chair, struggling to control the sub as it tore through the narrow gap between the cove's headlands and sped out to sea. The force of the acceleration was incredible. Within seconds, the speed dial was registering seventy... eighty... ninety knots and climbing.

On the GPS navigation monitor, he could see the little white blip leaving the shores of Harmsworth behind. Then the auto-guidance system took over, rotating them smoothly onto a westerly bearing. He held his breath. Time seemed to rush past on the slipstream.

"Have we lost them?" Ava shouted.

Darya turned and peered out through the rear screen. "I think, yes," she replied at last. "I cannot see them now. We are too fast."

"You can say that again!" Callum said.

By now, their speed was just under 110 knots, 127 miles per hour. Callum was sweating with the effort of holding them level. But they were doing it. They were escaping.

He waited another thirty seconds before finally easing off on the throttle.

Ninety knots... eighty knots... seventy... sixty... fifty...

At around forty knots, he released the throttle lever and maintained speed. The warning siren faded out and, besides the low hum of the engine, only Ava's sobbing now broke the silence in the cabin.

They cruised on without a word, until, gradually, the new reality began to sink in: Harmsworth was behind them. The realisation overcame Callum in a sudden rush. It was unlike anything that he had ever felt before. In that instant, everything that had happened, all the pain, all the heartache, all the horror, was forgotten, and he threw his head back and howled with joy.

Behind him Darya joined in. Her broken wrist must have hurt like hell. But that too was forgotten as she reached her good arm across his chest and kissed him again and again and again until the side of his face was numb.

They cruised on. Every metre between themselves and the island felt like a million miles.

Still hugging on to Callum, Darya pointed to the navigation screen. "Look."

His gaze moved to the digital map and he smiled.

"Ava, you must come and see," Darya said.

Ava leant forward, wiping at her eyes, and peered over Callum's shoulder. Her sudden laughter surprised all three of them.

Cheek to cheek, the survivors watched as the final, pixelated crags of Harmsworth Island crept towards the edge of the monitor and then disappeared from sight.

2

The journey to Nagurskoye sapped the last of Callum's strength. While Darya and Ava quickly succumbed to sleep, he forced himself to remain awake, clutching the flat, white pebble tightly in his hand. The sub's auto-guidance system navigated them westwards, weaving in between the islands. Still Callum kept alert. After everything they'd survived, he was determined not to take either the technology or the last few hundred miles of Arctic Ocean for granted.

Hours passed. Fatigue set in. In the silence of the cabin, his joy began to wane and in its place came uncertainty. Harmsworth was behind them. No more creatures. No more Volkov. But there was more to come. As well as survivors, the three of them were now the only remaining witnesses to the loss of a manned icebreaker. And an entire Spetsnaz contingent. People would want answers. Not just any people. Powerful people. Government people. And they would not like the answers. He tried not to think about it. In this remote and unforgiving landscape, survival came at a high price.

Ten miles from Alexandra Land, they received a transmission. Callum roused Darya, who listened intently to the message and then began to reply.

"It is the base," she reported. "They see us on radar. They want for us to stop and go to the surface, then they send a boat for us."

On her advice, Callum eased the throttle right back and took them cautiously up.

As the sub's nose broke through the surface, they emerged into a breathtaking world. The surrounding water was speckled with icebergs. The summer's warmth had sculpted them into supernatural forms, hunched figures, Celtic swirls and precarious forked spires dripping with melt-water; they glistened as they drifted in their thousands, in eerie silence across the brine.

Beyond them, the southern horizon was studded with islands. A hundred Harmsworths, each with secrets of its own, their glaciated peaks perched on nests of ice-free tundra. And far off to the north, the edges of the northern ice sheet sat patiently, waiting for winter to spread it back across the sounds.

"Isn't that something," Ava said.

Callum and Darya kept silent, gazing at the scene before them in awe.

"I guess this is what Dan was fighting for."

When the frontier boat arrived, the three of them were ordered from the sub at gunpoint. They were then transported the last few miles to the base, with the *White Squall* in tow.

En route, Darya tried again and again to explain their situation, but the guards were clearly not taking any chances. They kept their mouths closed, their sympathies to themselves, and their weapons trained on the three unknown quantities and their improbable tale.

3

Mainland Russia

Callum awoke. He was lying in an unfamiliar bed in an unfamiliar room. The last thing he remembered was leaving the mainland hospital in a people carrier with blacked-out windows. After that, nothing.

The room was obviously under surveillance, because no sooner had the soles of his feet hit the floor, than somebody was at his door. The smartly dressed woman was holding a mug of coffee and a change of clothes, and he gratefully accepted both.

"You are need anything else today, Doctor Ross?"

"Can I speak to my son?"

"Soon. There is meal for you in one hour."

She smiled briefly and pulled the door closed.

To his right, daylight was streaming in through the frosted windows, blanketing the sofa within the embayment. He moved into its path, took a deep breath and closed his eyes. He welcomed the rays' warmth, their cleansing effect on his skin. After living with the midnight sun for the last month, he was unnerved to find himself still relishing the kiss of sunlight. By all logic, he should have been craving darkness. But he had the feeling that from now on it was the dark that was going to be a problem for him.

He seated himself at the table in the centre of the room and surveyed the fragmented canvas cityscape on the wall opposite. The shelves around it were set with decorative bottles and other awkward ornaments. Nothing quite fit. Nothing matched. The whole setup was a far cry from the comforting sense of homely that was the obvious intention. Of course, it didn't help that he could see that the doors and windows were firmly locked.

He took an uncoordinated slurp of coffee, then stood up again and approached the mirror on the back of the bathroom door. He hardly recognised the face staring back at him. The overgrown stubble, which he had last glimpsed in the bottom of his whiskey glass on board the *Albanov*, had blossomed into a beard. Brindle and lank, it was every bit as unbecoming as his greasy hair. His lips were cracked, the skin on his face was taut and grey, despite being tanned, and his eyes looked sunken. If there had been anyone else with him, he might have attempted a hangover joke, if only to stave off his growing sense of unease. But he was alone in the room, the large, spotless bedsit, wherever it might have been.

A sudden thought occurred to him and he walked over to the pile of clothes at the foot of his bed and rifled through his jacket pockets. Everything was gone. Ngana'bta's flint blade. The letter for Lungkaju's daughter. The fossilised tooth. Everything. He felt around his neck for the tooth pendant. But it too was gone. The only thing left was the quartz pebble, which he snatched up in both palms and brought to his chest.

Showered and shaved, Callum was escorted down the hallway to another room. He was shown inside and the door was closed behind him. In the centre of the room were a series of desks pushed together to form a refectory-style dining table. Somebody was already seated opposite.

"Darya!"

When she looked up and saw him, a wide smile blossomed

on her face and she jumped to her feet. He raced past the table and threw his arms around her. They kissed. He'd forgotten how beautiful she was.

"Are you okay?" He stroked his hand through her hair and let the dark strands trip from the tips of his fingers. "I didn't know if they'd let me see you."

"I am fine," she said. "The doctors come to see me this morning. They think that I should have full movement again."

He looked down at her cast supported in a sling. She wiggled her fingers.

"That's wonderful," he said, still holding her tight. "But where is *here*?"

She shook her head. "I do not know."

The door reopened and a third person was escorted in.

"Ava!"

The Canadian looked even thinner than when they had first met on the *Albanov*, but the colour had at least returned to her cheeks. She burst into tears of joy as she rounded the table towards them, and the three survivors hugged each other.

They seated themselves at the table and began discussing where they thought they were, what they thought might lie ahead. None of them knew anything for certain, but Darya suggested that they were likely to be somewhere near Moscow.

Moments later, they were served with plates of hot food.

"What happens now?" Callum asked.

"Now I think we must explain."

Ava looked worried. "Do you think they'll let us go then?"

"This I do not know. I hope, in the end. But I think that we will be here for a long time."

"I think you're probably right," Callum said.

"What do we tell them?" Ava asked.

"The truth," Darya replied forcefully. "Anything else and they will know."

"But they'll never believe us," Ava said, "about the creatures...

or anything. Somebody's even been through my stuff. They've taken anything I could've used as evidence."

"Same here," Callum said.

"Me too."

They shared a look.

"It doesn't matter anyway," Callum said at last. "Darya's right. There's no point trying to hide anything. We tell them what they want to know as many times as they want to know it and hopefully we'll get to go home. Besides," he threw a suspicious glance around the room, searching for the cameras that he knew must be there, "something tells me they'll be a lot more interested in Peterson."

4

That same afternoon, the interrogations began. The Ministry of Natural Resources and Environment, the Ministry of Energy, the Ministry of Foreign Affairs, the Ministry of Defence, and the Federal Security Service, not to mention representatives of the G&S Corporation, all took turns examining and cross-examining the survivors individually, probing into their accounts in excruciating detail.

The interviews were draining and repetitive, each conducted by a single po-faced interrogator and, where necessary, an interpreter. After only a few days, Callum had repeated the same story so many times that he'd begun to question it himself.

His description of the Troodon colony raised eyebrows, as did his mention of Ngana'bta. But, as he'd suspected, the main focus of interest had been Dan Peterson, Volkov and the data stick.

"So Mr Peterson alleges that Mr Volkov set him up?" the interpreter said for the hundredth time.

Callum dropped his head into his hands and kneaded his temples. "Again, I can only tell you what Mr... what Dan Peterson told me just before we escaped from the island."

"Please."

"He said that Mr Volkov had contacted him under the codename *Finback* and tasked him with destroying the *Albanov*, which he did using high explosive."

"And why would Mr Volkov do this?"

"I don't know," Callum replied. "But the way Peterson told it, it was just plain greed. The environmental impact assessment for such a massive project was due to be long and costly, pushing back the construction date by several years and costing a small fortune. And that's without the cost of any subsequent mitigation measures."

"And?"

"And so Volkov figured that if he could engineer and then expose an American terror attack at Harmsworth, he could legitimately renounce the Arctic Council requirement for a foreign-led EIA. He could then expel myself and the rest of the team and replace us with one of his choosing."

"So then there would still be team at Harmsworth."

"Yes, but this one would be in Volkov's pocket," Callum continued. "They'd do the job in a fraction of the time at a fraction of the cost, saving him millions. Peterson mentioned something about twenty billion rubles minimum."

The interviewer and interpreter exchanged glances.

"Like I said before, because of the weight of evidence that Volkov could produce on Peterson, he could do all of this with the sympathy and full understanding of the international community, instead of their condemnation. The man was a monster. He tried to kill us, all of us. He didn't care about the damage he would do to international relations in the Arctic, or to the Arctic itself. He just wanted to make a saving."

"And what about Stuxnet?"

Callum sighed. "When Peterson was on board the *Albanov* he uploaded the virus from a simple data stick. Seems he did it without Volkov knowing."

"And tell us again what is happening to this data stick."

"He entrusted it to Doctor Lee before destroying the *Albanov*. It was a precaution, so that it didn't fall into the wrong hands. Anyway, Ava didn't know anything about it and neither did myself or Doctor Lebedev. He just hid it in her survival tin. When Volkov shot Peterson and left him for dead, he came after us next. He must've worked out that one of us would have the stick."

"And where is it now?"

"As I told you before, I've no idea. Last I saw of it, Volkov put it in his pocket. The last I saw of Volkov, he was fleeing into a tunnel beneath the southern end of the Hjalmar Ridge. It's like a maze down there. If he hasn't been killed already, then I wouldn't be surprised if he was still wandering around in the dark."

There was a brief silence while the interviewer and the interpreter exchanged a few words in Russian. All Callum knew was that they didn't swear.

Then: "So Mr Peterson alleges that Mr Volkov set him up?"

5

Edinburgh, Scotland

Callum awoke. It was 4:30am. His chest was tight and painful. His sheets were soaked with sweat. He sat up and threw his legs over the side of the bed. With one hand clasping at his chest, he flailed the other around him, scrabbling for a weapon. "There's something in here."

"*Solnishko*, there is nothing," Darya said. She pulled herself up from where she lay next to him and wrapped her arms around his shoulders. "It is okay. It is just bad dreams again."

"No, there's something," he shouted. His heart was pounding. He could hear the terror in his own voice. "Something…" He pointed to the far side of the room. "Look! In the corner…"

"It is just bad dreams," she repeated, kissing the back of his neck. "Just bad dreams."

It was maddening. How could she be so calm? Her voice seemed miles away and her fingers stroking through his hair barely registered.

"But…" He felt the kisses on his nape grow bolder. He focussed on the thing in the corner, draped in shadow. Gradually the face vanished, the eyes shrivelling away until they were nothing but knots in the wood of the wardrobe door.

Breathing heavily, he reached up and placed a hand over

Darya's. She was right. There was nothing with them in the room.

It had been three months since the two of them, and Ava, had at last been released from Russian custody and thrust back into their former lives.

"Anything from Ava?" he asked. The last he'd heard, she had gone back to Alaska where, despite their warnings, she had gone ahead and published a paper on the discovery of the living fossil *Troodon Avaleensis*. With no hard evidence, it had been unanimously renounced as crackpot by the palaeontological community and had effectively ended her career. Within weeks of returning, she had been forced to accept a face-saving redundancy package from the university. This had included a generous subsidy towards private psychiatric treatment, which all concerned had insisted upon, besides Ava herself. Since then, Callum's contact with her had dwindled from daily to weekly to now, when he wasn't certain when, or even *if*, he would hear from her again.

"Nothing," Darya replied. "You know that she lives with her brother?"

Callum nodded. "In Toronto."

"I think that she does not sleep well either."

He took a deep breath, still trying to shake the nightmare. They were getting worse, more vivid, more intense than ever since he had returned home. It was as if the greater the distance he put between himself and that awful place, the stronger its hold. Harmsworth was stalking him, head bowed, eyes wide, mouth full of razor-sharp memories.

"At least you can run from the real ones," he whispered.

Darya shifted behind him and began massaging his shoulders. Her hands were soft and he could smell the reassuring warmth of her skin. Of the three of them, she had suffered the worst physically, but she seemed to be dealing with the psychological aftermath well. She had the nightmares too, but then she also had a steadiness about her that Callum had to admire. Credentials intact, she had resigned her post at the Russian Academy in Novosibirsk and been granted a visa endorsed by the Royal Society. She was now living with Callum and working with Scottish Natural Heritage on a pioneering new climate change project.

He would never tell her, but night after night she would slide from his grip. As he hung over the precipice, straining to hold on to her, she would plunge down into the magma. She would stare up at him, her green eyes flashing, screaming as the liquid fire ate into her skin. And when only her head was left, it would twist impossibly on the surface of the molten current, still crying out for help.

Some nights he would fall after her, his stomach turning, clawing at his own face with the pain of her imagined loss. On others, the magma would congeal before him and shatter into a bed of shingle. The disembodied head would become Peterson's, the harpoon emerging from below his chin. The Texan's eyes would roll forward in their sockets and he would hold Callum's gaze. Then his hand would shoot up and close around his throat. *Harmsworth is my creation, McJones! You got that? My creation!*

"The worst ones aren't about the creatures," Callum said.

Her fingers stopped caressing his skin. "Not for me either. I see the people. I see Dan, I see Volkov, I see Starshyna Koikov, I see Lungkaju… all of them, all of their faces…" She paused. "The creatures, they are only background, in the shadows."

"Behind the faces," Callum added.

She let out a long sigh. "Perhaps in our stomachs we understand these animals better."

"Than ourselves?"

"Maybe," she said. "I look at these creatures and I know why they do what they do to me, but then I look at the people and I am no longer very sure. I think that it is this that is real nightmare for me."

Callum sat quietly, digesting her words.

At length she pulled him down next to her on the bed and

hugged onto him. "You have your interview tomorrow, then we take Jamie to Loch Ness. It is busy day, *solnishko*, so you should rest while you can."

Soothed by the sound of her voice, he settled his head back down onto the pillow. The interview was at the Edinburgh University Archaeology Department. It was for a part-time role, which he could tell would be largely administrative. Career-wise, it was a colossal step backwards, especially as Clive had offered to promote him to Jonas's old position if he'd stayed in Aberdeen. But, if nothing else, the last few months had taught him a thing or two about sacrifice.

He lay in bed for a while, eyes closed, searching for sleep. But it was too far beyond him. He waited until Darya had drifted back, then he got up and quietly made his way downstairs. He poured himself a cup of coffee and sat in silence at the kitchen table, sifting through the job specification for his interview.

There was a sudden thud as the *Daily Herald* dropped through his letter box, and he grabbed it and sat back down. As he scanned groggily over the front page, his eyes widened:

RUSSIA WITHOUT GAS. Millions of homes across Russia, Europe and Asia are without gas as the state-owned Unified Gas Supply System (UGSS) goes into shutdown. There has been no official word on the cause of the systems failure, but analysts suggest that it may be the result of a crippling cyber-attack...

6

Loch Ness, Scottish Highlands

Doctor Callum Ross selected a flat, white pebble from the shores of Loch Ness. He brushed the silt away and held it in the flat of his palm. He dug his other hand into his pocket and produced the pebble Jamie had given him as a gift, on the same shore, four long months previously. He compared them. The two pale, sub-circular discs of water-worn stone were virtually identical. But to Callum, what they were, and what they represented, couldn't have been more different.

"Here you are, son," he said, offering up the new pebble.

The boy threw another suspicious look at Darya, who stood watching them from the top of the beach. Then, in his own time, he walked over and took the pebble. He turned it over and weighed it in his palm.

It was hard for Callum to believe that they were back at Dores Beach, the place where Jonas had first broached the subject of Harmsworth Island. In contrast to the heat of that fateful summer afternoon, it was now cool and breezy. Winter held sway over the loch; only a handful of dog walkers plied the beach around them and the tables in the Dores Inn beer garden were all but empty.

Jamie crouched down and did a few practice skims. He

reared back as if to go, then he stopped. "Are you going away again?"

Since arriving home, the process of rebuilding his relationship with Jamie had been an understandably slow one. The nightly video calls that he had promised while aboard the *Albanov* had ended suddenly and without explanation. What was an eight-year-old supposed to think other than that his loser of a dad had lost interest? Again. And even though there was a good reason for the break in contact, there was nothing Callum could really say; as Darya had pointed out, the truth would either put the boy in counselling or freak his mother out so badly that she'd stop them from seeing each other altogether. For the time being then, the best thing that he could do was simply be there, be patient and let time do its thing. *Just give to him time.*

He walked over, knelt down and wrapped his arms around the boy. "Not without you," he replied. "But you and I are going to go places together."

"Where?" Jamie asked.

"Oh, faraway places. Timbuktu. Australia. Perhaps even the moon, if you're interested?"

"And the North Pole!" Jamie said. "Can we go to the North Pole?"

Callum did his best to maintain a smile. After a brief silence he gestured towards the skimmer in the boy's hand. "Come on, let's see what you've got."

Jamie turned back towards the loch, took a final practice skim and then spun the pebble out ahead of him. It dipped down onto the surface, leapt up high, impacted and leapt again, before tripping along and disappearing into the silty water.

"Eight, nine, ten, eleven!" they shouted together.

"Go on, Jamie!"

Jamie beamed and jumped up and down with excitement. "World record! World record!"

"Aye, it is, son. Definitely a new world record."

They took it in turns to skim a few more, before heading back up the beach to Darya. Then, together, the three of them began walking north along the shore.

"You are very good with him," Darya said, taking Callum's hand. "You are good father."

He smiled at her. "I guess only time will tell."

As they walked, the sun began to set. Besides the moon, only a few dark smudges of cloud sat bold against the purple sky above. The water glistened and the surrounding peaks were tinged with a pale light. Hand in hand, they watched as Jamie ran ahead of them, kicking at the shingle and sending it tumbling towards the edge of the ancient loch.

"Do you think that you will ever tell him?" she asked. "About what happened on Harmsworth?"

Inside his pocket, Callum's hand tightened around the pebble and he withdrew it once again. Releasing Darya's hand, he strode the short distance down the beach, and looked from her to Jamie.

It's just a stone, Dad.

Then he crouched down and slung it with all his might out across the water.

The pebble skipped along the surface, above the shadows and the silt, and through the moon's reflection, before vanishing forever from sight.

As the string of ripples faded, Callum returned to Darya's side and took her hand once more.

"One day," he said. "One day I'll tell him everything. If he'll listen."

Then they carried on along the shore.

Acknowledgements

Thanks are due to Richard and Louise Lorne, Andrew Needle, Karen Summers and Tom Morley, for taking the time to review early drafts of *Colony* and provide their invaluable insight.

Thanks are also due to those amongst my family, friends and colleagues who have expressed their interest and encouragement during the writing of this novel.

Huge thanks to my agent Joanna Swainson, for her faith in me, her encouragement, and the time and effort that she spends reviewing, editing and promoting my books.

Finally, special thanks are due to my wife Hannah, whose enthusiasm for my writing is a constant source of inspiration, and whose love and support allow me to follow my dreams.

Reach out to Benjamin Cross:

Website
www.benjamin-cross.com

Twitter
@BenCross_author

Facebook / Instagram
/benjamincross.author

GoodReads
author/show/20869812.Benjamin_Cross

COMING 2022 from Benjamin Cross…

The Anaconda Tree
A Ryan Miller Thriller

*Subscribe at **www.benjamin-cross.com** to receive updates
on this and other upcoming Benjamin Cross titles…*

Sam was told that Crichton and members of this organised group have been recruiting dealers to sell acid in specifically allocated areas. And offering them a percentage of the profits. They've been bragging to these recruits that they will become the sole supplier of acid across all of Essex, East London and a lot of the South East. With so much supply, they will flood the market and undercut all the other dealers around.

"Does this mean that he's been lying all this time and never *was* a Young Conservative? Has it all been a front?" I asked Sam.

"No. He has always been serious about his politics and he plans to become an MP," She replied in a serious tone.

"In light of these recent events, this ambition now seems highly unlikely... even for a Tory," I jokingly replied in my best newsreader voice.

She wasn't amused. She doesn't like any sarcastic remarks about the Conservatives; she proudly shares her affluent parents' politics. She probably thought I was being unfair and insensitive to Crichton's predicament as well.

It had all been going well for Crichton and his mystery partners, until the police started paying attention to the local drug scene. There was such a lot of acid about, so much careless talk and so many stupid kids having bummers and getting hospitalised. Not to mention the angry, influential and well-connected parents who made sure the police did something about it.

Following the first raids on frightened schoolkids who instantly grassed, they found out who they tripped with, who they scored it from, the dealers that those kids got it from; and the police started to work it all out. After some parents gave more information and after some more selected arrests, all the information came together and the pigs followed the trail to Crichton the Mr Big, and to other dealers and to our friends at college.

But where else did that trail go and who else would be busted? Who are these mysterious dealers at the centre of it all? Who are the acid manufacturers? Who knows them? Who do they know? Who else will get busted?

Those were the big questions over the next week at college. During which time, paranoia reigned and drug consumption went down. Not to mention supply.

During this time, several more people at college were taken in for questioning, including Silly John, Captain Trix, Mad Hatter and Paul and Sarah. But they were all released after a few interviews.

When they got back, they talked little of their ordeal. They didn't say what they were asked, or what was said. They had no tales of vicious police brutality. They did have angry accusations about police insensitivity, lack of respect and time-wasting.

I think that under their angry exteriors, they were all very relieved to be let off.

For a few days, it really shook everyone up.

But after some time had passed and there'd been no further house searches, busts or arrests, life went back to normal for everyone.

For everyone, that is, except Andrew Crichton. Who was still being held in custody. And for Kate and Rick, who were still waiting to hear confirmation that no charges would be made.

19

QUESTIONS

On Saturday, Samantha and I went to Kensington. We both had things we wanted to buy, and the really nice thing was doing it together.

As soon as we left High Street Kensington Station, I closed my Afghan coat tight and snuggled into its fur, but Samantha was wearing nothing to keep out the chill wind. The contrast of her blonde Pre-Raphaelite locks draped over her short black velvet jacket made her really stand out in the crowd.

It was a freezing cold day with a clear bright blue sky. A pale sun provided an oblique winter illumination, but no warmth. A biting wind whipped down the high street. Samantha must have been freezing; I wondered why she hadn't dressed more sensibly for the weather.

We walked down the road, like lovers holding hands. And every single guy we passed turned his head to look at Sam. This really boosted my ego.

She looked fucking fantastic as usual. Her jacket was open and her nipples were pushing through her thin, tight top. So sexy and horny; she really turned me on. She wore a long skirt decorated with Walt Disney characters. It was a very thin crepe material, and as the wind blew, her skirt clung to her body, clearly revealing the shape of her long, slender legs. Wow!

She walked with her head proudly up, blonde locks flying and with a sexy, confident swagger.

As we moved along the pavement, she left ripples of sensation behind her. Every bloke, of every age and every style, looking back, mouth open.

I looked at them, coming towards us, and behind after they'd passed. All leering and staring at her body. They didn't hide their dirty thoughts.

It might have been good for my ego at first, but now I felt that the continual leering was disrespectful to Sam. It was also disrespectful to me, her boyfriend.

I found myself getting angry. Both at the guys staring at her, but also with Sam. I wondered how she could not know she was inviting this attention. Inviting a very negative attention, that made them lust after her and see her as a sex object. Which is what she told me, when we were first together, is the thing she never wants to be seen as.

I wondered if she might, actually, be consciously doing this. Might she be inviting the stares and leering on purpose? Might she be getting a buzz out of it? And if so, why?

How could she be so brazen and not think about what was in those guys' minds? Or how I felt about it?

These questions were buzzing around loudly in my mind.

Does she like it? Is she being honest with me? Is it nice behaviour on her part?

Why is she still being prudish with me, after all this time?

What's going on in her mind?

I turned to her and asked:

"Sam, you must be really cold. You can have my coat if you want."

"I'm warm enough in my jacket… And I like the way I'm dressed. But, thanks," she replied. It felt like I was being told off.

Okay. I wasn't going to say anything else.

If I told her about the men staring at her, she would say I was imagining it, or that I was just being jealous.

If I told her that she dressed in a way that attracted the wrong attention from men, she would say that I was imagining it *and* being jealous *and* trying to control her.

If I asked her to be more respectful towards my feelings, she would say that I was being insecure.

In summary; I would be told that I am imagining everything and that I am jealous, controlling and insecure. Even though I felt that I was right to voice my concerns, there was no point saying any of it.

No man can argue when those accusations are put to you: imagining, jealous, controlling and insecure. It's not exactly what chicks are attracted to.

And anyway, part of you wants to believe them, because you don't want to be right. Even though your instincts tell you that you are.

And if you do say something, it will be the beginning of the end of your relationship.

We arrived at Kenny Market, and went inside, passing by the regular phalanx of pushers with their whispered invitations:

"Wanna score, man?"

"Need any trips?"

"Want any weed?"

Inside Kensington Market, no matter what the weather outside, there prevails a single balanced ecosystem. Summer or winter, it's always the same. A constant humid and murky subtropical atmosphere and a twilight gloom at all times of the day and night.

The labyrinthine layout is confusing, with stairs going down and up in different parts of the huge multi- floored building. Passages leading off at all angles and a maze-like layout where you can stumble upon, or never ever find, the different stalls, small shops and much larger shops that all live there.

There are weird and wonderful people of all shapes and sizes and all manner of dress, wandering around, or sitting and staring, or standing, or smoking, or rapping, in multiple different sizes of groups. And there are mysterious corridors and passages; dark alcoves and shadowy corners out of which peer strange barely defined faces.

This otherworldliness is the very essence of Kenny Market.

There's something almost mediaeval about it. The feeling is accentuated by the feudal hierarchy among the inhabitants. At the top are the noble elite, owners of the shops and stalls. Then under them, the bonded staff selling the goods. Then further down, the cheerful peasants who run the snack bars. And on the bottom rung, the pitiful underclass, who manage a meagre sustenance by selling what little they have from makeshift roadside kiosks. This last class are of course the drug dealers, the most precarious of them being at the entrances and the more established operating from the coffee shops and snack bars.

Just like those mediaeval cathedrals, the whole enterprise is built to cater for the many pilgrims who visit this holy place every day, and in huge numbers at the weekend. Because that's exactly what we are; we are pilgrims, come from all the suburbs of London, drawn to this unique and weird hub of alternative London.

Kenny Market is a fantasy world out of time and space. You get the impression that the entire building exists as a world unto itself, a bit like those weird parallel dimensions you read about in *Doctor Strange* and other offbeat American comic books.

It might even be possible to live your entire life in Kenny Market without ever venturing outside. Everything's provided: music, drugs, chicks, food, clothes. In fact, I suspect that some of them really do live here permanently and don't know what year it is, or what the world now looks like outside.

I'm only trying to paint a picture of how I see the place; which is that it has a sinister and slightly forbidding undercurrent. You can visit just for the current fashions and new kooky looks, such as the platform shoes and boots, glamorous clothes and shiny outfits. But I am sure that even the casual shopper for clothes still senses something a bit odd and out of synch, when they come on their weekend visits.

It isn't just a place that sells clothes; it is a whole alternative world. Kenny Market isn't just another building: it exists, it's alive. It exists out of time and space in a parallel universe. And it represents something. When we visit, we're not sure what it actually does represent, but it feels different and dangerous. And at the same time, it is also exciting to visit, walk around and explore.

The truth is, *We* don't really belong here. It's not really a place for trendy and hippie-looking teenagers from the suburbs. But it exists because we do visit; to hang out, to find the very latest looks, music and drugs here. To spend our money here, which is mostly given to us by our parents.

But it *belongs* to *Them*. Those authentic inner-city hippies, the ones who were there in 1967 and experienced the Summer of Love. They don't live with their parents in neat semis out in the furthest suburbs. They don't get pocket money and a grant from the local education authority. They are not worried whether Marc Bolan is the biggest thing since The Beatles. Or what shade of satin jacket to buy. Their biggest concerns do not revolve around how cool they are, or how long it will take to finally lay their girlfriends.

I don't actually know where *They* are at now. But I do know that *We* are moving further away.

We may still look a bit and dress a bit like *Them*, but even that is changing very quickly. We might once have liked similar music, but our tastes have diverged and are now very different from all that sixties stuff. We don't think the same anymore, or get angry about the same things. We don't share their earnest protest and revolution politics. We want fun and a good time, cool clothes and new shock tactics. We *are* from different worlds and *We* have been growing further apart from *Them*.

The teenagers come on Saturday as pilgrims and immerse themselves in this strange atmosphere. They move through, and it feels uncertain and volatile, but at the same time they're excited by this brief contact with a more dangerous, older world. They buy the clothes and sometimes the drugs, and hang out and pretend to belong. And then they get the tube and go all the way back to the end of the line, to tell their stories: *Guess who I saw in Kenny Market. Guess what happened to me in Kenny Market. Guess what I scored at Kenny Market. Look what I bought in Kenny Market.* But do they really *get* what Kenny Market *is*?

Sam and I wandered along the passageways, stopping and turning into a stall whenever something caught our attention. Samantha tried on some clothes and some thigh-high platform boots with very high heels and thick soles. I tried on a jacket with the same cut as a leather biker jacket but in red and yellow cotton, and some stacked heel cowboy boots. But the only things we bought were Smiley badges; one more for me and the first for Samantha.

A lot more people are now wearing the Smiley badge (the 'Mr' prefix and 'Face' suffix, having now been officially dropped). It looks as though Smiley will be the new symbol for LSD. Perhaps a full replacement of what had been Mickey Mouse's exclusive role. And somehow, Smiley looks like a more fitting and more English interpretation of a mindless, wasted and spaced-out grin.

We left Kenny Market and headed for Biba, where Samantha bought many tops and a large number of dresses. I was quite surprised at the number of pound notes she handed over the counter. It all came, she explained, from the very considerable pocket money she got. And I could see that she had many more wads of notes still in her bag.

We then went to Mr Freedom, the shop that Janine had told me about. It is at the bottom of Kensington Church Street and it looks like a cross between a pop art exhibition, a comic book and a boutique. It is decorated in comic book colours, has amazing pop art furniture and a huge sofa that looks like a pair of big red lips. Dotted around everywhere are loads of other similarly zany comic book-inspired things.

This is where the fashion for cartoon and comic book characters and primary coloured clothing started. It is also where you could first find wedge-soled shoes in superhero colours, and those ridiculous over-the-top platform shoes with wings. As well as clothes like the silver jacket that Janine bought here, plus the rest of this new glittery, pop art and glamorous fashion style.

Samantha bought some velvet dungarees, a hot pants suit and some more dresses, which were covered in images of comic book characters. I bought a tight-fitting blue t-shirt covered with yellow stars, and another tight-fitting mauve t-shirt with Lichtenstein's 'Whaam!' on the front. I tried on an amazing silver and sky-blue satin jacket, and a pair of outrageously high black and white platform shoes. Not having enough bread for these, I decided to get a Saturday job and save the money to buy them.

We looked in a few more shops, and then Samantha offered to buy us both afternoon cream tea. It seemed like a good idea, but I asked Samantha about the cost. She said I shouldn't worry about the bread, because her parents were paying anyway.

We went into one of the big stores, Derry and Toms, and entered a hushed, unrushed and delicate world. Everything seemed to be happening in a very slow and civilised manner. It is a place where the sales people treat their customers with almost subservient deference, and where the customer treats them with a colonial superiority and a patronising and polite rudeness.

I didn't like it and felt uncomfortable. A lot more uncomfortable than in Kenny Market, because here I felt a judgemental atmosphere prevailed and rules at play that I had no knowledge of.

Just like the museums down the road, it is home to a carefully preserved bygone age. All those quaint customs and manners, all the things you thought had died out before you were born. All those clipped voices and superior upper-class mannerisms; they are all here, preserved in aspic.

An odd thing occurred to me: it was the weirdest of comparisons, but this place was the same as Kenny Market. They were both separate worlds unto themselves, both preserved and unchanging. Both gave you the same discomforting feeling of being lost in time and space.

Could this be saying something about England? I wondered. Could both be representative of something very British? Could these two seemingly total opposites be, in a strange way, the same thing?

Were Kensington Market and Derry and Toms both in some way an accurate representation of English society, of our class system?

Did these two superficially opposite institutions actually represent the same things? Hierarchy, deference, reverence, order, ancient customs, everyone knowing their place, never-changing.

Were the same obscure customs, abstruse rules, arcane behaviours, dubious morals, all essential parts of the fabric of both institutions? And of Great Britain?

I didn't know, but I felt there was something there, something actually quite original. Something with which I might really surprise them in my next Sociology essay.

Samantha noticed none of this, but strode confidently through the store to the tearooms. She knew the route; she knew the protocol; she had obviously been here many times before. She belonged and was taking her place. She politely requested and was courteously offered a table.

All around us sat well-dressed matrons and proud old dears, modish parents with their well-behaved children and well-groomed and polite young teenagers with friends and on dates. All talking politely in low voices, creating an unchanging, hypnotising background noise.

We talked about the coming evening. Judith Weiss was having another evening-in, and I asked Samantha if she had any gear on her. In response, Samantha rummaged in her bag and calmly placed on the middle of the table a plastic bag containing some grass and two tabs of blue microdot.

I couldn't believe what she was doing. I freaked out. It was fucking mad! She'd done it as if it was nothing, in full view of everyone. The puff was bad enough, but acid as well?

"What are you doing. You've put the tabs where everyone can see them!"

I snatched the stuff off the table.

Samantha was highly amused at my concern, and laughed as if she found my reaction ridiculous.

"What are you worried about?" she asked.

"Christ! Do you wanna get busted?"

"Oh, come on, Mark… no one's going to do anything."

"It's… it's just stupid, Sam… put it back in your bag," I pleaded, while passing the bag in my hand over the table to her.

"All right, if you *insist*… I'll do it because you are so upset… But *you've* attracted more attention now… than I ever did."

And she was right. One or two of the heads were turning around to look at us, at what the fuss was about.

We'd made a commotion. I'd made a commotion. I had been the one behaving strangely; they wanted to know why.

"Anyway," she said, "the tabs are *for us*."

"Really?"

"Yes." She smiled. A loving smile that confirmed *we* were an *us*.

We left it at that. We didn't arrange a place or time for the trip, but I felt very secure with the idea. I would be tripping with Samantha; it would be perfect. We would wait for the right time and place.

We finished our cream tea and scones and then walked through Kensington Gardens and into Hyde Park.

As we crossed the road that divides the two parks, I felt a strange sensation; a kind of relief. A feeling that having crossed the road from Kensington Gardens to Hyde Park, I was now much closer to home. That I'd left the foreign and unfriendly behind me.

Because we were crossing a very important demarcation.

That road between the parks runs like a border between two distinct halves of London. On one side, The West, where I never feel that I totally belong. But on the other side, The East, it is all reassuring and familiar.

The side from which we had come represents a certain type of London. One to which I am both attracted but not invited: Kensington and Chelsea, the Royal Boroughs, Swinging London, The King's Road, Notting Hill, Portobello Road, Performance, Mick Jagger, the Chelsea Drug Store, Oliver Reed, Battersea Bridge, Chelsea Bridge, Julie Christie, John Steed and Emma Peel, and beyond that, Putney Bridge, Wimbledon, Esher, the stockbroker belt and the Home Counties.

But the side into which we now walked is home: Hyde Park, Oxford Street, Marc Bolan, Rod Stewart, Soho, Charing Cross Road, Budgie and Charlie Endell, The City, Tower Bridge, The Lane, The East End, Michael Caine, Terence Stamp, Beigels in Valance Road, Wanstead Flats, The Hollow Ponds, Gants Hill, and beyond that, Epping Forest, the A12, Southend and the train on the Pier.

Holding hands, we strolled through an almost empty Hyde Park. We walked along the paths and underneath the bare branches, in the last weak rays of the late afternoon sun.

Samantha went to the ladies' loo to roll a joint. We sat under a tree by a pile of leaves and smoked, getting stoned and feeling at one with the wintry melancholy and desolation.

After that, arm in arm and lost in our own warm and comforting sense of contentment, we walked slowly and silently to Marble Arch.

We took the tube back to Gants Hill and walked to Judith Weiss' house.

Judith's parents were out; it was to be another famous evening-in. Steve was there but nobody else had arrived yet. They were coming much later.

The girls, who had met before at the Hawkwind concert and were getting on well, disappeared off together to Judith's bedroom.

This left Steve and I in the Jewish Through-Lounge. Steve immediately congratulated me again on having Sam as my girlfriend.

"Not bad, Mark, not bad at all. You've had her for a while now. How have you managed it?"

"I think she really fancies me, you know?"

"One very sexy chick, Mark."

"Yeah, she is."

Then he got to the point. "Well?" He leered meaningfully at me.

"Well what?" I replied with mock ignorance and innocence.

"Well, what's she like? Have you done the business?"

"No, not yet."

"Come on, man. I don't believe it," he exclaimed with exasperation.

"I don't think she's ready yet."

"You must be joking. You must know that she's fucking asking for it?"

I didn't like the questions he was asking.

I didn't like him talking about Samantha like that. It reminded me of how angry I had been, walking with her in High Street Ken, and all the leering looks she got.

Now my best friend was saying exactly what I knew all those men were thinking.

"I think you're wrong, Steve."

"Look at how she dresses, showing out and teasing everyone. She is definitely very hot stuff and you need to give 'er one."

I really *did not* like how Steve was talking about my girlfriend. It was disrespectful, even if he made it seem as though he was offering me friendly advice.

"No, she is not at all like that. In fact, she is quite shy and not ready… and I respect her for that."

"Get in there, mate."

"I will… when the time's right," I argued.

"I'm warning you, man, she is a hot babe. Do it before somebody else does, that's what I say."

Before somebody else does! Oh Christ. I didn't want that to happen.

It could. There were so many who wanted to, and Sam didn't exactly put any of them off the scent. Especially that pseud Keith, her ex and still a close friend who she so obviously flirts with. He's been there before and if I didn't act fast, he might be there again.

Why, I suddenly wanted to know, was Samantha messing me around?

These questions were racing through my head as the girls returned. Samantha sat down next to me, snuggled up and held my hand in her loving way. I was surprised to find that I was actually angry with her.

Samantha rolled some more joints. How much dope does she have in that bag? I thought. And just how much pocket money does she get to pay for all her clothes, drugs and other luxuries?

We turned the lights out. From the heavy breathing and the sounds that Judith and Steve were making, things were getting very hot and sticky over there. But with Samantha, I had again reached that wall.

A wall of ice.

The others arrived; most of the same group as last time, but with the exception of Spud and his friend. It seemed that certain ex-boyfriends, certain members of Judith's 'ex-boyfriend club', are now not so welcome at her famous evenings-in. She's so into Steve that she is now banning the exes who might present a threat to him. How nice.

Judith got out the hash cakes, the music was turned up and everything started buzzing.

That is until Crispin Winkworth and Denise arrived. They brought some very heavy news with them. We listened in silence and shock.

They told us they'd just visited the commune and were horrified to discover that some days earlier, it had been busted and everyone taken by the fuzz. A few of the members had just come back and told them what had happened.

It had been a sudden and really heavy raid, with lots of police cars, two Black Mariahs and loads of police. The officers were running around, breaking down doors, searching everywhere, smashing everything and arresting everyone. The returnees told Cris they thought the police must have had the farm under surveillance for some time, because they obviously knew so much about what was going on there.

"Daryl's been busted along with all of the others at the commune. Most of them are still in custody," an ashen-faced Cris explained.

"The pigs turned everything over, brought in the dogs, roughed them all up, carted them off. Took all the equipment, everything. The pigs also raided the homes of everyone connected," Cris concluded.

"What about you, Cris? You know those cats well… and you told us you thought the fuzz have been following you… maybe you were right?" I said.

"He *was* right. They *were* following and they did take Cris in for questioning… not that long ago," said Denise, answering for Cris.

Everyone looked at Cris with surprise and sympathy. Cris himself looked a bit uncomfortable with what Denise had just told us. As if she wasn't supposed to mention anything.

"What happened, Cris?" Judith asked.

"It was nothing really… they were pretty heavy… but they had nothing on me… and I didn't tell them anything. And they had to let me go," he explained.

"With all your contacts at the commune, you were really lucky, Cris," I said.

Because I had a feeling that Cris was hiding something about what happened to him. And what he might have said to the Old Bill. After all, he knew a lot. And he had tried to recruit me as one of their dealers, although I'd never mentioned it to anyone.

"Yes, I *was* lucky… I suppose. But they had nothing on me," Cris replied very bluntly.

"Why did they come down so heavy on the commune?" Judith asked.

"They were after acid," Cris said, "and looking for the chemicals. The fuzz found all of that and the equipment in the labs and confiscated all of it."

"You had labs?" asked Steve.

"The labs in the barns… and where we kept the microdots from Holland… and where they've been making the strawberry fields."

And then I began to realise what all this was about. It wasn't a bust out of the blue. It must be connected to Andrew Crichton and his European Economic Community study tour, and side trip to Amsterdam. And also connected to all the busts at college.

It was now obvious to me how it all hung together.

The commune was the mysterious organised group of dealers and manufacturers that the CID said Andrew Crichton had been working with. They were *entrepreneurial hippies* after all. They were also entrepreneurial acid manufacturers and importers with plans to get rid of all the competition and build new markets for themselves. They were, in fact, capitalist entrepreneurial hippies. Working together with the equally capitalist and entrepreneurial Young Conservative, Crichton.

From her expression of realisation, I could tell Samantha was thinking the same thing as me.

"Where is this commune?" she asked.

"Near Ongar. In Fyfield."

"Do you know the people there well?"

"Yes, I was going to join them. I was going to live there."

"Have you ever met Andrew Crichton?" she asked.

At this comment from Sam, the others from college looked puzzled. Surprised at hearing his name being mentioned in the context of the commune. Then I could tell they were also thinking about it. And the pennies started dropping as they began to put it together.

"The guy who looks like a straight?" Cris asked Sam.

Samantha nodded.

"He used to go to my school. I know him," said Cris.

"He was busted at college… and is *still* in custody," she stated, her words foreboding.

"He was there at the commune a lot of the time. His cousin lives there," explained Cris.

"His cousin… lives there?" I asked with incredulity.

"Yes, he's a real head. Cosmo, Cosmo Crichton. His father owns the place… Owns the farm and gave it to them to use… for the commune."

"And so *they* are the acid makers and dealers with whom Crichton has been working," said Sam, stating the link.

"What a fuck-up. So how did it happen? How did the police find out?" asked Janine.

"Someone must have told the police. But who?" Terry asked.

Of course, nobody knew.

"Crichton knew the commune, he was busted and has been in police custody… so perhaps…" Cris insinuated.

And with that statement, the others started speculating how the bust might have happened.

"Could Crichton have grassed up the commune?" asked Steve.

"That certainly appears to be the case," Cris quickly answered.

The others gave their opinions and there was general agreement that Crichton had grassed up the commune when he was arrested. Or that the police had forced it all out of him.

"Maybe not… " Sam suggested. "Crichton might have been… well, his own man… but he has always had principles… and I cannot believe he would sell out his family… or the commune."

Sam added this character witness as a contrary opinion to what everyone else now thought.

"Perhaps the fuzz did work out a lot, but needed to get more information and so busted Crichton and he told them everything," said Steve, ignoring Sam's interpretation.

"Or they had been working with Crichton as a grass and their spy for a while," Terry suggested.

"The Old Bill must have been planning it for a long time, gathering information and waiting for the right moment to strike. Which was after they interrogated Crichton and he told them everything," said Steve.

"Yes," Janine added, "first the busts and house searches and interrogations, then Crichton in custody."

"And when all the pieces were in place, and they had all the information from Crichton, and all the tabs and chemicals were at the commune..." said Steve.

"The fuzz made the big raid... turned up with Black Mariahs and arrested everyone and shut it all down," said Terry.

They seemed proud of their collaborative sleuth work. Each accepting the story, speculating, coming to the same conclusion and finishing off each other's revelations.

That was their consensus. The police had been on the case for quite some time. Crichton had been working closely with the commune, and he was almost certainly the supergrass. He sold them all out.

But I noticed that Sam wasn't happy with the way they enjoyed discussing it. I could tell that she was irritated by how clever they all thought they were and their self-congratulatory detective game.

She looked irritated and displeased.

I knew that Sam was personally involved in this because she obviously cared about Andrew Crichton, who she saw as a friend. And who, let's face it, is seriously deep in shit. The others had no idea about this, but from Sam's point of view, they were showing no empathy.

I didn't want Sam to feel outcast and upset, so I tried to help her and the situation.

"No. I agree with Sam. Perhaps Crichton didn't grass them up," I said.

"Yes, I suspect there are still many questions to be answered on that," added Sam.

"If Andrew Crichton was really a spy for the police and a grass, then why is he still in custody? Sam is right, there is more to this story and I think you are all wrong," I added.

"You're only saying that, Mark, because that's what Sam thinks," said Steve, very unhelpfully.

And the others were not convinced, either, and were happy with the story that Crichton was the grass.

I kept my further suspicions to myself. I was sure that *someone else* could have grassed everyone up and sold them out. To save their own skin.

Someone who had been continually followed by the pigs. Who may well have been stopped by them early on, brought in for questioning and started talking.

Someone who didn't live on the commune, but who knew all the connections and what was going on. Who knew the whole set-up. Someone who had been arrested, and then let go. Perhaps all for show.

Someone who is normally very quiet and introverted, but gets very emotional and aggressive at the mention of certain things. Who has weird political views, about entrepreneurial hippies and especially about Israel. Someone who has the sort of personality to save his own neck while selling out everyone else.

Cris was obviously pretending to be shook up and concerned. In order that we wouldn't even guess what his role had been. That the real reason he walked away from the pigs, without any charges, is because he did a deal with them. I looked at Cris and thought: *Yes, the grass might be you.*

But, meanwhile, Crichton and his cousin were still in custody. And in serious trouble. Daryl the spaced-out freak and most of the others from the commune were also being held. Many of them likely to be in the nick for a long time. And Kate and Rick were still waiting to hear their fate.

But after all the speculation and guesses...

After arriving at the agreed consensus of what happened, everyone turned to a more important and immediate topic: where would the acid come from now?

This last question did not concern me.

I was untroubled. I had Samantha, and she had 'our' tabs.

20

SUNSHINE

On Sunday afternoon, Samantha came round to me. Down in Bag End, we talked, then smoked a joint and then started necking. Again, she wouldn't let me get past the outside of her jeans. This was a barred passage, and she was determined about that.

I couldn't stop thinking of what Steve had said: how she is happy to attract lewd attention, but behaves like a prude with me, how she flirts with her ex-boyfriend and seems to throw herself at him, but is still putting up ridiculous barriers with me.

I'd been brooding on a lot of things: what Kate had said about her tarty outfits with the advertising exec, with the E-type Jag. All the stories about her.

Could she just be pretending to be prudish with me? Could she really be taking the piss?

"*Come on,* Samantha, why won't you let me?"

"I thought you understand," she said, almost pleading.

"I do, but I feel you are taking it too far. What are you scared of?"

She didn't answer but withdrew into herself… for two full album sides. I tried to talk to her but she was completely closed. This was not good.

Then eventually she appeared to be more relaxed and came out of it. I opened the discussion again, but this time I was less direct and more conciliatory.

"Samantha, you know I really fancy you. You know that I really…"

I desperately wanted to say that I really loved her, but I sensed it was too stark a statement. It was a declaration that could only have two outcomes; either she tells me that she loves me too, or she backs off completely and thinks I'm going too fast.

Or she could think that me declaring that I love her is an ultimatum to fuck me. And the way she was feeling, it could push her in the wrong direction.

I said instead:

"You know that I really… like you… and I love being with you… and I feel that we have something special going on between us… so why won't you sleep with me?"

"I like you too, Mark, but it's difficult for me. Try to understand."

"But I don't understand, Sam… I don't understand why after all this time you still keep stopping me from going further. Why do you get so frigid? Why don't you want to do more?"

She stopped and thought for a while and then said:

"I've never… I am a virgin."

"But," I said with astonishment, "I thought you said that you and Keith…"

"No, I lied, I made that up."

"Why?"

"I felt that I had to lie to you… because I liked you… But the truth is Keith and I never made love, he wanted to but I wouldn't… That's why we split up."

Steve was wrong. No one had slept with Samantha.

This made me more relaxed and helped me understand better why she kept stopping me. Why she got so tense, and why we never got any further than kissing and a bit of titting up. And why she wasn't ready to sleep with me.

I still wanted to have sex with her, of course. But I now thought that maybe I'd been unfair and had pushed too hard. I felt that I should give her more time.

I did have this uncomfortable feeling at the mention of Keith's name. It seemed to me that from the way Samantha spoke of him, that he was very important to her. That he still had an influence over her, and that she still had strong feelings for him.

But I let that worry pass and we just cuddled and smoked another joint and sat and talked. Then we went out to join the others at the Odeon.

We had arranged to meet up there to watch the film *Fantasia*. It was showing at cinemas to celebrate its thirtieth birthday. We'd heard about it being really psychedelic, and it was indeed a very far-out film, especially the weird bits at the end.

Samantha was very loving and affectionate to me. We sat holding hands, caressing our fingers and pressing our legs and arms against each other. It was nice and we were both relaxed and had a good time.

Dave had brought some of his old ex-skinhead friends who spent most of the film shouting out stupid but funny comments, which got the whole audience laughing... nervously. Janine had a joint which we furtively passed between us, but the thick smoke and the smell of the dope was obvious. It was pretty clear the reason the manager didn't bother us was because he was wary of Dave's rowdy friends. At the end of the film, we outraged the older members of the audience by not standing to attention, but instead walking out during the *National Anthem*.

At college, there was double good news.

Kate Baker and Rick Jones were both now out of trouble. They were free.

The other good news I heard first from Silly John, and then I heard it from Kate Baker.

Very soon, everyone was buzzing with excitement about it: the coming Saturday, Paul Henderson and his sister were having another party. Their last one at the start of autumn term was now legendary, going down in the annals of Loughton history as one of the wildest and maddest parties ever. Expectations were high for the next one.

All the people who had been at the first now couldn't wait to do it all over again. And all the people who had missed it the first time and had been vicariously living off its legend now had their opportunity. Of course, that first party was legendary to me, because of my night with The Girl in the White Mac.

This time, Steve would be taking Judith, but that was okay; I would be taking Samantha. We discussed it with the rest of the crowd. Dave said we should all trip there. We knew the vibes would be cool, the people laid-back and the environment would be perfect. So why not?

Everyone agreed; we would score acid and trip together, at what would be the second greatest party ever held in Loughton. Steve remained silent and noncommittal throughout this discussion.

I was happy with this state of affairs. With or without Steve, I would be tripping with my friends, my water brothers, responsible people in secure and sympathetic surroundings.

And I'd be with Samantha, tripping for my first-ever time, with Sam. Who had tripped many times before. I'd have nothing to worry about; I'd be in the hands of an expert.

Then there was the matter of the acid; where would we get it? I kept quiet about Samantha's two tabs. Someone was bound to score some more and if not, well, at least me and Samantha would be okay. Worst case, we could cut our tabs up to share.

I went off to find Samantha, to tell her about the party and the plans for all of us to drop acid together. But when I did find her, I didn't approach. I stood and watched her from a distance. She was walking across the college playing fields with Keith. They were close together and deep in conversation and I didn't like it.

I felt stupid; what would everyone else think? I felt angry; why was she always so close to Keith? Why was she always in such deep and intimate conversations with him? What was she doing with him? What about my feelings and what about *our* relationship?

I had a sense of impending doom. What if Keith was at the party? What if I couldn't control my jealousy? What if something sparked it all off at the party? What if Samantha misbehaved… with Keith?

I talked to Samantha later. I didn't mention Keith, but I sensed something different about her; something different in the vibe I got from her. It felt as if she was taking one step back, away from me. It was hard going talking to her. It was hard going getting back to that affection we had.

It felt as though she was wiping the slate clean, rewinding the tape, as if everything we had done together didn't matter anymore, wasn't important, didn't add up to anything. I felt as though something was disappearing, and I had nothing to build on and had to start again from square one.

I told her about the party on Saturday.

"We can trip there," I said.

"I'll have to get some acid… unless you can get some."

"What do you mean? We can use our blue microdots."

"I just sold them."

"What! You said they were for us!"

"I did, but I sold them to Keith."

"To Keith! Why to Keith, when they were *ours*?"

"I can get some more."

"But why did you sell them? What if you can't get any more?"

"I will. I promise."

And that was it. I was hurt and upset.

Those had been 'our' tabs; she'd said so. Now they were gone. Samantha didn't appear sensitive to this. She didn't realise that she'd done more than just sell two tabs of acid; she'd broken a plan we'd made together. Sold them to Keith, her ex. When it was something we'd agreed to take together.

Later on that day, I saw her again with Keith, walking along, close together, sharing secrets and laughs. This time, I was not going to keep quiet. I watched them walking through the foyer and then they parted. Keith went one way and Samantha another, to the college library. I waited a bit and then followed her into the library.

She was sitting in front of a pile of books. I walked up to her, stood by her desk.

"What's going on?" I demanded.

Samantha looked up, surprised.

"Shh," she said.

"What's going on? Why were you with Keith... again?"

She looked at me, horrified that I should be bringing this up, and horrified that I should be breaking the silence of the library. The other people there were looking at me; accusing faces that said be quiet.

Samantha took a piece of paper, wrote something and handed it to me.

I don't want to discuss it, it read.

I do, I wrote on the paper, and handed it back.

She ignored me.

"I do," I whispered as loudly as I could, directly into her ear. But she just leaned forward into her books, indicating that there would be no more communication.

I walked out. Really angry and upset. And went home.

The next day, she came up to me in the foyer.

"I want to talk," she said.

She said no more, turned and walked ahead, and I followed her to an empty common room.

As soon as I shut the door, she started.

"You won't let me talk with whoever I want," she stated.

That was, I supposed, fairly true. Or was it true? It was only Keith that I was pissed off about. So how was I to answer?

"That's not fair," I tried.

"I think we should split up."

"Why?" I was aghast. I hadn't expected this. "Everything's okay between us, isn't it? Why?"

"I don't feel that it is. You're too possessive."

"No. I... I... ah... just don't see why you have to spend so much time with Keith."

"I've told you that I have other friends. I won't cut them off," she said flatly.

There would be no debate about this and then she added:

"And another thing... I can't give you what you want."

"But. I can wait."

"No. I want us to split."

So that was it. She was ending it. What could I do?

Beg? No, at least I had my pride. Besides, I knew there was no hope.

Samantha could be very strong about certain things; I knew she was not going to change her mind. Or who she was close friends with, especially Keith, her recent ex.

I was depressed, but the party was only a few days away. I was totally psyched up about dropping tabs at the party with my friends. I naturally would have preferred that I did it with Samantha. But I couldn't let myself get down about this, and back out. I wanted everything to be okay. I was determined to have a good trip, with or without her.

"What about the party?" I asked. I meant: *What about the*

acid for the party?

"I'm still going." She *would be*, wouldn't she? I really would have to get her out of my mind.

"What about the acid for the party?"

"I'll bring it as I promised. You'll like it too… I'm getting some tabs of sunshine… Californian sunshine."

"Sunshine!"

I was amazed. Rick Jones had said you couldn't get it anymore. He'd spoken of it wistfully; he said it was something really far-out, but now lost forever. It is the fountainhead of acid; it is the LSD they took in 1967; it is what fuelled the Summer of Love.

"How are you going to score sunshine? No one's got any."

"An old boyfriend," she said.

I tensed.

"Not someone from college," she said reassuringly. "An ex-boyfriend who works in my father's agency. He's bringing it in directly from the States."

This was both bad news and also good news.

The sunshine was the good news. The ex who works in her father's advertising agency, the bad news.

"Mark, I promise that I will get the sunshine, for you and your friends… and I promise that I will bring it to the party."

And with that, she turned and left.

And I stayed and thought about my relationship with Samantha. From beginning to end.

How I had gazed admiringly at her from afar, that first exchanged look and smile, meeting her in Ilford and that initial flirtation. From the first conversation between just the two of us, and all of our subsequent times together, when we got closer and closer, until she became *my* Pre-Raphaelite girlfriend.

I thought about what we discussed in our very first deep conversation: sex, virginity and ex-boyfriends who didn't understand and only wanted her for her body. I thought about how I had been so very attentive, concerned and interested. And also wary of Keith and how close they were.

Perhaps deep down, Stripes sensed that the real threat was from Keith. Perhaps I always had too. Had I been wrong in believing that I had something real and special going on with the beautiful, aloof goddess called Samantha? Or 'Sam' to her close friends.

Then I blew it as well, by getting too jealous of Sam's antics. Or 'too possessive' as she put it to me, which sounded a lot worse than being just jealous. Because being 'too possessive' made you sound like an old-time chauvinist from the fifties. Not like a hip, understanding, modern dude at all. And that accusation broke any confidence I might have had. Could it have been part of her game?

In normal circumstances, I would have gone mad with anger and jealousy and sought some kind of apology or reconciliation. And tried even harder to win her back as my girlfriend.

Either way, Samantha was still going to the party. And she was scoring some Californian sunshine and bringing it with her for us to trip on. And I was desperate to drop Californian sunshine for my first trip. The true and actual essence of 1967 and the Summer of Love.

I still fancied Sam.

But, if I was going to trip, at the party, in the right environment and with the right people; if the first trip was to be on that mythical sunshine; and if it was not going to be a bummer; then I had to finish with Sam.

She had of course already told me that we were over. But *I* had to finish with *her*. In my mind.

I had to finish with all of the lust, desire and love I felt towards her. I had to finish with the excitement I felt when I was with her.

Could I do all of that?

If I was going to drop the acid with my friends and have a mind-expanding, consciousness-awakening, doors-of-perception opening trip, then I had no choice.

I had no choice but to make all of my feelings about Sam just go away.

I decided to wear my Budgie jacket to the party. It is the best jacket I own, and with its colourful lilac and purple suede and cool cut, it seemed just right for my first acid trip. Where I would be back where I lost my virginity, in the largest and most impressive mansion on the edge of Epping Forest.

The party was buzzing. It had the same electric atmosphere as the party here before. Only more so.

The same crowded, buzzing, energetic, excited and overflowing party.

Overflowing with people, talk, drugs, booze, music.

Flowing around the house and into every room and out into the garden. Flowing into the night air and into the hearts and minds of everyone there.

I was actually one of the party's core now. I came as one of the flower children; they were all here, including Janine and Terry, Dave, Sarah and Paul and Steve with Judith. And virtually everyone from college, including Silly John, Captain Trix, Kate and soon Samantha… and whoever she came with.

This time, I was much closer to the party nucleus. This time, I was not a gatecrasher. This time, I was part of the party hub. This time, I felt different, more confident, more grown up, part of the scene.

I was a participant. Last time, I was a suspect gatecrasher. More like a visitor or spectator. This time, I was *with* the main party groups and acidheads.

We went upstairs, toured the hallways and found a large bedroom with an attached bathroom. We took it over and made camp there. Base camp, before our ascent.

Sarah had brought along loads of psychedelic games and toys; she said these are things for heads, things for us to play with while tripping. Sitting on the floor in the middle of the huge bedroom, she removed from her carpet bag an Etch A Sketch, a round hand-held thing that contained coloured oils and water between two panes of glass, so that when you turned it, it created psychedelic patterns like from a light show; an intricate device made of connected metal rods, that you could twist and turn to make different geometric models and shapes; a Spirograph so we could draw far-out patterns, with which Sarah said we could make our own mandalas to look at. It was all fuel for the trip.

We made everything ready. Put all the toys for heads out on the carpet. Rolled a couple of joints and talked and waited for the tabs to arrive.

Everyone was excited about the sunshine that Samantha was bringing. It was legendary, almost mythical. None of us had tripped on it before and we shared what knowledge we had so we would all know what to expect.

Our communal knowledge of Californian sunshine, its impact on the sixties and its importance to the whole hippie and psychedelic movement, had been gathered, absorbed and digested by all of us over several years. Starting as stuff heard in passing when we were not even teenagers. Then over the following years, fascinated when hearing it described as the major influence on the art, music and films we were getting into. Until it took on the mythical qualities as the holy grail of all acid.

We sat and discussed all that we had pieced together, everything we had gleaned from different things we had heard and read. From first-hand reports told to us by the older and original hippies. From extracts from *Oz* magazine and *International Times*, from books someone had read, from anecdotes and stories passed down from the sixties and the Summer of Love.

Sunshine was the original LSD from San Francisco, the stuff that Timothy Leary told everyone to turn on, tune into and drop out to. The very acid that Ken Kesey and the Merry Pranksters had tripped on. The stuff they'd put into the Kool-Aid Acid Tests. The acid they took on their road trip across America in 1964 and turned on American youth, single-handedly creating the whole hippie movement. It is the very same acid that kept all of Haight-Ashbury tripping. It is the acid about which The Beatles wrote a song about tripping; *Good Day Sunshine.*

It is the very essence of those times. The real spirit of 1967. The purest form of LSD.

And soon we would all be dropping it. Once Samantha arrived.

We waited for Samantha to arrive with the sunshine.

We waited.

And we waited.

Where was Samantha? Our excitement turned to tension and then to anxiety. Where was she; where the fuck was she and where was the acid?

We went to stand on the landing and looked down at the front door. Waiting for Sam to appear in the entrance hall.

A long time passed.

Then the doorbell rang. It must be Samantha.

I knew that her arrival could indeed shatter any semblance of calm. My nervous system was in disarray, my stomach a churning sea. There were too many emotions and issues that I had to suppress.

I must stay cool, I said to myself. Must stop my heart from racing, must not get uptight. Because I had a good idea where she'd been and who she'd been with. And who she was arriving with.

The familiar emotions threatened to overwhelm me: jealousy, embarrassment, anger and betrayal. And I knew they would, if I let them. Those emotions would fit me as snugly as my old jeans. If I let them.

But I won't, I told myself, not tonight.

I would dismiss all negative emotions, and have a great trip on sunshine with my friends.

I would stay cool and detached from it all. I was ready for the trip and I wasn't gonna let these petty emotions fuck it all up.

I ran down the stairs with the others as Samantha stepped through the front door. She was with Keith. I knew it. She had arrived with Keith. Fuck. She was with Keith. I must not let this freak me out.

Everyone else was angry; she was supposed to be here hours ago. But I was too busy getting myself in a relaxed frame of mind to get uptight about all that. I forced the jealousy and anger out of my mind. I wouldn't let myself brood or even think about what she might have been doing. With Keith.

Samantha looked strung out and strangely nervous. Keith just stood back and looked blank.

She looked at me with an expression that I thought spoke of all that had passed. An expression that looked a bit lost. An expression that said *I am already out of my head.*

She came up to me and spoke.

"I'm tripping," she said. Releasing herself from any discussion.

Okay, I'd go along with that. I wanted to go along with that. No arguments, no hassles, no bummers.

"Have you got the acid?" I asked.

"Yes," she replied, holding out a small glass phial in the palm of her hand. It contained two large yellow tabs; one complete and the other with a small bit missing.

"This one's for you," she said, handing me first the complete tab, and then the other one.

"They are strong… a half is probably enough for you."

I placed them on my open palm.

Samantha stared at me, her pupils huge black saucers, her eyes wide and distant.

What did she feel? About me, about this?

I looked at her face; it was beautiful but blankly serene. She was now detached from emotions and discussion and feelings.

I thought that I could still sense a vibe, an understanding, that there was still something between us.

But there was no point in thinking about that possibility.

Soon I would be serene and detached from emotions. Wouldn't I?

Dave pestered me for one of the tabs. He wanted the whole one. I didn't have time for squabbles so I gave it to him. He ran off to the bedroom upstairs with Paul and Sarah to share it between themselves.

Samantha was still looking at me and still standing close. I sensed she was wishing me peace. She didn't speak but her eyes and energy told me everything; she wishes me peace but she's not with me. She won't be with me on this.

Then she took Keith's hand and wandered off into the party.

I had the other tab in my hand and went back upstairs. I took it to Steve and Judith who were waiting on the landing.

As I looked at him, I knew instantly that he was going to let me down. He's scared; he's not ready. I knew that; I had known that for a long time. But I *was* prepared.

"I've got something in my eye. It's really bothering me," he said.

He was saying that he wasn't gonna trip. Even though it was what I expected, it still threw me off balance. Whoosh. My stomach sucked in and the juices broke their dam to wreak havoc. Perhaps I was not as prepared as I thought.

I had really wanted to trip with Steve. We were best friends, and when it came to tripping, I knew that I would be close to him, closer than with the others.

But I was resolute. There is no debate, I told myself. I'm gonna do it anyway.

I felt that I was playing out a part and the decisions had already been made. It was my part in a cycle that had been gaining momentum; that's how I was beginning to see it.

"So, you don't wanna trip?" I asked Steve.

"I don't think I should... not now, you know... not if I'm really worried about my eye," he spluttered.

"And well, Judith doesn't think it's a good idea anyway."

It was a lame excuse; we both knew that.

But I said, "Okay."

Because I was no longer interested in the endless debate over should we, or should we not drop acid. Which even now Judith still wanted to have.

"But I've got some good gear," he added. "I'll get high and keep up with you while you trip."

"Yeah," I said. Thinking he'd have as much chance of that as a balloonist would, keeping up with a Saturn Five rocket blasting off on an Apollo moon mission.

I went into the en-suite bathroom that was connected to the bedroom we had made our home. The others were already in there, and with a razor blade were cutting their tab into three.

They swallowed the acid as nonchalantly as they might eat a piece of chocolate. I decided this would be my attitude too.

I cut my tab with the razor blade; it split into two unequal halves. Samantha had told me it was strong. That a half was more than enough.

"Give this to Janine and Terry," I said, handing Paul the smaller half. They left with the tab and returned to the bedroom.

Now I was alone. It was echoey and cold.

I could feel the tension coursing through my body; I could almost hear it. I was nervous and uncertain, facing the unknown but determined to go ahead.

I stared at myself in the mirror.

My face looked back at me, already disconnected. The face I saw in the mirror was examining me, looking into my eyes, reading my mind.

Without breaking eye contact with myself in the mirror, I stuck out my tongue and placed the tab on it. It stained my tongue yellow. I left it there, my tongue still outside my body, the tab waiting on the tip.

It's because of Samantha that this tab is on my tongue, I thought. But she is only part of the story; everything else has come together too. And now we're all here. In the right place, with the right people, back in this house.

I looked into my eyes; they stared blankly back. Was there any message for me?

No. Just go ahead, swallow, dive in at the deep end. It's the best way, right?

I brought my tongue in and swallowed, hardly feeling the tab go down. I tuned my mind into a good vibe.

It wasn't difficult, because I really was happy to be tripping here, in this house, with these people.

A cycle was completing, and this is where it had begun.

I thought back to that earlier party. What would I have said then if I'd known I'd be back here dropping acid? Was it what I really wanted then?

Let's say I'd kept a diary and documented everything. How would I have recorded the events? How would I have described how I felt, where I was at? What sort of story would it be?

What account would I have made? Would I have understood the path led back to here, now, to this moment? With a tab of acid about to begin its work.

How would I describe that party, and everything that has happened since? And how would I describe myself? How I had changed, learnt and grown. What I had experienced.

I thought about how we are all changing.

How we have been moving out of the shadows of the sixties. Led by confident, cocky, outrageous and shocking rock stars, to more glamorous fashions, new music and different attitudes.

When the trip was over, I would record that cycle, write everything down.

I knew this was something I needed to do.

It suddenly felt very important.

There was a meaning here, and I didn't want to lose it.

And then I joined the others and waited for the trip.